TENEBRÆ MANOR
IN THE DARK TREES DEFINITIVE EDITION

P.S.Clinen

Tenebrae Manor – In the Dark Trees Definitive Edition

First published in 2014 by P.S.Clinen

This edition first published in 2017 by P.S.Clinen

Illustrations and annotations by P.S.Clinen

ISBN: 0-646-97839-X
ISBN-13: 978-0-646-97839-0

More from the author can be found at
www.psclinen.com

Also by P.S.Clinen:

A Boy Named Art

The Will of the Wisp

Once more for Del,
who I still miss every day.

CONTENTS

❦ APPENDIX

- Character Profiles
- Compendium of Poetry
- Illustrations & Sketches
- Interview With the Author
- About the Author

ACKNOWLEDGEMENTS

The biggest thanks belong to my sister Elizabeth who is constantly bombarded with all kinds of writing from me and manages to edit and make sense of it all. As always I thank my wife Edie for encouraging me with all things art – *you, strange as angels*. Thanks to family and friends for their encouragement. To the online folk – those from Goodreads, Amazon, Wordpress who provide a wonderful platform for aspiring authors. And to my LORD; my salvation is found in you, my rock, I will never be shaken.

Praise for *Tenebrae Manor*

❖ *'A poetic, other-worldly song; macabre and mysterious.*
★ ★ ★ ★ ★ *'*
- Reader's Favorite.

❖ *'An exquisite tale that is not easily forgotten.'*
- Book Viral.

❖ *'An amazing and original story of friendship and family with a group of unforgettable characters.'*
- Feathered Quill.

❖ *'Eerie and highly evocative.'*
- Awesome Indies.

AUTHOR'S PREFACE

I drew before I wrote. In many ways *Tenebrae Manor* existed in my head before it was written down as a novel. '*A bunch of weird characters in a house*' – that was the story I always wanted to tell. Creative writing was a compliment to my drawings; it breathed life into two-dimensional scribbles and eventually usurped drawing as my creative forefront. *Tenebrae Manor* was written over the better part of one year, under a rather intense pressure that was solely self-inflicted. *You can't write a book. There's no way you'll have the energy to finish it. It won't be long enough to be anything worthwhile.* Such is the inner-critic when a creation is young and a craft is rough and unhoned. If anything, stresses from my life compelled me to dive into this little world I was building, and it was a most therapeutic escape. I adored it, I finished it, life moved on and got better; but what to do with my first opus? Would people want to read this? The answer that came from the route of traditional publishing said no. I get that. The book is a strange beast, not one that fits into any sort of mainstream niche. But to be honest *Tenebrae Manor* wasn't written for a mass audience. I wrote it foremost for myself (as any writer should), and decided that (with an impossible amount of nerves!) it was something I wanted to share with others. The first edition of *Tenebrae Manor* was put together by myself and as such the somewhat rough quality of it reflects an author who still wasn't quite sure what he was doing. It is one thing to write a book; marketing a book requires an entirely different skillset. So why this updated edition? Well hopefully I've just answered that; the book in your hands is the best way to experience the story. *Tenebrae Manor* is not the best thing I've ever written, but it is a personal favourite, and it will always be my first little darling. Through compiling sketches, interviews, reviews, etc. from the journey made since its publication, I believe this new edition of *Tenebrae Manor* does a far greater justice to the book than its original edition did. I hope you enjoy reading this definitive version of *Tenebrae Manor.*

-     *P.S.Clinen, Halloween 2017.*

"Eternity is a frightfully long time to spend alone..."

Part One

I - Bordeaux Speaks With Crow

The epochs pass. A certain higher-sensed creature records its progress. And though a time has been reached where this creature can safely assume that all has been revealed to him – namely that modern man has tread upon all the earth, certain locales have been deemed but futile to the progression of his culture. As such, there are places dotting the planet that have remained ignored for centuries.

One such region exists somewhere where coniferous forest and unyielding rock have deemed exploration and habitation impossible. Lost among these mountains, seemingly teetering on the edge of the world itself, stands Tenebrae Manor. Pertaining to the architectural caliber of styles introduced centuries apart, the mansion dons an immediately unique and timeless appearance. Upon observing characteristics seen on the ancient keeps of the dark ages, to whimsical features native of Georgian and Gothic decor, it is at once discernable that Tenebrae Manor must have stood for centuries. But the epochs pass, and that umbrageous façade remains untouched by the populace, merging into a sort of sickly castle-mansion hybrid. The uninviting mansion is home to a handful of surreal apparitions, doting the darkness with twilit minds set only on utter seclusion from the outside world around them. They are a ghastly bunch, floating aimlessly down the endless dusty corridors.

Who are these beings? These immortal wights of a half lit world? They are like the centipedes that scurry about their way in the soiled gloom as anti-supernal apparitions, avoiding the ways of the vagabond through strict adhesion to their immemorial home. Through a torrent of time so punishingly unrelenting, yielding not to the bemoans of ennui, of stagnation, these vapid spectres of shadow trudge ever onward. Adrift as they are in the vast cosmical sea of tree and rock, they gather. They gather because there is no one else. There is nothing else. This is the world they know, the world so omnipresent that any previous memories of a life before have been lost to the swampy recesses of the mind - like old dreams that one almost certainly forgets upon awaking. Their world is Tenebrae. They are the residents.

One such apparition, his name being Bordeaux, strides perfunctorily through the gnarled trees speckling the countryside. Aquiline of face, topped with a tangle of messy hair coloured to his namesake, Bordeaux carries with him an air of whimsy unmatched by that of the typecast demon. His skin is pale, hued white. His horns, violent as blood red, are small and curled as the twisted branches of the trees surrounding him. A burgundy coat is pulled taut across his narrow yet strong shoulders, which are hidden at times by the charcoal scarf draped about his collar. And as his fine black shoes crunched on the needles littering the forest floor, he turned his eyes skyward to observe the omnipresent canvas of night encompassing him. No moon shone at the present time, but it was no matter to Bordeaux. The years of darkness had left him with a seemingly enhanced vision. As such, a monochromatic gloom hung in the atmosphere, a tone of inescapable indifference.

Bordeaux's scarlet eyes squinted earnestly as his face contorted to a grimace. It was not the night that was troubling him but rather the heat wave that had enveloped the region of late. Seemingly unending, much like the night itself, the heat had sapped much of the demon's usual effervescent demeanor.

"Insufferable eternity!" he sighed, pressing a red silk handkerchief to his sweating temple before stuffing it back into his coat pocket.

His day had been a busy one. 'Day', it should be noted, referring solely upon twelve hours of time passing to where he stood now. For the forested regions of Tenebrae are shrouded in an everlasting blanket of midnight sky. Knowledge of such reasons surrounding this phenomenon trace their way back so far in time that they elude the present residents of Tenebrae Manor. Yet in spite of this, comprehension of an archaic magic spell has allowed remaining descendants to revivify the nightfall to a constant impenetrable strength. Yes, *why* the region is coated in night remains a mystery but the residents know that they *prefer* the darkness and choose to keep the spell active.

Bordeaux's hours had been stretched to their limits. His position in Tenebrae's walls as master of affairs was a most demanding vocation. However suiting it was to his pedantry, Bordeaux still found himself positively exhausted after the long hours working. And now, with the sudden arrival of a certain… guest, Bordeaux felt his frustration begin to overflow.

His spidery stride continued through the forest, steadily approaching the foot of the mountains. Out of the perpetual gloom before him a wooden hut manifested into view. Hearing his feet crunch on the pine needles, Bordeaux soon noticed another metronomic sound, namely that of steel splitting wood. As the hut came within reach, the demon slid his wispy hand along the log wall and circumnavigated it, shuddering at its splintery touch. And behind this hut a man came into view. Lean and muscular, two arms rose and fell, aimed and struck as an axe whirred down into the log chunk below, splitting like it was butter.

"Surely the firewood is unnecessary," said Bordeaux.

The man, not even flinching to the sudden appearance of a demon at his side, brushed his hands onto his green tunic. His face was coated in a fine film of sweat, dripping from his chestnut curls. "Bordeaux."

"Crow."

Crow nodded and scratched his scalp, the star-shaped ivy leaves which sprouted from a crudely made cap rustling. "Better to cut the logs now than leave it until the snows arrive."

His visitor began to pace casually in a semi-circle around the humble campsite. Crow had certainly set up a homely residence.

"They are saying things," said Crow.

Pondering a moment, Bordeaux replied, "Yes, I am aware."

"I heard this one's alive. More likely his sanity is on the decline but he lives."

"It has been an age since we last had a live one," said Bordeaux.

"I most definitely haven't met one. Or should I say, another."

"Ha! Hmm!" chuckled Bordeaux, "Yes, well, not all humans have your indifferent composure to the supernatural! Your decision to remain in this dusky locale bewilders me, then again, men are very strange creatures…"

Crow grinned. Mortal he was and comely for a youth in his third decade of life. Crow had assumed the role of a forest hermit, living under the black trees in a hut he had built himself.

"A human, yes. That is why I am here," explained Bordeaux.

Crow had resumed his wood chopping but continued to listen to the master of affairs.

"I have received reports regarding his arrival. And as I am yet to lay my eyes on him myself, I ponder whether you have any information this demon may find interesting."

"I had only a glimpse of him. Wandering through the trees, he was. He vanished from my sight quite quickly."

"And you thought not to engage a conversation with him?" Bordeaux inquired. "Surely the familiar face of man would have strengthened his resolve?"

Crow slouched his shoulders and let the axe swing at his side, "Bordeaux, you know I like to be left alone."

"Oh! Well pardon my intrusion!" the demon exclaimed, turning to walk away.

"No, wait!" called Crow. "Not you, the human. That is, I did not want to talk to him."

Bordeaux grinned.

"And no sooner than I'd seen him, I heard his cowardly scream off in the distance," the wood hermit continued.

"Hmm, yes. Well, I had heard of his arrival within the manor itself."

Crow's brows raised. "Bordeaux, within the manor?"

The demon nodded, hands clasped behind his back.

"Is he mad?"

"How am I to know?" said Bordeaux. "I was hoping you could divulge such information."

"I am not your messenger."

"No offense was intended," replied the demon. "It is just that I am so busy at present. Preparation and such."

Crow grinned. "He he, yes. The lady's birthday?"

Bordeaux nodded again, flicking a mote of dust from his burgundy coat. Another log split beneath the blow of Crow's axe, until the hermit hesitated.

"Were I in charge, I'd merely ignore the human's presence."

"Just so?"

"Yes. With the Lady Libra being so demanding, I'd be inclined to attend to her matters first. The human will deal with himself. In the end, they all die or go insane."

"And you, my dear Crow?" sniggered Bordeaux.

Crow smiled in return to the jest. The wood hermit seemed eager to induce Bordeaux's leave and he began to cut logs yet again. The crimson demon was not ignorant to his subtleties, though feeling somewhat deterred from his duties at the manor, remained idle within the campsite.

Bordeaux turned his gaze to a furnace glowing with embers, their dull glow reflecting off the iron braces strapped across a wooden shield that lay propped beside a stoker and bellows. Approaching it almost cautiously, he peered lower to obtain closer inspection. It was a fine shield to be sure, a product of expert craftsmanship. Carved into the three-pronged star shape of a sycamore leaf, curled iron braces clung to its painted surface to create intricate venation. Dotted along said steel veins, glossy emeralds lay embedded.

"Why, Crow," Bordeaux gasped.

Crow had turned away from his axe work and was presently mopping the sweat from his brow. His visitor turned his head towards him. "Your work?"

Crow nodded.

"Magnificent."

"Just something I have been working on."

Bordeaux shook his head. "Quite remarkable and no doubt suitable for an apt swordsman such as yourself. Or perhaps it is intended for decorative purposes?"

"No, the former, Bordeaux."

The hermit became animated in a heartbeat, tossing the axe aside to present the fruits of his skills as a smith. He carefully picked up a lengthy strip of metal from the ground nearby and held it before him. "This, this is to be the sword to partner my masterpiece."

"Impressive," replied Bordeaux. "I have little reason to doubt it will be a spectacular weapon. I must interject though…"

"As to why?" Crow finished. "It is a precaution more than anything, I suppose. There have been more frequent sightings of Wood Golems recently."

"Ahh." Bordeaux hissed and rubbed his thumb and forefinger between his eyes. "More worriment."

"Slow creatures, Bordeaux. Slow of mind and stature. I would not let it concern you."

Bordeaux looked up and blinked with a sigh, "As you say, my dear Crow. I must ask you to be swift with your tempering of this weapon. For perhaps I may rely on you to keep these detestable things away from Tenebrae Manor?"

"I have enough to do about my own home."

The demon simpered in a way that made Crow grit his teeth.

"Don't be so coy, Bordeaux. If it pleases you, I will keep an eye out."

"There's a good lad."

Bordeaux and Crow stood erect and stared intently at each other for what seemed like several minutes, before the crimson demon broke their locked gaze, turned and took a step back towards his abode. Crow returned to the chopping block and, for a moment, the only sound was the crunch of their feet upon the fallen pine needles.

Bordeaux glanced over his shoulder. "Certainly, should you hear any more news of the human…"

"I will inform you immediately," Crow cut in. "But I'd say your fellow lodgers within the manor are likely to be more helpful."

"Indeed. Goodbye."

"Goodbye."

The splintering crush of dried conifer trunk beneath the cold blow of silver steel filled Bordeaux's pointed ears as he set out on his return journey. Shuffling his shoulders within his coat, the sweat enrapt him as he groaned in

discomfort. The heat was certainly playing on his nerves.
And now, these Wood Golems! What impropriety had
Bordeaux done to deserve such anxieties? As he wandered
through the forest he slashed at a nearby tree trunk with
his nails and hissed venomously through his teeth.
Tenebrae Manor loomed ahead out of the darkness, a
macabre relic towering atop a small hill jutting from the
jagged canopy. Bordeaux barely spared a glance at his
immemorial home, too lost in his own reverie to enjoy the
comforts of the dusky surroundings. Something was
different. The demon could feel it in the atmosphere.
Hidden amongst the suffocating heat, there was an
unshakable feeling of foreboding, one that puzzled the
fretful master of affairs.

Just as his mind began to turn back towards the tasks
at hand, namely the birthday preparations for the mistress
of the manor, his foot scuffed against a rough
protuberance in the ground. He looked down in
frustration at the interruption to observe a decayed shape
crumble under his heel. One could be excused for thinking
it merely an old tree branch or stump. But Bordeaux knew
better of the surrounding regions and the creatures that
lurked in the dark.

The creature in question at his feet was none other
than a wood golem and its proximity to Tenebrae Manor
only heightened his angst. The head, somewhat cylindrical
and topped with dusty root like branches, had
disintegrated significantly. It was most like that the
creature had perished some time ago, for the bulging eyes
of the thing had all but disappeared, leaving a pair of
uneven hollows. Its body was indistinguishable from the
soil about it, so decayed it was.

"So close to the house," muttered Bordeaux.

He kicked at the corpse, dislodging the head from it and sending it hurtling down the hill.

"Ah, I do not need this!" he repeated to himself. Surely Crow would be of some help to keep the golems at bay but their increased frequency was troubling Bordeaux. Deadly though these creatures were, the golems were so slow that they were usually destroyed before they could wrap their claws about the throats of their victims. It was a favoured tactic of theirs, as some sick revenge for their own existence. They were essentially animated tree trunks, ripped from the ground by a noose and brought to life with the dark magic of a long gone baron of Tenebrae. Bordeaux resumed his homeward stride, having formulated a plan of action in his mind. Yes, the golems could wait, if only for a moment. He had a celebration to plan and the mistress of the manor, the Lady Libra, was not wont to any form of patience or consideration.

II: Inside Tenebrae Manor

Imposing, sinister and infernal, Tenebrae Manor stands perched upon its hill, a beacon of darkness quintessential to the surrounding lands. Monstrously enormous in its dimensions, it is the very spectre of antiquity, a ghastly abode, unsettling in all aspects.

It is within the mansion that a majority of strange beings take up their residence, some having lodged there for centuries on end. The history of its construction and the architects that designed it were long lost to the ages; even the eldest eldritch being of the house had no knowledge past a certain point backwards in time. Bordeaux wove his way up the powdery path to the front steps of the castle. His physique remained crestfallen; his hand clasped his chin, his red eyes transfixed on his steps. The floor of the threshold groaned under his shoe and, without a hitch in his spidery stride, he continued through the massive archway as the heavy oak door swung inwards as if on its own. He stood in the doorway and sighed before looking towards the hulking being looming in the shadows over his left shoulder. "My thanks, Usher."

"Master Bordeaux, welcome home."

A mountain of a monster, the Usher had all the traits associated with an oafish and ugly man, though the scars upon his skin and the stitches at his joints betrayed his immortality. His gaze was permanently deadpan, as if his creator had neglected to teach him the thrills of joviality.

Bordeaux had to grin at the beast. "Always a steadfast servant, dear Usher."

"Thank you sir." Usher grunted in return, his hulking hand remained latched to the doorknob, as though he were awaiting another order.

"News?" asked Bordeaux.

"A message. The Lady Libra wishes to see you, sir."

"The self-absorbed gourmand. Very well."

He took a step further into the entry hall and Usher dutifully closed the door with a thud, resuming his erect stance as doorman of the manor. So lifeless was the Usher's expression that he could easily be mistaken for mere decoration, not unlike the suits of armour that lined the wall against which he stood. Ever vigilant, the Usher had become just another part of the furniture in Tenebrae Manor. Not the most physically pleasant receptionist to newcomers to the manor but unmatched in quality of service. It was these traits that Bordeaux admired greatly and found himself thinking of as he began his ascent of Tenebrae's main staircase.

No light shone down on the stairs at the present point and the house was as silent as it was dark. Flits of charcoal grey night sky illuminated the windows to some small extent, casting shadows that sculpted dimensions into bannister and step. The stairs slid down hypnotically beneath Bordeaux's shoes, black then white, black then white, as his ascent to the higher floors of Tenebrae drawled on.

He came presently upon a junction in the staircase, a landing where a vast arch window looked out upon the southern forest. Bordeaux came to a stand still to absorb the adrenalin that came from such a dizzying height. Below the window, sheer wall dropped for the four storeys he had already climbed, before plummeting further down over the cliff face to jagged pines and boulders below. The edge of the world, with Tenebrae Manor teetering upon the precipice, a sea of black trees and mountains spreading further than vision permitted and threatening to obliterate any who may fall into the pitch.

Bordeaux pursed his lips and looked back the way he had come, the black and white steps trailing down until black conquered and light penetrated as far as it could. Forgotten candelabra stood soldier silent in the four corners of the landing, ancient tallow gripping their vine-like arms. One such candelabrum had become the inverted perch for a colony of bats that squalled affectionately to Bordeaux's caressing claw.

"My pretty little things," he whispered, as one bat gave its leathery wings a good stretch before hugging itself back into slumber.

Bordeaux knew that the left junction of the landing would take him to the quarters of the awaiting Lady Libra. Yet, again he felt deterred from his duties. A fatigue had enveloped him, one quenchable only by a glass of red and a dusty old tome awaiting him in his own room.
But things had to be done, such was the responsibility of his position and, as such, he decided to inquire upon

another of the preparations for Libra's birthday, undertaken by another of the manor's darkled characters. So it was the right hand stairs he took, stairs that ascended ever higher to the very zenith of the house, into the immense auditorium at its pinnacle.

At a glance, it seemed that the auditorium in question had been a poorly calculated add-on to Tenebrae Manor's façade. So garish and out of place it did seem that it stood like a boil upon otherwise blemish free skin. A mighty, vacuous cavern, ghosts of an echoed past were all that occupied its dark red seats. Every sound was discernable from its outer circumference, proving it to be more than acoustically sound. But so unnecessary it was, a theatre of such size. Forgiving the fact that Tenebrae's residents were small of count already and that visitors were indeed so rare as to render the auditorium redundant to all but one apparition.

As Bordeaux passed row upon row of empty seats, he found a soothing relief in the soft echoes of his footfalls accompanied by the muffled sound of gentle piano keys nearby.

"Such a capacity, this cave could certainly house my woes."

His whispers surprised him; though low, they were still carried far in the ever-hearing eardrum of a hall. On the stage, a spotlight shone down onto nothing save for flakes of dust that captured its rays along a cyclical journey through the air. A loft in the high corner of stage left, hidden amongst rafters so that only a dull candlelight betrayed its existence, concealed the perpetrator of the aforementioned piano sounds.

Bordeaux stopped at the foot of the ladder up to the

loft and cringed at observation of its rungs. He was not a man of physical exertion; even more so, he was not one for sullying his prim appearance. Nonetheless, he rose to the task and made his way to the loft as the sounds of music grew ever louder.

The simple and dusty loft greeted him, in such untidy state as to leave him hesitant to handle any objects with his bare hands. Across the floorboards, sheets of musical score lay everywhere as if thrown in a fit of rage. The piano, or rather, the immense pipe organ that stood with all its girth along an entire wall of the loft, had seated before it a passionate mantis-like man hurling his fingers along the keys with apt precision and speed. The tails of the man's green cardigan shifted and swayed over the bench where he perched; waves of sickly brown hair sprouted and spread horizontally from a part where the roots of said hair bore deep into the magnificent mind of its owner, the composer.

Bordeaux stood silently for a moment, admiring the elegant tones floating forth from the instrument, before clearing his throat loudly.

The composer started. "Who is it? Who, I ask disturbs the melodic thought train of the irrepressible Arpage Espirando Notturno?"

He rose with emaciated hands aloft, convulsing, yearning for some lost and impossible dream. Green lights flew from betwixt the keys of the pipe organ, wisps of curled haze spewed from the pipes and a new sound, a ghastly wail exhumed from the composer's cadaverous mouth. His mouth appeared to contort itself to inhumane dimensions, perhaps by a trick of the lights.

He now turned to face his intruder and, as if his jaw

were merely elastic, the shriek increased in volume as his mouth stretched wider.

Unperturbed to this monstrous behaviour, Bordeaux clicked the thumb and forefinger upon his crimson hued hand and the lights, the flames, the wails from the composer and his instrument ceased.

"I…"

"Sit down, Arpage."

"Sir."

Arpage slouched back upon his stool and swung lazily around to face the keys.

"I am honoured by your visit, sir. Indeed, honoured! My apologies, Master B," he mused, poking apathetically at a key on his piano, where a B note sounded over and over again. *Bernt, bernt, bernt…*

"It is just this blasted humidity," he continued. "It places both my mind and instrument positively out of tune."

"Arpage."

"How can one think in this stifling heat?" Arpage interrupted, hissing through his teeth at the abhorred adjective. The B note rang again and again. *Bernt, bernt, bernt…*

"Arpage," drawled Bordeaux.

"… When this dank auditorium alters the very sounds of my vision! Sounds of my vision? How perfectly ridiculous!"

"Arpage!"

The composer leapt from his reverie with a start, the monotonous B note breaking into a disconcerted squeal. "Oh, sir! Sir! A thousand pardons!"

Bordeaux grinned. "How is the composition coming

along?"

Arpage was nonplussed by the question, "T-t-the composition?"

"You are a composer, are you not?" Bordeaux mocked. "The irrepressible Arpage Espirando Notturno?"

Abashed, Arpage was struck with realisation. "Oh, the composition! Of course, of course!"

Here, Arpage stood and strode to the cobweb encrusted writing desk in the corner of his small abode. He scratched at his head and stroked his ruff before his hands set into actions more erratic than those of his delicate music making. Rummaging through papers and knocking over one unfortunate vile of ink, the jittery man turned about face and threw his chest out with pomp and circumstance. The tails of his bottle green cardigan swayed to a halt and he straightened out a sheet of paper in his hands.

Inhaling to speak, he hesitated on a sudden. "Ah sir, I must warn, it is rather... Erm how to say? Unfinished?"

"Just what you have so far will be fine, my friend."

The composer grinned, cleared his throat and proceeded to fling his limbs about himself in some whimsical dance. His voice boomed in baritone:

> *'tis blood I'm told*
> *that perks the soul*
> *with life entwined*
> *upon the divine*
>
> *As eternal epoch*
> *Tick-tocks the clock*
> *A jubilant lark*

Springs forth from the dark!

Radiant lass
Of luminous class
Tonight we boast
To your beauty, a toast!

Arpage finished his recital by holding himself in position similar to that of a flamingo standing upon one foot and spreading its wings.

Bordeaux's thin mouth curled at one corner before peeling open into a smirk of fangs, his hands clapping in slow applause.

"Very good sir," he said. "The Lady will be most pleased."

"Yes, Yes. Thank you, Master B. Yes," stuttered Arpage. "But the length, sir. The length is not quite, hmm, long? As to its continuation, I find myself suffering from writer's block! Oh woe! Oh the intolerable!"

"There there, my good friend. Patience, good citizen!" Bordeaux reassured, "You have plenty of time remaining until Libra's birthday to complete your task! I merely arrived into your quarters to inquire on the progress!"

"You are kind, Bordeaux, sir." Arpage rubbed his hands together.

"There's a good lad."

The slit of Arpage's mouth split open like a wound, his ghastly crooked teeth beamed in a sour and yellowed smile. A hesitant utterance escaped betwixt those two craggy rows before the corners of his mouth collapsed as if of exertion and his shoulders hunched ever further.

"Now now, Arpage, there's no need to be uncivil. A few minutes of entertainment is all that is asked. Surely you can hide your tepid feelings towards this project behind tricky lyrics and giddy strains."

Arpage was feebly indignant, throwing an arm into the air and turning his back to the demon visitor. "Sir, I am afraid that goes against all my musical instincts. I'm troubled, sir. Troubled, I say again! To conjure this, this, piece! This piffle! How can one summon passion to draw forth quality when one is so, so…"

"Indifferent?" offered Bordeaux.

"Indifferent! Marvellous, sir!"

The loquacious Arpage seemed set to roll off into another prattle, before Bordeaux silenced him with a finger to his lips and a hush. "My dear friend - confidentially, all of us are somewhat, disinclined, shall we say, towards the lofty importance Libra has placed upon her birthday. But need I remind you of her position in Tenebrae? It is she who keeps this night sky strong for us, only she knows the spell!"

"She could do something about this heat, surely."

"Ha, my friend. Your churlishness amuses me. There are things we simply must withstand with Libra at our hierarchic zenith and her birthday is but once a year."

"But Master B! Each year it is more! More and more she wants! I cannot keep up at this rate!"

Arpage was becoming flustered, stamping his feet like an unruly child.

"Arpage, I am aware of her increased appetite for all things but what are we to do? Surely you see the predicament I am in?"

Arpage considered his master's words a moment

before sighing longingly and, having been beaten into submission, returned to his post at the foot of the monumental instrument.

Bordeaux clapped his hand upon the composer's back before striding back to the ladder, sighing. He retrieved his red silk handkerchief from his coat pocket and mopped his skeletal brow. "It is hotter here than outside," he groaned.

Arpage had ceased to remember his master's appearance all but immediately, the notes of intense invention again spewed from the garish instrument and Bordeaux took it upon himself to leave the composer to his work.

III: The Lady Libra

It could be delayed no longer. Bordeaux had to act upon the Lady Libra's summons.

As the distance closed between their inevitable meeting through step by spidery step of Bordeaux's skeletal legs, the perpetrator of the forthcoming meeting lounged lazily within her quarters at the top of the mansion in Tenebrae's finest wing. Reclining on a chaise lounge dwarfed beneath her ample girth, Lady Libra, the mistress of Tenebrae Manor, stretched her arms luxuriously. Her dusky eyes were like pools of dark amber; this accompanying her plump red lips, upturned ever so slightly at the corners, gave her an air of unshakable confidence, of peerless wisdom. Her body, hugely fat, curved sinuously beneath her alarmingly snug charcoal dress, clinging to her like a second skin. She was all things beauty in a woman, albeit exaggerated to their polar extremes, so as to create a sort of overripe diva - like a piece of fruit left upon its branch but a day too long, so as to be left too sweet, too ripe. Hedonistic in all respects,

Libra was not wont to being denied her sensual surfeits and her lofty position within Tenebrae left her lapping up all luxuries her reluctant servants languished upon her. She lay now, fanning herself apathetically with one hand, draining a glass of cherry wine with the other. Surrounded as she was in her comforts, Libra was a shade flustered, attributing to the stifling heat wave. "Madlyn," she called shiftlessly.

Seconds passed and only a vacuum devoid of sound came in reply. She shifted her weight onto her elbow. "Madlyn," she called, louder this time but to similar result.

Libra squeezed as many seconds out at she could before her patience was exhausted and struggled into a sitting position. Her movements were graceful, albeit lumbering in a way. Slowly, heavily, she rose to her feet and stiflingly gave her back a stretch; it had been some time since she had stood up. "Where is that wretched girl?"

She took two steps forward before an answer came, though not in the form she had anticipated. A courteous knock upon the oak door of her bedroom was followed by Bordeaux's imposing entrance, whereupon the demon stood formally and awaited acknowledgement.

"Oh, it's Bordeaux," murmured Libra, as if to herself and she slowly flopped herself back onto her chaise lounge.

"My Lady, how do you fair this hour?" Bordeaux bowed with great panache and stepped closer to Libra.

"Surely something can be done about the heat, Bordeaux?"

"Others were hoping that you would remedy the

situation."

"Ah, B. I never catch a break now, do I?" she sighed.

Hold your tongue, Bordeaux, he thought. Since ascending to Tenebrae's highest perch, the gorgon had shown little activity in the way of leadership.

"Well, don't just stand there being so formal, take a seat." Libra gestured to a less than comfortable wooden stool, upon which Bordeaux propped himself and planted his chin into his hand.

"Futile as it may be, for the sake of the others, I must ask; can you do nothing about the heat wave?" he asked.

"Madlyn!" screeched Libra.

Bordeaux moaned inwardly, his attempt was indeed futile. This time though, at least for Libra, an answer came to her request, as a young blonde girl in a navy blue dress and white apron staggered in on clumsy legs. Her knees seemed to buckle under the load she carried, that of a platter of glistening pastries. The girl placed the platter down onto a low table next to Libra, who proceeded to greedily grasp a delicacy in her fingers and stuff it generously into her plump mouth.

"Coffee, my lady?" the girl asked.

"Where have you been, Madlyn?" spat Libra.

The girl's empty, sunken eyes rolled back mischievously. "Oh nowhere, really… Hi Bordeaux."

"My dear Madlyn, how do you fair?"

She tried to hide her smile, yet her attention was so arrested on Bordeaux that the coffee cup beneath her overflowed with a hiss.

"Stupid girl," hissed Libra. "You may take your leave, once you tell me where you have been hiding, ignoring my calls."

"The kitchens are busy is all. There's talk of another human in the house." Madlyn brushed her hands on her smock and pulled at the blonde pigtail that sprouted out the side of her head.

"A human? Is that all? Is that the reason for your tardiness? Your depriving me of these fine sweets? Go now, silly girl."

"Bye Bordeaux," simpered Madlyn, paying no attention to Libra.

The order must have settled into her feeble brain somewhere though, as the girl tottered out through the door she had entered with a silver tea tray in hand.

"She is so insane, one could mistake her for a monster," said Libra.

"Yes, well those humans do have fragile temperaments. I believe it is safe to say that her year at Tenebrae Manor has frightened out what was left of her wits."

"Stupid girl to begin with, really. But she is dutiful when she feels like it and lord knows, I've needed a servant true to their duty."

Bordeaux sipped his coffee quietly as Libra crammed another cake into her overweight body. The demon was not surprised that she had not offered him one. Libra's ravenous appetite was startling to nobody.

"Now, about my birthday…" she began.

"My lady, please. I must interject. This matter of the human."

She threw her arms into the air. "Oh, the human, the human. What of him?"

"As master of affairs, I feel I must deal with him swiftly so as to carry out more important matters," said

Bordeaux.

"Well I don't know much," replied Libra. "Only that the lad is scampering about the walls somewhere. Like a rat in a maze, trying to escape I'd say. I had thought you'd be more informed. How did he get in here?"

"I would hazard the guess that Usher let him in."

"The halfwit."

"A youthful sort, from what I gather, " added Bordeaux. "Probably a simple farmhand. Not rugged enough to be a wrangler."

"Indeed."

Libra licked her sticky fingers and began to drain her cup of coffee. It was increasingly clear that Bordeaux's presence was frustrating her as much as it was he. Bordeaux rose to leave, such pleasantries with Libra were beginning to grate on him.

"Sit down, Bordeaux, you fusser! You're too sensitive."

Bordeaux stood still for a moment, before turning back to face Libra and rolling his eyes. "I suppose I do put the boy in flamboyant."

"There's the sweet young man I know. Now, I can tell you that Edweena found the man out in the forest but last I heard, it was Deadsol and Comets that were looking after him."

Bordeaux grinned. "That ought to scare some of the youth out of him."

There was a pause.

"So Bordeaux," Libra smiled. "Since I have so aptly divulged your required information…"

"… The preparations are coming along satisfactorily."

Libra stared up at him through her pool-like eyes,

smiling vampishly. She seemed to be attempting to gracefully roll onto her stomach, no doubt hoping her alluring charm would wheedle more information out of Bordeaux. Though she was so engorged, that movement was difficult, unaccustomed as she was to her increasing centre of gravity. As such, there was a distinctive delay in her physical being, demonstrated in this ham-fisted attempt at seduction. Her plump abdomen pressed down into the chaise lounge beneath, as the mountainous shelf of her rear end quivered slowly upon her hips. Propping her head upon her hand, her white fingers twined through her dark curls. "Just… Satisfactorily?" she asked.

Bordeaux had observed this charade with indifference, his begrudging respect for the lady forcing him to indulge her curiosity. "Satisfactorily," he said. "Swimmingly, smoothly, without hitch, like clockwork. What more can I say?"

Libra seemed content with the response. "Such a hard worker, B."

Bordeaux shifted uncomfortably.

"Yes, go then," said Libra. "I see you want to leave. Go do whatever it is you always do. Bustle here, hustle there. Once you discover life's simple pleasures, you will be much happier. Eternity is a frightfully long time to spend alone."

She poked another pastry into her mouth and simpered.

"Would that my schedule permitted it, dear Libra."

"Oh B, nobody likes petulance. Not when your fabulous queen keeps this house underneath a lovely blanket of night." A broad gesture of her arm drew the shape of the lengthy window occupying most of one side of her room.

It was this comment that anchored Bordeaux reluctantly into his position one rung lower than Libra, even though he had to look past the excess of luxuries in the lady's room in order to see out the window. Her private bedroom was more like a mansion in itself, pressed into a single expanse. Her tables lay adorned with ornaments of great beauty, of metals most valuable, gems most lustrous, trinkets she had gathered prior to her resignation into this comfortable locality. It was here, in the most opulent section of Tenebrae that she was able to live as she desired, in torpid bliss.

As Bordeaux's eyes circumnavigated the interior, Libra rose from her seat to lean softly against him. Bordeaux recoiled from the touch of her prominent belly pressing into his side, her deep eyes oozing with the innocence so well feigned by a charlatan.

"I don't doubt that you'll get the rest you've earned," whispered Libra. "Until then, you'll handle the issue of the human, won't you?"

The demon pensively scratched at his chin. "Such trivialities always seem to need my endeavours to ensure proper undertakings are achieved."

"It is not unnoticed, love. Now go, I wish to doze."

Libra shambled to her sizeable bed, an ocean of crumbled quilts whose quantity almost diminished her remarkable plumpness. Collapsing down onto it and sinking softly into its billowy down, she exhaled a sigh of utter content, as though Bordeaux had already made egress. He remained steadfast to his post for but a moment, a qualm begotten by the abundance of disruptions to his regime choking the last remnants of aplomb from beneath his ribs. Lady Libra was snoring softly within the minute, her assurance of tranquility doing little to influence her emaciated counterpart.

He had taken upon himself to proceed directly to the ground floor drawing room, where he would undoubtedly discover the very being of his botheration. The human. The drawing room in question was a favourite rendezvous for Deadsol and Comets, who were, no doubt, interrogating the poor man this very moment. Bordeaux would do well to advance immediately to this room. That is until a rare display of revolt overcame him and the renegade within instead led him to his own quarters, to amass a warranted reprieve. Guilt swam in his lungs with each step away from his vocation.

His room was a simple one. An apt description when compared to the abundance of his most recent visitation to Libra. A round tower jutting from Tenebrae's northeastern foundation pointed skyward like a guard's lance, it was here in this turret that Bordeaux ventured to escape the pressures of life in the manor as master of affairs. If he were allowed but one sliver of personal joviality, one err in the staunched tourniquet of his loyal disposition, it would lie somewhere within the spherical grey stone of his own walls.

He could not help but smile in relief at the sound of his leather shoes reverberating the stone spiral stairwell entering the room. Up and up he went until the curtain of black ascent was peeled away and his eyes fell upon his nook with blissful nostalgia.

"There is something in Libra's words," he muttered.

He shook his head though, for he was well aware that were he to adopt Libra's languid disposition, Tenebrae

Manor would swiftly fall into chaos.

Bordeaux removed himself from the confines of his burgundy coat, further revealing his slim frame, wrapped as it were in his grey waistcoat. The shirt beneath, streamlined in elegance, was of a red so dark as to put even his fine coat to shame. The passion of the most violent primary colour shone from his clothing as the very definition of the word. Were blood to have soaked the fibres of it, it would appear insipid by comparison. The demon carefully draped his coat over its rack and placed his shoes beneath it with precise pedantry. His wrists turned outwards as if to absorb the very feel of his room in all its creature comforts. They were comforts of simplicity. His room was decorated with meaningful ornaments acquired throughout his extensive life. On his writing desk, a set of panpipes tied with feathery tassels, a skull of some long dead human being, its eyes dripping with the tallow of a candle placed upon the scalp like a pointed hat. Pendants of sincere craftsmanship displaying the care and love that went into their creation. Within a pearly clamshell, Bordeaux plopped ring after ring of brilliant silver as he removed the ten that he usually wore. One on every digit, each engraved with patterns of paisley or intricate ivy. Inks and paints sat orderly placed upon a drawing board covered in unfinished sketches and manuscripts. Crimson curtains swayed like ghosts in the open window on the northern facade, their movements drawing Bordeaux to the ledge where his extravagant telescope was assembled. A wind was concocting its gusts in the atmosphere beyond and for a fleeting, exciting moment, Bordeaux thought it was the signal of a long awaited cold change in the weather. Alas, the currents were a scalding variety, churning up the torpid air from its stagnant hibernation.

"A change of sorts," Bordeaux reasoned with himself. The heat was still sapping, sweating out its wild fever but at least there was movement in the air. The pond had been disturbed, a current created, no longer did it sit like static tarn.

He placed his ruby eye against the eyepiece of the telescope and scoured the watercolour canvas of the night; there were no stars. The clouds were indistinguishable wisps of grey, appearing as brush strokes of some masterful deity's hand.

With a flick of his hand, Bordeaux sent the sepia globe next to the telescope spinning on its axis. Continents and seas blended into each other and the demon let out a sigh. Gathering his pan flute in his claw, Bordeaux sat on the windowsill and deftly blew upon a note of somber tenor, the beauty of its echo drifting off outside with a tribal husk. The flute swayed beneath his pursed mouth like a metronome as his eyes transfixed themselves onto the large painting hanging on the eastern wall. It was a favourite of the artistically inclined demon, a piece of vibrant impressionism. A seaside scene of serenity leapt from the canvas in a burst of light and colour. The waves that crashed onto the grainy shore snaked into the horizon in serpentine curls of gold and blue, reflecting the sun as it rose. It was all Bordeaux remembered of the day. The sun, the celestial orb of brilliant fire, was still intense on the morning backdrop of the colourful painting. The brushstrokes were jagged stabs, as though the painter had vented all fury upon the work and conjured the exact opposite of the aforementioned emotion, a scene of pristine contentment. Its intensity threatened Bordeaux, though he felt exhilarated to gaze upon it. It was a world he had known once, so very long ago. A world so different to the present, a present blended into the past with its monochromatic rigidity.

The throaty rasp of his pan flute, the inviting tranquility of the painting, drew Bordeaux into a peaceful mood. His tasks were forgotten; his mind was at ease. Yet just as his reverie was about to take off into palatial expanses of navy blue space, there appeared from the stairwell a head. A head, neck and two shoulders sprouting from where the floor split open into a cavern of spiral stairs. It appeared slowly, like a dream, with an unsettling grin of menace peering from beneath a moustache of brown and black. The nose was aquiline, a bird-like prominence on the face of its owner, though not pointed like the beauty of the raven but rather rounded. The nasal phenomenon had more in common with the clumsy ugliness of the spoonbill or perhaps the shoebill; namely any apparition of the stork family. This curved snout contributing to the overall unappealing bust of the being that had drifted upwards into the room. He is the demon, Deadsol. Equivalent in some respects to Bordeaux, though he displayed not much of a muchness in other faculties. His hair was parted upon the side, a slimy pelt of dark brown grease crowning his head above rounded eyes whose lids were puffed with shadow. The grin parted, his mouth opened and from within Deadsol came a drawling, sandy voice. "Bordeaux."

The other demon, though castaway in deep reverie, was not startled by Deadsol's appearance in his room and turned from the window to face him.

"Deadsol, my brother. Pray, tell. What do I owe this pleasantry?"

Deadsol's grin returned to its perch below his thick moustache. "Bordeaux, you most agreeable gentleman, you are required in the drawing room!"

Bordeaux sighed. "When, my friend? Surely you see me here in the throes of recline?"

"On the double! At once! Immediately, good citizen! What more can I say? A human is here! A fresh one, at that! You must alight your abode, alight. I say it twice!"

Bordeaux exhumed an internal and lamentable sigh, his ensconcing had been cut so rudely short, his responsibilities called, as a child screams for its maternal overseer.

"In a moment, good sir."

Having received the response he had set out for, Deadsol, seeing no further reason in loitering in Bordeaux's presence; disappeared down the stairs.

"My work is never done," bemoaned Bordeaux. "Though it is gratifying to be necessary." The sweat was draining down his body; his coat would no longer be needed. Although Bordeaux found a great boon in confidence when appearing dressed in refinement, his waistcoat seemed up to the task of his amiable presentation.

Taking one last gulp of his homely turret and promising swift return to his roost, Bordeaux left for the drawing room.

IV: The Muse & Ruse of Two Different Women

Madlyn ran clumsily down the stairs, flight upon flight, each step taking her further away from her abhorred mistress and closer to the clammy depths of Tenebrae's kitchens. Compared to her matchstick legs, her knees stood out like bulbs and she had to stop briefly on a landing to adjust her stockings. Panting erratically, she poked at yet another tear in the clingy material, a ladder cascading down her shin. She would need a new pair, yet again, though the stockings did little to hide the purple bruises upon her kneecaps. So maladroit was her infantile gait that her knees were constantly clashing upon each other like some sick instrument of primitive percussion. Like most things though, Madlyn was numb to the pain, her mind seemed eternally bound in a gauze of ignorance that rendered her indifferent to the strains of her macabre reality, allowing her juvenile thoughts to remain enraptured in the fantasies of her whim.

Forgetting her duty, she flung the tea tray she had been carrying over the banister and into the darkled void to her side. The cymbal disc whistled through the gloom before bursting into a most audible clatter as it crashed onto an unseen floor below. Madlyn squealed at the sound before hurling herself forward again, down more and more stairs as the air began to grow thick around her. Dampness settled upon the atmosphere, a soupy sickness accentuated by the heat encompassing.

Madlyn jumped down the last five steps onto black cobblestone and retrieved the medallion of her violence from the floor where it had landed after its drop. It seemed unaffected by the fall, a small dent here and there, a scratch or two but it was Madlyn's own reflection in the tea tray that transfixed her eyes. A grin crept across her mouth, a malevolent piercing sliced across her face.

"Ugly, *ugly* girl!" she said huskily, her voice scolding with the same appraisal a mother might use to reprimand her renegade child.

Yet the sinuous smile still remained on her comely face. Surely, she wasn't all that hideous. Far from it, a skinny little thing to be sure, blonde and gangly but it was her eyes that betrayed the instability that dwelt deep within her fledging heart. She toyed with her misplaced pigtail and smoothed her collar before skipping gaily along the floor into the sweltering kitchen ahead.

The kitchen of Tenebrae was a spacious cavern, though the blanketing humidity of its sweating dimensions gave its two frequent inhabitants a sense of claustrophobia that a more stable person would find unbearable. The kitchens were all that Madlyn knew of Tenebrae, although her curiosity had carried her around the vast interiors of the manor, her memory was severely lacking at the best of times.

She had appeared at Tenebrae a year earlier, a weeping adolescent long lost within the forests and no doubt given up for dead by whoever might have thought to search for her. Madlyn had made an instant and lasting impression upon Bordeaux, who always found it humorous that an insane young girl was the only stable mortal dwelling within Tenebrae's walls. Even Crow had shuddered to learn and observe the imposing house and its ways, choosing instead to hide away in the blackness of the trees. But to Madlyn, Tenebrae was her world. The girl gave no hints as to her life previous, whether that was due to madness or suppression was not known. Yet she had wanted to make herself useful, Bordeaux delegating her to a kitchen hand. Once the gluttonous Lady Libra had discovered the servant girl, she had taken it upon herself to keep her as a personal maid and Madlyn, being as impressionable as she was, was unquestioning in the errands bestowed upon her.

Like a sea cave in a cliff face, the kitchen dripped and oozed. The steamy murk brought the walls alive, pulsing like the heavy body of a slothful animal. The room was breathing, sighing, whistling with the sounds of creation - a laboratory of twisted edible experiments.

In the wild fever of the uncomfortable kitchen, a mound of a man stood at the long bench chopping vegetables with incredible dexterity. Several pots spewed and simmered in watery chorus upon the stove and a great wood fire oven roared angrily. Yet the man gave no indication of panic and one would be excused for believing him to have more than two hands, so swift and precise was his work. He was the silent chef of Tenebrae Manor, a fleshy triangle of filleted corners, propped on absurdly small legs.

Madlyn crept behind him and slammed the tea tray down on the bench. The clamour echoed slightly, muffled by the moisture in the air. It was a noise that would have startled anybody, if not for the fact that the chef was both deaf and mute. Yet the man seemed calmly aware of the girl's presence and turned to her. His face was bland, a leather bag of forgettable features. His eyelids drooped so low it was a shock to learn that the man wasn't blind as well. His lips pouted and sagged from years of disuse and his globe of a nose, the only distinguishable protuberance, jutted prominently. The mute chef handed Madlyn a scrubbing brush and pointed to a pile of dishes awaiting her. The pile was higher each time, as Libra's appetite increased, though the chef himself was guilty of mess and excess when it came to his craft. The kitchen was riddled with rats, although most lay dead in the traps set about the floor. Despite the deplorable working conditions, the mute chef was unmatched, his concoctions highly heralded by all Tenebrae's residents.

Madlyn hummed tunelessly, completely out of time with the pace set forth by her scrubbing arms. Elbow deep in suds, her sunken eyes traced the beads of condensation on the wall before her, as the droplets moulded shapelessly within brick bulge and mortar crevasse. In her mind, the perspiring walls were her tears, as Bordeaux brushed them from her cheek and swept her from her feet. He could always fly in her reveries, a talent obviously amiss in his real world counterpart. The girl lived at Tenebrae Manor, a nightmare world of frightening visions and impossible supernatural beings. Yet still she yearned for the fantastic contours of her daydreams, a world where even her hopelessly romantic notions were possible. Her infatuation with Bordeaux kept her vigilant to her tasks, a pitiful hope of gathering up his forever absent affection.

As inattentive as she was ignorant, Madlyn soon grew bored with the repetition of dish washing and stood momentarily still. The mute chef and his eloquent conducting clicked away like clockwork, unaware of the maid's increased ennui. She brayed apathetically, an unlikely attempt to grasp the deaf man's attention. She sighed louder and begun to tap her foot against the cobblestone floor. Still no response. Why would there be when the object of her assault was stone deaf? The chef's bald scalp sweated as profusely as the walls around him as Madlyn flicked a billowy cloud of suds his way. The effervescence plopped softly onto his greasy smock but still he paid no attention to Madlyn. Her face then contorted with a glower of violence as she hurled a sopping plate at the wall in front of the mute chef. The plate shattered to pieces and was enough to grab the mute chef's attention as he turned furiously to face the kitchen girl.

It may have been only the cobwebbed haze clinging to the air that gave him the appearance of a bull snorting steam from his nostrils; in any account, he was livid. A pudgy finger trembling with rage patiently gestured her to take her leave, the chef was obviously trying his hardest to restrain his wrath.

Madlyn was astute enough to understand the chef's moods. He would never act upon his fury, despite Madlyn's frequent provoking. There were no losers in the current situation. Madlyn was briefly free of responsibility and the mute chef could manage better without her in the way. Stopping only to swipe a few withered orbs of varying fruits and cram them forcefully into her apron pouch, Madlyn bolted out the doors of the kitchen from whence she'd come.

A labyrinth of stairs connected Tenebrae's half-lit rooms with steps akin to creaking tendrils. Spiders mused quietly in the high echoing ceiling corners, their cobwebs adorning peeled wallpapers of brilliant red and decayed grey. Shadow sank into shadow, a tide of macabre drifting deep into impenetrable umbra.

As Madlyn disappeared into the dark ground floor dungeon of her humble abode, another femme fatale brooded soundlessly in a forgotten drawing room in the whispery southeastern corner of Tenebrae's third floor. A ghastly wind rattled the perimeter of the room's arch windows, as though it were attempting a hideous intrusion. Its sombrous sound spiralling about the window ledges gave an impression of polar chill but the ashen darkness of the unused fireplace in the room confirmed the heat wave's continued presence.

The woman sat on a large leather chair; her form slouched upon the slender white arm that propped against the wooden armrest like a pale mast. She was the vampire Edweena.

Short of temper yet steadfastly composed, Edweena

had wrestled with an unquenchable blood lust for several centuries. Indeed, she was one of Tenebrae's oldest inhabitants, locked eternally within the lusty body of a lass in the prime of her youth. As the wind tore ever-onward outside, she sat content with the contrasting stillness of the room and the equilibrium the two composed. Her fingernails tapped rhythmically on the surface of a dusty book and although the candle that had served as her reading light had been extinguished for what could have been innumerable hours by now, Edweena stared vacantly into the blackness of the night outside. Still no moon. The present times had been taxing on her; the unexpected appearance of a live human so close to Tenebrae Manor had interrupted her regular hunting. The very idea of a ripe, hot-blooded mammal in her reach made her bloodless eyes dilate. Years of feeding on the awful scum around her had tested her patience thoroughly. Rat blood was tepid and repulsive and the occasional livestock she encountered had usually been dead so long that their life fluid was significantly decayed.

Why did I not just finish him when I had the chance? Edweena cursed her hesitance. Now the man was in the care of those two harlequins, Deadsol and Comets.

They care only for the cheap thrill of frightening the pathetic vagabond.

She hoped that death would steal the human's breath swiftly; she would be there in a second to devour the remains.

It had been Edweena who had discovered the lost man. Observing his aimless wandering from her perch in the conifer canopy, her mind had argued within itself on what actions she should take. A thread of remorse, a reminiscent remain of her past humanity had kept the man alive long enough for him to stumble upon the manor itself. And only then had she realised her responsibility towards Tenebrae.

The man had made it all the way to the front foyer, the Usher allowing his ingress as he did to all who appeared at the front door. The Usher had been civil to be certain, menace was not of his composition. Yet the mere sight of the hulking monstrosity had thrown the intruder into wild panic, galvanised by the sudden entrance of Edweena. She had leapt down in front of him, delighting in the pale terror that pasted itself onto the man's pallor.

"W-who are you?" he had stammered.

Edweena had hissed venomously in response, flashing her razor sharp teeth with such ferocity that the man had wailed and collapsed. She nudged the pile with her foot, confirming his vital signs before pondering her choices.

"Do you just allow anybody to waltz in here?" she hissed at Usher.

The doorman stood vigil with an expression almost of hurt, a rare showing of emotion on Usher's stitched face. "It's my job."

Edweena sighed apologetically. She did not mean to vent her frustration on the simple servant. She knew what she must do.

Curse my abiding devotion to this forsaken house!

It had been an act of moral duty that made Edweena present the human before Lady Libra. It had been her first encounter with Libra since the latter's ascension to ladyship of the manor and was, as one could expect, a reluctant encounter.

Ugh, she's gotten so fat.

The Libra she remembered was the svelte, though voluptuous gorgon with which she had once been loyal friends. What was this overweight thing lounging before her? It had been Libra's hedonistic lust and Edweena's unwavering restraint that had divided the two.

I saw ourselves as better off serving Tenebrae as we always had, probing the countryside for predators who may somehow threaten the secrets of this land; its erasure from all the world's maps and minds.

Libra had seen opportunity. When Malistorm, the previous baron of Tenebrae had disappeared so abruptly, she had no problem swooping in and taking his post. Ever since, the gorgon had no time for her vampire companion and Edweena was not one to let go of a grudge. Bordeaux should be the baron. He does all the work. Lady Libra has merely assigned herself the superfluous title and does nothing but eat and laze.

If she had blood, it would be boiling as she mused upon such memories. Their reunion had been a loveless encounter, fraught with a tension that Libra had tried to coat in glossy voluptuaries.

"Dear Edweena, what am I to do, my love? I am already so positively preoccupied with the running of the manor that I am bewildered as to what to offer!"

"Such responsibilities are native to your position. What am I supposed to do with this man?"

Libra ran a finger over his forehead and cheek, "Oof! So sumptuous, I could just eat him alive."

Edweena rolled her eyes. The thought of robbing the man of his life had enraptured her more than once but again the pang of humanity struck her and the idea of killing him seemed barbaric.

"Oh Edweena, why do you look at me in that sneaky way? Make your decision. I find I am at a loss to help you, after all, someone has to make sure this lovely night sky remains intact."

Edweena sighed, she knew the spell must not be all that complicated. Yet Libra had continuously hid behind the notion that it kept her too occupied to attend to other affairs.

Malistorm had managed and he used to bustle about as much as Bordeaux!

With the unconscious man dragged behind her by the arm, Edweena hurled him across the hallway outside Libra's lavish quarters, abandoning all reason and baring her viscous fangs.

"No! Stop!" wailed the man.

He had come to so suddenly that Edweena was knocked back into composure. Her mind raced with temptation, the man's warmth emanated from him, his life was there for the taking. She cursed herself again, grabbing him by the collar and dragging him screaming through Tenebrae's halls, down past the Usher to the front most drawing room of the manor. She kicked at its door and stared into its interior with incredible fury bristling in her eyes.

"Deal with him."

She threw the man into the awaiting arms of Deadsol and slammed the door behind her.

My last great error.

She sat bemoaning in her seclusion. Life seemed so unfair at times that Edweena cursed her immortality, toying with the idea of racing away from Tenebrae until the blanket of dawn washed the night sky away and she crumbled to ash. Was eternity worth such sufferance? Of what worth was everlasting life when she was unable to completely enjoy it? A rat scurried across the dusty carpets at her feet. Its fearlessness in the face of impending death mocked the vampire. She sneered at its ignorance to the fatal predator above it. No, she would spare this one. Her hunger was unabated, though her apathy overwrote its pangs.

It was too late anyway. From the dusky opening of the cracked door came a stately owl, which resolutely ignored all other instincts and pounced upon the helpless rodent. A squeak at the deathblow, a hoot of the reaper, then the room was silent again. Edweena was unmoved. Elsewhere, Madlyn had flung herself onto her simple straw mattress in her windowless room and scribbled into her journal with childish penmanship. She sung softly to herself and kicked her feet about like a limp rag doll as she drew spirals in her book. Her only quill was a haggard old crow feather she had found one evening between trips to Libra's room. Falling apart though it was, the quill was Madlyn's favourite treasure as its red inked tip scrawled across sepia page. All her drawings were in red ink. It was her favourite colour, the colour of her hero. The spirals she drew almost looked like horns.

V: Irksome Harlequins

In the vast, empty miles of isolation that surround Tenebrae Manor, a world where all is countless pine and prickled crag, hazards of grave fatality protect and conceal it from mortal eye. The woods are still. The woods are quiet. But life is there. Lives of creatures both conceivable and nightmarish, no less brutal than each other, lurk within the sea of gloom. As night is unending, bearings are near impossible to confirm. And it is the night that is oft the death of intrusive fools who venture into Tenebrae's forests by intent or fortuity. Such natural circumstances have galvanised the defence of the mansion and established a veil of concealment upon it and its relation to the world beyond.

Still, there are times when, from some divine prank of the deities there comes the arrival of a mortal whose resolve is unyielding to the pressures of insanity and as such, find themselves interloping to the highest degree. It becomes a taxing affair on what to do with such a human and has long been considered a scenario of incredible abhorrence to all of Tenebrae's residents.

There was a live human wandering in Tenebrae

Manor. From all accounts, Bordeaux had gathered that he was a man, one of mental stability in spite of raw fear. One whom, if not dealt with swiftly, could escape, back to his reality and uncover the secret world.

Bordeaux cursed to himself. Usually one of calm composure in the heat of confrontation, the crimson demon had found his patience dwindling to an alarmingly short order. His rank as a head servant of sorts meant that it fell upon him to resolve the present situation. The previous baron, Malistorm, had been of such soothing authority that Bordeaux had rarely felt the fabric of his anxiety torn down to its very fibres as he did now. But Malistorm was gone and in place of his paternal overseeing there appeared Libra in all her grand proportions. And it was with her portly appearance as head mistress that Bordeaux begun to feel the strains of concern for Tenebrae's wellbeing. In his years as master of affairs, he had not dealt with many cases of live humans within the walls. The most recent had been Madlyn and the girl had been of such frazzled disposition that she could easily be dealt with without resorting to fatal measures. The Usher had not moved from his post; not that he should have either, as Bordeaux reached the front foyer of the manor and made his way to the imposing doors of the eastern drawing room. He acknowledged Usher with a tip of head that was observed but not returned by the deadpan doorman.

Bordeaux's claw-like hand clutched the lion head doorknob and slowly turned it. The burgundy oak creaked thunderously, the echoes of its cries flying off into the spacious black of the hallways.

The first evident feature of the drawing room was

that of a sickening heat. Deadsol and Comets had lit a fire in the mantelpiece, a fire that roared with such vehemence as to singe the wallpaper surrounding and cause it to bubble and melt away in peels. A shadow stood before the flames. It was a most irregular shape, a body like that of an inverted light bulb, a chemistry flask, supporting a melon of similar dimensions upon its thin neck. Sprouted from the melon's sides, a pair of rabbit ear protuberances where the distinct jingle of bells could be heard chiming from their tips. From the mouth of the melon, for it was in fact a head, came a squabbling collection of squeaks and rambles, as the shadow's small arms thrust a poker into the glowing embers with violent repetition.

"My boy, that fire is prominent enough," said Bordeaux.

Visibly vexed at the interruption of his stoking, the small creature heaved his chest in flustered breaths and throwing aside the poker, turned to face the demon. Standing as he was, the creature appeared to be intimidatingly lanky in stature, the light of the flames outlining his unusual shape. His shadow stretched to an end at Bordeaux's feet. As the creature advanced forward, the shadow receded, until it became discernable that a two-foot tall jester stood beside the crimson demon. The imp's eyes were mismatched in size, his face seemingly locked in a mischievous smile where two fangs upon a lower jaw sprouted like weeds.

Bordeaux smiled affectionately and ruffled the red and yellow motley cap of the runty jester, his bells jangling obnoxiously. "Comets, my boy."

Comets attempted to recoil from Bordeaux's welcomes but instead became unbalanced on his curled silk shoes and fell onto his rear with a thud. He shook his head, sending the rabbit ears of his fool's cap rattling away again, before running back to his post by the fire.

"Bordeaux!"

Deadsol grasped him suddenly by the shoulders and welcomed him warmly. Bordeaux had to reach for his counterpart's wrists to remove his hands from digging into his shoulders.

"Deadsol."

"Why, sir? And why what, you ask? Why are you here? Here, in this very room, when the clock strikes on this very hour."

"I am but answering to your summons, my brother."

"Summons? Summons, he says! I made no such summons!" Deadsol flung his arms flamboyantly and placed a hand on his chin. Bordeaux was nonplussed.

"But a few moments ago, with your bust appearing so suddenly in my quarters! Surely you – "

"I am certain I would have remembered such a visit, my dear friend. Now! I am pleased you are here. A most important matter! Of a grave and vital urgency, citizen! A chief concern! The human, sir! Bordeaux, he's here!"

Deadsol pressed his palms into Bordeaux's back and gave him an encouraging shove towards a corner closet, where a brouhaha of bangs and bumps rattled the inanimate object into life.

"Now see here, Deadsol; I can manage! Now, this man. What is the state of his cognitive composition?"

"Critical, citizen. Dwindling by the moment, good man!"

Now there's a good sign, thought Bordeaux.

The cupboard rocked, the teak groaning under the

internal throes of the human.

"Pray, tell. Have you spoken with him? Reasoned with him?"

"Lo! Listen to the words he says, 'Have you reasoned with him?' To what avail, you pray tell?" Deadsol replied. "To what avail do we ever reason with such fallible fellows? Their lives are far too fleeting to tax oneself upon such matters as the man's feelings. The very idea!"

Bordeaux tilted his head in a display of chastisement, "A little mercy on his life, brother. They only get one. Fleeting though it may be, you surely see that they deserve at the least a quiet life of settled banality?"

Deadsol, clearly distracted, was curling his fingers together with an inhumane dexterity. His moustache twitched involuntarily. "Sir, a thousand pardons. You must have bored me with your vapid bemoaning of human sentimentality."

There was a pause in which the two demons stood and stared at each other.

"No need for that look, Bordeaux. I know what that means!"

Here, Deadsol's voice took on a rather sinister tone. "The human is, shall we say; under wraps."

He planted his foot against the cabinet door in the form of a forceful kick, causing the doors to burst open and a sweating pile of horrified human to collapse outwards onto the floor. He exerted himself in futile squirms, pallor pale with terror.

"And this be him." Deadsol grasped the man by the scruff of the neck. "Helloooo, mister!"

A frantic cry pattered meekly from the man's mouth.

"Come now, Deadsol. That's enough," said

Bordeaux.

"Fiddlesticks! You can be quite the killjoy at times, Bordeaux."

Deadsol let the man drop back down into a crumbled heap on the floor and Comets had his turn of terrorizing the poor soul. The jester rocked to and fro on his heels with the man's collar in his gloved hands, grunting like a rocking chair with each sway. The human whimpered like a child.

"Pathetic really," said Bordeaux, almost sympathetically.

"Hmm, yes, quite," replied Deadsol, distrait. He had procured a pipe from his brown wool coat and was puffing upon its tip with unwarranted self-importance.

"Now, then, the matter of this elephant in the room," said Deadsol.

"Elephant? The man?" squalled Comets.

"A metaphor, you imbecile!" Deadsol scolded, uprooting the jester by the rabbit ears of his cap. Comets struggled like some animated turnip before Deadsol gave him a savage swat with the back of his hand. Comets spun across the room like a meteorite and crashed headlong onto the carpet. Seemingly unhurt, he leapt to his feet immediately and ran back to where he had been standing next to Deadsol not a moment earlier.

Bordeaux remained erect, a towering intimidation over the crying man, "Sir, can you tell me who you are?"

"I'll handle this, Bordeaux." Deadsol's interruption was followed by a slow jaunt in a hemisphere around the man, pipe glowing in a beacon of vermilion in the hazy heat of the room. Halting suddenly, Deadsol prodded the mouthpiece of his pipe accusingly at the human.

"Citizen, explain yourself! Who are you?"

The man's lips quivered in terror.

"Come now, sir. Edweena didn't pull your tongue out did she? Your name!"

"J-j-j-Jethro."

"J-j-j-Jethro, he says. How many J's in that?"

"My stars, those humans give themselves some strange titles," said Bordeaux.

"J-Jethro! Jethro Ulysses Hammond."

"Sounds English! You are far from home… Well, J-Jethro! A hearty name you have. Oh yes, a genuine Prometheus! Robust, diligent, heroic even!"

The man shook his head in a look of quizzical bewilderment that Deadsol ignored.

"Your business, man! Where are you from?"

"A farm, sir, on a hill. Oh, I don't know where it is."

"Aha! A likely story, scoundrel!"

Comets, craving the attention being poured upon the intruder, begun to leap about the room noisily,

"The hill! The hill, he doesn't know where! A deserted hill is where!" His bells rattled on and on.

Haggard eyes of sand - look!
At blackened, brittle trees shook
With gusts of groaning, ravaged fury,
Bursting with the leaves they took!

"On a hill it seems. Well that is less than helpful," said Deadsol. "The world is one of many hills, many mountains, innumerable even to the birds who fly over head with the greatest vantage point!"

Comets sung;

Like golden stars, they spin and swirl,
Glide on violent gale hurl!
Through grey force, the birds drown
And slide on through maelstrom curl!

"But more, sir!" continued Deadsol. "Indulge me further. On what wind did you ride into the realm of Tenebrae, eh? What zephyr?"

The man's terror was increased further more by Deadsol's eloquent speech; he was clearly a man of simple composition, true to his occupation as a farmhand.

Comets sung;

The wind chases onward forth
From empty, endless miles North.
Ivy, creep! Cling to ruin,
Strangle dead a long lost worth!

"I am lost, sir! So lost! I was sent on an errand across country. Oh, what is this awful place? Which way is my home? How long have I been here?" rambled Jethro.

Deadsol smiled, "All are questions that only you would know, young man. What would I know of your fool's errand, of your hill?"

Comets sung;

Warmth forgotten, time is still,
Sun shine weak onto the hill.
Dim as a silver coin in the sky,
Yearning for sleep debt to fulfill!

Comets hereupon grew bored of his recital of the desolation hill and, seeing that neither Bordeaux nor Deadsol seemed likely to give him the attention he desired, he returned to his fire stoking.

"Well, this was a wastrel interview," huffed Deadsol. "Excuse me." He snatched up from Comets the fire poker, which was in fact his walking cane and moved to egress.

"You're leaving, Deadsol?" asked Bordeaux.

"But why not?"

"The human. Surely you see we are, in fact, not finished here?"

Deadsol thought a moment. "Oh, very well."

He returned to Jethro and again lifted him by the scruff of the neck, proceeding to scream a ghastly wail into his face. His fierce baritone droned on, bloodcurdling in its volume, joined in turn by the tenor squeal of Jethro, a squeal that wavered off pitch into frantic falsetto.

Deadsol released grip on the man, who fell to the floor, weeping like a child. The demon laughed victoriously and shoved him back into the closet before moving to complete his exit of the room.

"Deadsol…."

Deadsol chuckled with great mirth. "What is it now, Bordeaux? Look at him! He's not going anywhere! Did you see the fear in his eyes? It would pluck the very strings of my sympathies, if I were in possession of such things! I bid you good health."

Bordeaux turned his head from the departing demon to the closet. His mind raced away on the subject of what to do, red eyes looking down to see Comets the jester staring back at him indifferently.

"Well, what is it, Comets?"

Comets' head tilted to the side but his expression was unchanged.

Bordeaux shook his head at the imp's folly. "Enough of his nonsense."

More than ever, Bordeaux felt the eager urge to return to his belvedere and waste a few hours on rest. Observing Comets barricading the cabinet doors with a stray oddment of firewood to the chagrin protests of Jethro, Bordeaux left the drawing room.

In the halls the air was mercifully cooler, though the heat had become too much to endure once and for all. Usher, the ever-loyal vigil, stood and acknowledged Bordeaux's presence with eye contact.

"Enough for the while, my friend," murmured Bordeaux.

"Yes sir," Usher replied. "Maybe you should sleep."

Bordeaux considered returning the offer in kind, before realising its impotent nature when applied to Usher. The stairs greeted him.

"I am very weary. Goodbye, Usher."

"Goodbye, Master Bordeaux."

VI: At the Summit

Time is a most enigmatic phenomenon at Tenebrae - comparable to a stallion-hauled chariot, indifferent to the poor souls who become trampled under the wheels, balanced in turn by its cold absence and maligned cruelty. The grains slip through the neck of the hourglass with incredible briefness, leaving behind feelings of happiness and joy in the upper bulb, never to be revisited barring regretful reflection. And of the other direction - through the neck, to the present, where the hourglass becomes so clogged that time itself would appear to have halted its chariot altogether. It remains still as scum-skinned tarn, the languid revolutions of clock arms the only betrayal of life, cycling across the face of the clock as dragonflies over the stagnant swamp. These insects are the only vital giveaway to the presence of a future, its composition - be it bleak or promising, is unknown.

Perched on a balcony overlooking the southern cliffs of the mountains, where a prominent spire looms atop as the apex of Tenebrae Manor like a ghastly, rusted blade, two shadows sit in a sombre assemblage.

It is Bordeaux and Deadsol, brothers of the eternity, companions of the twilit melancholy. Bordeaux - a man of whim and reserve, of refined panache. The rascal Deadsol - cut of the same vibrant cloth, albeit with threads of mischief, of ravenous appetite for destruction. Time in its most mysterious nature has blurred the hours together, so that the haze encompassing has absorbed memory; how long had it been since this pair had met in the drawing room?

The only conclusion one can be assured of is that it is now closer to Libra's birthday celebrations and their interrogation of the intrusive man ever further in the past.

"The summer must end shortly," said Bordeaux.

"End?" Deadsol replied. "Whatever does end in this place? It merely drips onward, down and down. Unending, my friend."

"Hardly an optimistic response." Bordeaux procured a cigarillo from his coat pocket and ran two fingers down its rough side.

"Will you do me the pleasure? Fine smokes, these."

"My thanks but I have my own," said Deadsol, retrieving his own pipe as though drawing a pistol.

Bordeaux clicked his fingers like flint, igniting a flame upon the tips, with which he lit both his cigarillo and Deadsol's pipe.

His pipe lit and illuminating his face with its glow, Deadsol continued.

"Even were we to be relieved of such a heat wave, what would follow? I ask you; what would naturally tail a summer of such intensity?"

Bordeaux thought a moment. "One would hazard to guess at a blizzard."

"Exactly. The weather will do as it pleases, Bordeaux. And even if we were to possess some powerful magician who could control such phenomena, say - a glutton whose self-importance is as inflated as her abdomen, why would she concern herself with our troubles?"

"Hmm, yet Libra informed me the control of weather was beyond her skill."

Deadsol guffawed. "And you my friend? You believed such piffle? She can maintain a night of everlasting proportions and you thought a simple heat wave was beyond her skill?"

"I suppose I had not seen it that way."

Deadsol had struck a blow on Bordeaux's dignity and though they had conjured a friendship capacitating of such honesty, the crimson demon seemed eager to move onto other subjects.

The two blew slow wisps of indigo smoke into the void beyond them, swollen as it were with pines of infinite number. Bordeaux's thin lips parted and from his mouth slid a smoky serpentine dragon of terrific tooth and whisker. Above them, the dragon took on a life of its own, as rabbits of smoke snorted from Deadsol's prominent nostrils leapt forward only to bounce into the stream of indigo flame of the dragon, perishing instantly. Some were constricted by the beast, some caught in its savage jaw. Others simply took one hop too far and found themselves caught in the embers of the dragon's fiery breath. The two demons were pleased at their puppet show, before Bordeaux's eyes focused beyond the curls of smoke into the trees below.

"Do you think he'll find it?" he asked.

"He always does."

As though he knew he was being spoken of, Comets hurtled over the banister and plopped onto the balcony, breathing heavily.

"Well, speak of him and he comes," said Bordeaux.

"Comets, what of this intrusion? Did you find the shiny thing?"

A triumphant Comets held forth a silver coin, gleaming as bright as his smile. "Found!"

"Quite good, lad." Bordeaux turned to Deadsol.

"Your turn or mine, my friend?"

Deadsol gestured an invitation with the sweep of a hand. "Let it be yours, fine citizen."

"What joviality. See here, Comets. Hand it over."

Comets snatched his hands away, cradling the coin like a bird egg.

"Come now, Comets, you disagreeable scoundrel," said Bordeaux.

"The shiny is mine!" said Comets with defiant finality.

Not one to sway towards random physical violence, Bordeaux simply stared intently at the jester until his intimidating gaze became all too much for Comets and the coin exchanged hands.

Comets took a step back; head down like an obedient canine as Bordeaux tossed the coin up and down in his hand.

"Last time, Comets," Bordeaux reminded.

Swinging his forearm in revolutions like a pendulum, the crimson demon wound up his strength and let loose an almighty throw. The coin whistled into the night, cutting the cobwebbed gloom like a sickle. Its reflection lingered a moment, before sight of the medallion was lost to the black trees.

Comets darted over the precipice with unrestrained vigor until he too disappeared from view.

"Deadsol, I had wanted to inquire - the man?" Bordeaux sat back down.

"He is not going anywhere," Deadsol assured. "He's right where we left him, bound with ropes now, too."

"Be sure to spare him, Deadsol."

"Cease this fussing, B. You and your sappy sentiment! He's being fed. Madlyn is taking him the scraps of Libra's excessive meals. Scraps though they may be, with Libra's hunger as it is, you can be sure that he is well fed indeed."

"I must thank you for your restraint, Deadsol."

"You are welcome, my friend. Much as I'd like nothing more than to prey upon such a fragile mind, I realise you need one less stress on your mind at present."

Bordeaux smiled, "You are far more charming when you suppress your ribaldry." The wisps of indigo smoke drifting from their mouths continued to play at their ventriloquism.

As though of need of vent, Bordeaux opened the floodgates of his angst on Deadsol and words began to cascade from his mouth. "Personally, I will be glad when this farce is over."

"The birthday?"

Bordeaux nodded slowly, his face curled with vagabond smoke.

"Were that ghastly banshee not so short of temper and abundant of magic, I would give her a piece of my mind," said Deadsol.

"If we pay her no other compliment, we must say that she does keep the sky dark for us."

"Yes, the spell. Bah! If only the old bat would divulge

the secrets of her witchcraft."

"Old bat? She's the vigour of a lass in her mid-twenties!" said Bordeaux.

"Ah yes, of two or three lasses I might say and I speak not of her mental structure," chuckled Deadsol.

"Another jab at the physical decline of our fair mistress."

"I'd call it a physical increase."

"Enough."

Deadsol was visibly amused with his antics but held his tongue from further insults. The demons sat in silence, gaze hypnotized by the nighttime scene surrounding. Somewhere in the gloom, Comets was scavenging for his coin.

Comets tore through the conifer maze with adroit agility, paying no notice to the whips and lashings of pine needle striking his person, his eyes bore into the darkness, searching, hunting. It was a trivial game to be sure but to a being of Comet's juvenile disposition, chasing down a silver coin in a forest was the highest calibre of fun. The imp was an enigma, a humanoid of disproportioned features, grotesque in their peculiarity. Did his mind bulge with knowledge and press against the very inside edges of his scalp? Or, encompassed as it were in his melon like skull, was his mind more akin to a rattling bead in an egg-shaker, chiming like the bells of his motley cap and echoing off the cavernous walls of unused head? The eloquence of the monologues poured from the angular slit of a mouth in beautiful and nonsensical phonics; were they of purposeful poetic prose or merely the ramblings of an ignorant fool? Despite an attention span of extremities so opposing that one could deem it as suspicious trickery of a changeling, Comets found his focus enraptured upon his little game for hours at a time. While other exploits came across to him an ignoble nuisance, his shiny coin held him in hypnagogic state. Wont of his character, he was drawn to such relics as a moth is to flame and no matter how long it took, he always managed to uncover the treasure he sought.

The moon made navigation less challenging at present, for it hung in the sky as a perfect disc, a flawless swirl of vibrant paint, a blinding white at its centre. And that white faded out in a circle through brushstrokes all shades of grey and into the impregnable black canvas of night. It was as though it was a pebble, dropped into a still pond where the colourless hue was ever changing like ripples across the water's surface. The moonlight gave the forest a cloak of navy blue, electrifying in its intensity, giving new animation to the trees, sharper edges to all objects.

Comets came to a halt and stood statue-still on the matted floor of dust and needles. There it was. The moon had betrayed its reflective friend and shone a noticeable beam from the coin's surface. Betwixt weed and gnarled root, the coin was exposed in all its foreign, metallic glory. The jester hopped forward on one foot until his shadow blocked out the shining silver. Triumphant he stood, yet as he reached forth to scoop up his prize, his wrist was grasped by a hand of knuckled root and wood.
Comets, true to form, was not in the least startled by this

movement of usually inanimate tree branch, a mild nuisance, nothing more. The hand was rough and splintery on its petiolar arm and Comets' gaze sought the source of the thing that had grabbed him. On a stump stood an awkward, squatted humanoid shape where two bulbous eyes revealed themselves with the peeling back of papery bark eyelids. The eyes were round as the moon above, penetrating with an intrusive deadpan. They were mismatched in shape, just as the eyes of the jester, so that it almost seemed to Comets that he was staring into a mirror.

His grin unabated, Comets titled his head to the side and let forth a trebling trio of staccato grunts, high in their pitch and responded in turn by a mimicking boom. The tree stump, the creature, mumbled a moan in response to Comets' through a mouth of jagged and stitched dimensions. Unbeknownst to Comets, the monster that stood before him was a Wood Golem; an animated tree stump of a frightening potency quenched somewhat by a body sluggish in movement. Draped about the thick neck of the creature was a noose of frayed and petrified rope, a morbid adornment atop the bole that was its body.

The jester shrieked a bloodcurdling warning to the ligneous creation, his little fangs displayed in a simian-like sneer of intimidation. Unhand my coin, the sneer said. The Golem responded in turn with a baritone bellow that thundered through the surrounding woods. Unchanging in its deadpan expression, the Wood Golem brought back its other arm and initiated a swing. A bludgeoning blow was ensured, a blow that would have crushed Comets' skull like the ripe melon it resembled, had the thing not been so cripplingly slow and predictable of movement.

Comets, of lithe limb and adroit agility, threw his tiny frame at the creature that stole his shiny thing, freeing himself of its grasp and jumping onto its shoulders. With another venomous hiss, he sunk his jaws into the golem's head. Like a vice-grip they squeezed, unmercifully biting down into the monster's face, from which came the crunch of splitting wood. The Wood Golem languidly thrashed in a vain attempt to throw the imp from his perch but Comets' fangs were latched down ruthlessly, showing no quarter. Further and further Comets let his teeth penetrate, one fang straying from wooded mouthful and piercing the eye of the Wood Golem like a knife through jelly. The creature let out a sickening moan of pain, the insides of the eye secreting down its face, a weeping wound.

Resorting to other attacks, Comets unhinged his jaws and snatched at the noose tied about the Golem's neck. He pulled with all his strength, until the creak of rotted wood splitting arose and the head of the creature burst off its thick neck. The cries of the thing were no more; the rooted claw relaxed and the coveted coin plopped to forest floor.

Indifferent to his thievery of a life, Comets snatched up his coin and stared victoriously at the mound of death at his feet. The eyes were still open, still intimidating in their stare, the punctured one leaking its fluid in a hideous puddle. From the thing's head sprouted branches twisted and deformed and it was from these handles that Comets picked up the skull and examined it. Deciding that it would make a fine trinket, a symbol of his triumph over adversity, he took it with him on his return journey to Tenebrae Manor.

The moon thrust its beams like swords through the demented conifer canopy, a grin of unsettling satisfaction was illuminated on the face of Comets the jester. Deadsol and Bordeaux would be most pleased. His coin was warm, clutched tightly in his sweating palm; the manor loomed ahead with its shadowy outline blotting out part of the lunar orb behind it.

But when Comets climbed to the summit, he found that the balcony was empty, devoid of the demon duo. The butt of recently extinguished cigarillo still released its smoky wisps from the tip but all else was still. His gratified countenance was replaced with one of feeble frustration, for there were none to share in his victory over the Wood Golem.

Sighing deeply, the imp took one last look at the totem of his battle, before flinging the head over the balcony. It struck against the jagged cliff face below and tumbled earthward with a dull thump.

VII: Of Tête-À-Tête's

It won't close, my lady."

"It fits," snapped Libra. "Try harder, you stupid!"

Madlyn's clumsy digits trembled with exertion, feebly attempting to close the laces of Libra's corset. The fitted material squealed in protest, struggling to maintain her girth. Flesh bulged from wherever it could find escape in swathes protruding from betwixt fraying seams. Try as she might, Madlyn was unable to properly assist the short-tempered Lady Libra, who resolutely ignored the simple fact that the corset in question no longer fit.

"Oh forget it!" huffed Libra. "I'll wear the dress instead. Fetch my belt."

"Belt, miss?"

"Don't 'belt miss' me! You know the one I speak of! The ivy leaf!"

Madlyn entered Libra's spacious wardrobe and was met with mountains of cloth and fabric. There had been a stage in Libra's life when she had been in possession of much less excess, a stage when her clothing was hung neatly upon racks and pressed finely until the wrinkles were naught. As her lust for life increased evermore, conversely her enthuse towards keeping her belongings in order declined. She had once demanded that Madlyn were to tidy things up but the simple servant girl had not the ability to match the lady's expectations and, as such, disarray ensued.

A flurry of panic descended onto Madlyn's hummingbird heart; there were dozens of belts before her! Strewn across threaded rock and hillock like serpents lounging in the heat. There were buckles of many shapes and these emblems of antiquity confirmed that Libra had certainly gathered many fine things in years gone by. Belts like snakes with heads of bone, of silver sun, of minuscule bas-relief.

It was through what some call good fortune that Madlyn found the belt in question, a scaly strap of interwoven leather, like the host vines of the brilliant emerald ivy leaf that served as adorning buckle. She snatched it up and returned to the bedroom where Libra had struggled back into her form fitting dress of dusky charcoal.

"You are slow but just in time, I suppose..."

Libra took the belt and wrapped it about the spherical orbit of her waist, clasping the two halves of the ivy leaf that would lock together to become whole. There was a struggle, the leaf halves reached for each other's grasp in vain, as Libra sighed and tugged harder. The leather strap of the belt dug into her soft sides until it was all but hidden beneath fleshy bulge. Still the belt would not close. She inhaled deeply, holding in her paunch back as far as possible, her face turning a flushed fuchsia from both exertion and held breath. The buckles came close, so close, quivering in her strained fingers until finally, they met and interlocked. Libra's breath was short but her face showed an expression of triumph.

"There!" she gasped. "I did it."

Madlyn stared expectantly at the quivering Lady, who was holding herself as still as possible. She looked perfectly ridiculous, as though the belt would slice her soft body in half, squeezing her like a vice grip. Soon her face contorted to a grimace, a wince and what followed was a relieving sigh, an exhale that expanded Libra's belly to its original dimensions. In a blink, the belt burst open again, detonating like a barrel of gunpowder and flying to a far corner of the room, relieved of the pressure of the ballooning stomach it was subjected to contain. Libra blushed redder still, as Madlyn's accusingly stupid eyes continued to stare.

"What are you looking at?" huffed Libra.

It was a look of vague vapidity, although the combination of Madlyn's globular eyes and the small mouth with its upturned corners would have her perceived as a girl of smug intellect to any who didn't know her personally. Her gaze was broken in an instant response to her superior; her eyes cast downward and gawky feet scraping at the ground like a mule.

"It must be the heat. Yes, that's it. It must have shrunken my clothing somehow."

Madlyn smirked and was, no doubt, fortunate that Libra didn't notice. The Lady of Tenebrae Manor had become rather flustered after her episode of wardrobe malfunction and was, as such, further startled when Deadsol cascaded into the room.

"Damn it all. It's you," hissed Libra.

"A prominent man should always make a prominent

entry!" replied Deadsol gallantly.

"You should have knocked. What do you want?"

"But a moment, Lady Libra. A tête-à-tête, it would seem!"

"Ugh, be quick. I'm very busy." Libra made no attempt to hide her contempt towards the demon.

"She has requested a three tiered cake," said Bordeaux. "She took the liberty of procuring a sketch."

The mute chef accepted the crumpled sheet and examined it, squinting through his weakening eyes. His countenance bore a weight of responsibility, seasoned with a dash of revolt. The picture was crude, as though penned by a child but its message was coherent enough. The chef nodded astutely.

"You have my thanks, good sir."

Bordeaux patted him on the back and winced at the touch of greasy kitchen attire, that of sweat and food spillage. The crimson demon held his hand away from his person as though it were some foreign article he wished to dispose of, before eyeing an apron hung upon a nearby rack with which he proceeded to wipe his hand clean.

"This is, to me, only worsening her situation," said Edweena.

Bordeaux allowed himself a smirk. Leaving the chef to his work, demon and vampiress trudged through the dank corridors of Tenebrae's lower ground floor, where no ventilation gave fresh breath to its sweating walls. The floor, black as coal with the grime of insects, coated in dust moistened by perspiration and footsteps numbering in their thousands; seemed to absorb all colour, as though it were ready to swallow up careless travelers into a doomed quicksand.

Withdrawing further from the kitchen, Bordeaux and Edweena began to discern certain echoes flitting in the sombre melancholy; the echoes of their sedated voices, their shambled footfall.

"You mustn't overdo it," said Edweena.

"It is my duty."

"Be that or no, you must give yourself rest at some point."

They entered the wine cellar and Bordeaux took up in his hand a torch that hung at the entrance. The roars of the kitchen gave way to a bellowing silence, in pitch as inky as the ocean floor. Shelves of bottled antiquity faded into a sickening black. None argued that the chilling macabre in Tenebrae's cellars was without peer; its foreboding horror lay sick with feverish darkness, as though the gates to the very underworld itself stood rusting nearby.

The solitary torch shone meekly, of such dull orange that no comfort could be taken from its light. Bottles shone with its reflection, sidling silently past as the two friends plunged further into the cavern. Their eyes stood out in the gloom, ruby and sapphire, both in their respective pairs.

Bordeaux stopped before a portion of shelf no different to the rest and retrieved a certain vintage. "This is the one," he mused. Then, as though remembering Edweena's recent statement, replied, "It is but once a year I must endure such stress. I will rest after."

Edweena's eyes shone, intense with the blue fire of her discord.

"I simply could not handle it if Libra were to fly off into another juvenile rage," he added. "Regardless of the injustice arisen each year from her birthday, I find answer to her every whim at this time of year much less taxing than rebellion. Wouldn't you agree?"

Bordeaux stared intently at Edweena, whose internal fury was churning with each thought of the unjust mistress of Tenebrae Manor.

"But it isn't fair," she implored. "Why should you have to do all this work? We stand in this darkled cellar, searching for some wine long lost to the ages, while she is upstairs, no doubt, lounging in luxury as we speak."

Bordeaux thought a moment, a moment where the silence became deafening, a torrential ocean crashing shoreward in booming waves.

"One must do something to pass time here."

Libra sat upon the edge of the chaise lounge with a slow elegance met with the groan of chair beneath weight. Madlyn obediently filled the gorgon's coffee cup and timidly placed a pair of sugar cubes towards the beverage with little tongs.

"Give that here, Madlyn. I'll do it. Deadsol and I will speak alone."

Madlyn stared blankly.

"That means you leave."

Upon realisation, the girl started for the door, her kneecaps clashing against one another below her greasy smock.

"Ah, miss! Wait! Allow me the honour," said Deadsol, showing a gentlemanly care in escorting Madlyn to the door. With a gentle push on her slight back, the girl was gone and replaced with the noisy ingress of Comets. The imp made no hesitation in advancing to Libra's vanity and rummaging through the various trinkets there.

"That accursed little rodent," Libra hissed. "Why have you brought him?"

Deadsol feigned abashed shock.

"Comets, you capricious lout, you forget yourself!"

The imp rolled his eyes and bowed with unsettling grace, were he capable of lowering himself further, it seemed doubtless he would do so; only his legs were far too short, his feet far too long, to allow a comfortable bend of knee.

"Ditch the facade, little man. Deadsol! He must leave as well."

Comets needed no invitation to leave, scuttling out the way he'd come with the bells of his cap rattling. The door was slammed.

"I do not know why you tolerate that boy," said Libra, still filling her coffee with sugar cubes.

"Ah, if only you knew, miss. A couple of peas we are; Miss Libra. Peas of a pod, birds of a feather, a chip off the old..."

"That is quite enough, Deadsol."

The demon corrected his posture but was instantly on the move again, pacing about the lavish room. His eyes searched, his moustache twitched. In short, the man was rummaging and making little attempt at discretion. His exaggeration of motions was unbearably overt.

"Deadsol."

"Miss?"

"Why are you here?"

Deadsol was taken aback. "Why, she asks? One can not inquire on his ladyship's health and well being?"

"One can, but that isn't why you're here. The Deadsol that I know does not simply *'inquire upon his ladyship's health.'* Explain yourself."

Her coffee had morphed into a sugary pulp, thick as syrup, not that Libra had cause to object. She downed the potion swiftly before the cup was refilled with a wave of her smooth white hands.

Deadsol stood before a vanity where an assortment of perfumes and jewelry lay dormant in an aroma of scented powders. He began to dexterously assort the trinkets as though searching for something of utmost importance.

"Come now, Deadsol. Don't do that! Don't make me get up."

"This!" shouted Deadsol, facing Libra and holding a brooch in the shape of a black rose aloft.

Libra's confusion was matched only by her frustration.

Deadsol remained still as a statue, the brooch held high, eyes fixed upon her.

"Yes. That. What of it?"

"It must be this very wonderful thing that controls the eternal night!"

Here, Libra snorted a laugh of gaiety not often seen in the presence of Deadsol. She covered her mouth daintily but that did nothing to cease the spray of coffee that shot from her lips.

"Ha! I knew you had ulterior motives, is that what this is about? You think you can waltz in here, disturb my peace and march out with the secrets entrusted to me? I thought more of you, Deadsol."

The demon appeared embarrassed, his arm slowly lowering the brooch back to its place on the vanity.

"Unfortunately for you, the spell is one of knowledge, not of tangible substance," said Libra. "Perhaps you should commit more time to thanking me than interrogating me."

Deadsol remained silent.

"Truth be known, it was I who was entrusted with this archaic knowledge, a successor for Malistorm was needed and who better than I, one who had studied the happenings of Tenebrae for centuries. Power comes to those who seek it, Deadsol. But such endeavors are wasted on the ignorant. The cunning always emerge victorious."

"Oh folly! Woe to me, woe to my mind of severed tendrils!"

Madlyn stood at the head of the great stairwell and drifted off into a vacuous reverie. From the outside of a window came a tapping and a muffled hoot, the ghastly shape of a great owl fluttering ominously behind the pane. Madlyn's own owl-like eyes started at a door slam from where she'd just made egress. Out of the shadows there hopped Comets, having himself been abdicated access to Libra's bedroom.

In the blue light of the moon, which cast its shadows in the shapes of grotesque puppets across the bleak stairwell, there stood girl and boy. The servant girl. The harlequin. An alien tension held the pair in a state of caution, for neither of these two had ever laid eyes on the other hitherto. Madlyn relived memories of a younger day when she, a little girl, traversed a tent of funhouse mirrors. Such was the distorted shape of the little man before her, that these memories were relived. Madlyn raised a finger as if to prod Comets' face. In return he did the same. She tilted her head in inquisitive inclination. He did also.

"It was last year when I had decided I would not attend the next celebration," said Edweena. "The very atmosphere of the auditorium made me cringe. And so minimum was the entertainment."

"Perhaps that is why she seems much more demanding this year. I agree it was not Arpage's magnum opus. You will not attend this time around?"

Edweena sighed. "I suppose I must. If anyone inquires, I am there to assist you. Let it be known I still hold my grudges..."

'It is appreciated, to be sure."

Bordeaux and Edweena slowly made the return journey to the light of the kitchen corridors, dim as it may be, yet a revered salvation from the pitch-blackness of the haunting cellar. A voice seemed to drift from the dark, a whisper that crawled across the necks of the two beings. *Forget the light,* it said. *Stay here in blinding doom; give yourselves up to the enveloping morbid sleep. Down here there is no light, not in this far corner, these most deep confines, this very perimeter of space and time. Not even the dim moonlight of the Tenebrae night can penetrate this lull.*

The bloodcurdling murmur was unanswered by both Bordeaux and Edweena, immune as they were to all horrors after centuries spent in darkness. Any other weak mortal would swiftly perish here, this place where sanity was so easily surrendered. Where one finds themselves dashing wildly into unseen surroundings in panicked attempt to find an escape, to expel all terror from the hot blood of their warm bodies, for they are so foreign in this cellar devoid of heat and pulse.

No, Bordeaux and Edweena did not turn towards the voice. Their backs remained facing the darkness, morphed into hulking shadows against the backdrop of the torchlight.

Deadsol clasped his scalp in anguish; his erratic composure had flown from bold intrusion to pitiful depression. Libra watched this charade with indifference; Deadsol's exaggeration of all emotive faculties was well documented amongst the residents of Tenebrae Manor. Her patience was dwindling, the urge to be rid of the man stirring the cauldron of her bubbling anger.

"Deadsol, cease this blubbering! Cease!"

"Blubbering, she says! Blubber, the very word carries hypocrisy. Oh ho lo! Pot calls the kettle black! A pot indeed! Oh woe!"

At last, Libra's temper reached boiling point. She stood from her recline and raised her hands skyward. Deadsol gasped as he felt his feet leave the ground, as though some unseen force had plucked him up by the scruff of the neck. He thrashed and wept like an infant, his leather shoes clacking together as he kicked.

"You forget yourself, Deadsol. I should give you such a thrashing." Libra's voice was one of unwavering control. "Your priorities should direct themselves towards that of my birthday! Busy yourself with something, anything. Bordeaux would no doubt appreciate it."

"Ah he he! Busy. Yes, yes. Bumblebee-busy, to be certain. A proposition, yes! A comedic performance, starring me - Deadsol! And of course the plucky assistant, Comets!"

Libra was indignant, "You will do no such thing. The thought of you two deplorable harlequins poisoning my celebrations pushes the bile to the back of my throat."

"Then what, miss? Oh please let me down!"

The demon fell in a heap on the floor and continued to weep.

"I want you out of my way, Deadsol. Colloquies with you are most vexing."

Libra stood pondering a moment. "You will decorate the auditorium. Go. Take that hideous imp with you. I do no wish to see you until the event. And fear my reprimands should you perform poorly at your task!"

Deadsol peered up from the floor at the hefty lass, "Decorate! Yes! Colours abound, light and sound! At once, my dreary deary!"

"Good. Leave."

"Very good, Lady Libra. Most benevolent are your reasonings!"

"I find that you've drained me proficiently of said benevolence. I say again, leave."

Deadsol made for the door. "Why yes! Rest, my dear; regain the reasoning! The sleep of reason produces monsters!"

The door slammed, its voluminous blast taking all sound with it, so that only echoes were left reverberating in the now silent room.

The jester and Madlyn lingered on the stairwell. Their gazing upon one another was intense, wide-eyed and silent, that is until Madlyn wrested the energy out of the dreamy atmosphere and uttered, "Who are you?"

As though Comets were indeed her reflection, his reply came. "Who," he mimicked, "Are you?"

"I am Mad," said the girl.

"So am I."

"How is that so? When we are so very different?"

"Who says we are different?"

Madlyn had to think. "Why… Nature. In our appearances. We are different."

"You saw the black rose," said Comets.

"Yes. It was very pretty."

"I saw it too. We are the same in that way… If only

that way."

But their reverie was broken by the emergence of Deadsol. He raced by them and swiftly swooped up Comets by the ear of his cap.

"Come along, my boy. Bustle, I say! We've errands!" Madlyn watched as they sailed off down the hall, Comets never removing his gaze from her.

Edweena and Bordeaux had returned to ground floor, away from the stifling air and into a realm much dryer, arid even. The dust of neglect clung to every surface in Tenebrae's foyer and cutting through the melancholia came an anguished wail from the direction of the rooftops. A spider stirred, a suit of knight's armour rattled, an ancient portrait of a forgotten baron appeared to incline his painted face in the direction of the noise. From his vigil post at the front door, Usher turned his head slowly and emitted a barely audible grunt.

"That sound," Edweena whispered.

Again there was a shout, preceding a rumble like that of a great stone column tipping over. Bordeaux stood and focused on the noises echoing through the mansion. There was no doubt in his mind who the perpetrator of such obnoxious volume was, as he and Edweena begun the ascent of the central staircase. Bordeaux's leather shoes clicked rhythmically on each step, washed over with the hush of Edweena's long black scarf trailing behind her. The years of unending movement about the house and its surroundings had left both of them in peak physical condition, svelte and tiring not to the overwhelming summit of stairs.

The noise was coming from the auditorium, its expansive brouhaha increasing evermore as demon and vampiress drew closer. It became discernible that there were a multitude of voices, rumbling about the other, trying to gain dominance through increased volume. The great door to the theatre was ajar and Bordeaux, taking a look at the face of Edweena, who stood bemused, pushed it open.

VIII: Decorating the Auditorium

The auditorium - an introverted atmosphere and cavern of acoustic desolation, a monstrous eardrum infinitely scouting, searching for a change in the ominous quiet. Where any difference in the still atmosphere would have it transformed into that of a menace of booming throat bellowing. Spewing forth echoes of tremendous bass that reverberate in the common time signature. The seats red and empty, hollowed out like upturned mollusks. Its lights, draped through high ceiling as glow worms trapped in the silk of a spider's thread. And the composer Arpage - ensconced in his loft and staring blankly at a scribble cluttered score sheet.

This cave where time is frozen, all is silent, a vacuum devoid of sound and all is still save the dust motes sailing endlessly about the walls, seemed to portray within its confines a small galaxy. A forgotten void as dimly lit as the heavens with their faraway stars.

When it appeared that nothing could penetrate this

curtain of laconism, when the very idea of sound was fast becoming lost to the ages, there came a low drawl. It was that of a man singing and increasing in volume as he drew nearer to the auditorium. Then, with a blast of prominence came Deadsol in mid-song.

"... And the night mourned the sorrows of the earth! Now here's a cadaverous colosseum! What say you, Comets?"

The jester trailed in behind him. "Dusty, sneezy but we can manage."

Deadsol clapped his hands and at once there was a burst of light about the theatre, all unlit lights shot up with a fresh glare that gave the room a dull gold glow.

"Now see here, this place is simply not up to scratch. Surely you'll agree Miss Libra deserves a tidier jubilee? Comets, you scoundrel, what are you doing?"

Deadsol's lackey had clambered onto the stage and was scaling the curtain to its summit. Perhaps he was exerting some form of downward tug, because his light frame alone could not have encouraged what followed, that of the curtain rod dislodging from its perch at one end and sending Comets crashing to the stage with it. Deadsol could do nothing but guffaw as the imp jester struggled to untangle himself from the curtains. Overcoming any structure or patience shown in his attempted egress, he simply tore at the cloth with his teeth and ripped his own escape from the threads. Deadsol laughed so loudly that his shoulder made forceful impact on the nearby wall and caused several lights to plummet earthbound like meteorites and shatter on the floor. The general clamour that followed echoed about the interiors of the theatre and instantly destroyed the reveries undertaken by Arpage, who remained hidden in his loft as the unseen third inhabitant of the auditorium.

The musician had, of course, heard the commotion beneath him and a switch had been struck in his composition, one that threw him from quiet contemplation into a pool of artistic frustration. His rage was suppressed into his core until the pressure was all too much and something snapped. Maybe it was his neck twitching involuntarily, his pencil breaking entwine under his furious grasp or perhaps this snap was merely an onomatopoeia best suiting to his sudden mood swing. In any account, the composer flew upright and stormed to the entrance of his loft to discover the instigators of such racket. Deadsol and Comets had created from the orderly auditorium a chaotic ruin and Arpage's yellow teeth bit down on his lip until the blood trickled to his chin.

"What is this? This impropriety? Here I am, the boulder barricading artistic flow just beginning to give when this, this! This commotion that tickles my very underarms, drains my strength and all ideas go up in puffs of smoke!"

Arpage carried on in his fury. "This heat enrapturing, suffocating! These demands, demands for a magnum opus expunged from my bones, gifted to her, her of all undeserved people."

Here, he broke into sobs. "I am so weary; sleep beckons me! But how? How can I engage in slumberous activities when time drags me screaming closer to the date of my doom! How, when such noise whips at my ears?"

Comets jumped on one foot and tittered softly, as though reciting a lullaby,

The composer grows weary,
But fret not, my deary.
For in his dreams and slumbers
Come his greatest scores and numbers!

In response to this poem, Arpage felt his eye flinch and his brain thrown backwards in time. It was as though he was reminiscing of a forgotten childhood, memories of a young poet flexing his academic grey matter and concocting his first works.

"Such phonics! Such locution!" he stammered. "You! Little man! Meteors may just be my salvation."

"His name is Comets," said Deadsol.

"Pah! Irrelevant! The point is this little man has inspired me! More, more, I say! Uh, if it please, of course... Ah he he, yes." Arpage's hands flailed upon his skinny wrists as he dashed back to his piano and called "Another verse, young Comets!"

The jester turned to Deadsol, who shrugged his shoulders. Comets thought a moment before inflating his chest with pomp,

Slaving away through toil and trial
In such heat! Gives rise to my bile.
And all for a girl so mean and so fat
And incredibly cranky at that!

"Yes! Eureka!" Arpage called from his loft.

An eerie green glow gave ushering to a sombre legato of notes from the piano. The composer played a carnivalesque waltz most haunting in its lumbering. Comets continued in time;

A reluctant posse
At her feet, so to see,
Mutiny! They pray, we'll betray in the day
But victorious morn' is astray.

The music continued and Comets flung his body about the auditorium, throwing confetti conjured as if from nowhere. Deadsol laughed like a hyena as the room began to look more and more like it had been struck down by a gusty blizzard. A whirlwind of chaos had descended, with Comets in the eye of the storm as a figurehead - a deity of tornados. From the keys and pipes of Arpage's instrument came zephyrs of colour and butterflies of noise.

Comets was swinging from a rope whereupon a light sat at its end resembling the luminary lure of a deep-sea angler. Back and forth he swung, until there appeared in view a pair of figures draped in maroon and black, standing vigilant at the door of the auditorium. Despite his vantage point, the jester could see naught but a pair of deep red eyes penetrating him with intensity to paralyse. Close then far, big then small as he swung.

The music stopped, the confetti settled to the floor and three rebels stood stunned under the piercing glare of Bordeaux.

"Who fashioned this disobedience?"

Deadsol turned to him nervously. "Ah, Bordeaux! Just in time, I dare say."

Behind him came a dull thump. Comets had plummeted to the floor.

"This place must be presentable for the jubilee! What have you done?" Bordeaux said.

"A calculated adornment, Mr. B," replied Deadsol. "A verbal contract, as it was. Libra instructed us to prepare the auditorium for her birthday."

Edweena, who stood with Bordeaux, snorted. "Prepare, indeed. This place is a wreck."

"Where is Arpage?" said Bordeaux.

None replied and in the little loft above, the composer crouched frantically behind his piano. Deadsol and Comets inclined their heads slowly in time towards the loft. Bordeaux followed suit.

"Arpage."

The composer would have remained concealed, had his cowardly sobs not betrayed his location. He stood upright and, shaking woefully, he moved in sight of the crimson demon at the top of the ladder to the loft.

"There's our man," smirked Edweena.

"Master B, please -"

"Enough." Bordeaux silenced Arpage with the uprising of his palm. "My boy, what part did you play in these shenanigans? Or are you innocent?"

"Guilty! Guilty!" Comets cried. "A trio of deeds, most awful indeed!" He realised no one was paying him any attention and began to jump about the place.

"Oh sir!" wailed Arpage. "Young Meteors is right! They pranced in here and encouraged such blasphemy against my lady."

"Blasphemy, you say? I referred to the destruction of this very theatre. Perhaps there is more I should be livid of?" said Bordeaux.

Arpage flung his hand to his forehead. "Sir! Forgiveness, I implore! A song, sir. A most insulting song towards Libra!"

"The turncoat!" said Deadsol. "He's ratted on us!"

"Turncoat! Spin! Spin!" Comets twirled until he was dizzy.

Bordeaux pondered a moment with Edweena grinning beside him. Rebellious as these three had been, she found much humour in the degrading of her former ally, Libra.

"But why should that matter?" said Deadsol. "She isn't here to hear. Here to hear! Oh my! Besides, she is but a mere shadow of what she used to be."

"Shadow! Shadow! What is shadow, when all is night? Nothing is shadow at all!" cried Comets.

"Alas, a lumpy midday shadow at that," said Deadsol.

"Midday! Midday! What is midday? So long in the dark! I've forgotten!"

Bordeaux had heard enough. "That will do, Deadsol. In any account, this room must be made presentable."

He now pointed at both Deadsol and Comets. "You and you. Tidy up or I will lock you both in the cellar until you deafen yourselves with the sound of your screams!"

Arpage tittered.

"Arpage," said Bordeaux.

"Ahh! Master B?"

"Concentrate, sir! We have spoken already about this! And you know better than to involve yourself with these two misfits."

Comets moved to shout something in defense, only to be silenced by Deadsol.

"As much as all of us dislike these annual demands of Libra, we must abide by them!"

"The night is quite essential for some of us," added Edweena. "If not for Libra, do it for Bordeaux. The man is exhausted!"

"I did not seek pity, my dear Edweena but I thank you," said Bordeaux. "The show must go on. The reward is another year's reprieve from the wrath of Libra. I ask that you would all galvanise yourselves with me. We can do it together."

"Here, here!" cried Arpage.

"Well said!" echoed Deadsol.

Five silhouettes gathered close in the vast auditorium and, lit by the glowworm lights that remained overhead, they conversed. The reprimanding was at its end and now this quintet stood and permitted themselves but a few minutes grace from their individual demands. The eleventh hour was near, soon the fruits of their labour, which had been nourished with a sickening heat wave, would blossom for better or worse. The yearly episode that they had grown to dread was beating upon the door to their composure. Soon it would break through and, like a blast of southerly gale, it would pass on by and exit through an opposite window. The results of its chaos would remain but the threat itself would be gone and recovery could commence.

IX: The Undercurrents

In the palatial cosmic, the baubles of celestial beauty dangle about their orbits as though on the strings of a mobile. Megaton spheres contradict their own weight with an effortless float through vast expanse. The host star bristles from its own heat with fiery needles like that of the porcupine, spewing forth spectres of light, of energy. The sun blisters the closest pair of satellites with searing flame until their surfaces crack and weep the pus-like magma of their boiling insides. And pertaining to similar tragedy, those orbs furthest from the sun's proximity dwell in vacuous and forgotten darkness. The cold locks them in an eternal sleep, their frigid expanses sustaining no life.

In a fortunate setting, riding a slipstream of equilibrium, the final rock in the host star's initial treble glides comfortably like a leaf on a breeze. Slowly it spins, on axis and orbit, a dancer so carefree, so oblivious to the seething envy of the other planets. It is of a perfect balance, one hemisphere sleeps peacefully in the umbra, one soaks in the warmth of the sun's rays and each take their turns, selfless in their swapping. A deity twirls the sphere in his mighty hand, taking notice of a blemish upon the surface. It is polished again and again, yet the blackened spot remains as a dirty bruise on the skin of this apple. A sun spot, the surface of a dark, deep sea.

It is the eternal night of Tenebrae blanketing its portion of earth's surface. The sky is still, the surface of this impenetrable ocean. Stars skim the shallows in ignorance to the mournful souls who are drowning in the depths. Their lungs fill with the water of regret as they press for the surface, for breath, for life. It is too late - their struggle is in vain, they wallow in their despair. The surface is still; below, the currents pull and tug in restless wanderings.

Our characters are unmoored. Be they pertaining to a calculated chart, or aimless in their off-course drifting, their individual vignettes share a similar destination. A celebration draws near and they are each in varying moods relating to this forthcoming jubilee. Their accounts hang like ornaments on a tree, enveloped in their own mysterious beauty - a red globe for Bordeaux, the crimson demon. And what else? There is a copper coloured globe for Deadsol. A smaller one trails behind it in motley red and yellow; it is Comet's bauble. A brooding black for Edweena and verdant greens for Arpage and Crow. And on a branch far lower than the rest, where the lack of light robs it of any distinct colour, is a bauble representing the Mute Chef.

Above them all, a certain branch sags under the weight of a dusky charcoal sphere. It is of course the elevated Libra, a honey-eyed Venus. They sit together on the same tree, leaves of a common bole, though perfectly encapsulated within their individual spheres, unaware of each other's presence.

A candle burned, its tall and slender frame diminishing slowly, spreading horizontally as it spiraled downward. On the wooden surface of the vanity, where wax was beginning to congeal and stick, two elbows rested. The forearm pillars held within their hands a head of remarkable beauty and the mirror reflected the face of the Lady Libra. Within her fingers, a tangled curl of darkled brown hair wove its serpentine form, one of many elegant strands that dangled gracefully about her neck. Her face a perfect form, softened in its contours, heart shaped and full with a pair of hypnotic topaz eyes. Their pupils were drowned, swallowed up by an encompassing pool of amber that could lull weak of will mortals into submission. It was these eyes that gazed distantly into their own reflection. Did their own beauty amaze them? Or was Libra merely off in pleasant reverie, dreaming of a future more extravagant than her present? The mirror was a canvas, a portrait of the voluptuous, a celebration of life. But what else had the procurator of such a portrait hidden amongst his brushstrokes?

The background, the half lit gloom of Libra's bedroom, camouflaged another being. A being noticeable only at a second glance, a deeper look. Yes, there she is. Madlyn is behind Libra. The candlelight was not strong enough to illuminate her gaunt features, despite a white gloss of Madlyn's own eyes emerging from shadows. Her hands performed a different kind of brushstroke, brushing through Libra's cascading curls.

"It will be an extraordinary event. A jubilee of abundance!" announced Libra.

"Yes, Miss," replied Madlyn.

"A splendiferous episode of worship! Worship of me!"

"Yes, miss."

"And everyone will be in awe of my beauty and announce unyielding devotion and love to their perfect mistress!"

"Yes, miss."

"And my cake will be wondrous, a dream! And - come now you silly, don't brush so hard!"

"Yes, miss."

"Nobody does anything right. But my party, my party. It will be perfect, nothing wrong and I - Madlyn, you deplorable ninny, what are you staring at?"

"Nothing, miss. Sorry, miss. Yes, miss."

The servant girl's flimsy mind was a noticeable absentee at present; it had run off into the colourful throes of imagination. Madlyn's mental stability, frail as it may have been, had been lured into daydream by the transfixing of her eyes on the brooch sitting on Libra's table. It was the ornament of brilliant black, the ebony rose brooch that could rival any gem in regards to beauty. The petals of the rose twirled and intertwined into each other, spinning into the centre and absorbing conscious thought with its hypnotism.

Madlyn was infatuated by such a piece of jewelry. She

had never owned many jewels herself and this particular brooch captured her lust for the surreal, her thoughts crying out to her. You simply must have it!

The candle burned weaker by the minute, collapsing into itself in melted tallow. Madlyn's arms turned like gear shafts of an ancient machine, a monotonous repetition, a cycle of brush through hair and brush again. Libra was powdering her face with pomp and circumstance, the sweet aromas of her cosmetics lightening her mood ever still.

"Where was I, now?" said Libra, "Oh, it has but slipped my mind... Oh yes! The cake! Well..."

"Yes," came Madlyn's repetitious response "...Miss."

In the foyer, another picture was painted. It is a surreal piece of caliginous gloom, the very definition of still life. The mighty oak doors of Tenebrae Manor loomed ominously from their host wall, moonlight stabbing through its pellucid stain glass features and casting demented shadows across the black and white tiles of the marble floor. All around there loomed a sense of warped reality, a charlatan playing tricks with gravity, with perception, so even the most steadfast being would find themselves bewildered in their bearings.

High in a corner, a spider silently spun silk with its eight emaciated legs. It stood intimidating and triumphant over the foolish fly, which had become numb from poison, immobile in the sticky confines of arachnid rope.

Perhaps it could see its own mocking reflection, multiplied by the eight oculi of its captor, cruelly reminding it of an inevitable doom.

A cockroach scuttled across the tiles and the clicking of its legs sounded off beat with another very similar sound nearby. A grandfather clock swung its pendulum back and forth, a monotonous metronome of cogs turning and hands cycling about face. Through the gloom there came the muted chortle of an owl that had found some ingress into the mansion and lay concealed somewhere within the room. From the doorway, one could observe the eternal staircase of Tenebrae Manor beginning its inclination to the zenith point of the house, the banister adorned with the heads of griffins and busts of harpies. A chandelier hung motionless from the ceiling like a dead man, collecting a foliage of cobwebs and taking on an appearance of an inverted shrubbery.

The Usher stood vigil. One more figure in a line of armour. How was he any different to the suits of mail and steel that stood in a line next to him? His eyes remained locked in a vacant deadpan, his stance unchanged as the hours drifted by. Through all, he must wait. At any moment there could be a rap on the door and what would become of it if he were not there to respond? Not another thought plagued his mind. No memories of a life been and gone, no yearning for a favourite past time with which to waste his hours. He was the Usher and he must wait. The clock struck the hour and bellowed like a gong. The owl started, the spider stirred and the Usher stood unchanged.

"And another!" bellowed Arpage. "Louder, I say!
Stronger!"

From below, on the stage, Comets jumped on the
spot and stamped his feet down fiercely onto the
floorboards. Items lifeless and static hitherto rattled with
life given them by the pulsing vibration of Comets'
stomps.

"Yes!" Arpage boomed.

He struck the keys of his piano with malevolence,
their noise adding to the commotion of the room. Deadsol
danced with whimsy through the seats, contorting his
limbs extravagantly, tossing feathers and pine needles
conjured as if from nowhere.

Above them, the ceiling was hidden by a supernatural
cloud, swirling and raining down strings of spider thread,
which grabbed at the feathers greedily and left them
permanently suspended mid-flight. Pine needles spun
frantically from their cobweb puppet strings as the air grew
thick with colours of tawny, silver and emerald.

"Tawny owl, do not howl!" Deadsol cried. "Shoots of
pine will do you just fine!"

"Spider leg and spider crawl," added Comets. "Veil of
web a spindly shawl!"

The noise of this auditorium treble had finally found
cohesion amongst their individual bellows. The senseless
chaos had become a controlled, tense dirge - Comets with
his percussion, Arpage's instruments pounding out a
foundation of bass, Deadsol contributing rhythm with his

dance and melody with his rhyme.

The theatre was inundated with decoration and the clean cold air had been replaced with a wilderness of embellishment.

High up in his room, Bordeaux had bargained with himself a moment's rest from his duties. From his vantage point on the windowsill, he was able to fully absorb the rays of the moon, which was dripping with a pale yellow sweat. Bordeaux's foot dangled from the perch of his window ledge, teasing the abyss as it swung in time to the notes of his flute. He had done all he could, all other facets were now completely beyond his control. These had been weeks of torment, the lofty standards that he applied to his work, combined with the frantic and unusual commotion about the manor had planted a seed of fear in his mind. It was a fear of the inadequate, a fear that he may fail to live up to the expectation of his post. But now, as he sat on the window ledge adrift in reverie, his refined composure had returned.

Weary of his instrument, he let his hand fall to the side of the wall opposite to his dangling leg, the flute hanging precariously albeit firmly in his grasp.

Melancholia had overtaken him, the painting on his wall a constant reminder of what had been and what was now so far behind him. The sinuous sea, the taunt of the morning sun peering over the horizon, seemed to mock him with oblivious fancy.

Beyond the window, the trees stood like soldiers in the moonlight, silent and still, guarding him from escape. He felt as a prisoner, his heart filling with a primal urge to crack the ribs of confinement and disappear into the forest. The great trunks of closely pressed pines stood as bars across any adventure into the world beyond the night. Soon the pangs of his dutiful guilt quenched the callings of the wayfarer and he dropped from the sill to ensconce in his favourite chair and delve into another reality that could be found only between the pages of an old book.

The branches jutting from the aforementioned tree trunks, those twisted spearheads jutting into the underbelly of a dark sky, proved more than efficient as footholds in the swift clambering of Edweena. The stealthy vampiress cut through the canopy with the deft precision of some lithe panther. Within her burned a fiery passion, a wild bloodlust that smoldered in her core and clouded her vision from any sightings of contentment.

It was unknown even to her where she was heading at present; perhaps she merely wished to exhume the overflow of her anger and resentment through her vigorous climb. Edweena had drowned in frustration since Libra's ascension, her ebony haired skull slipping beneath the waves after a mighty struggle. What remained was a bitter grudge, not that of jealousy but of abandonment. The forest floor was but a blur beneath her leather boots and Edweena regaled times when she had not been alone in her scouting. As though they had represented the shadow of the other, Edweena and Libra had been inseparable.

Was her anger justified? Surely, she thought to herself. Why had Libra changed so much?

Edweena came to a halt on a branch, lungs gasping profusely from exertion as the sweat poured in streams down her face and body. Her tight grey pants clung to her legs, the black ribbons adorning the top of her black ensemble brushing to a standstill as she sucked in air. The heat only emphasised her sweltering fatigue, pouring down her face in beaded drops. Libra has always been prone to excess, she thought. Perhaps the years of nocturnal escapades had dulled her desire towards physical movement. But that doesn't explain why she suddenly stopped seeing me. Aren't friends supposed to converse? It was no doubt possible that Libra did still care for her friendship with Edweena but certainly, her selfish impulses were stronger. And isn't that exactly the point?

Further out in the forest, where Tenebrae Manor stands only as a prominent backdrop rather than an all encompassing surrounding, the hut of the hermit Crow is alight with an orange glow. Its sickly light illuminates the undersides of pine branches, forming an intermingling tartan of orange and black. The shadows expand and retract with each crackle of the fire lit within the outdoor furnace.

As smoke spirals lazily into the night air, a sharp sound can be discerned; Crow is tempering his blade with hammer strokes. The sword has taken shape since the hermit's awkward meeting with Bordeaux, obtaining a fine edge that will soon be honed further into an enviable sharpness. The fire was beginning to die, until Crow threw more kindling to the flames. His firewood, much to his chagrin, was composed of wood golems he had slain recently. His skewbald mare brayed uneasily from its stall. Crow winced at the ever-growing pile of scrap wood and gazed anxiously out into the trees, where the calls of ravens echoed through the dry atmosphere.

Flanking the western wall of Tenebrae Manor, a crude trail of sorts rides up alongside, covered by a cold stone roofing formed by the bulging overhang of the auditorium above. A pair of forgotten carriages lay cobwebbed beneath the lot, shielded by rain to an extent, though the muddy ground about their wheels had splashed up to the axles. A macabre carriage saunters up the path from the trees as a does a bear crawling from the hibernating mouth of a cave. The clatter and snort of horses quenches the silence and the carriage groans in agony under the weight of its cargo.

The driver is curious specimen; an impish fellow hunched and frail, spine curved to such extent that he seemed to be coiling towards complete omission from any mind. His eyes balloon forth, locked forever in an expressionless gawk. Pocked with the evidence of removed stitches, his lips protrude - yet the mouth never moves. The imp has clearly lost the ability to speak - perhaps out of fear of punishment of the anonymous tyrant who had stitched his mouth previously, so that he was regarded as completely mute.

He pulls at the reins of his horses; they come to a stop beneath the canopy of stone, where an enormous pair of doors opened up into the cellars of the manor. And, as though he premeditated the imp's arrival, the doors creaked open and the mute chef shuffled out onto the drive. The chef pushed heavily on the doors, though even with his ample weight they were difficult to budge. He then moved to assist the small visitor, who had drawn the cloak from his cargo and revealed the quarterly larder of Tenebrae's supplies. The mute chef pouted, not of disappointment, rather concentration as he counted with his pudgy fingers. Crates of wine, barrels of fish, sacks of grains, hefty cuts of meat, wheels of cheese, assortments of vegetables; it all seemed in order. They nodded silently to each other and proceeded to unload the larder - laborious work for such decrepit souls. And once the last barrel was rolled down into the cellar, the imp man mounted his carriage once again. The reins cracked, the horses brayed and away he went back into the trees from whence he came. The mute chef waved him off and closed the doors; the driveway was still and no words were spoken to give evidence that the scene had ever changed - only the newly imprinted tracks in the mud betrayed as such.

The night sky above Tenebrae Manor was still but beneath, the currents were moving. The pull of water streams interwove and stitched together, an ominous foreboding that was stirring something; the atmosphere thick with a sense of forthcoming change. The undertow pulled in all directions, it was only a matter of time before the seams frayed and tore apart into unmitigated anarchy.

X: Libra's Birthday

The doors swung wide open and a gust of air was sucked into the vacuous auditorium, its presence felt only by the leaves and feathers that hung from the ceiling. There was an empty echo, repetitive and solemn, that of fine leather footsteps clicking on the floor.

Bordeaux glided to the stage where he was able to look out on the arena where Libra's guests would gather in a few hours. The spotlight shone down on him, his fiery hair alight with cherry red curls. Shadows cast by the sharp contours of his face were thrown in a way that accentuated his gauntness. Of streamlined refinement, his coat and trousers clung to his slight body as he moved from the spotlight and continued to pace about the stage. In the umbrageous darkness next to the spotlight, Bordeaux could not shake a sense of impending doom, a cloud of forbearance hung above his shoulders. Were he to turn his head to confirm the storm's existence, the clouds would shift about their axis, remaining hidden in the umbra, the dark side of the moon, so to say, behind his head. He felt his senses sharpen in the silence; his ears filled with a quiet as encompassing as a roaring ocean, only the soft sound of snores were detectable.

Up in his loft, Arpage was sleeping. Head down on the desk, his quill smearing ink across a score sheet. The ruff about his neck had ridden up in his slumbers and was now the victim of his dribbling mouth that expanded and retracted with each breath.

On hearing the composer's gentle snores, the corner of Bordeaux's mouth upturned into a grin. He only hoped that the proceedings would run without hitch and that life could return to its usual lull afterward. Matters were waiting to be acknowledged; too much time had been exhausted in this fickle celebration. Bordeaux gritted his teeth and swallowed back a choke of angst, before flinging his arms in the air and calmly making his exit from the theatre.

The light sought refuge from the night tide and just as the dull orange glow of a candle brooded in the presence of its own exposure, so too did Edweena lament in her isolated drawing room. Through the mirror, the full-length portal into an opposite reality, she critiqued her profile. She brushed dust from her grey pants, adjusted a ribbon upon her black bodice and ran her arms down the tight black sleeves of her undershirt. Her hair, a crop of onyx, coupled with her practical dress sense could have her mistaken for a figure of masculinity. However, one look at her slim curved frame and there was no doubt she was woman. A woman who, upon staring into her reflection, realised that there was no opposing reality, the glass was merely a cold reminder of what was. And even if this fanciful notion of a happy dreamland were true, the figure staring back at her did not show the signs of such heightened joviality.

Her inspections were brought to a halt by the emergence of a series of dull thumps, not unlike the sound of scratching on sandpaper. Beyond the sealed windows of silent room, the night wind uttered no breath. It could not be the wind that tapped so impatiently on the panes. She strode to the window and cautiously peered about.

It took a moment for her vision to focus beyond the reflection of her own haunted face and eventually there came into view a twisted branch. On observing the branch, its undeniable movement in the absence of wind, Edweena was dumbstruck. Before her, this ligneous limb clawed at the outer wall of the manor. It was grasping blindly just as one fumbles for light in a dark room.

There was then a sharp crack, a piercing through the air that made Edweena jump. From the gap created by the probing arm, a sinewy tendril curled into the room, weaving like a green snake before settling itself close to the floor. The vine clung to the interiors as ivy is wont to do and as Edweena regained her composure, she noticed more sounds, more scratching. All along the windowed wall there crawled ivy vines and skeletal branches attempting to find any ingress to Tenebrae Manor.

The wall transformed, streaked now in a green hue that bulged its ruffles in shoots of ivy leaves, until one side of the drawing room looked like a forest itself. The glass broke further; the branches that had been tapping so urgently seemed at peace now that they had found entry into the room.

Edweena stood bewildered, although a steeled resolve prompted her to inspect the verdure phenomenon that had so suddenly intruded upon her musing. Her slender hand reached for the wall, until her white fingers brushed against a vine. It shivered under her touch before returning to stillness. Edweena snatched her hand away stared perplexedly. How long she would have remained there was unknown but her trance was broken when the boom of the foyer's clock came echoing through the halls, its fainted whisper reaching her ears. She was expected in the auditorium. Absorbing one last glance at the green wall, she strode swiftly back out into the halls.

The clock had indeed blasted out its battle cry and down in the foyer, a mountain stirred and began to move. The very idea of a mountain moving presented a most unusual picture but that was indeed what was happening. A hulking figure that had stood steadfast indefinitely now groaned into life. It is of course, Usher. The hour of Libra's celebration was nigh; his duties were required at another door, namely that of the auditorium.

There was a twitch in his thumb and a creak in his neck as he slowly lifted his leg to make the first step towards his summons. Usher's limbs ached from disuse and though his face still held fast to its eternal deadpan, a new feature had augmented with it. A faint detection of cripplingly determined focus; he simply must reach the auditorium to welcome the guests. He ambled forward like an invalid, his suited shoulders snow-capped with dust; the light reflecting from atop his scalp, where only a few black reeds lay plastered in slimy grease.

Reaching the stairs was the easiest part but now as he stood at the foot of the mountain. He sighed perplexedly and attempted to lift his foot high enough to gain elevation. Gripping the banister for balance allowed him to take the first step with minimal struggle but his celebrations of such an effort were snuffed out as a brisk green shadow rushing past him.

Crow had entered the house and sprung out of the blocks in the race to the summit. The wood hermit barely noticed the Usher, who received a rather rude brush on the face by Crow's golden cape as it fluttered like a flag behind his shoulders. Up the stairs he flew, shrinking from Usher's view towards the distant pinnacle.

It had taken Usher a quarter of an hour to reach the first landing. He paused for breath and tried to ignore the taunts of the candelabrum-hung bats that squealed at the blundering disturbance. They mocked his stunted attempts, shook the darkness from their wings and settled back into sleep. As he continued to climb, another apparition stormed past; Edweena in all her sullen beauty spared a word for Usher at the very least, unlike Crow before her.

"Come now, slowpoke... That's you, you know..."

Her appearance startled Usher, her intimidating eyes thrown over her shoulder as she ascended above him before she too was lost to the upper shadows.

Surely he must be close to the top. He was presently overtaken again, this time by Deadsol and Comets. The imp jester imitated Usher's sluggishness by jumping up the steps with both feet, one at a time until Deadsol snatched the runt by the ear and hauled him up the stairs. Next came Rune, the ancient zombie, Tenebrae's mummified librarian, who was not known to venture farther than the confines of his books. Still, despite the old age of Rune, he still shuffled with greater speed than the doorman.

Usher had reached the top floor of the manor and now shuffled urgently towards his destination. The goal was so close now. Again he found himself giving way, this time to an enormous cake propped on a trolley. The ghastly thing towered like a sickly ghost of cream and sugar, quivering as it rocketed down the hall as though of its own accord. But no, the sweet slab was not endowed with such ability, for hidden behind the thing and pushing the trolley with meaty hands, came the mute chef. Despite his speed, the man moved with precision, deftly rebalancing the cake whenever it threatened to tip. Madlyn trailed behind, somewhat amiably dressed in her smock and dress of white and navy blue.

By now the Usher was forlorn. Who was there left to arrive? His frustration welled within him, were he capable of secreting a tear of emotional ventilation he would by now have drowned Tenebrae Manor.

Finally, Bordeaux arrived beside him. Prim as always, the demon gave Usher an encouraging pat on the back before entering the auditorium, which was now a few feet away. Usher's face showed nothing but inside he was smiling. He triumphantly clasped the handle of the great door and hauled it open. This action of victory was met not with applause but rather an unearthly quiet, broken occasionally by the sporadic coughs of those already inside. Soon Bordeaux returned to his side.

"Usher."

The doorman directed his gaze to the crimson demon. "Yes, Master Bordeaux?"

"Usher, we are all here. Come inside and take a seat."

With all the haste he had left to muster, Usher joined those sitting amongst the seats. Though they all sat together, the characters appeared so isolated in the sea of vast red felt. The seats jutted their heads above one

another like ripples in a mounting ocean wave where each
row pushed further towards the crest. Busts of the
characters floated above the tide, attaining to no particular
pattern, just as jettisoned barrels bob in the sea. Upwards
the wave rose to its tipping point, where it remained inert.
Above, the cobwebs lay draped in such thickness as to
emulate a storm, the feathers thrown by Deadsol could
very well have been seagulls trying to escape the coming
rains that would inflate the turgid red sea beneath.
And now, from the zenith of the wave appeared a
prominent shadow that blotted out the entrance with its
roundness.

On the stage, Bordeaux stood tall and announced
with a voice of smooth baritone, "Lovely ladies and grand
gentlemen. I present to you, our approbated Lady Libra."
The shadow at the door moved and exposed itself in the
light to be none other than the Lady herself. Met with a
flaccid applause, she marched with a grandiose oblivion
down the aisle to the jubilant chords of Arpage's piano.
Libra was dressed magnificently and adorned with trinkets
of jewelry that reflected the light as she moved. She was a
confronting sight, somewhat jarring in her protuberance;
the pot of her fleshy paunch lay generously bulging over
the waist of her black and billowy pantaloons. In all, she
had attained the look akin to a gypsy belly dancer, her hair
tied high on her head where dark curls burst forth like
reeds of a pineapple or the lava of a long dormant volcano.
Her arms remained aloft, absorbing what applause and
cheers she could hear, until she reached the steps of the
stage. Hereupon she required Bordeaux's assistance up the
stairs, for she was so heavy that such effort brought about
fatigue. So much so that once she had reached the stage

where a throne awaited her ensconcing, she stood for a moment panting for breath. Soon enough though, she sat, flushed with a light sweat on her face and brushed a strand of hair daintily from her face.

"Lady Libra," Bordeaux recited, "You, our glorious mistress, our steadfast leader. To you we cling in the epochs of uncertainty. To you we turn for the assurance of blissful night. May Tenebrae never disintegrate under your reign, may our ancient home outlast time itself. To you, on this day (although we really mean night), we celebrate the anniversary of you and no other. May the evening be a most excellent jubilee! May the night know no end!"

Libra was grinning as feverishly as a child, though she was not listening entirely to Bordeaux and his well-rehearsed speech. Rather, she had spied the mountainous cake that stood centre stage in a glistening glory.

"Yes, very good Bordeaux. Now you there! Wheel that cake this way!"

She was of course speaking to the mute chef, who stood with his arms behind his back next to his masterpiece, unhearing and therefore unmoving to Libra's request.

"The imbecile! Never mind!" she huffed. "Madlyn!"

The servant girl spluttered into action, pushing the cake to within reach of Libra. In her clumsiness, she had almost tumbled headlong into the thing, until a merciful regaining of balance held her upright.

Libra produced a fork as if from nowhere and proceeded to pick away a prominent mouthful from the body of the cake. As she placed it into her mouth her eyes rolled back with gluttonous delight.

"Oh my. That blind buffoon did it again!"

"He isn't blind," said Madlyn.

Libra's eyes cut through to the servant girl's very core, "You correct me?"

Madlyn was startled back into an attentive stance, her eyes wide and anxious after speaking out of line. All the while the chef stood unknowing of the conversation going on and that it had been he who had been readily insulted by the person he had worked for weeks to please.

"Moving on." Bordeaux swept in just in time to save Madlyn from punishment. "As you were all readily informed, you will now line up to present our Lady Libra with presents. Who would like to go first?"

It was Comets who made the first movement, leaping from his chair and scuttling down the aisle cradling something dark in his gloved hands. Whatever it was, he held it like a newborn or perhaps a bird that had broken its wing; his usual erratic nature seemed to have been replaced by a doting regard.

Libra watched him sullenly as he approached the throne and laid at her feet a large pinecone, before turning and leaving the stage.

The silence that ensured was varied in its chief emotion - Bordeaux's brow raised bemusedly, Libra's lip curled with disdain, Madlyn stared absently at the ceiling. Comets was unmoved by any of this and simply returned to his seat.

"Bordeaux…" hissed Libra.

For a moment, Bordeaux was frazzled. "Uh, perhaps we should move on? Our always astute composer, Arpage Espirando Notturno has prepared yet another of his resplendent musical pieces. Let us welcome him now!" Up in the loft, Arpage kicked at his instrument and the pipes bellowed into life; the piano was playing of its own accord. Arpage slid down to the stage by means of a well-placed rope, his legs kicking frantically as he did so, until he plopped onto the same level as Libra and Bordeaux. "Ahem!" he cried. "My lady, it is always an honour! My only hope is that you enjoy the fruits of my long hours!" The spotlight that shone down onto Arpage did little to hinder the prominence of his unappealing features. His eyes lay sandwiched betwixt a bony bulge of cheek and brow and seemed possessed with a demoniac focus. And from his dried and cracked lips, which did little to cover the glossy yellow crags of his teeth, came phonics of beautiful cohesion. The auditorium became hazy as his words flowed like quicksilver to the metronome of his flailing hands.

Those in the audience fell into a spellbinding trance - Crow paid no heed to a large spider that was crawling across his tunic. Rune the mummy was distracted so much that he failed to notice Comets attempting to pluck at the fabric strips that bound him together.

Bordeaux found himself standing static, though confused by an unshakeable feeling that he was swaying; he too was oblivious to that of Madlyn staring longingly at him from across the room.

There were in fact only two citizens present that seemed uninspired by Arpage's recital; the rascal Comets of course and the Lady Libra herself. The pompous mistress of Tenebrae Manor rolled her eyes and puffed her exhalations with frustrated boredom. Her black fingernails tapped on the armrest of the throne as she grew increasingly impatient. She looked to Arpage and saw he had finished and was taking his bow. The piano keys ceased their sounds and the audience applauded louder than they had at any point that evening, much to Libra's envy.

"Thank you, Arpage," said Bordeaux. "I believe we can all agree that you've surpassed all previous efforts with that stunning recital. Lady Libra, we hope you are impressed."

Libra snorted, "Impressed? I could barely stay awake through that senseless dribble. More praise! Bad, just bad! I demand you all stop applauding him at once!"

Arpage took each verbal blow like a punch to his person, keeling further down with each assault. "B-but, Madam Libra," he stammered. "That opus took me months to complete!"

"Well it sounded like you slapped it together without thought or consideration, you dullard!"

The audience watched with increased intrigue as Bordeaux stepped in to defend the quivering composer.

"Now Libra, be reasonable! Surely you see -"

"Silence!" stormed Libra, "This is my birthday! You should all be on your knees! Not trashing this auditorium with filthy feathers! Not presenting me with pinecones! And not piddling out worthless piffle!"

Her fury was as directionless as a toddler's tantrum but Arpage's shoulders convulsed in a mounting rage, his narrow chest wrapped in cardigan heaved violently; his hair went flaccid and disheveled as he tore at his own scalp.

"This will not stand!" he cried.

Libra's eyes began to smolder, her own misguided outrage alive in her features; her lips contorting, her neck twitching, "Mind your words, little man."

Arpage's animosity extinguished his usual cowardice and he stamped his foot defiantly. "No! I will not mind my words. Minding my words is all I've done for weeks, months! And for what? Some selfish beast of a woman accusing me of piddling out piffle! Well you Miss Libra; are a right villain! A big, selfish waste! You, you, you fat girl!"

Libra's bristled with disbelief, "You insolent -"

"Ah! But wait!" interrupted the composer, "Since my composition displeased you so, perhaps I should read the other song I wrote, the song I wrote with Deadsol and Comets as they decorated this lovely venue."

Confounded with disbelief, Bordeaux was powerlessly slow to intervene, for Arpage had already withdrawn a crumpled piece of paper from his pocket and begun to spew forth a torrent of insults towards Libra.

The others gaped, fearing Libra's inevitable wrath yet were infatuated by such rebellion from the usually tepid composer. Edweena tried to hide her smile, Deadsol and Comets cackled like hyenas and Bordeaux could only cringe and wait for this disaster to be over.

Once Arpage had finished his outburst, all eyes were on Libra - what colossal punishment awaited the renegade composer? What monumental reprimand? With bated breath they moved to the edge of their seats and waited.

Libra stared venomously at Arpage, then scanned the room and felt the ocean of eyes boring into her. But it was not the attention she had demanded. On the nonce, she felt completely exposed and intimidated and, in an inverse reaction to what anyone would have expected, her face winced and she burst into tears. Sobbing wretchedly, she rose to her feet with a struggle and ran, or rather, waddled to the exit.

There were none who tried to stop her as she wailed uncontrollably and disappeared out into the halls.
Bordeaux was left incredulous; the night had been chaos. He had failed, though it had been others who had dragged him down to such depths. The crimson demon considered this a moment, before his obliging hands helped Arpage to his feet. Deadsol and Comets were still laughing, though all present began to feel a change in the air.

It was a forgotten ardor, déjà vu as it were, like a dream long passed that lingers in the back of the mind until its emergence years later and it is though it was never absent. It became cold. The heat wave, seemingly unending, had, in a split moment, abated and the residents of Tenebrae Manor felt the anticipated soothing of a winter wind. However, the effect was all too temporary. For only a few minutes later, the air turned sharper still, the temperature plunged into boreal depths.

In the confusion of the theatre, Madlyn, more out of curiosity rather than care for her sovereign, had wandered out into the halls briefly. Only she would dash back immediately, having observed something that everyone simply must know.

Though her voice failed to prevail over the verbose ramblings of the others, still she yelled excitedly. "It's snowing, everyone! It's snowing outside!"

END OF PART ONE.

Part Two

XI: Out in the Field of Pumpkins

The blizzard that struck its blows on Tenebrae Forest was as unrelenting as it was potent. As though the planet had been hurled to some far corner of space in remote proximity to the sun's warmth, no such life giving fire would welcome the now freezing citizens of the manor. What had been a punishing summer heat wave had somersaulted so abruptly into its opposing season that one had barely enough time to appreciate the relief from the heat before lamenting the unbearable chill. As red hot steel is quenched in soothing water, the forest of Tenebrae, littered as it were with pine needles, singed upon contact with those first few snow flakes, flinching as warm flesh convulses in reaction to a cold hand. The wind carried its savage bite and wormed its way through every nook and permitted no relief from its icy jaws.

Tenebrae Manor stood inundated with flurries, its shoulders burdened with the heavy cloak of snow. The drifts grew plump with baroque crystals of beautiful powder until the forest was near unrecognisable. Conifers drooped with excess weight; rooted feet were hidden, as the boles were buried trunk deep in the wintery tide. They remained upright, yet were undeniably slipping into a hibernated state, silenced by the gripping fatigue; disintegrating away from life's pulse by the firn's lull.

Subsequent to the apparent death of the trees came the disturbed silence, peering out from around each corner, as though it had been in waiting for the heat to dissipate. The quiet was so encompassing, a nightjar's breath was free to echo over the drifts and added to the ghostly firmament that was Tenebrae. The night sighed and the façade of the jaded manor creaked softly under its gelid burden.

Libra had ordered the cake be delivered to her bedroom, a task that Madlyn apprehensively completed; the wails of Libra's melancholia poisoning the manor with their sombrous echoes as Madlyn brought the cake to her bedside.

"Miss?" she tittered.

"What do you want?" sobbed Libra.

"Um, the cake."

"Leave it there and go away!"

And besides this brief colloquy, none had made contact with the Lady of Tenebrae Manor since her disastrous celebration. Bordeaux had initially been relieved to see the back end of this abhorred party; he was finally alleviated of its stresses and able to perform what he had deemed more important errands about the manor. Regardless of how calamitous it had been, the allaying of his anxiety had been worth it. Even so, a pang of remorse struck in his heart and in spite of Libra's less than respected image in the eyes of the residents, he still felt somehow responsible for assuring her happiness as though she were any other friend of his. He was making his way down the hallway towards Libra's room when his countenance reversed on him yet again.

Why do I trouble myself with the extent of her mirth? When there still remains the issue of this human intruder? And when wood golems are running amok about the manor?

Bordeaux walked crestfallen, the silhouette of his slouched shoulders illuminated by the dull candle glow of the chandelier above Libra's door. About the floor beneath his feet lay puddles of fresh tallow from the dripping candles above and he did not concern himself to knock on the great door.

The light in the bedroom was just as dim, a gloom hung in the air - a gloom that shouldered a significant warmth when comparison to the rest of the house. The Lady had not denied herself the pleasure of warmth in her days of isolation. Lit by the fire that crackled in the mantelpiece, a mountain of frumpy sheets lay upon the opulent mattress of Libra's bed, cut with trails leading between valleys and also to the summit of this mound of cloth. The mountain was too large to consist only of sheet and this was, of course, due to the sniveling virago that sobbed pathetically beneath.

Bordeaux bided his time, glancing at the destruction of the room with an indifferent patience. It was clear that Libra had broken any number of her possessions in a fit of temper.

"Libra."

A whimper of acknowledgement responded from the pile of quilts.

"Come now, this is improper behaviour for the one who claims to be our leader," said Bordeaux. "Leave your quarters. Get up and about. Tenebrae requires it."

"No! Why should I care what happens to this place? After such mean things were said about me!"

"Then perhaps you'd be right in relieving yourself of such lofty echelon. I'm sure someone else would enjoy such privileges even more than yourself."

Bordeaux got the reaction he wanted. Libra shot up and kicked the blankets away, staring at him imploringly. The mascara on her eyes ran in streams down her full face, riddled with days of tears; her hair was disheveled in its mess of curls in agreement to the hours spent pressed into the pillow.

"But I'm the queen here! No one else!" she whimpered. "Don't they realise that? Oh, Bordeaux! Did you hear what he called me? *Fat girl*, he said. Fat! You don't think I'm fat do you, Bordeaux?"

The crimson demon spied the empty cake pan that sat on the table next to her bed. A fork lay across its icing dotted face and pointed accusingly at Libra, who looked visibly plumper than the last time he had seen her. Libra had seen his hesitance in answering her question and flung herself back under the blankets and began to sob some more.

"This cold front has seized hold of our very bones," said Bordeaux. "Surely you see it is quite, hmm, coincidental that it arrived on the moment of your exit from the party?"

"Go away, B," moaned Libra.

"You assured me that you had nothing to do with the insufferable heat. I can only curse my own gullibility for believing you."

"I only wanted to instill the emphasis of the occasion! Keep you all focused on the work before you; surely you see nothing wrong with applying a little pressure to ensure a good job. Yet you all failed!"

"I'd call it oppression," said Bordeaux.

Libra only grunted in return and remained huddled in her shell of quilt.

"*Oppression,* Libra," he continued. "And now you've inundated us with this freeze, why must you maltreat your supposed subjects so?"

"What have you done with that piteous little composer?" asked Libra, sitting up again and seemingly ignoring Bordeaux's accusations.

Bordeaux sighed and paced the room. "What would you have done with him?"

She slammed her fist down onto the table, sending the fork flying from the cake pan and caking her fist with remnants of icing that she presently licked clean.

"Why punishment of course!" howled Libra, "Put him out in the wilderness for all I care! Let him freeze. He can slave away in the pumpkin patch with that belligerent scarecrow."

Bordeaux started. "Work with Sinders? Surely no. Arpage is not one for physical labour."

"Exactly! Let his foppish hands toil in the cold until they crack and bleed, let his timorous voice break with cries of his own anguish!"

She made little effort to hide her mounting excitement, flinging the cake pan with deadly swiftness until the silver discus hit the wall with a clatter. Libra now stood so close to Bordeaux as to make him uncomfortable, he could not discern what made the gorgon smell so sugary. Perhaps it were a well suiting perfume she had adorned or, more likely, the scent of sweetness on her lips, which were encircled subtly with icing sugar as they spoke.

"See that he is reprimanded severely, B," she whispered. "The lout Sinders just might be the ticket…"

Bordeaux shrugged his shoulders, clearly displaying an air of defeat. There would be no reasoning with Libra but could he really doom Arpage to work through this blizzard?

"As for Deadsol and Comets," continued Libra, "Because I know they had some influence on that musical fool, well, I'll let you choose the penalty."

"Miss." Bordeaux nodded reluctantly.

He turned to leave before the dusky voice of Libra's voice chilled the back of his neck again. "And B."

"Miss?"

"Take that boy with you. That human boy."

"To the pumpkin field? Is that wise? He would be free to escape at will!"

"With Sinders nearby? Ha, I think he'd more likely die of fright!" laughed Libra. "Do you really think he's going anywhere in this snow?"

Bordeaux rubbed his hand over his forehead, "As you wish, my lady."

That seems foolish though, he added, though only to himself.

"Really sir, I fail to see the justification in this! I have begged apology, pleaded! I did not mean, I mean I did not intend to express such malice!"

Bordeaux pressed open the doors of the ground floor drawing room with Arpage sniveling in his wake. The composer's reluctance in leaving his auditorium was more than obvious as he had shuffled behind Bordeaux, sometimes on his knees, sometimes crawling and other times dragging his feet along with shoulders slumped.

Inside the drawing room, Deadsol sat smoking his pipe while Comets tested his endurance by holding his hands out into the fireplace. The hands of the jester quivered with pain before the flames became too much and he would snatch them away, only to try again moments later.

"Bordeaux, my good man! I bid you the finest health!" paraded Deadsol. "And our master of eloquence, none other than the composer himself, Arpage!"

"Ignore him, Arpage," said Bordeaux.

From his comfortable vantage point, Deadsol watched with disinterest as Bordeaux removed the barricades of the forgotten closet and opened its doors. Jethro tumbled out and his defeated body hit the floor forcefully with a clump.

"See here, Bordeaux. Look at this mess you've made," said Deadsol from his chair.

"Mess, a mess. His mind's a mess!" Comets sung quietly as though only to himself. His eyes remained transfixed on the fireplace.

Bordeaux prodded the human with the end of his fine sword cane, which was topped with the golden head of a falcon.

"Jethro," said Bordeaux, "Do you remember where you are?"

"Where he is?" laughed Deadsol. "He never found that out in the first place!"

The human looked up at the crimson demon and whimpered softly; he remembered this nightmare too well. He had hoped it had all been the fabric of a violent imagination but the cold floor under his hands confirmed a reality all too real.

"Oh dear God! Who are you people?"

"There he goes again about that God fellow. Mentions him every time we throw him a scrap of food. Haven't the slightest clue to whom he refers," said Deadsol.

"Home," whimpered Jethro. "I want to go home..."

"And here I was thinking confinement might speed up the onslaught of insanity... I've a new home for you lad, on the authority of Lady Libra. Come with me."

Bordeaux grabbed the man by the scruff of his neck, pulling him to his feet before flinging him over his shoulder with a surprising strength.

"Good tidings, Deadsol, Comets," Bordeaux nodded. "Come along, Arpage."

The rugged hills that riddled the southwest topography of Tenebrae presented a scene far more devoid of life than the other regions of pine-speckled country. One mile in this treacherous direction will bring the foolhardy adventurer to a clearing where the ancient pines disperse, as though the soil in this brief circumference were poisoned, leaving behind a silent field. Somewhat offset from the centre of this circle, yet still noticeable to even the most unobservant spectator, there stands a decayed facade of brick and mud.

Crippled with ivy, this small house stands merely as an outer shell, gutted from the inside so as to leave naught but rotted wooden flooring behind. The foliage of parasitic vine clotted so thickly to this shell, the host had been drained and overcome by their creeping tendrils.

Encircling the hut and reflecting the moonlight with crystalline luminance, there jutted the orange skulls of a thousand pumpkins. Distended to awkward shapes, the vegetables groaned as if they were the living dead climbing out of the ground with the gaunt and leafy arms that were their vines. Worm eaten holes gave the pumpkins eyes and wailing mouths, locked silent in a twisted expression of mortal agony.

Hung across Bordeaux's shoulder like a sack of grain, Jethro whimpered in fear; Arpage too, seemed unsettled by this place.

"Keep up, Arpage," said Bordeaux.

The composer followed apprehensively. "Master B, it is so cold, so very cold. And my feet! They're unfamiliar to walks of this length. Rest, sir! That is what I need. But this place, something about it gives me the jitters."

The hut drew closer, Bordeaux weaving his steps carefully between the pumpkins, which grew in no particular pattern.

"Eyes, sir," Arpage continued to ramble. "They are staring, sir. Erm, that is the pumpkins. They are staring is what I mean."

"Be quiet, Arpage. You're less coherent with every syllable. I would get used to this place if I were you, for this will be your new home until Libra sees fit for you to return to the manor."

No door shielded the entrance to the hut, so Bordeaux rapped his clawed knuckles on the frame and called out.

Inside the house was one large and very bare room, lit in shafts by ribbons of moonlight piercing through the holes in the roof. The air smelt of rotted wood and earth and to the immediate horror of both Arpage and Jethro, a crouched figure stirred in the far corner. Remaining low to the ground, the emaciated figure moved two steps forward and, still concealed by darkness, called out in a chilling and raspy voice, "Who is there?"

"It is I, old friend. Bordeaux."

In a flash the figure shot forward towards them, as if in one frame. Arpage tottered back in fright and fell on his haunches. A shaft of moonlight illuminated the face of the figure; it was a weathered portrait and skin sagged like old leather, of orange faded to brown. Straw like hair arrowed downwards from under a black-rimmed hat. But it was the eyes that were the most frightening. The eyes or lack thereof one should say, were merely black hollows in the old leather, for the head of this creature was indeed a pumpkin; before them stood the scarecrow, Sinders.

"Bordeaux! My old friend! Why would you venture out into the snow with this dismal field as your destination? This must be an errand of vital importance."

Bordeaux dumped the dead weight Jethro to the floor and shook hands warmly with the scarecrow.

"By the order of the Lady Libra, these two are to work the fields under your supervision."

Sinders eagerly clasped at Jethro's hand and shook it. "How do you do my lad? Ah! A human! So warm, a dead give away! Or rather a live one, ah ha!"

In his barely conscious daze, the human was petrified to find clumps of straw in his hand after the scarecrow withdrew.

Arpage backed into a corner and whimpered pathetically as Sinders crept up to him. The scarecrow probed the composer's limbs with sharp prods before seizing up as though from an electric shock.

"Wait! The Lady Libra? Pooh on her, I say! Why should I listen to her?"

"First, I was hoping you could explain your absence from her party," Bordeaux said firmly.

Sinders shielded his head, though there were none attempting to strike him, "No sir! Have mercy, I merely didn't attend because, well, because I simply can't stand her! My attendance is nothing, Bordeaux. I'm all the way out here, no one remembers lamentable old Sinders!"

"Damn you, fool. Enough of this charade," Bordeaux barked. "Fact being that you should have been there. Considering the circumstances, I'd say that having these two lackeys under your feet should serve punishment enough for you."

Sinders scraped his foot along the groaning floorboards and let his arms swing dead from slumped shoulders.

Jethro, who must have passed out on the journey to the pumpkin field, roused presently and joined Arpage cowering against the wall.

"Oh lord! Dear God what is that thing? What is it? Oh save me, wake me up from this nightmare!" he cried.

"None too social, is he?" said Sinders.

"He'll learn soon enough. Now. He is human. As such, he needs warmth. Food. Water. You will make sure his needs are at hand."

"Soft little things, people are," said Sinders. "Erm, there's a fireplace over there and I suppose most of the pumpkins are ok to eat. Why he'd want to eat them though is beside me..."

Bordeaux peered grimly into the ashen fireplace.

"There's your first task, Arpage. Go get firewood."

The composer lay on the floor in fetal position and moaned softly, "No..."

"Now!"

At Bordeaux's command, Arpage started up and dashed out the doorway. Leaning upon one wall were a variety of gardening tools and it was here that Sinders retrieved a sickle and made egress too. Bordeaux following him out into the moonlight.

"Well until Mr. Man over there finds his wits, I'll have to pick up his slack," said Sinders.

The field was a mine of exquisite gemstones, for the sparkling crystals of snow speckling the choking ivy of the house capped the scalps of pumpkins and lay upon the leaves like dew drops.

Arpage wandered about cautiously; seemingly eager to fulfill his task (for fear of punishment alone), yet he was too inadequate to get his hands dirty. A pile of logs lay vigil nearby to the hut and the composer inspected them with a wince.

"Eek! There are spiders here!"

"Spiders; hairy, gaunt and tiny," chanted Sinders, swinging his sickle amongst the pumpkins with questionable aim and purpose. It was true; at a second glance, the brilliant crystals glittering in the moonlight were not only snow granules. Closer inspection would discern the presence of thousands of minuscule arachnida plaguing all surfaces. The smallest embodiment of life - legged white capsules so fragile and camouflaged that their presence was forgettable despite all encompassing.

Still dancing about with his scythe, Sinders swung the blade sickeningly close to Arpage's face.

"There's the wood, Mr. Arpage. Hop to it! They won't harm you!"

Arpage hesitated, complying eventually and attempting to lift the first log. His arms quivered, matchstick thin next to the burly timber and unable to exert the strength necessary to lift. In an effort to hide his feebleness, the composer quickly hopped to a smaller scrap, more branch than trunk and placed it on his shoulder. As he stumbled for balance his neck ruff tangled with his green cardigan, his swampy hair drooped at from its usual horizontal jutting but he seemed to hold an air of accomplishment. Arpage was doing all he could to ignore the spiders, which now, disturbed from their host log began to crawl all over his person.

"Tell me, Mr. Arpage, what malevolence brings you here? I say, why are you being punished?" asked Sinders.

"Stupid beast that I was," moaned Arpage, "That I had the hide to insult Lady Libra in song."

Sinders convulsed with laughter, "Splendid! Ah ha! Then you and I will get along just fine."

Here the scarecrow broke into a tune;

There are spiders on the lawn,
But love, don't look forlorn!
Though their webs may be a tangled mess,
Intent was to adorn!

Arpage smiled and joined in;

There are spiders on the lawn
Don't look at them with scorn.
Beads of dew beset silver ribbons
Glowing in the dawn.

Sinders, in a mounting crescendo;

There are spiders on the lawn
And one would think they warn
That to forget life's simple beauties
Is your heart left torn to mourn!

Arpage finished with a grandeur coda, dropping his log and puffing out his chest;

There are spiders on the lawn!
I accept them with a yawn.
Where web ends, eight legs defend
Waiting static in the morn!

Jethro remained in a fitful sleep, yet Arpage had already begun to enjoy his supposed punishment. He found himself thinking that it wasn't all so bad and surely he would get used to the cold of the ivy crippled hut and its field of demoniac pumpkins.

"Marvellous!" said Sinders. "Bordeaux, now I know you can hold a note. Have you a verse to contribute?"

But his words were lost to the night, for neither he or

Arpage had noticed that Bordeaux had taken his leave some time ago and was presently wandering back through the trees to Tenebrae Manor.

In the forest, the night was aglow with a phosphorous blue that hung in wreaths through the frigid air, betwixt branches that reached for one another, uniting against the deep freeze. Through his sharp vision, Bordeaux was able to discern the clustered members of a nocturnal company; owls of ruffled distinction burying their heads deep in the savored warmth of tawny plumage and the bats; jet black ornaments inverted in the canopy, shielded from the wind's bite by leathery wings.

The breath of the crimson demon lingered in the air, he shivered and pulled tighter the confines of his fine burgundy coat. His charcoal scarf and fiery hair were crusted with dusty snow that had fallen so gently onto him; the flakes were mild mannered, brutal in their potent frost yet intruding softly onto the warmth of his body like a guest who feels he has outstayed his welcome.

The night held no fear for the tireless demon, though the particular hour harboured the chill of uneasiness; perhaps it was only the winter weather but Bordeaux felt possessed by the idea of evil lurking in the gloom. Was there any foundation on which to lay down his concerns? Or was it merely a fanciful flight that enraptured his soul?

Tenebrae Manor emerged like a shipwreck in the distance, the house that Bordeaux had called home for centuries, sturdy and immemorial. The sharp angles of the roof could quite easily be mistaken in the darkness as more pine trees, though Bordeaux knew the lay of the land well enough to find comfort in the camouflage of his home. He was only a few minutes away from the front door.

Steadying himself with his cane, Bordeaux scaled the steep incline on which the manor stood king, the southern cliff face breaking away to his left as the house towered on the brink of the precipice. The frontage of the house was less tree-choked than the surrounding forest, yet as the demon wound his way up the crooked path towards the threshold, he became aware of a certain unusual occurrence. Those trees that stood closest to Tenebrae Manor seemed to be leaning inward, as though reaching for the house with petiolar limb. Whether this was worth considering, Bordeaux had no time, for another strange happening entered his senses. A sound, one of scratching.

Veering from the pathway Bordeaux crept, apprehensively following the noise that seemed to arise from the side of the house. A creature, a flitting shadow of bemused grunts was huddled against the wall, preoccupied with a hasty endeavour. It did not take Bordeaux long to realise, with a sinking heart, that the creature was a wood golem. His pulse raced; what was this thing doing here and so close to the house? Never had he seen such practicality and determination in what was usually a mindless monster. The golem had heard the intrusion of Bordeaux and turned its bulged eyes towards him.

Turning to leave, Bordeaux would rue a momentary lapse in reflex that saw the golem lunge at him, grasping him by the throat and wrestling him to the ground. He and the monster struggled in the dirty snow. The cruel hand of the beast closed its grip about Bordeaux's neck with vice-like strength and left him gasping frantically for breath. Bordeaux pressed his free hand into the wood golem's face, trying desperately to gain an advantage. Despite his best efforts to ward away his panic, it was mounting as each of his frantic efforts to fight off the monster fell short of effect. The demon managed to withdraw the rapier from his sword cane and soon his wild swings found contact with the wood golem's body. The creature's hide was of thick wood and his best blows seemed wastrel and ineffective. He needed to breathe, his vision began to blur, until, by freakish luck, he was somehow able to thrust forth his sword into the beast's side. It was the moment he needed, as the wood golem reeled away but for a moment and Bordeaux stole away his throat from its clutches and gained back precious ground. He leapt adroitly to his feet and charged, his instincts kicked in and landed a calculated blow on the neck of the golem. It attempted a counter shot with a lumbering swing of its cudgel arm but Bordeaux was too swift. The crimson demon kicked forcefully at the beast's chest, throwing it helplessly onto its back, before plunging his blade straight through the chest, impaling it to the ground where it expelled a deathly groan.

Bordeaux gaped for breath, keeping his cautious eyes fixed on the dying wood golem. His strength was sufficiently exhausted and feeling not the fangs of the cold snow, collapsed to the ground. He had won; his life had been spared.

Dazed as he was, eventually he made a move to inspect just what the golem had been doing before its death. He stepped past where his sword jutted like a flagpole from the lifeless golem and ran his hand over the wall of Tenebrae Manor. The rough touch of wood and stone was blistered with shards of snow, unchanged under the touch of Bordeaux's fingers until for a moment, when his hand slipped into nothingness. Nothingness where there very much should be something. With a realisation both confused and concerned, Bordeaux understood immediately; the wood golem had been tearing apart a wall of the manor.

XII: The Perimeter

Spread like a spilt pot of ink, Tenebrae's night creeps across the land, staining the hills black and the trees a mess of greys, deepest greens and navy blues. The manor is that pot - exuding the darkness from its very core, standing at the centre of the stain as the antithesis of the sun. From the summit of the house itself, where Libra resided in luxury, the ancient spell channeled the murk in its impenetrable shades bereft of geniality. Through the icy forest came the sound of slow footsteps, crunching softly in the deep snow. A svelte shadow slid between the trees, head hung in deep and melancholic thought. What possible reason could this figure have to be out in the harsh taiga, roaming with such directionless and mechanical strides? Such remained a mystery. Where the warmth of mortal would soon perish from the chilling fatigue of the winter snows, the bloodless soma of Edweena was indifferent.

Edweena's movements lacked the tenacity of her

mission, her steps were heavy and weighed down upon by the thick snow, which rose to her waist at some points. Haste was noticeably absent, the vampiress was fighting an internal apprehension that possessed her faculties and prevented her usual enthuse - namely leaping with speed through the treetops. It was this apprehension that nagged in the back of her mind. Turn back, it said; naught will come of this little expedition. And while Edweena was most certainly within her own element out in this unpredictable wilderness, she felt now a looming vulnerability, a disclosure of mortal weakness. She had walked further in the last few hours than she usually dared to, each step bringing her closer to peril; she was toying with her own death. For the concealment that came with the night's darkness did indeed have its outer limit, Edweena knew that every step away from Tenebrae Manor brought her towards the wide world, where blackness encompassed only half the time and hours of deadly daylight would instantly disintegrate her body to ash.

What was it about this very moment that directed the sails of her determination towards this destination? Her brooding had found a channel and, no longer willing to remain in an idle ferment, had churned to life and surged headlong into ambition. It may have been that the sky was indeed a shade lighter, though perhaps it was naught but a trick of the mind. She had not kept track of time. And why should she? When Tenebrae was so indifferent to advancement, content in its shadows, why would Edweena bother herself with acknowledgement of hours? Yet there lingered the frustration of her oversight; had she taken note of the time when she left the house she might have been able to gauge the progression of her journey somewhat more effectively.

There was something so foreign about the sky, as though it had been replaced with a twin so subtly differing in appearance, yet altered enough to evoke a nagging in the back of the mind and suspect the trickery of a duo of charlatans. Yes, there was something unusual about its hue. For the first time, Edweena became aware of the clouds that stretched across the canvas of sky but it was a certain reflective quality that held her transfixed. It was only a colour, a simple pink that lined the clouds on one side and contrasted brilliantly with black shadows opposing it.

Edweena's breath slipped from her lips in an exhalation of intrigue; could she have reached this fabled perimeter, which had eluded her until now? Her Valhalla, the unseen reward of the faithful, could very well greet her over the crest of the next hill. She was by now quite unable to disguise her excitement and her slow trudge broke out into a dash. The slope and the hindering depth of the snow made her ripe with frustration, though it did not slow the pace of ambling, nor the pace of her racing mind. The crest was several metres away, at which point stood two pine trees that were not unlike any others in the forest, yet held the significance of a gateway, parted to form a path over the summit.

Edweena stopped suddenly, her reckless legs restrained by a flood of caution. Her life was at risk; she had to remember that she was indeed a vampire and that she would be swallowed up by the very power she hoped to observe if she were not careful.

As she crept up the last steps of the hill, she felt a strange heat, not of the weather surrounding, for it was still most certainly wintry but a heat from within her core. Edweena winced at the sting of this heat that only increased as she neared the peak. Then, steeling herself, she took the last step that brought her to the top.

The other side of the hill was exactly the same - an ocean of trees heaved by the waves of mountains. But this did not concern Edweena, for she was hypnotised by the light before her - the dawn. She had reached the outer perimeter of Tenebrae's night.

The sunlight was subtle, only as discernible as the hour before dawn, though Edweena had to squint her eyes to absorb what lay before her. The sky was a magnificent forum of pinks, oranges, navy and grey. True, there was no sun visible; it would appear if she travelled a few miles further but its presence was undeniable in this twilit portion of Tenebrae Forest. The pines glistened with snow like fragile figurines in a stain-glass scene. Not since the commencement of her accursed vampiric afterlife had Edweena gazed at such marvellous colour. The earth that had covered memories of a life long past was shoveled away, leaving behind a euphoric realisation; the world was still out there. With all its rapid pace, its inconsiderate change, the globe spun and naught was stagnant outside the Tenebrae night.

Sweat soaked Edweena's skin as the heat from within her being increased to near unbearable limits. Still she stared in wonder at the morning and its endless possibility. Her skin was aglow with a vermillion that smothered her usual whiteness with its vibrant brushstroke. It was only when the pain became all too much and her skin began to burn and hiss that she took a few steps backwards into the shade of the hill. With a sigh she drank in the darkness of the umbra as feverishly as she had the dawn, the burns on her skin suddenly more intense, as though her amazement had numbed her pain receptors hitherto.

It was there in the gloom that she pondered the possibilities laid out before her. Would she wait until the outside world fell under the coverage of nightfall? Only then would she be able to make a break for it, run the risk of instant incineration and pray some refuge from daylight would appear to her in time. There would be twelve hours of darkness at her disposal, surely she would run into some cave where the sun's rays wouldn't reach and she could hide safely until the next night. The restrictions were there to be sure but the challenge they imposed excited her; dashing from refuge to refuge with no promise of a tomorrow. There would be no more boredom; the idea of mortality was almost relieving to her.

Either way, she had hours to wait until the dusky horizon fell into blackness and the ensuing time added hesitancy to her ambition. She had responsibilities at Tenebrae Manor; what if her vagabond nature ended up being accountable for the revealing of the manor to the world, of its supernatural oddities, of its impossible residents? If the forest were revealed, what hope of refuge would these immortal wayfarers have and where would they go if their immemorial home no longer offered concealment?

Edweena turned her gaze to the crest of the hill, where the light shone like a halo between the two trees. No, she was not ready to meet the challenge. Not this time.

With the pang of defeat she turned her back on the dawn and trudged back into the oily tide of darkness. Her stride was slow and crestfallen, her composure drained significantly by the physical sting of sunlight and the harsh criticism she so often struck herself with.

The vampiress felt painfully daunted by the endless sea of trees surrounding her, unchanging as she moved like a somnambulant. Anguish tore at her heart with an aggression that threatened to burst from reticent ribcage. The trunks of black trees stood dominant over her until it all became too much and she collapsed down onto a fallen log. The rotted wood gave slightly under the dead weight of her exhaustion; she buried her face in her hands. Edweena could not recall a time when she felt so lethargic and it was this weakness in her carnal disposition that only heightened the sense of failure in her mind. The arch of her slouched back heaved with laboured breathing, as she convulsed with sobs an ignorant squirrel descended the neighbouring tree and nosed about Edweena with a perilous mixture of confusion and curiosity.

Even in her debilitated state she made no error in seizing the rodent in a flash and savagely snapping its spine, leaving it lifeless in her hands. She tore at its flesh eagerly and sighed as the red life fluid filled her with renewed vitality.

Edweena stood, strong again, focused suddenly on her present; she was bound to Tenebrae Manor. The scales had tipped back in favour of her ancient home and the fresh ideas of a new world of danger to explore seemed less appealing. Perhaps it would only be a short time until the yearning to escape crept up on her again but until then, the darkness had won.

XIII: Bordeaux Amongst Old Books

Through darkled shadows there flitted a movement. Though no light reflected upon it, a certain change in the hazy gloom made it discernible, as one is aware of wind only by its brush on the cheek and the shuddering of treetops. This apparition moved all but silent, only a click of clumsy footsteps and short bursts of breath broke through the echoic halls.

Madlyn crept with haste. She made her descent down and down the stairs into the pit of the manor without a second thought, a route so familiar to her. This time however, the urge to escape the wrath of Libra had doubled and her heart fluttered furiously like a rabbit racing away from a gnashing greyhound. Each step drew her further away and it was with great relief that she reached her room and slammed the heavy wooden door shut. She was safe now. Lady Libra was not one to leave her quarters unless absolutely necessary; her distaste for physical exertion coupled with Tenebrae's innumerable stairs meant that Madlyn could breathe easily in her own abode. It was a dank and windowless cavern of grey brick, more likely to have served as a storeroom before Madlyn had made it hers. Its proximity to the kitchen was only the lesser of its two advantages. The other of course was the room's isolation from the rest of the house.

Madlyn plunked down heavily onto the straw mat that served as her bed and tenderly removed a clump of cloth from her cradling smock. She unraveled the cloth covering with the embellished gentleness and gasped when she caught sight of the hidden token within. The sight of it confirmed in her the rebellion she had undertaken. A flash of glossy ebony caught her sunken pupils and held her completely hypnotised by coveted beauty. It was the black rose brooch that had sat on Libra's vanity and Madlyn had stolen it. The kitchen girl had been overwhelmed with fear up until this point, where she was able to gaze at the thing's great beauty and let the thrill of her rebellion surge through her veins. Her breaths were still short, her mind too feeble to comprehend why she found this brooch so captivating. What she planned to do with it was now her main concern. Stealthily snatching it for herself while Libra was preoccupied with her own reflection in the mirror had been the easy part.

The walls of her room would have driven the more claustrophobic being into a frenzy but to Madlyn, this room was all she had to call her own. Wrapping the brooch in its protective cloth and stuffing it under her pillow, she presently stood and made her way to a pitiful little desk in the corner. It was not a long trek, to be sure, for so small was the room that she was there in two steps. On the splintered surface of the table lay Madlyn's meager and adored possessions. A few scraps of paper whereupon she had scribbled her thoughts and creations, a quill - merely shed plumage of a no doubt long dead owl and a small shard of glass that had once been part of a mirror.

Madlyn contorted her back to an awkward angle as she reached down to scratch at the back of her shin. The pendulum swinging of her disorderly blonde pigtail failed to wrest her attention from the mirror shard. She smiled vaguely, an expression that would bemuse even the greatest psychologist. The stonewalls sighed in the silence, for a moment Madlyn felt a presence unsettlingly close.

Turning about her tiny room and confirming no visible haunt disturbing her silence quenched her momentary fear, so she was able to return her gaze to the reflection in the shard. Swimming through its triangular surface, the swollen globe of Madlyn's right eye reflected back at her a dead expression. The effect of the sunken skin about her ocular jellyfish, darkened by fatigue, was one that seemed to smolder with a billowy smoke encircling. The blue iris dripped with a malice that frightened her, a malice she did not know herself capable of. But it was a poorly developed malice, more like the expressionless hostility reserved for strangers in which one has no desire to acquaint.

As though only to fill convulsive impulse, Madlyn dashed to her bed and leapt onto it to confirm the presence of the brooch. It was still there. Her heart tingled with a glow. The virgin innocence of her misled love had its embers rekindled. The black rose brooch, which was to become an embodiment of her very affection, should be gifted to the crimson demon. Her love was a confused thing, oblivious to its blatant notions that left it obvious to others. He should have the brooch, Madlyn had decided.

Of the consequences, she was untroubled - even of the obvious fact that Libra would no doubt see the stolen brooch on Bordeaux's lapel. Such considerations were abated by her incubated innocence. The seed of her love had been planted long ago but only now was action to be taken; the plant was to be watered, tended to, with every hope that it would soon spill forth in pulchritudinous blossom.

The wind that howled about the castle wailed like a newborn, having only whipped itself to life an hour previous. And yet its cold hostility carried with it an omnipresent air, as though it had always been hurtling its gusts across the surfaces of land and sea, only to have just reached Tenebrae Manor, where it would soon pass on through and around the cavernous seashell and never be seen again. The gale moaned with an aptly intimidating warning; a warning of a danger that threatened the very livelihood of the castle's residents. A danger that had filled Bordeaux with an increasing sense of doubt and pushed him into action. It was this dread that sent him on a grave errand to the library of Tenebrae Manor, where there stood the hope of answers; any answers would assuage the fears that weighed his heart.

Much has already been described of Tenebrae Manor, its echoed corridors, its stairwells of eternal incline, drawing rooms rotted by their own antiquity but what of the manor's western side? It has been said that the auditorium juts from the house like a boil upon the western side but what can be said of the rooms that stood in its shadows several storeys below? Through a maze of halls, penetrating far and deep, identical in their adornments of stone and wood, there lies an immense library. Access to this archaic cavern would seem a confusing pathway that would turn any jaunt sour and indeed it seemed that it were only Bordeaux's years of acquired knowledge of Tenenbrae Manor that had ingrained the correct path to the library into his head. There were four of them that made their way through the candlelit darkness, though three of them were unaware of the other that completed their tetrad.

Accompanying Bordeaux were not only the tweed clad Deadsol and Comets the jester, whose composure was one of lesser apprehension but also Madlyn. The girl lurked in their shadows, a few paces behind them, following on a restrained tiptoe that took up all of her lagged concentration. Though she pursued three, she saw only one, the man with his deep red coat - the figure of her affections. She wrestled with her shyness and spent every step trying to exert the extra effort that would push her into his presence. Oh, to be noticed by him! But every time she thought the time had come to burst into their candlelit view, she hesitated and slunk defeated back into the gloom.

Deadsol, possessed as he was by a self-righteous ramble, had provided more of an irritation to Bordeaux's frazzled mind than any manner of support and he prattled endlessly.

"To relax, Bordeaux. That is what one needs! Oh yes, my yes, I know, oh! Let matters deal with themselves, I

say, or better yet! Let us let Libra deal with it! But no!
Stupid fool that I am to suggest the very idea, that idea that
she would take action!"

"You will do well to follow quietly," said Bordeaux.
"Your joining me was by no means compulsory."

"Always trying to be rid of poor Deadsol! You are
lucky I am so patient, B."

Bordeaux paused before the great oak doors of the
library, "Maybe you are right, Deadsol. Maybe you are the
patient one."

They entered the library and stood a moment near the
door. Rows of shelves loomed around them, from which
innumerable books stared silently. The smell of literature
lingered, clinging tenaciously to the air with its mustiness.
Faded leather wings hugging dried pages and ink, these
books perched themselves on their shelves as the three
apparitions moved towards a light glowing faintly in the
heart of the aviary-like library.

Madlyn hung near the entrance, still able to discern all
conversation in the echoes of the room. A far corner of
the room established itself as a small sitting area, where a
fireplace roared with life and flung shadows of book
towers across the carpet.

It was there that the mummified zombie, Rune, had
ensconced on the floor and stared absently into the flames.
Enveloped in gauze, he displayed the patience of his age
through his quiet hours of reading. Rune was the eldest
remaining resident of Tenebrae Manor and after several
centuries of restless wandering, he had settled for a life of
researching the history of the mansion and its
surroundings. His jaw hung listlessly open at all times, as
though it were tired of conversing with that upper row of

yellowed teeth. Above his gaping maw, betwixt rows of bandages, two yellow eyes peered from a decayed blackness.

There he sat, legs crossed and ignorant to the company behind him and yet once their presence was made clear; namely by Comets prodding at the mummy's arm, he showed signs more akin to annoyance than fright. His head turned about its axis and seemed to slowly consider his intruders.

"Is that Bordeaux and Deadsol?" he croaked in a strained voice.

"The very same, Rune," replied Bordeaux. "Well met, my friend."

The mummy rose to his feet, rising higher and higher until he towered over them all. He was a creature of great lank, pushing towards eight feet in height, his arms hung low beside him, reaching the knees of his spindly legs. With a considerable delay, Rune limply shook the hands of both Bordeaux and Deadsol.

"I have not had a visitor in some time," he said. "Yet something tells me that this is more than a casual meeting."

"You are not wrong in that assumption, Rune," said Bordeaux. "We come with a request for information most critical. The very livelihood of Tenebrae Manor depends on it."

Rune scratched his head absently, though he was not wrestling with the words of Bordeaux but rather the actions of the jester Comets, who was making a nuisance of himself about the library.

"Comets!" barked Deadsol.

Comets leapt upon the shelves as swift as a simian

and with unmatched zeal, began to fling unfortunate tomes about the floor. The fluttering of the soaring pages contradicted the dull thud of book spine upon carpet, as birds of printed words, stitched and bound, crash-landed upon the floor.

"Must the young boy do that?" said Rune.

"Comets, you rascal! Descend from your perch at once, good citizen!" Deadsol ordered.

The jester made several unmentionable gestures of ribald obscenity before obeying the command of his friend, stamping down onto the ground and jumping on the spot repeatedly. He muttered an incomprehensible curse and scratched crudely at his rear. Rune was visibly peeved at the actions of the imp; though his body was old he showed no apathy in reprimanding the lad with a swift clap across the head. Comets slurred dizzily as the bells of his cap jingled.

"These books are all that connects Tenebrae to the world beyond the night! One would do well to treat them with respect."

Comets wasn't listening but had calmed down significantly now that the others were paying attention to him.

Rune turned back to Bordeaux. "My friend, I have lived here for centuries. I remember your arrival to this place like it was yesterday. You know that I have devoted the long years of my afterlife to researching the history of not only Tenebrae but also the entire world! If there is some threat to my old home, I will do all I can to bring my knowledge forward in assistance."

He rung his hands passionately, causing the bandages swathed about his limbs to rustle softly.

"Then please, divulge all that you know about Wood Golems."

"Wood Golems?"

There was a hush amongst them. For Rune, it was an air of perplexity that plagued his mindset. Bordeaux was pressed with grave concern and, in the shadows, Madlyn gasped with fascination. She had climbed a nearby shelf and crouched behind dust-coated tomes so she was able to look down at the others. The ceiling was within her reach, pinning her somewhat between shelf and roof, amongst the decades of dust that irritated her nose. Madlyn fought back the urge to sneeze and continued to observe Bordeaux with her bulbous eyes.

"Wood Golems, you say?" repeated Rune, "Well for one, I know that they can be quite deadly if you give them a chance. But what possible threat could they pose to us?"

"My friend, I found one trying to destroy the walls of the house. I was then attacked by the creature and was startled by its aggression."

"It was destroying the house?" said Rune.

"I kid you not and their increased numbers throughout the forest lead me to believe that there is something very wrong. We must act fast, lest they destroy the foundations of our home and it collapses."

"They have removed a certain *joie de vivre* from our lives," chimed in Deadsol eloquently.

In the meantime, Rune had produced a stepladder and propped it against a shelf. It was a shelf not unlike any of the others, though it was seemingly obvious that the zombie knew what he was searching for. His knees trembled under the weight of the monstrous book that he had slid from a high shelf. It was a mammoth thing of brown leather, precariously balancing on the shoulder of the now top heavy Rune, who presently fell from the ladder with the book landing heavily next to him.

Bordeaux rushed to help the old citizen to his feet but was waved away and soon Rune had arduously returned to his feet with the book in his arms pulling him floor-bound like a sack of flour. He stifled a grunt and plopped the huge book onto a table and ran his fingers across the cover.

"Wood. Golems." he said strenuously.

The book fell open at a random page but again, Rune seemed to know exactly where he had turned.

"An ancient monster to be sure," he began. "Although only recent to this area. They are born of the Black Rose Tree - an archaic magic in the form of a mighty tree. It says here that Wood Golems sprout up around its roots like shrubbery, before they are ripped from the ground with noose-like vines of the host tree. They are endowed with life from that moment."

"Well yes, all well and good to know where they come from…" bustled Deadsol impatiently.

Rune ignored Deadsol's impropriety and continued. "The host tree is said to sprout beautiful roses upon skeletal branches, black as onyx. The entire effect is very pleasing to the eyes; the Black Rose Tree is both stunning and deadly. It is known to strangle intruders from its mighty branches and display them as ornamental warnings to any foolish enough to venture near it."

"Interesting," said Bordeaux.

"Indeed," replied Rune. "I had always known Wood Golems to be very territorial but they rarely venture past the boundaries surrounding the black Rose Tree. The host tree feeds the golems with the hearts of intruders. This is very much a perplexing conundrum."

"Perhaps their revolt is something territorial," suggested Deadsol. "I don't know why Tenebrae Manor is in their line of fire but perhaps, perhaps, perhaps fire! Of course!"

"What are you on about, Deadsol?" sighed Bordeaux.

"Why B, we could set them all on fire! That would be rid of them!"

"Unwise," said Rune. "While such a move would surely exterminate their excess numbers, what of us? What would become of us all if Tenebrae Manor went up in flames? The risk is too great."

"But the destruction, oh what fun!" cackled Deadsol.

"Be quiet, Deadsol," said Bordeaux. "Rune, might I borrow this book from you? Perhaps further reading will reveal some clues and offer a path to solution."

Rune grunted hesitantly. "Normally, I would not lend my books to anybody. But for you Bordeaux, I will allow it this once. You are far more level headed than the other rabble rousers in this manor."

All eyes turned to Comets, who was tearing pages from an unfortunate novel and eating them.

"Rune, I apologise profusely for the actions of my little friend here. I assure you that your book is safe with me."

As Rune accompanied them to the exit, Madlyn fell from the top shelf with a squeal and hit the floor forcefully. She winced through her teeth and clasped at her elbow, which had born the brunt of her weight in the fall. She was mostly unhurt and fortunately remained unnoticed by the others. Her mind swam with the promise of great beauty. There were more black roses out there. She could get another to impress Bordeaux! If only she could find the courage to give him the one she had already!

Rune sighed. "Bordeaux, you and I have lived here so long, I can tell you this; never have I felt so uneasy about the future. Libra, lovely girl I am sure but she lacks a certain something that has left me apprehensive."

"I know," replied Bordeaux. "She does not fill me with confidence but what choice do we have? She is untouchable. Her magical skills have spiked so much recently, who is there to challenge her leadership?"

Deadsol shook his head, "Tut-tut, if only Malistorm were still around."

"Yes well there is little benefit in dwelling on his disappearance," said Bordeaux. "I hold the belief that he simply ran away to pursue other things. That said; he was a fine leader."

"Could the loyal Bordeaux finally be showing a little rebellion towards our lovely Lady?" taunted Deadsol.

"I will stand firm to whoever reigns Tenebrae. For the good of the manor, for the retention of our seclusion from the outside world."

"Malistorm was the best we ever had." Rune was reminiscing and had not followed the conversation. Next to them, Comets sung softly to himself,

Deep in the forest
Where all is still,
The wood golem lurks
Against its will.

Endowed with life

By some magical curse
And ripped from the ground
By a noose made it worse!

Wandering restless
And instilling fear,
It isn't quite certain
Just why it's here!

They hide in the fog
And emit chilling grunts.
They'll devour the hearts
Of lost folk they confront.

It doesn't know better,
So don't blame this creep.
All that it wants
Is to go back to sleep.

The poem, eloquent in its form, confused the listeners who had just witnessed unruly ribaldry from Comets not moments earlier.

"Very nice, young man," said Rune. "If only your manners were as graceful as your poetry."

Comets ignored him.

"I would love very much to hear from you, Bordeaux. Should you require anymore assistance…"

"Of course," replied Bordeaux.

Their footsteps echoed in the hallways and Madlyn was able to disguise her own as just another echo. Bordeaux clutched the great tome under his arm, his other hand clasped at his crestfallen chin, his eyes locked on the ground with an expression of repressed turmoil. Comets and Deadsol were many metres ahead of him, prancing whimsically through the gloom. Madlyn capitalised on her chance and ran up to Bordeaux, tapping him on the shoulder. He stopped and turned.

"Madlyn?"

Without a word, she held the brooch before him in both hands. Her knees quivered as fast as her heart, which raced like a butterfly.

Bordeaux stared at the black rose brooch and took it in his hands. Madlyn hid a smile behind her emaciated hand and turned her head from him.

"What is?" began Bordeaux, unsure of how to finish his sentence.

What is this? What is the meaning of this? From where did you appear? Is this a present for me? But before he was able to elaborate with any form of question, Madlyn had run off into the distance, pushing past Deadsol and Comets. Bordeaux stood nonplussed, gazing into the black, the book under one arm and the beautiful brooch in the other. From the darkled hallways there drifted the sound of Madlyn's nervous laughter.

XIV: Libra's Dream

She travelled an obscure route, hidden from waking consciousness. A path concealed by sweeping branches draping moribund in the haze of narcosis. The mountain of sheets that covered her twitched and reformed in reaction to her weighted but steady breathing and conjured up frightful visions of a living crag overwhelming in its girth.

Libra's face glowed amongst the mess of dark linen - a moon and sky fallen from the heavens laying lethargic on the bed. A convulsion of her eyelid, lasting only a second, belayed how deep her slumber was. Between her softened cheeks, her lips had set in that smile of content; the smile that covered her ignorance - be it intentional or no, to the chaos that was going on about the manor she claimed as her own.

In her mind's eye she recalled the life preceding luxury. It appeared to her in flashes, vignettes of times past that were vital to the plot of her life's outcome. It always began at the same point, her memory only managed to recede so far; what lay beyond the shallows of the lowest tide were hidden to her, she could not say why. But Libra remembered an agony seemingly unending and when that pain was all too unbearable, it had ceased. What was left behind was a euphoric rush of adrenalin, a feeling of unstoppable strength and vitality. Just as a branch is pruned with the expectation of it returning in greatest blossom, so too had she endured pain for the greater result.

Tenebrae Manor had always been her home, at least the only home she could remember. Then there was Malistorm, the former baron of the house - who had taken her under his wing and taught her the ways of magic and the extent of her potential. He had been a world-weary sorcerer who had never divulged more than his intention. As such, Libra never did discover how Tenebrae Manor came to be or how Malistorm had become its baron. All she knew was that the house was old - perhaps older than time itself or of some other realm where time is negligible. Then, pervading all other thought was the insatiable thirst to have the house as her own. She remembered Bordeaux from the beginning, Edweena and Rune too. And Malistorm, with his crest of shock-greyed hair and a cloak of brilliant violet....

The violet curtains in the bedroom fluttered with the arrival of a frigid wind from the open window. In her sleep, Libra twisted her face with discomfort as the wind brushed her cheek with its icicle fingers. Under the spell of the gale, Libra's dream turned bitter and her wanton violence aimed itself at those who threatened her. She was the Lady Libra; Tenebrae Manor was hers. Behind her eye lids in the depths of her dream, the gloom swirled and

from its syrupy murk emerged the malicious grinning face
of Deadsol. His thumbs plucked at the lapels of his copper
coloured vest as he bounced gaily upon his feet, his mouth
silent yet moving as though prattling on excessively.

Though no words were discernable, the sight of the
demon revolted Libra to such an adequate degree that she
began to toss her head about on the pillow. Deadsol
rambled on and on, carrying the same sanguine
countenance that Libra found repulsive. Her heart lurched
in fury as the apparition of Deadsol was suddenly plucked
off the ground by his moustache. He thrashed about
feebly; his attempts to free himself resulted in a prominent
lengthening of his whiskers, so that soon he found himself
strung by the neck and swinging from a gallows.

Libra rolled over in her bed so that her heavy body
faced the other direction, having conquered Deadsol, she
hoped to return to a more pleasant dreamland. But almost
immediately she was met with the ghastly vision of
Comets, who stared at her vacantly with his hollow eyes of
mismatched size. His head twitched, the bells of his red
and yellow cap chimed and he began to hop from foot to
foot. The jester circumnavigated Libra, so that she could
only see him each time he passed the hour mark - gliding
from left to right out of view then appearing from the left
again.

"Away! Pest!"

She caught him by the ears of his cap and spun him
in the opposite direction; her speed increased as she
wound up her shot like a hammer-thrower. With a flick of
her wrists, the jester went flying and screamed as he was
struck down in mid flight by a bolt of lightning. Comets
burst into a shower of fireworks that fell like rain onto the

shoulders of Edweena.

Edweena – she who had been her loyal friend from the beginning. The vampiress stared at Libra with those accusing eyes. Why did she hold such a grudge? It had to be jealousy, what else? Well, that was her own fault. Someone had to reign over the Manor, why couldn't Edweena be happy for her friend? Libra spared her from her dream wrath and became immersed in melancholia. Edweena turned and took her leave, the stately Bordeaux taking her place.

"Ah, Bordeaux. Such a gentleman. How could I delegate harm unto you?"

It took only a moment for her sympathy to reek with envy. Bordeaux stood as the biggest threat to her position!

"But so weak-willed, my sumptuous little B. Weak as water, I say! Yes, you are naught but a sponge that mops the mess of peasants! Mop you shall!"

In her mind's eye, Bordeaux transformed into a soiled cloth that was held firm in the scrubbing hands of Madlyn. "Madlyn, the stupid girl! She could snap like a twig, let it be!"

Libra was on a roll now and had reserved her most potent destruction for last; appearing before her was the composer, Arpage.

"You!"

The ghost of Arpage fidgeted nervously. Libra took a lustful delight in the howls of his anguish as she dragged him by his bottom jaw through fields of jagged glass and scolding coals.

"What was it that you called me, Arpage? Be gone!"

When she clapped her hands the composer vanished into dust as though he were never there.

The Lady Libra awoke. Her amber eyes glowed from the tangled mess of her dark curls. Her beauty was flushed with the rose-cheeked flutter of her fury's wing beats. She arose to her feet effortlessly, as though her bulk was a thing that did not trouble her and flew to the open window. The wind struck her face and carried the blanket of her lush hair in the same direction as the purple curtains. She did not feel the cold. She would not be defeated. Raw tenacity surged in her veins, culminating in a bitter clenching of hatred, jealousy and arrogance. Libra was the queen of Tenebrae Manor; nobody would take that from her.

While the calls of crows clawing through the air were prominent, it was discernible that another cry had uprooted itself and joined the dirge. A gravelly moan with such depth of baritone hummed repetitively in the forest. The wailing was not of a single anguished creature, echoed innumerable times; it seemed almost certain that a manifold of voices had compiled themselves together and dispersed to random outposts in the trees surrounding Tenebrae Manor. Carrying with them a chill to the spine more bloodcurdling than the growl of a hungry wolf, the cries nestled into the hearts of the manor's inhabitants and left behind a residue of anxiety that affected Bordeaux more violently than any other.

It was true that his recent brush with destruction at the hands of a vagabond golem had shaken him. He sat in his quarters, coughing with each turned page of the book leant to him by Rune, as the ageless dust spun away in spirals. There was little room left on the surface of his desk but the efficient demon had found a space for a leather-bound notebook and quill with which he was taking notes. At the head of the desk sat Madlyn's brooch.

From the other side of the room, his painting of a seaside dawn impressed into him a new beginning of change; an emancipation from responsibility and anxiety, away from the burden of eternal night. Bordeaux lifted his head from the book in an effort to rest his eyes momentarily from his intense reading, when his vision became locked onto the colourful canvas. The painting called to him, of that he was conscious; it beckoned him with fanciful notions that he refused to yield to. Bordeaux would certainly find enjoyment in the outside world, he knew from centuries long past the thrills of travel, the blessings of the sun's kiss.

But to what purpose would a return to the wayfarer's life achieve? Eternity was indeed a long time and even reclusive figures such as himself found themselves in need of companionship at times. The stability of Tenebrae Manor was of great comfort to Bordeaux; he could not leave it, yet now it seemed he was confronted by the possibility of its annihilation. He picked up the rose brooch and twirled it in his fingers, sending a kaleidoscope of blacks shades into weavings of impossible patterns.

The moaning outside his window continued its omnipresent thrum. Bordeaux removed his person from the chair and stood at his window; the painting behind him bore into his mind, though now there was a polar force that tugged him in the opposite direction. Framed as it were in his window, the nighttime forest lulled Bordeaux into maudlin reminiscence. The pines cut their saw-toothed verdure; the snow cloaked the land in silvered brilliance. Though the moon did not shine at present, the forest was alive and however foreboding its atmosphere was, it remained his home. In the corner of the window, a spider spun its web quietly, oblivious to the adoring eyes of Bordeaux.

"How beautiful the night is."

For several minutes he stood enraptured. The moans grew louder on a sudden and knocked him back to his senses. Bordeaux knew where they were coming from. The echoes were the very same unmistakable groans that were uttered by the wood golem that had attacked him. What could have possibly disturbed them? On a sudden he became aware of another disturbance; he leant out the window to get a closer look.

The trees nearest to his room were bending inwards towards him. On the outside walls surrounding, their branches gripped at the house's facade like vines as a parasite constricts its host. Soon they would enwrap the entire residence in their ligneous limbs. As an experiment Bordeaux snapped off a small portion of branch within his reach and gasped as it reeled in pain, only to reposition itself and stretch out to the house again.

Bordeaux started as though struck by revelation and strode back to his desk. He flicked back through a few pages in the book and read furiously.

"Wood golems are steadfastly loyal to the Black Rose Tree that begot them. They will defend the host with their own lives."

He looked up in thought and found himself staring at

the brooch given to him by Madlyn; its black petals
appeared suddenly menacing.

XV: Arpage Struggles to Adjust

With one hand clasped in a feeble grip, Arpage drove his other into the gaping maw of a cloth sack and clutched at a handful of seeds. He withdrew his closed fist and sighed inwardly as the majority of grains he had grasped fell through his thin fingers like sand in an hourglass. By the time his hand emerged from the sack he was able to open his fist and count but a few measly seeds lying dormant in his palm. His eyes scanned the field before him, hillocks of pumpkins reared their orange heads and for a moment he was reminded of an impressive crowd in some grand auditorium. But no, these pumpkins would not congratulate him, even if he were to bow or blow kisses. They would not throw roses at his feet nor hurl confetti to rain down onto his shoulders. Instead, it would be he that threw the confetti of seeds at them.

Arpage sighed again and tossed them with a weak underarm swing and pretended their clatter on the dried earth was the applause of his ghostly audience. His shoulders slouched and his mouth, a capsized smile, sunk further into dissatisfaction. He turned his head back towards Sinders' shack and weighed up his progress of work with what remained. He had only thrown the seeds over a tenth of the vast field and the crows, having recognised the familiar sound of scattered seeds falling, wasted no time in swooping down from their blackened perches to scour the ground for bounty. The slimy pelt of Arpage's greasy cowlick drooped with frustration.

"Away, you beastly birds!"

His hands flailed but the black birds resolutely ignored him. Some swung perilously close to his face while others more confident with the aim of their beaks were able to clip him about the arms and hands, further fraying the fabric of his green cardigan.

"You'll never scare them away like that. Look at the fear in your eyes! They know you are not a threat." Sinders emerged from his darkened home and into the moonlight. The crows instantly dissipated with his appearance. Arpage hurled the sack of seeds down in anger.

"Well maybe you should be doing this then! After all, you're the scarecrow! I simply despise this cruel punishment, oh woe!"

The composer had fallen to his knees and begun to sob gently.

"Well what am I to do?" replied Sinders. "I was ordered to keep you busy, what else can I have you waste the hours on?"

"I'm tired, sir," moaned Arpage.

"You are a namby-pamby."

"I beg your pardon?"

"A fop! A wimp! Insipid!"

Arpage was taken aback. "I am no such thing!"

"Nonsense, my friend! I've never heard a man complain so much." Sinders turned from the crestfallen composer and entered his home again, continuing, "This is meant to be punishment, no? Now our young man here is a model citizen! Jethro, how goes it?"

Arpage crawled through the doorway on his hands and knees to see Jethro huddled over a small flame, with Sinders looming in the shadows behind him.

"You managed to light the fire, lad!" said Sinders, placing a hand of straw on the man's back.

Jethro flinched a little. "Yes... Yes the fire is lit..."

"No need to tell me, you dull boy! Now Arpage, why can't you move with the same quiet obedience as our mortal friend here?"

Casting his glance this way and that, so that he was able to absorb the entire picture before him, Arpage analysed the bleak shack. Its interior had undergone a vast increase in homeliness since his arrival, due in part to Jethro's work. The mortal man had recovered from his fitful delirium and seemingly accepted his present fate, busying himself with cleaning and upheaval of Sinders' shack. The fireplace was now aglow always; the room kept warm with a new door and patched windows to keep the heat in. No longer did the moon throw its beams through the roof holes in shafts, nor the snow lie in patches upon the rotted wooden floor - Jethro had patched the roof of its many failings and trimmed away at least some of the excessive ivy that choked the entire facade. For his bed, Jethro had compiled a collection of old sacks and filled them with leaves, while Arpage had shown no such resourcefulness; he continued to sleep on the floor like a forgotten canine.

The composer turned his nose up. He refused to accept that this intruder, who now sat wearily by his little fire, had upstaged him. Sinders allowed himself to lean into the fireplace in such a way that he unwittingly set his hand aflame.

"Such perilous balance... Those inches separate comfort and pain! Such is the heat of the fire!"

"S-sir... Your arm is on fire," Jethro mumbled nervously.

"Oh my it is!"

Sinders dashed the length of the room and flung his limb into a bucket of water recently used to mop the floor.

"Stupid old pumpkin head," huffed Arpage.

"What's that, Mr. Arpage?" replied Sinders. "Don't you have seeds to sow? Ah ha!"

"A plague on you both," sneered Arpage as he returned to the field.

Once Sinders had successfully extinguished the flames that had enveloped his arm, he returned to the fireplace and once again stood dominant over the cowering Jethro. The man turned his head and looked up timidly; the hollow caves of Sinders' black eyes held him in a trance, while his stitched zigzag smile made him shudder involuntarily.

In due time, Sinders grew weary of standing and slumped to the floor next to the flame, never once taking his eyes off Jethro. The scarecrow was merely enraptured by a child-like curiosity in the young man; but to Jethro, Sinders stared with a sinister malice. Jethro's hair, once a mess of dirty blonde, had been drained of all colour and was now a shade of grey pushing towards white. He stared right back at Sinders with eyes that openly expressed the deep state of shock he was in. They were glassy pearls; where once an oceanic blue had flowed an ice cap had glassed over his pupils in a useless attempt to stave off insanity. They bore into Sinders all the same, though Jethro's curiosity held far more disbelief than Sinders' naive examinations.

Jethro's mind raced, he had considered means of escape, more so now that he had been removed from Tenebrae Manor but he was at a loss as to where he could flee. Which direction could he possibly take? He had no bearing whatsoever, remaining baffled and directionless under the eternal night sky. Where was the sunlight? Had the sun risen and set as he always knew it to do, he would be able to gauge which way was north and that would at least be a start. But it was always dark! How could that possibly be? At any moment he expected to awaken and cry with relief of the fact that this had all been a nightmare. Since Jethro was unable to recall the events that led him here, he could not be certain what reality was and assumed that he would not simply wake up and have his troubles taken from him. He was a farmhand; he knew that reward came only with hard work. He would take his chances and escape.

He was growing increasingly uncomfortable of Sinders and his constant staring. Clearly the scarecrow had limited social skills, the common rule of keeping one's business to one's self did not make his list of appropriate manners. Yet Jethro could think of nothing to say to break the awkward silence. Several times he opened his mouth to speak but no words came.

"Perhaps you should check on Arpage," he finally managed.

"You think so? Well okay," replied Sinders.

The scarecrow took his leave and left Jethro alone with his fire. He let out a sigh of relief, at least Sinders was easily persuaded. Within his chest he felt his heart pang with remorse, the fire before him gave a nostalgic memory of the sun and its all but forgotten warmth.

It was only once he had delved deeper that Arpage had become suspicious of Jethro. What was dismissed as fickle jealousy by Sinders had in fact had taken root into the fertile soil of the composer's brain and, nourished with the food of his thought, had stirred from its torpor into confirmed distrust. Between the staff lines of his veins where blood flowed legato, he had shoveled away the rabble of quavers and clefs that lay cluttered, waiting to be assigned their position in some unwritten song and found that these dubious feelings towards Jethro were as certain as the music that had forever enchanted him. It had been expected that the human would show the myriad of frantic emotions he had displayed hitherto but Arpage now found himself at a loss to explain Jethro's conformity to the rules of his imprisonment.

Arpage stood as stone-faced as a Venetian mask, his eyes quivering about their sockets, firing icy glares at the crows that had returned from their roosts and settled on the pumpkins. The internal rage that burned within him was but collateral damage. His suspicions had no real proof; on what plausible notion could he place his feet stably? A dreadful sigh pressed past his crooked teeth and whether it was this sigh or his haggard appearance that had done so, he could not tell but numerous crows flew away to his sudden surprise.

With naught to distract him but his mind, Arpage retrieved his sack of seeds and once again found himself hurling granules through the air. And upon hearing again the scattering sounds on the ground, the crows swooped anon.

XVI: Suspicions

Sleet tore down and although their watery needles thrust cruelly onto the rooftops of Tenebrae Manor with an unadulterated malice, there was perhaps some comfort to be drawn from them. For though the rain was frigid and piercing to the skin, it foretold the presence of a warmer clime. Of those living within Tenebrae Manor, those eternally clinging to any foothold of hope, none were bold enough to assume that the wintery spell was nearing its end.

The manor stood marooned, shipwrecked in a grey-green sea; stony turrets jutted skyward as masts, reaching heavenward with rusted spires and apexed roof. The struggle against drowning - drowning in the torrent of forest, was weakening.

For all of Tenebrae's haunting tenacity, the clinging tendrils of ivy and branch that had entwined themselves to the façade could not be forced back. They coiled about column and constricted; as though to asphyxiate, to drag the house down further under until it lay smothered and indistinguishable amongst the wild forest. The vines crawled from all sides and slithered up rampart in search of ingress, while those branches that flourished higher up had found their way over parapet and through broken window. It was as though Tenebrae Manor were victim to colossal arachnid and lay in helpless paralysis as the web was spun all consuming.

And throughout the subtle chaos there still murmured the same throaty groan of the Wood Golems, their echoes penetrating even torrential rain and adding to the shivering fear settling upon the hearts of certain residents.

In the third floor drawing room, where one wall had become verdant with ivy, Edweena sat in the glow of the fireplace and observed Bordeaux, whose profile suckled at the darkness and lengthened its shadow cast by the flames. Across her face there glowed the hint of a smile, accentuating the pale beauty of her face.

"I saw the sun," she said.

Bordeaux stirred from his owl-like stance in front of the fireplace. He looked at her from over his shoulder and laughed softly. "That old thing. And how is our negligent lantern?"

Edweena shuffled in her seat and thrust her reddened forearms at the demon. "Hot as it ever was. Look, it burns."

Her skin had taken on a pink glow and developed a stinging itch where the dawn's light had burned.

"Well, I didn't actually see the sun..." she continued, "but the dawn must have been right past the next hill."

"A ghastly look for you," said Bordeaux, preoccupied

with Edweena's sunburn. "I think I much prefer your pale pallor."

The crackling of the fire joined the hush of violent rain that filled the gaps of silence between their words. For some minutes following, the pair said nothing. Edweena's sapphire eyes stared intently at Bordeaux; he could feel her gaze and adjusted his stance. Tension mounted in the silence.

"We could leave, you know," Edweena said eventually.

Bordeaux did not react immediately but slowly turned away from the fireplace and sat down in a leather armchair next to her.

"Well, certainly not now."

Edweena tilted her head in vexation.

"It's raining," said Bordeaux.

The vampiress smirked solemnly. She was not used to Bordeaux making jokes.

"I cannot leave," he continued. "Not while I am needed."

"You could be needed for centuries. I don't see anyone standing up to the pedestal where you find yourself perched."

Bordeaux's face pained with longing, he poured the weight of his depression into the fire with his deadpan stare.

"Why care so much, Bordeaux?" pressed Edweena. "This house, home to be certain but so depressing. Are we wasting the hours by staying here? We have all the time in the world, yet we choose to lurk in this half lit dimness."

He considered her words and searched his mind for the appropriate response. "The longer one stands still, the harder it becomes to move again. My friends are here and they have need of my duties. Especially now."

Bordeaux retrieved Madlyn's brooch from his coat pocket and spun it in his fingers. Having grown weary of such weighted topics, Edweena turned to other things.

"What is that thing you're carrying around anyway?"

"It was given to me by Madlyn."

Edweena laughed bitterly. "That poor girl. Reaching for you - untouchable you."

"Be civil."

"Oh lighten up, I know what you think of the girl."

"In some other life, perhaps a clumsy little sister?"

She laughed harder. "I could not have put it better!"

Bordeaux became serious again; "It perplexes me, where she could have gotten such an item."

"Clearly Libra's," replied Edweena. "But what does that matter? It's just a brooch, a perfect little trinket for your emasculated taste."

"I hardly think that was necessary."

"There there, B," said Edweena. "Go on then, tell me all about it."

Bordeaux leaned forward in his chair. "I had thought as such; that is, that Libra were the owner of this brooch. I resolved to approach her about it, having received little help from Madlyn herself. When I made my way to our lady's quarters I was puzzled to find the room vacant. It was a rare occasion, I suppose, that I happened to chance upon an hour where Libra was not in her usual reclining and I was at once stumped as to where to search for her..."

Bordeaux called out but no response came. The room was still, devoid of light and cold as though neglected for years. He struck his fingers like a flint and lit the lantern hanging closest to the door. Libra's absence was most irregular; yet he could not pass up the opportunity to snoop about her opulent home. She had certainly hoarded an admirable quantity of fine treasures. It seemed such a waste to him to see such brilliant paintings stacked in corners as though they were mere firewood.

Bordeaux inspected her dresser, finding to his surprise that it lacked the clutter akin to the furnishings that surrounded it. The mirror was tall and on the counter lay a hairbrush, perfumes and a garish jewelry box, baroque as a bohemian church. He imagined Libra, ensconced on the stool before the vanity, marveling her own self-absorbed beauty.

Shaking his head, Bordeaux wondered whether Libra had noticed the effects of her excess - was her confidence born of denial or ignorance? Yet he could not blame her inactivity at times, having grown tired of travel himself and finding limited resources with which to whittle away the hours of eternity.

His own gaunt cheekbones cut a reflective portrait in the mirror. The face that stared back at him was the very same that he would have seen hundreds of years earlier. He suddenly ached for rest and found himself weary of his own youthful looks; looks that rarely showed the torments of his years. It was only his eyes that betrayed his fatigue.

The years gone by flew past in his mind's eye, smothering his vision like a murder of crows swooping upon him; he recalled his first meeting with Libra. The way Malistorm had introduced her so highly, the initial attraction he felt for the slim and shapely beauty before him, the fierce competition that plagued the early years of their friendship and established the foundation of their future strains. She had been on a par with him for centuries; in intellect, magic, wisdom, power.

Only recently, namely the two or so years gone by, had Libra stood unmatched in her challenge to the headship of the manor. And once she had gotten there… In the reflection he thought he could discern a figure but upon turning around it was only a hulking wardrobe looming over a mountain of discarded clothing. Libra's bed, perennially unmade, lay in a shamble of sheets in the centre of the room, illuminated by the light of the night seeping through rain-smeared windowpanes. The place was hedonistic shamble smothered in its own gluttony.

Bordeaux tried to remember the Libra of old, determined and hotheaded, half her size in both physicality and status. She already seemed long gone; perhaps Libra had been his friend then but he knew now she was no more than a difficult colleague.

Moving across the cluttered floor, Bordeaux slammed his shin into the side of the lady's favourite chaise lounge. He swore through his teeth quietly, face flushed with embarrassment. But there was none who saw his momentary lapse in dignity and, doing his best to ignore the throbbing pain in his leg, he regained his composure.

Once it became apparent that he could not find

anything tangible in unraveling his mystery, Bordeaux decided to take leave. He gritted his teeth, his mind nagged at him, told him to go find Libra, if only to ask a few questions. Maybe she would know nothing; such a response would at least quench some of his angst. It seemed unlikely that he could find Libra in Tenebrae Manor, the house where hundreds of rooms weaved together into an unsolvable maze. Adding further to his misfortune was the stammering question of where Libra could be, considering her disdain for leaving this place. If she were not here, Bordeaux could not think where else to look.

Back out in the hallway, closing the door behind him, he considered for a moment a trip to the kitchens downstairs but he presently tossed the idea to the wind. He knew Libra's apathy would not last the entire return journey up the flights of stairs. The girl was lazy; he had to remember that.

Bordeaux was at a loss – he knew he could only return later and hope for Libra to be present. He had only taken a few steps in the direction of the main stairwell when he was brought to a halt by a sudden noise. It was a creaking that he could not be certain of, for at that very moment thunder clapped outside the window at the end of the hall, cloaking the sound.

He turned, staring back down the long hall and saw the silhouette of a figure opening the bedroom door and shutting it softly. Lightning flashed through the window and a face was illuminated, hanging suspended within that fleeting second like a moon against an inky backdrop of space - the face of Lady Libra. The unshakable confidence that was oft so prominent on her features had vanished with the confirmation of an intruder, it was obvious she had not expected nor desired any visitors. Best she could, Libra resolutely assumed the façade of her confident composure and tried to smile at the crimson demon.

"Bordeaux," she whispered. "You've come to see me?"

Bordeaux eyed her suspiciously. "I had just left."

"You were… In there?" asked Lady Libra, her eyes widening and finger pointing gingerly at the door.

Bordeaux nodded.

"I was just, uh, looking for Madlyn," said Libra. "Returned just this moment."

Bordeaux stood musing. The bedroom door was the only door between himself and the lady, until the hallway ended at the large window beyond. He would certainly have seen Libra pass him in the narrow hallway, yet she was not in the bedroom moments ago when he had been there. How it was that she now stood where she was flexed the logical limits of his mind.

"A brief visit was my intent, Libra."

"Oh well, B, could it wait?" Libra continued to turn her head distractedly towards her door but changed her mind. "Oh fine, be quick."

Bordeaux held the black rose brooch aloft, "Is this yours?"

"My brooch! Yes! Give that here!" said Libra. She reached forward and greedily grasped the air in front of her. "Come now Bordeaux, that's mine!"

The crimson demon did not hand it over immediately, gauging her reaction best he could.

Libra frowned furiously, then seemed to decide against anger and instead, produced a sickly sweet smile.

"Fine. Keep it. Like I care!"

"Might I ask where it came from?"

"I found it," said Libra. "I've had it for a long time. Can't possibly recall where I got it…. It was only a plant if I remember, I made it into a brooch myself."

Bordeaux paused and replied, "It is very nice."

"Don't stare so, Bordeaux. You know it's rude. So is going into other people's rooms! and another thing - how did you get my brooch? You stole!"

"I did not steal, my lady. Madlyn gave it to me."

"That sneaky witch!" snapped Libra, "And she is supposed to be bringing me my supper right now!" Libra stamped her foot and pouted. She sighed, shoulders slouching. "I have to do everything around here."

It was with a struggle that she maneuvered her ample form around Bordeaux and made for the stairwell, the barely audible sound of her footsteps betraying the heaviness of her tread.

"Come away from there, Bordeaux," she said, looking sternly back at him.

"I suppose it was just her own conceit that had her commanding the brooch to be returned to her. One moment she was so despairing to get it back and the next…"

"I can vouch. In years past, she'd keep whatever caught her fancy," said Edweena. "Quite obsessive if you ask me…"

"You miss those times?"

Edweena looked away from Bordeaux, who, seeing the discomfort of her suppressed anger, returned to his own musings. He twirled the brooch in his hand.

"It was a wastrel endeavour. All I discovered was that this thing does, in fact, belong to Libra."

"I don't quite understand, Bordeaux. So give her the brooch back, what has it to do with anything?" asked Edweena.

"She can't have been in the room, I surely would have seen her..."

Edweena sighed. "You're talking to yourself, B."

"What's that?" said Bordeaux. "Oh. Excuse me, Edweena. Just thinking out loud."

The rain ran ceaseless in its lashings; the fervent fire the only offering of comfort to them.

Rising from his chair, Bordeaux stripped away a few stray branches from the ivy-clad wall and tossed them to the flames. The wallpaper peeled away with his pulling, as the vines clung desperately to their host. The intricate patterns left behind ran like a network of veins between the scraps of burgundy wallpaper still pasted to the wall. Bordeaux stoked the fire.

"My apologies, Edweena. I suppose it's just fruitless suspicion. The trees latching themselves to our home, these monsters outside and increasing in number and violence."

"You really thought Libra would offer any help?"

"No. I thought Libra might have something to do with it. That brooch, I believe, may be related to the golems."

XVII: The Rascalities of Deadsol & Comets

At the end of the sandy pathway that winds along the gentle downhill slope from the manor's threshold, there stands a most curious vigil. Rusted to the colour of dried blood, a postbox perched on a bent pole reaches out as though waiting on a handshake. Out of place as it were, one could assume it to be Tenebrae Manor's last remaining outreach to the world beyond. Disused for so long that none quite knew how it got there, the effect of its salutation was diminishing by the year as thorny bracken reached their sinuous claws out of the dried ground and smothered it. Tenacious it stood, though fighting a losing battle; it would not be long before it buckled and was lost to the overgrowth.

And yet for all its neglectfulness, for all its years in isolated abandonment, the hinges of its lid still spoke like clockwork, groaning loudly as it was flung open. Flung open at the hour before moonrise by the dutiful Usher. The postbox had stood so long and seen so little, that when Usher opened it, there was nothing further to say; empty it remained, frustratingly choked for words.

As for Usher, never had he been rewarded with the sight of mail; his stony face stayed the same, his hand reaching into the rusty void was always met with nothingness. This was how it always was at the hour before the rising of the moon and Usher, having completed the task trudged slowly up towards the castle. There was no softness to the scene, only rotted remnants of flaky grass. Corroded fence and disintegrated tree branch cluttered the landscape with dry angularity. The dirty snow laid clumped in patches, its bitter cold sharpness enough to slice skin and give dull ache to weary bones.

The return journey was always taxing for the ambling Usher, due to the inexorable rigidity of his unfortunate knees. Had his neck allowed further skyward inclination, he would have noticed the branches that clung to his home so; but oblivious he remained, continuing the only pathway he knew to take. Past the last gnarled tree root, twenty-three more steps until he was back at his post in the foyer.

All was as it should be, that is until a slight moderation to the scene caught his eye. Ahead of him, the mighty oak doors of Tenebrae Manor stood ever so slightly ajar. Had he erred? He always closed the door behind him when he went to check the mailbox. His simple mind faltered at the discrepancy and for a moment, he was unable to move. But readily he shook away the clotted shackles of his paralysis and proceeded through the archway, paying close attention to his closing of the doors.

Usher would have simply returned to his post, had the upright funeral pall not been occupied by the shadow of another statue. What was this madness? Had he been exorcised from his physical being and left to observe it from third person? He scratched at his flaking scalp with a meaty hand and leaned further forward to where the shadowy intruder stood still and silent. Usher recognised the face in the gloom, the eyes of it flickering on a sudden and a wretched grin peeling across it.

From the mouth of the shadow face came a voice. "Boo!"

Usher gaped and stumbled backwards, almost losing his balance before a strong hand caught him from falling. Speechlessly he composed himself, as though his words had been stolen by the cackling laughter that now filled the hall.

"Capital, Usher good sir! Just capital!" Deadsol guffawed. "What a simply splendid reaction!"

The demon clapped his hands in glee, as the Usher appeared desperately perplexed. The words were caught in his throat, so that he could only utter, "Have I been replaced?"

"Replaced? Why no, my good Usher! Not by the hairs of my moustache! It was simply a jest, a joke in good faith to be sure. Really my friend, you must learn to condone such conviviality! Well now, is that the door I hear?"

Usher had heard it too and reached awkwardly for the doorknob. Beyond the open door, the threshold was empty; some phantom had played knock and run. He shivered as something brushed past him; turning at once to where Deadsol was, Usher found the demon replaced with the squatted posture of Comets the jester.

"Half a man could still do this job proper," grunted Comets.

"Mind your words, Comets you simpleton. Our Usher is a fine servant!"

Usher turned his head again and found Deadsol somehow standing just outside the front door. The bewildered doorman shivered. He could not even begin to understand the magic of these two charlatans.

"Knock knock," said Comets.

"Who's there?" replied Deadsol.

"Usher."

"Usher who?"

"Usher-da learnt to dress proper."

Through this volley, the Usher had turned his head back and forth but when the punch line had been delivered, he looked down to discover his suit was on backwards. He gasped.

"Ha-ha! Delightful!" Deadsol was laughing so hard he begun to wheeze.

Comets too, cackled like a hyena. "How ever did you do up those buttons, Usher?"

Before Usher could reply, Comets had dashed his way down the hallway past the great staircase.

Deadsol called after him. "Comets, we surely can't leave our dear friend in such disarray!" before turning to Usher. "There's a good chap, got to run!"

The doorman cried out to the fleeing Deadsol to no avail but as soon as he looked down, his clothes had returned to normal.

Hallways in Tenebrae ran like rivers weaving through cragged valleys and Comets had plunged headlong into the torrent, his little feet flying over the floors that changed from carpet to stone to tile. And just as a scrap of driftwood strikes heedlessly at boulder and river bend, so too did the jester bump himself against wall and ornament. Around the corner there, where he failed to correct his direction in time and knocked a forgotten clay pot from its podium. Tripping over a square of carpet here, he clutched at curtain as he fell and pulled the entire rod down with him. His tiny lungs wheezed with exertion as he tested the extreme limits of his body with this renegade sprint.

Then, as though all energy had been truly sapped from him, he stopped at the top of a great staircase and stared through bulging eyes at the black chasm beneath him.

As for Deadsol, he had only to follow the trail of destruction that his impetuous lackey had left in his wake. Bereft of any haste or concern in his catching up with the speedy harlequin, Deadsol removed his pipe from his vest pocket and lit it leisurely. The clay pot that Comets had sent plummeting to the floor lay in the demon's path, miraculously intact and he took a moment to bend at knee and restore its arrangement in the cobwebbed corner.

"Ah, these aching joints," he mumbled to himself.

He did not show the same care towards the fallen curtains, a brush of his foot kicking them to the side as he continued on.

Upon reaching the stairs, he found Comets jumping down them one at a time at a sluggish pace, taut as a spring as he threw all of his small weight into each step as he jumped. The jester turned and squawked when saw that Deadsol had caught up with him. Shaking away his moribund daze, Comets leapt onto the rickety banister and slid down into the blackness with his echoing voice diminishing in volume as he went. The foot of the stairs with which the two rebels were currently descending marked the entrance to the great kitchens where the mute chef was no doubt busy dealing with both Madlyn and his own vocational demands.

The mute chef, being quite the forgettable and enigmatic tenant of Tenebrae Manor, had not received company in some time. He possessed the loyalty of a bulldog and, pertaining to such steadfast ardor, had tirelessly busied himself with the food preparations required of his post. On recent occasions it had appeared to him that his work had somehow become more difficult, more intense. The monotonous nature of his vocation, the unchanging surroundings of sweltering kitchen meant that he could not be certain. Yet his fatigue increased and it was this fatigue that had led him to retire early for once, to cast aside responsibility if only for a short while and sleep in his room.

He was wrapped in an over-tight set of pajamas that were not unlike his cooking attire; the addition of stripes and lack of grease stains being the major distinction. The candle in his hand quivered in his weak grasp as he breathed a silent sigh and shuffled purposefully to his room - a shallow hollow just off to the side of the kitchen.

From his disused throat there bubbled a sort of low gurgle, a groan of relief to his aching joints as he took the weight of his fat body off his feet and sat down on his bed. His was a drooping obesity, his elder years sagging far beyond the ripened swell of Libra's fatness; and the chef seemed to recede inwardly as hermit crab withdraws into its shell, weighed down by slouched shoulder and sluggish stomach. The senses of appetite were all he had - taste and smell. All the while the pleasures of speech and sound had long abandoned him and, now too, his sight was having its own doubts. He could not read anymore - at least not comfortably and the absence of music and conversation in his life left him joyless. It was always upon retiring to his bed that he felt so melancholic; the chef took solace in the fact that his work kept his mind occupied.

There he lay on his bed, a great dome in the dimmed candlelight, his absent gaze absorbing the outline of the doorway where his kitchen lay beyond. Although he was unable to conjure any irritation from the repetitive faucet that dripped out in the kitchen or of the mice that scampered noisily about the floor, he began to develop an acute awareness that had been unnoticed hitherto. It was an awareness of a presence stalking the shadows with ham-fisted stealth. Yes - there was someone nearby, an intruder.

He sat up slowly and pursed his flabby lips; it could not be Madlyn. At this hour, the girl was usually upstairs attending to Libra's grooming. It was obvious that whoever it was that lurked in the darkness cared little about his or her exposure, for so recklessly did their shadows fling themselves about the kitchen beyond the chef's doorway that even he was able to see them.

With the precision of an assassin, the mute chef placed in his hand a sickly impressive cleaver that he kept glisteningly sharp on the floor next to his bed. He rose to his feet and began to creep slowly into the kitchen, his own stealth benefited by the padded sponginess of his foot soles absorbing any sound he could have made. He delved deep into the kitchen without being noticed, moving softly towards what he presumed to be the intruder.

Raising the knife above his head with astute concentration, he prayed that his eyesight was not playing tricks on him and that the object of his strike was indeed the enemy he had heard. The knife dropped like a guillotine, before the lights came on suddenly and the blade fell from his grasp.

The mute chef rubbed his eyes to adjust to the light, before fumbling about the floor for his knife.

"Woah!" came a voice.

The chef grabbed his knife and leapt to his feet in a fighter's stance.

"Easy, chef!" cried Deadsol, who had reeled backwards with his hands aloft in defence.

The mute chef, quivering in his rage, only just managed to recognise Deadsol and hesitated before lowering his weapon.

"Easy now, Mr. Chef!" said Deadsol. "Now then, I hardly see that thing doing any real damage."

The chef, bemused, lifted a fleshy brow towards his extended knife arm and saw his cleaver had been replaced with a leek. The vegetable went limp in his grasp and he dropped it to the floor with a gasp.

Turning in his confusion, he saw Comets the jester stamping about the long wooden table that dominated the kitchen floor. The harlequin found no issue in pressing his feet down onto whatever he found, squashing several plates of food and kicking away various utensils to the floor. Comets then espied a large cream cake at the end of the table. He and the mute chef both dashed directly for it, the jester's eyes hell-bent on its destruction. The chef cursed his slow reflexes as Comets got to the cake first and did not hesitated not in his jumping into it and causing its tiers to collapse within themselves. He grabbed handfuls of the cake and threw them at his own face.

"Look at me, I'm Libra! Gobble-gobble-nom!"

The mute chef slouched in defeat and let out a heaving sigh. Deadsol found himself shuddering with hysterical laughter, clutching at his stomach as tears streamed down his face and into his moustache. He moved to clap the crestfallen chef on the back.

"Never mind, chef! Had you objected, you should have said as such!"

The chef's lips quivered with a curious mixture of sadness and rage. His depression had pushed him to the very brink, whereby the simple nudge of Comets' destructive antics had sent him tumbling over.

Covered with cake innards, Comets spoke. "All those in favour of trashing the joint, say I. I!"

Deadsol shrugged his shoulders at the chef, who strained to understand what was happening to his kitchen and why such anarchy had befallen him.

"Sorry, chef. I must say I. And with two being clearly the majority amongst this lovely little treble of men, it must be said that you are tragically outnumbered! Aye! Aye!"

"Aye!" cried Comets, "Aye! Yah! Hurrah!"

"Avast there, Comets. We must distance ourselves from this swampy lagoon where we layeth marooned! Thou art gentle and understanding oh chef! You'll clean this up will you not?"

Deadsol pressed for the exit with Comets, his curled silk shoes leaving behind prints of greasy cream on the already putrid floor.

Deadsol sighed cheekily as he left, whispering as though only to himself, "Never mind about the mess. In the dark, all cats are grey. Good night, good night."

XVIII: Madlyn Attempts an Avowal

Bordeaux had suspected for some time now that, to a certain extent, the black rose in his possession was responsible in part for the outbreak of golems. His time had been consumed; enveloped by the stony confines of his room in the high tower, reading the mighty tome borrowed from Rune, so that his eyes ached from the excessive strain. Time and again he lifted his head from his desk and rubbed gingerly at his forehead, wondering whether the ancient ink of the book's pages had imprinted itself on his forehead as he slumbered heavily upon its open face. The wood golems worshipped something known as a black rose tree; they were notoriously territorial. This he knew from his studies. The resemblance of the brooch to the sketches drawn in the old book was undeniable - the onyx hue of the almost crystalline petals, rough and unyielding to the touch. And such properties and notes had led him to believe that the brooch was a random blossom from nothing other than a black rose tree.

From this accusation there bloomed a budding hope; perhaps, should the rose be returned to the golems, they would cease their attack on Tenebrae Manor. This attack, of which the effects were increasingly prominent, was a slow disintegration. Just as rust bites at sword and shield with an omnipresent corrosion, so too did the golems claw at the walls of the house and the vines and branches of nearby trees tightened their stranglehold on the facade. It was fast becoming a dire predicament; several rooms of Tenebrae Manor had become completely inaccessible, due in turn to a smothering overgrowth invading. The manor, once so abundant in isolated rooms shut off to all life, now felt the tightness of its constriction to such extent that the residents had to choose their paths carefully - lest they be turned about by obstruction.

Bordeaux was relieved that no golem had yet been able to find its way inside the house, where it may pose a threat to any of the more ignorant or invalid denizens such as Madlyn, Rune or the Mute Chef. Yet as the time passed and as the effects of the invasion increased, the crimson demon's cause for concern amplified to a point where he would try anything to save his home. Perhaps his propitiation would please the creatures.

He would admit himself that his idea was riddled with flaws. Who could say that a black rose tree actually existed? In his centuries of existence, Bordeaux could not vouch for its tangibility. Was there only one? This answer too, evaded him. The scribblings of the book were vague at best. Perhaps it stood concealed as one entity in the far reaches of a forgotten taiga or as manifold about the world's more isolated corners.

There then remained the question of the brooch. With no plausible evidence of a black rose tree, who was he to say that the brooch was one of its trimmings? Libra had been impossibly dismissive of the whole subject; unable or unwilling to disclose how the rose came to be in her possession. But most pressing on Bordeaux's mind was the motives of the wood golems. In his heightening pessimism, he failed to see how returning the rose would end the attacks. He had too little proof and too much to lose. If the golems remained abundant after his relinquishing of the brooch, then Bordeaux would be at a loss and concede that the golems' violence was purely a mindless survival tactic. Tenebrae Manor would fall, its residents exiled - and where else would there be appropriate isolation for the magic of an eternal night to flourish?

The crimson demon had travelled the entire world, happening upon Tenebrae Manor by purely desperate coincidence. He could not see lightning striking twice on his luck. Some would certainly perish; Edweena would turn to ash on the sunrise, while the fantastical horrors associated with denizens like Comets and Sinders could not hide amongst society as Deadsol or Libra could. Bordeaux winced at the thought; he had been in such a position before, living in human society - forced to remain enigmatic, only to change his identity every few generations. He sighed to think of the friends he had seen come and go, die in their own time, while he was cursed to live on.

With these thoughts plaguing his mind, Bordeaux resolved to give the rose back to the golems. How he would do this he was not sure. He could not risk a confrontation with them, after being taken off guard by a random golem almost cost him his life. Bordeaux had to leave the black rose in a place where the golems might find it.

It was beyond the furthest frontage of the manor that he found an appropriate pedestal. Further past the rusted letterbox and beyond the first cluster of birch and conifer, Bordeaux knew of a small clearing, surely no more than fifty metres in its radius. And it was here that there stood, rather forlornly isolated, a charred tree stump. Bordeaux had envisioned the stump to have once been another faceless tree in the forest, perhaps struck down by a thunderbolt and seemingly poisoning the earth about its circumference, so that no other tree dared blossom nearby. Yet its segregated status made it a perfectly exposed pedestal for the crimson demon to place the rose upon it, where it glistened as though a native plumage of the blackened tree stump.

Though appearing so natural to the scene, Bordeaux knew that if his thoughts were correct, its camouflage would not be of any matter. For he assumed the wood golems were drawn towards it and had they sensed that the rose lay within the confines of Tenebrae Manor, then they should be more than capable of locating it on a stump in an open clearing.

So as he placed it in position, the grass lay damp with dew, the air crisp with cold and Bordeaux's breath hung in the air like mist. Sidling slowly back into the trees, Bordeaux continued to pause sporadically and glance over his shoulder to confirm the whereabouts of the rose. It remained where he had left it, shimmering with moonlight, glaring menacingly as though it had sight of its own.

Patience was of utmost importance; he would have to wait a little while to see if the relic disappeared. And what if it didn't? His desperate plan would reach its end and he would be back to the drawing board.

Bordeaux sighed longingly and too pessimistic to pray for hope from any deity that would listen, made his way back home where he resolved to rest in his room.

She had deemed her theft as daring, however the inane Madlyn had afterwards found herself to be more wary of the venom of her superior to the extent of paranoid fear. She carried on about her tasks, answering to Miss Libra's impossible expectations with her native albeit reluctant servitude. There had been innumerable times gone where she had considered the possibility of a personal renegade towards Libra's demands, only to be hindered by the directionless performance of her hindered mind. In the all-knowing amber eyes of the lady of the manor, she would suspect rebellion.

Lady Libra had said nothing to her about the disappearance of the black rose brooch and Madlyn's immaturity suggested that just maybe she had gotten away with the deed. But something of the savvy coiled about her chest, though a feeling of very foreign nature to the maladroit Madlyn, she trusted it and spent the hours of her lengthening reprieve in fear of impending punishment.

Her knees shivering with a combination of fright and cold, young Madlyn carried a tea tray up the many flights of the central stairwell and timidly approached Libra's door. She knocked hesitantly, defying her own clumsiness by balancing the tray across the palm of her other hand. No response came. Madlyn felt a brush of adrenalin sweeping through her, pushing her into the dark room and placing the tray on a low table next to the chaise lounge. She spun about quickly, her ponytail whipping her in the back as she raced for the exit. Her egress was on the horizon and, for a moment, it felt insurmountably far away, the darkness of the room clawing at her from behind as she plunged through the yawning gap of the open doors. The door shut swiftly behind her; she had made it. Libra was not there.

Back pressed to the door, Madlyn's attention was arrested by a wayward bat that squeaked from its inverted perch on the window to her left. To her right, her shadow was dragged into the umbra by the cold steel shafts of moonlight that permeated the dusky air.

Kneeling to clip her shoe tighter and to adjust her stubborn stockings, Madlyn arose and ran back down the hall to the stairs from whence she had come. She felt a veil of cold sweat stinging her skin and her lungs burned with exhaustion as she charged back into her room at the base of the castle.

Struggling in vain to regulate her frantic breathing, Madlyn made an attempt to compose herself, wiping the sweat from her palms on her dirty smock. Her slowing breath filled the silence around her as she felt for a match with which to light the stubby candle that latched to her little table.

With the match in her grasp it became a struggle to steady her hand, for she almost dropped it twice before striking it on the stone wall. The match head burst into life and for a split second, Madlyn could discern an ominous shape of an intruder in the light of the flame. She screamed, the match whistling from her grasp and extinguishing on the floor. Yet it would only remain dark for a heartbeat; the candle sparked with a blood red flame that revealed Libra standing chillingly close to Madlyn, surrounded by those claustrophobic walls. Her eyes - the sticky globules of puddled amber pierced with violence.

"Hello Madlyn."

Madlyn gasped for air and felt her eyes heat up as if she were about to cry. Libra's stare bore into her with an intense hatred; venom that she had not seen before for her overbearing superior. Long had Libra threatened her but this was different. Madlyn was at a loss to predict what Libra would do.

"Did I startle you?"

Madlyn struggled for words. "I just left a tray for you. In your room."

"Very good."

"You weren't there."

"I wasn't."

They stared at one another for a second.

"So I just left it there."

"I am sure you did, Madlyn. You always leave things as you find them, don't you?" said Libra.

Madlyn gaped for an answer.

"I know you stole my jewelry, Madlyn. What else have you been hiding from me?"

"I didn't! I didn't mean to!"

"Shush." Libra raised her pale hand to Madlyn's lips, "Allow me to make something clear, Madlyn. This house is mine. Tenebrae Manor. You steal from me, I can send you back into the forest where we found you, left to fend for yourself. Or perhaps we can make it worse. I can make it so that you never see your little hero Bordeaux anymore. I see how you pine for him. Does that sound like an apt punishment?"

"No. Miss, please don't!"

"Just remember this, Madlyn. I always get my way. Don't you ever forget it, little girl."

As if to confirm her words, Libra's gaze continued to ooze with poison; Madlyn shifted uncomfortably, desperate for Libra to leave her alone. This was her room after all and her sanctuary; the very paramount of her discomfort had breached her only haven from the thrashings of strenuous demands.

"I am going back to my room now," said Libra. "You are not to disturb me for a few hours. Not for anything. Is that understood?"

Madlyn, who had pulled her lower lip into the clutches of her teeth, nodded quickly.

"Good."

Libra tossed a curl of her dark hair over her shoulder and left the room, leaving Madlyn to slouch and gasp for air. The kitchen girl was free of those constricting eyes and dropped like a rag doll onto her bed. Those piercing pupils appeared in her mind's eye and she shuddered to recall them. She knew she had to do something. She did not want to think of life without Bordeaux there, even were they to be distanced apart.

A thought dawned on her. He could protect her. If there were anyone to rival Libra's echelon, it would be Bordeaux. Madlyn's heart raced; she would have to confess her feelings properly. The brooch must have confused him, the message lost in translation. It was time to stop pretending, it had to be her that made the move. She had waited too long for Bordeaux to sweep her from her feet like the knights in her fairytales. Maybe, even in this world of shadows and fantasy, those knights did not exist.

"… Plumage of roses, coal black branches and a glowing heart made of wood that remains an object of great power… This is futile."

Bordeaux beat his fist on the great book and groaned with frustration. He drained the remains of his wine glass and stood achingly. Adjusting the lapels of his burgundy coat, he stretched, his back and legs pained from being seated for so long. The book he had borrowed was so long, yet several reads from cover to cover had revealed nothing prominent. Bordeaux had had no idea that there was so much recorded on wood golems; despite his now knowledgeable brain on the matter, he could not find any anchored reason as to why the golems were destroying Tenebrae Manor.

He took up the wine glass in his hand, forgetting that he had just emptied its contents and proceeded to clutch the bridge of his aquiline nose vexingly. His eyes remained shut fast and he tapped his foot impatiently. But then, flinging his arms skyward in a gesture of defeat he moved to the windowsill, where he appeared to leap into the open air. Yet he had merely clasped hold of the ivy that had grown so thick against his wall that he was able to climb to the roofs of Tenebrae Manor with ease.

Reaching a higher part of the roof where the pitch stood at a comfortable angle for him to stand upright and where he was able to brush the heart-shaped leaves of ivy from his coat, he hissed, "Let it burn to ashes."

Slowly ascending, Madlyn saw the spiraling stairs as a vortex that stirred her emotions and when she reached its apex, at that clinical point at the summit of the steps, there resided the very object of her affections. This vortex that she ascended, inverted so that the epicentre of this torrent, that point which would normally lurk deep below the surface, was now at the very top of the stairs to Bordeaux's quarters. Her eyes were locked on the destination, whirling as she climbed, her feet tripping more than once on the rough stones. Her hands clutched into fists, held timorously below the collar of her slender neck as though shielding her heart from the lugubrious blows her unspoken feelings provoked.

The top of the stairs lay before her, a square of light above her head where step and railing ceased and Bordeaux's room lay. When it became apparent to her that one more step would bring her head into view of the room, she froze and for several seconds the only movement seemed to be that of her frantic heart pounding in her chest. She was as a fledging, preparing to make that first leap from the nest and pray her wings kept her aloft. Boldness crept into her bloodstream and she stepped into the light and called out, "Hello," with a voice choked with nerves, as though her very heart were trying to jump out of her mouth.

Yet no reply met her. Any response she might of

heard was a mere trick of the phantom, her ears fabricating the greeting that she wanted so much to hear. By the cruel hand of that charlatan known as fate, Bordeaux had quit his quarters not moments earlier and stood atop the very peak of the manor's roof gazing out into the wilderness. The wind leapt wildly about him, a solitary figure in the elements and Bordeaux felt the wind on his face as he had many times over the centuries. The sensation that came with the lashings of the gusts, the sensation of being alive, despite the heaviness that weighed on his heart, provided apt palliation. For but a moment he thought of no danger or threat to his home; he could stand and appreciate the night sky he adored and like a weaning child, he was afraid of the change that would come with abandoning it.

He recalled the heat wave, now so long ago, when the sky was not of icy glass and rather dried haze. Preoccupied as he were, Bordeaux was entirely unaware of his doting admirer who now stood in his turret, in view of him if he were to only turn his head. But he did not turn. He closed his eyes and locked in his mind the image of the tree-choked valleys and knuckled mountains of his immemorial home he loved, as the gale gushed so forcefully around him.

Madlyn dropped to her knees, drawn down by the anvil drop of her heavy heart. A sensation unknown to her since childhood returned suddenly and her eyes burned with despair. From her sunken and drought stricken eyes there squeezed a tear that flicked the back of her hand and trickled to the cracks of the stone floor. It could hardly be called crying; her eyes stung with swollen tears and, once or twice, she was wrecked by the convulsion of a sob.

Something had been broken inside her; it was a

glimmer of maturity that had no choice but to build itself on an unstable foundation. And it had taken one kick of the cornerstone to send Madlyn tumbling back down to ignorance, so that she presently wiped the tears from her streaked face and sat up, the cold floor numbing her haunches. Her hour had passed and Madlyn had yet again overshot the mark and come up with nothing constructive. She sat there, her mind blanked of the thoughts that plagued her hitherto, incapable of any movement for the time being.

The wind howled outside the window and this sound, coupled with the sight of those wild trees swaying in the gusts possessed every faculty of Madlyn and she was unable to do anything but sit there, broken.

XIX: Judecca

When Bordeaux returned to his room some hours later, Madlyn was no longer there. The room was ruffled by the wind that fluttered through the window. The curtains licked like flames with their deep red hue and the pages of Rune's great book somersaulted over one another and sent dust flying into the air.

Bordeaux slipped in through the window and returned to his desk where the book lay. The chill of the breeze bit at him. Tightening up his scarf and closing the windows, he lit the small tallow candle atop the skull on his desk. Its warmth was ineffectual in the drafty room as the crimson demon flipped through the book to find the page he had read to. It was then that the spine of the book caught his glance; there was a minor imperfection in the binding in the form of a small paper tear that he flicked with his finger. There was a page missing.

For a moment he considered the jigsaw rip of what

remained of the page, clearly it had been torn out either swiftly or by a ham-fisted hand but what concerned Bordeaux was whether it was a recent injury to the book or not. Had he simply overlooked the missing page previously? He did not want to bear the blame for damaging Rune's priceless tome.

He would not have the time to properly dissect the situation, for at that moment the repellent bust of the brotherly Deadsol once again rose dreamlike into the room from the peak of the spiral stairs. Grin intact as always and eyes wide and empty with cavalier, he rasped slowly, "Bordeaux?"

"Deadsol," sighed Bordeaux. "I am in no mood for pleasantries. Pray tell, what brings you to my quarters?"

"Ah, my brother most patient! Most patient you are, Bordeaux but you are required. Required elsewhere! Oh no, not here!"

Bordeaux rubbed his temple and groaned inwardly.

"What could possibly be the matter? Can it not wait?"

"I fear not, citizen!" replied Deadsol. "To Libra's room, to Libra with haste!"

The overenthusiastic demon lifted his forefinger skyward and disappeared down the stairs singing faintly.

Enveloped in his own reluctance, Bordeaux began to feel an urgency fill his heart as he approached Libra's door. Familiar voices made their way through the walls in muffled drones, there was certainly more beings in Libra's room than just Deadsol.

As he opened the door, the conversations seemed to hush; an odd snigger here and there seemed to allay Bordeaux's concern.

Gathered in the corner of the room there stood the

quartet of Deadsol, Comets, Edweena and Madlyn. Not since Libra's ill-fated birthday party had Bordeaux seen so many of the manor's residents gathered in the one place.

"What is transpiring here?" Bordeaux asked of nobody in particular.

He was met with silence, yet the smirks on the faces of his friends left him bemused until Madlyn stepped forward, arms held behind her back, her body rocking on her feet like a mischievous child and spoke. "She's stuck. She doesn't fit, no, not at all."

Bordeaux parted the small crowd to observe himself what pleased Madlyn so. For a moment, he was unsure just what he was looking at; a mountainous protuberance, from which a pair of trunk-like legs kicked feebly, seemed to be pressed against the stone wall where Bordeaux remembered there to be a large wooden wardrobe. The wardrobe had been moved aside and in that instant Bordeaux realised the situation and broke into a smile of his own.

Libra, the owner of those kicking legs, was stuck in some sort of small entrance that had been concealed previously by her furniture.

"Are you fools going to assist me or not?" came Libra's venomous voice from the other side of the passage.

"Fascinating," chuckled Bordeaux. "A passageway! Where do you think it leads?"

"I cannot comment, I'm afraid," replied Deadsol, who puffed at his pipe.

"Madlyn found her like this," said Edweena.

"Oh yes, stuck I'm afraid," continued Deadsol. "Trapped, as Dis is trapped in the icy confines of Dante's ninth circle!"

Libra squirmed like a mollusk, her fattened body bound at her hip circumference by the unyielding dimensions of the entry. Powerless as she were; she continued to kick and complain, though it only added to the comical appearance on display for the bystanders. Comets sprung forth and began to tug at her foot, beating on her leg with his tiny fists.

"Such is a life of excess," he sighed reflectively.

"Get that damnable imp away from me!" Libra squealed. "Away!"

She kicked again, blindly trying to land a blow on the jester, who leapt from foot to foot and dodged each attempt. His bells rang excessively, blackening Libra's mood immensely. Appearing to be in deep thought, Deadsol smoked at his pipe with head back and arms folded as Bordeaux turned inquisitively towards him.

"Deadsol, do you deem this audience necessary? Why have you gathered so many here in this room?"

"Why, for a multitude of opinions!" burst Deadsol. "With which to conjure a plan of freeing our most trapped mistress!"

His words pleaded honesty, yet his smirk portrayed a desire to exaggerate the humiliation of Libra; of this, Bordeaux was most convinced.

Deadsol continued, "Having passed upon Madlyn in the hall, who announced her lady to be in a most dire predicament, I deemed that I make the noble dash to assemble assistance."

"A saint," muttered Bordeaux.

"It's too small there," said Madlyn. "She'll never get out."

"Serves her right if you ask me," said Edweena.

206

Libra retorted, "I can hear you, you know! Ugh! Do you want the night sky to weaken? Would you let the spell expire because you refused to help me - me, the very one who shields you from the light? Your life in darkness is in my hands, remember?"

"I am afraid that feeble frets will get you nowhere at this stage, deary," said Deadsol.

"Feeble frets, Deadsol?" said Bordeaux.

"Oh ha! No, a difficult loquacity, theeble threats perhaps?"

"Feeble theeble, folly and thimble!" chimed Comets. "Fumb and Thinger, thumb and finger!"

Deadsol pulled Comets to his side by tugging at his rabbit ear cap. "What I mean to say, lovely Libra, is that if you require our assistance, you have only to ask politely."

Libra did her best to ignore the demon; she would not back down so easily. She seemed to be attempting variations of freeing herself, crawling forwards or backwards, firstly placing her hands on either side of the plugged doorway and pushing against the wall in an attempt to gain a few forward inches.

It was undeniably apparent to the others that the girth of Libra's ample rear would not fit through the opening and from the vantage point of the trapped woman herself, her sizable paunch would not compress back the way she had come. Her face grew hot with frustrated tears; the cold reality of the situation fueled her futile rage, she was not used to such powerlessness.

"Humph, fine!" she hissed venomously. "My… Friends. Would you be so kind as to help me?"

Deadsol bounced on his feet gaily. "Help with what, my dear?"

Libra sighed. "I'm stuck, Deadsol."

"And why is that, my sickly sweet Lady Libra?"

"Ugh! Don't make me say it! Just help me!"

"There's a good sport! Not to worry, miss!" said Deadsol. "Say there, Bordeaux. Give me a hand here."

"Please excuse this impropriety, Miss Libra," said Bordeaux.

Each taking hold of one of Libra's ankles, Bordeaux and Deadsol readied themselves.

There were a few travailing seconds of exertion, with the demoniac pair pulling at Libra like she were a great anchor being hauled from the sea. Libra pressed her hands to the ground in front of her and pushed backwards with tremendous effort.

For all their valiant efforts, there seemed to be too much resistance about the doorframe to free Libra from its confines. Sweat crawled down Deadsol's temple and on a sudden, he fell backwards onto his rump; Bordeaux placed Libra's leg down with far more dignity than his counterpart but the unfortunate gorgon still stuck fast. The room was silent save for the treble's laborious breathing.

"How droll," said Edweena. "What now, geniuses?"

"Our most astute magician – foiled by a simple swell of stomach and rigidity of door…" sighed Deadsol. "It's a forlorn hope. We'll have to leave her there."

"What? No!" squealed Libra in protest.

"Never mind, lass! A few weeks of starvation and you'll be trim enough to fit through!"

"She's double the size of that hole," said Comets. "Half of her would fit."

Deadsol clicked his fingers. "Half of her, capital idea! We'll cut her in half!"

The Lady Libra shrieked in wild panic; Deadsol and Comets were erratic enough to go through with such an idea. She began to kick frantically.

At the same moment, Edweena plucked Libra's feet into her hands and pulled one last time. By some chance combination, it was enough to twist a considerable portion of Libra's abdomen back the way she'd come, so that she was able, with more great effort, to shuffle backwards and out of the small entrance.

Libra stood and brushed the dust from her charcoal dress, her chest heaving like a metronome. Her hair was disheveled; her face aglow with a pink hue of embarrassment and perspiration. Her mortified heart fluttered and she could only squeal timidly, "Leave! Leave me! All of you, now!"

"What's in there, Libra?" asked Bordeaux, pointing to the passage where Libra had just been trapped.

"Nothing! None of your business! Go!"

For the first time in a while, the others saw a flash of weakness in the composure of Tenebrae's chief lady. She lashed out feebly at Comets with a superfluous slap that the runt easily avoided.

Edweena and Madlyn, each for their own reasons, could not help but snicker at the hilarity of the scene, even though Libra's eyes threatened them with an intense abhorrence. Bordeaux stood bemused, while Deadsol had apparently forgotten the situation entirely and now stood smoking his pipe and staring out the window.

"Has wax blocked every ear in this room? I said go away!" cried Libra.

The others shuffled out from the room unhurriedly, Comets receiving a kick in the back as the door was slammed behind him. The residents stood bemused in the halls that echoed with the tremulous sobs of Lady Libra that came from the other side of the wall.

The joviality of the brief comedy that had transpired in Libra's room had little longevity for Bordeaux and he fell quickly back into melancholia. Bordeaux felt in his heart a greater fear and heaviness than he had hitherto, for the wood golems remained stationed about the ivy-choked manor in increasing numbers. As a bird is locked in its cage, Tenebrae Manor was slowly disintegrating. The once proud and archaic castle, brooding in reclusive umbra, seemed to invert into itself, weakened at the very core of its foundation. And just as birds locked in a cage will beat and scratch at the walls of their incarceration, Bordeaux felt his crestfallen chest cry for relief. In the back of his mind he knew that his idea had been hopeful at best and knew that he must now venture out to see what remained of the black rose brooch, lest he be at a complete loss to allay the decay of his home. He had no other plan and there would be no deus ex machina to save Tenebrae Manor from oblivion.

Bordeaux stood in his room at the window, where below he could observe the presence of an unsettling evil with his own eyes. They stood scattered as the disorderly trees of the forest surrounding; their camouflage betrayed by their bloodcurdling moans – the golems were everywhere.

XX: Chaos Descends

The stress that lay heavy on the heart of the master of affairs was not that of a solitary episode burdened only on his own accord. Nestled in her generous breast, Libra's heart also begun the feel the strains of weary pressure. However, both being of such a reclusive nature, they were unable and no doubt unwilling to share the load of the mounting tension afflicted on Tenebrae Manor. So that while Bordeaux stood at the window of his room and tried to process the torments conjured by the golems below, Libra paced her confines anxiously.

She chewed at the nails of her fingers while her mind raced erratically. Her thoughts were clouded by their own abundance, jostling one another from the pedestal of her mind's eye, so that they made her brain ache with similar effect of a jarring piano chord pounded repetitively. The chaise lounge she so often reclined on provided no comfort to her, Libra found she was back on her feet within moments and struggled to remain still. Fatigue made her shoulders slouch, her breathing laborious; yet she could not sleep. Libra's eyebrows arched in a way that stole her face of its phlegmatic glow; the major concern of her mishandled thoughts was that she had lost authority over the residents of the manor.

As she strode about the room she ran her hands down her fleshy sides before standing akimbo and cursing the lack of discipline that had led to being so robbed of dignity. In the corner of her room, the wardrobe remained out of place, the passageway she had kept in secrecy for so long still in plain view. From the small entrance, an eerie glow issued forth, flickering between shades of red, green and orange.

From the tunnel, she switched her gaze downwards to her considerable waist and cursed through her teeth. It was just momentary carelessness that had led to the passageway's revealing. Libra wished she could turn back the hands of the clock and carry out her initial thought of widening the hole. It would not have been that difficult to do, yet she had remained in resolute denial and refused to believe she had gotten too big to fit through.

She had traversed the doorway frequently and found herself recalling the previous time she had navigated into the small room beyond it, remembering how tight a manoeuvre it had become.

On the small table next to her lounge there sat an empty platter, the latest in a long line of gluttonous episodes involving the Lady of Tenebrae Manor and it directed Libra's thoughts towards a chance for personal redemption. She could try to enter the passage again and prove to herself that she still fit. No! It would be a foolish move. What if she became stuck again? That would certainly be the end of any restoration of dignity amongst her attendants and scullions.

Libra pondered how a life of such grandiose excess, of such lavish luxuries could carry such hefty consequences. Had she not earned her echelon at the apex of Tenebrae's hierarchy?

With the strange glow still filing out of the small entryway, Libra became self-assured. There remained but a single reprieve - she still had power. Having obtained such vast magical knowledge and with it, power, Libra knew that these qualities kept her at a distinct advantage over Bordeaux and the others.

She had staked her claim and whilst that still stood, Libra had time on her side. The room throbbed with the glow that pulsated from the tunnel and Libra realised the importance of staunching the wounds of her dominance before they hemorrhaged. So long as no other discovered the patron of her vast magical skills, Tenebrae would remain under her dictatorship.

Swiftly she leapt to action. With the thrust of her outgoing palm, the wardrobe, as if of its own accord, slid back into its original position. The Illuminant miasma of light that channeled from the passageway was concealed and for a second, Libra was in complete darkness. A candle came to life in her hand and she slithered like a cobra around the perimeter of the room, lighting any and all torches she discovered. A rope, rather a bell-pull next to her bed became adumbrated by her ominous shadow as she moved towards it. As the rope was plucked, a cold echoing resonated somewhere far away. The vibrations of the rope raced downwards from Libra's hand, through a small hole in the floor and down into the inaccessible bowels of the castle. The rope shook its way about corners where it was held by elaborate cogs and pulleys, plummeting down dusty shafts shut off for centuries. The head of this snake, a rusted bell, peeled into shrill discord and startled the occupants who were there to hear it - a scattering of silent spiders, cockroaches and the exhausted Madlyn.

She had settled into a restless doze, face down on the pillow with heart burdened with fretful fancies. The bell rattled her room; her original startling dissipating into a recalcitrant apathy, for the bell meant only one thing. The Lady Libra required her presence.

The bell chime had originally carried a dire dread on its resonate wavelengths, at a time when Madlyn was new to the manor and eager to impress her superiors. Yet as the months went on, Libra's demands became insufferable and Madlyn's mind became more preoccupied with impressing Bordeaux. As such, this present bell cry caused barely a twitch in the kitchen girl as opposed to the usual urgency it expected.

Madlyn clawed hesitantly to her feet and groaned inwardly, before removing her shoe and violently throwing it at the obnoxious bell.

Up in her room, Libra sat down on her chaise lounge and waited. In the oceanic silence that hung heavily around her, she thought that she could momentarily discern the distant peel of the bell. Yet she knew it must have been a trick of her senses; the castle was a vacuum of isolated echoes but that bell was far too distant from her to be heard clearly. She must simply wait for Madlyn's appearance.

A flustered sigh escaped her lips as she propped her head upon her hand. The fingers of her other hand tapped impatiently on the edge of the lounge; her black nails producing a satisfying click on the leather.

The minutes dripped by and Libra became increasingly frustrated; Madlyn usually did not take this long in arriving. There was a mountain of stairs between the apex and nadir of Tenebrae Manor - Libra of course knew this, having appointed Madlyn to carry out her errands for her instead. But there was something suspicious about the girl's tardiness.

Libra growled through her teeth; she had plans to carry out! She refused to be hindered by such stupidity. She cursed all reliance on anybody but herself and moved to stand up, before Madlyn entered that very second.

"Miss?"

"Madlyn. You are slow. Always so slow!"

"Yes miss."

"Explain yourself."

"Just tired is all, Miss Libra. The hour is late and I was sleeping." Madlyn remained close to the door.

Libra stood akimbo, "When the bell rings, you move. Is that clear?"

"Yes miss."

"The very idea that you must be reminded! Stupid... Anyhow, I have a new task for you. You will ready a cell in the dungeon."

Madlyn's eyes widened. "Ready?"

"Yes ready, you silly," replied Libra. "Clear out a cell and have it ready to receive a prisoner."

"W-which prisoner?"

"Deadsol."

Madlyn sighed in relief; she had feared that it was her that Libra intended to lock up.

"The cells have been in disuse for years now. Ever since Bordeaux decided that confinement within Tenebrae Manor alone was imprisonment enough - a laughable notion if you ask me."

"Yes miss."

Libra began to move closer to the kitchen girl, her eyes locked fast in an intimidating leer.

"Deadsol is a rebel, Madlyn," said Libra. "Do you understand what I intend to do with rebels in my mansion?"

Madlyn stumbled for words, struck dumb by the imposing presence of her Lady superior.

Libra eventually turned away, deeming the colloquy as complete and Madlyn spent a few seconds processing her orders. The kitchen girl remembered the embarrassment written on Libra's face but a few hours earlier and was, of a sudden, endowed with a flurry of courage. Libra had needed the assistance of the castle residents; she wasn't so daunting after all. Why did she so readily yield to every one of Libra's commands?

"I don't think I will, miss," she uttered.

Libra paused and turned back to face her, "You don't think what?"

Madlyn realised the finality of her statement; the leap of faith had been made, she had no choice but to lurch further into the darkness.

"I won't get the cell ready," she said. "Deadsol shouldn't be locked away... He didn't do anything wrong."

Libra seemed lost for words; Madlyn had never spoken back to her as such. A sound rattled through the air - that of Madlyn's knees clipping together as her legs shook with fear and defiance.

"You dare defy me?" came Libra's icy voice.

A rush of adrenaline pushed Madlyn into further throes of courage. "Deadsol said you're a bombastic mega-glutton."

Libra felt her nails dig painfully into her palms as her fists clenched. Her teeth ground together and a convulsion made her neck twitch, a vein on her forehead bulged. Her fury reached a cataclysmic pinnacle.

Madlyn feared she had pushed once too hard and would bear the onslaught of Libra's torrential anger. But Libra composed herself, stayed her menace and decided there and then to pursue a more tactical avenue. She needed to wrest authority back for herself and with a girl as dim as Madlyn, a Machiavellian approach would prove the difference. A sinuous smile forced its way across her pale face. "Did he now? Well Bordeaux certainly doesn't think as such."

It was only a small movement - the corner of Madlyn's mouth flinched but it was with the mention of the crimson demon that Libra knew she had steadied the ship.

"Bordeaux..." said Madlyn.

"Has proposed, my deary" said Libra. "To me."

"Proposed?"

"Yes, proposed. To be wed."

"Wed?"

"Married, stupid!"

The word cut Madlyn like a knife; Libra knew full well that she would buy into such deceit.

"Not t-true." Madlyn stammered. Her lips quivered

uncontrollably.

"Oh but I'm afraid it is true, Madlyn. Bordeaux said my beauty was matched by no other and that he wanted no more than to worship me as his queen!"

Madlyn stood dumbfounded; her shoulders slouched with defeat. Libra waited patiently for a reaction in case of any rebuttal but knew she had Madlyn defeated. She wanted to laugh, almost in disbelief of the ease in which she could trick the kitchen girl. But she remained coldly composed until the oceanic silence of the room returned, which was soon broken by the off-tempo sound of Madlyn's foot on flagstone as she ran deliriously back through the corridors.

When he took his first step from the front doors of the manor, Bordeaux was immediately aware of a certain baleful latency around him. The moaning of the golems had become as omnipresent as wind rustling through darkled branches, though their foreign call could hardly be dismissed so easily.

The sky poured down onto the forest in endless murk; no moon lit the path for the belaboured Bordeaux and no lunar light shone to kiss the blade of his sword cane with cold lustre. The crimson demon withdrew the weapon blatantly and held it before him as a warning to the violent creatures that observed him from the shadows. Scattered they stood, in no predetermined formation, yet they were innumerable. From their petiolar heads, where twisted branches sprouted with gnarled deformity, the eyes of the wood golems stared with deadpan benevolence. They stood still with the patience of Venus-flytraps as their asymmetrical eyes met those of the demon. Bordeaux's eyes, the colour of blood, scanned the surroundings like a sentry and he boldly moved forward through the trees with a threatening defiance. His cold footsteps seemed to issue a challenge to any monster that might lurch from concealment and attack. He could hear the scrape of root-like feet of those few golems who moved on occasion and that of another sound - the loose end of the noose that draped the golems brushing against the ground. Yet none approached him. He moved through the darkness with patient ease, his vision keen in the pitch black; the path before him memorised.

And slow as his journey had been, Bordeaux eventually reached the plain where the lightning-struck pedestal of the tree stump awaited his arrival.

The black rose brooch was gone and still the wood golems were everywhere. Bordeaux's heart sank - his flawed plan of propitiation had failed. The disappointment that filled him was not entirely despairing; he had known from the start that his idea had been hopeful at best. What bemused him now was how to approach the situation from here on in. There had to be some reason for the forest's assailment on Tenebrae Manor. Bordeaux had hoped in vain that by returning the relic to the mindless wood golems, they would recede back to whence they came and return to being a rare and docile sight.

In a flash of anger he lashed out at the tree stump with a vigorous cut of his rapier. Until recently, it had not been necessary to equip arms upon leaving the manor but since his random encounter with a violent golem and the increased aggression of its brethren, a weapon had become imperative.

Bordeaux heard the grunt of an alien presence frighteningly close to his person and he turned to find himself greeted by a quartet of wood golems. The monsters were all different in various ways; some more squat than lank, others of thicker bole - however they all pertained to the common characteristics of their kind. They all wore rope nooses about their necks and the bodies of the four before him were clotted with fresh soil, as though they had only recently been brought to life and ripped from the earth.

Bordeaux was swift to act; he would not be caught off guard as in his previous encounter. He leapt upon the first golem and swung his sword cane, the rotted wooden skull of the thing splitting with ease. The headless body falling to the ground seemed to enrage the trio that remained and they moved to surround the crimson demon. One approached and grabbed at Bordeaux's free arm; though the strength of its grip was horrific, the sluggish swinging of its other bludgeoning arm would be its undoing. Bordeaux plunged his blade through the chest of the beast and his arm was free again. Two remained; he skewered the head of his first victim upon the end of his sword and ignited it with a flash of fire from his hand. The head smoldered with flames as it was hurled at the pair of golems. Its strike ignited one of them who in its panic, thrashed onto the other and left both covered in fire. They began to writhe about with a speed that startled Bordeaux and the crimson demon soon realised the foolishness of hurling flames so carelessly into the taiga.

He had to act fast, lest the forest go up in flames. He frantically kicked both golems so that they lost footing and tumbled backwards down a slight incline at the meadow's edge. By freak fortune, the golems landed not on dry grass but a dusty surface that extinguished the fire as fast as it had been lit.

Clouds of disturbed dirt soon settled and Bordeaux feverishly drank in the quiet that descended; the golems did not move, he was safe for now.

The trek back to Tenebrae Manor was carried out at a quicker pace. The vines that choked the house had robbed it of its usual dominance, a sight that made Bordeaux cringe in anguish. What was left for him to do? Never had he felt so powerless, Tenebrae Manor was wasting away with nothing to save it.

From the highest window of the mansion, the crimson demon observed the menacing silhouette of Lady Libra, lit by the candles that guttered behind her. He could not discern whether the shadow was looking at him from the window or just gazing into the night but his mind soon swelled with thoughts of freedom. A realisation dawned on him and though the relief of that realisation was minuscule, Bordeaux suddenly felt the comfort of one final idea - a last ditch attempt to save Tenebrae.

From the vantage point of two copper eyes, a squat glass held aloft by a silent demon shone in the firelight with crystalline colours. Swirled by gentle gyrations of the hand,

P.S.CLINEN

the cognac within mixed its liquid luminance with the
reflections cast by gloomy ice and the glass sweated with
the feverish heat of its surroundings.

Behind the glass, the fireplace danced with the
shadows and within the confines of the cradling arm chair,
Deadsol seemed so small, shielded by the ghastly shadows
that played their tricks on the wallpaper. The infantile trust
placed in the sturdy nestles of the chair was one that
possessed the copper demon into an intoxicating lull.

Am I drunk? How can I be? This is the first I've had...

Like moth to flame he stared, the glass cutting a
kaleidoscope of sinuous patterns with the curl of the
flames contorting in the backdrop. When it appeared that
nothing would arrest Deadsol's attention from the charcoal
glow, his torpid head turned to the other arm where a pipe
was slowly dying in his grasp. Wisps of stale smoke crept
from it and sketched leaden shades onto the red fire
behind it.

Deadsol sat up presently, his sudden jolt startling the
runty shape of Comets, who had been sitting quietly at the
demon's feet. Deadsol's eyes betrayed his lack of cognitive
sense, his pupils dilated to minuscule dots that gave the
impression of a trance.

"It's time for me to go, my boy."

A bemused sneer peeled onto Comets' face and he
scratched his head. "Go where, D?"

"Go, yes, you are right!" replied Deadsol. "Go. Goal.
To the goal, I have to go."

"What trick is this, charlatan? Snap out of it, fool."

Deadsol got to his feet and somnambulated towards
the door of the drawing room. The fire shuddered with the
draft of cold air that rushed in as the doors opened, the

hypnotised Deadsol turning his head this way and that as though scouting for some faraway treasure.

"This caravan of charlatans, rumbling across the steppes of Little Russia," he rambled. "I need a kopeck from mother, the carnival is in the village tonight. And here it is today but gone tomorrow! Like chaff on the late summer breeze."

Comets dashed to the door in an attempt to block his friend from leaving.

"You're not making sense, Deadsol," he cried. "Come friend, sit please. Cease this sleepwalk and rest before the fire."

"Take your being from out my path, clown! It's the gypsies I want to see."

The demon shuffled into the hall and left Comets in his wake.

"Where are you going?" cried the jester.

"My home. So sick, sick for home," Deadsol's voice dropped to a mutter. "My past taunts me, rips at the very fabric of my soul, to tatters, ribbons! Shattered like glass that cuts me deep with its poetry. Oh son, the son of a gypsy risen to the rank of baron. But where are my lands? I must return, to home. I drift like a maudlin wayfarer."

A horrible insanity clung to him, yet Deadsol did not fight against it. There was a forgotten comfort in his hypnotism and he felt no need to rebel. His legs cycled of their own accord beneath him, carrying him through rooms he had never seen before, down corridors dusty with neglect. Haunting sounds reached his ears, though whether they were fabricated in his imagination or not, he could not tell. Screams rang faintly from distant corners of the manor with Deadsol walking dreamily though the haze.

Though his legs shuffled onwards, he felt as though he had forgotten how to move.

Behind his head, forever out of his own line of sight, he felt the presence of his hypnotist, whose dusky reeds of hair curled about with no gravity as bane. The dark tide washed over him and he was pulled down, down further into the depths of the house, until ancient smells of rotted wood, petrified stone and rusted iron permeated through his prominent nostrils. His moustache twitched, his eyes saw nothing for all their distant focus and it was then he realised that it was not the smells of his old home but rather something more sinister.

A cell. This is a cell. What ghost has led me to incarceration? To trick the trickster... I'd tip my hat, well done sir. But my hat is at home. Or perhaps I never wore a hat at all.

Deadsol rambled deliriously, never had he felt so powerless. In his daze there appeared before him blurry visions of some wicked figure. For a moment he was fearful, yet the sight of soft white hands swaying before him reminded him of a woman of his childhood, centuries ago when he was still mortal. The hands held his arms aloft almost affectionately, yet their engagement was that of chaining him to a wall. He became drunk with melancholia and despairingly wondered how many years his mother had been dead.

Ambling through the eternity… Salvation was naught, woe to this forgotten demon…

The hands were so strong and in this state he was completely unable to fight back, as they effortlessly turned archaic key through lock and the weight of disintegrating chains burdened Deadsol's shoulders. Soon his vision worsened, flashing between blackness and blurred sight;

the foreign hands fell to the sides of their owner. Those dusky curls of hair sighed through the dark cell like seaweed under a pier, a pair of heavy breasts before him lulled Deadsol further into child-like nostalgia. The ghost drifted from the cell and he heard one last crank of key turning. It was all over now. He was locked away, left to sleep a deathly sleep where he was not sure whether he would wake up.

Good night, little man. Sleep now or you may not wake up at all...

XXI: Exiled

Had Bordeaux known of the true whereabouts of the black rose brooch and of the dire consequences that would tail behind it, he certainly would not have raced so directly onto the course of his final desperate plan. For though the brooch had disappeared from the tree stump, it had not been gleaned by the sprawling wood golems. Rather, the relic was concealed in the dusky confines of an old messenger bag that rattled its way about the hip of Madlyn in time with her steps.

The girl had stumbled onto the black rose completely by accident and immediately taking its discarding by Bordeaux as a blow to her person, had plunged further into the forests of Tenebrae. She had done all she could muster; her heart had been left out on a limb in a desperate yearn for affection, yet now it sunk deep into her chest with a weight of bitter sorrow. If Bordeaux could not be hers, then surely she would have been able to live with that. But it was the thought of him alongside Libra that tore her apart. Madlyn's mindless acceptance of the grotesque woman's orders had withered slowly to a tipping point, where she had instead begun to loathe her. And now, now that the bane of her simple yet strenuous existence had stolen her one dream of happiness, Madlyn had resolved to run away from Tenebrae Manor.

Nobody had seen her preparations; no attention had been arrested by the sounds of her shuffling about her room, cramming her belongings into the bag, last of which being the page she had torn from Bordeaux's book. The sketch of the tree with black roses mesmerized her so much that she wanted to keep it with her. She somehow believed that things of such beauty – even just a drawing of such things - could imbue her with utmost happiness. Where she would flee to, Madlyn did not know. She had stepped out the front door of the manor, the door held ajar by the vigilant Usher. Tenebrae's humble servants had gazed briefly at each other, yet Usher made no inquiry into the intentions of young Madlyn, nor had she indulged him with a reply. And why should they converse? With both clinging to the lower most rungs of the house's hierarchy, what cardinal significance would be gained by any discourse? With both submerged in pitying selflessness, the Usher closed the door with Madlyn on the other side, his mind ignorant to the finality of the girl's impending mission.

Her initial wanderings had been indecisive at best. The paths were infinite, spanning all degrees of the compass, yet their likeness to one another had caused her to stumble. There stood naught but trees in all directions and she could not know the swiftest path to the forest shoreline, where the tide of trees would recede to less monotonous fortunes. The endless night that enveloped Tenebrae Manor was not without limit of coverage, this she knew from Libra. Madlyn would need to travel until the dawn broke but the miles that stretched under the extremities of the spell were unknown to her. Perhaps the cycle of night and day returned to normal on one trip to the horizon - she could traverse that in a few hours. However, there was nothing disputing the night sky stretching for leagues on end, perhaps the perimeter could not be reached promptly on foot.

Madlyn thought not of the dangers that lurked in the forest surrounding and with her thoughts clouded by the ideals of fairy tales, she foolishly assumed her own safety to be unthreatened.

As the stories she remembered circled through her mind, Madlyn mused over the direction of her adventure. Recalling no blessings of a warm place in the days of her sanity, she sighed longingly for the southern lands of children's stories, where fields drowned beneath a sweet sun. The place where evil was abated - she prayed that such a paradise could exist for her and, through no logical process, set off in the direction she assumed to be south.

The taiga was impossibly vast. Each tree she passed a mere drop in a deep green sea. Madlyn scrambled through terrain that grew steadily more resilient as she progressed. There were times where the trunks huddled so closely together that even her gangly frame struggled to pass. Grass grew thick in patches; waist high on one uphill slope that Madlyn spent a painful amount of time ascending. But then the grass would fall away and give way to stubborn shrubbery that gripped her frock as she tried to pass, grasping with hideous claw-like branches.

Madlyn was unable to say how far she had travelled when she first noticed the diversity of trees around her. Though overwhelmed with pines, there loomed other variations of birch and sycamore, elm and oak. There they stood, vigilant sentinels of a silent army, their formations disorderly yet effective in hindering swift travel through.

Soon the forest became alive with a silvery glow, as a full moon appeared from behind the canopy. Madlyn cast her eyes skyward and became drunk with its beauty as a moth to flame, until she lost her footing and stumbled down a small grassy slope. Tumbling head over heel to the nadir of the hillock, she landed with a thud into a muddy creek. The smell of wet soil was overpowering as she sat up unhurt yet startled. Mud had ruined her navy blue dress and white smock and she gingerly picked the leaves from her tangled hair. Her arm must have skimmed a sharp stone or branch during the fall, for a stinging graze ran up her right forearm. Although nature had tried to rattle her tenacity, she resolutely pushed back and rose to her feet. She had to press on, it seemed that nothing in this world was willing to show her any kindness.

The light of the moon made her travels easier and for a further few hours she trudged ever forward until fatigue began to envelop her. How long had she been walking? In the eternal night it was difficult to discern, though Madlyn knew that she should rest soon. She came upon a large oak tree whose massive roots were interlocked over the ground like tentacles. There, beneath the mighty bole she was able to comfortably sit in a nook of roots and drift into a fitful sleep.

The moon had set when she awoke but in the

darkness her eyes had adjusted and vision was somewhat clear. When Madlyn had walked a little further, she felt her foot kick at something in the dark and on bending down to inspect she picked up a large pinecone. It felt rough and weighty in her palm, yet the thing fascinated her so that she rummaged through her bag to try and make room for it. Her messenger bag was full enough already, stuffed with withered fruits and bread she had stolen from the kitchen, her quill, the mirror shard and a lantern. Acknowledging the darkness that had settled around her, Madlyn took the lantern from the bag and put the pinecone in its place. Only then did she realise that she did not have any oil with which to bring light to her murky perimeter.

The sounds of the wilderness overwhelmed her of a sudden and she became blinded by simple logic. Ill prepared as she was, a useless lantern was the first acceptance of failure that Madlyn recognised. Dryness cramped her throat; unease crept up slowly behind her. Madlyn had no water either. There was no saying how long she would have remained stationary, had a crow not suddenly swooped from a branch above and startled her into movement. Unease loomed and she hummed to herself in an attempt to ward off rising wariness;

> *Oh persnickety wickedly witch*
> *Who tried to stave off dandruff itch*
> *Used a cat to cushion her head*
> *And fell with a grunt out of her bed*
>
> *Oh persnickety wickedly witch*
> *Of flake and flurry scalp twitch*
> *Sought bats to beat the snow away*

But wings clapped her hair to grey

Oh persnickety wickedly witch
Heard the cure from a snitchy-snitch
On her crown she let perch an owl
That pecked her head and made her howl!

Oh persnickety wickedly witch
Who tried to stave off dandruff itch
Inhaled the dust with every breath
And promptly sneezed herself to death.

She fought on and presently the ground beneath her aching feet began to slope so that she was walking steadily downhill into the concave of a valley. Her steps fell heavily as she went, the weight of her tired body thrown onto her knees. Yet Madlyn felt drawn towards the pit of the valley by some surreal force. The grass became mere tufts of dry straw, sprouted from dusty outcrops of knuckled rock; the forest's shades of green receded to make way for a dried world of earthy colours.

Her legs throbbed with pain as she pulled up beside a large rock but no sooner had she leaned her hand upon it than she snatched it away. A sharp gust of pain pierced her palm and when she looked down, Madlyn noticed the boulder was covered with thorn-laden vines.

With her hands clutched to her chest, she followed the trail of thorns and saw that they were strewn everywhere around her. Jutting from thick black tendrils they protruded, sprawled across every rock and tree in sight. Madlyn felt overwhelmed by the parasitic nature of the tendrils, gripping the ground like the roots of a tree, seemingly draining the earth's very core to a husk.

For a moment she considered turning back, until something glistened in the corner of her eye and in a second, her heart leapt in amazement. When her eyes confirmed the astonishing sight, Madlyn dashed recklessly into the thorny bracken.

Blossoming effortlessly from the dusky gloom of one particular tendril was a black rose - not unlike the relic of Libra's brooch. Madlyn's heart beat like a hummingbird; plucking the rose from its host, the vine shivered at the disturbance. With her free hand, she rummaged through her bag and withdrew a crumpled piece of paper - the page from Bordeaux's book about wood golems. It had caught Madlyn's eye during her failed avowal in Bordeaux's quarters, displaying beautiful sketches of a magnificent tree that sprouted black roses from its branches. The plumage on this vine was the very same, it had to be and Madlyn had a sudden revelation. To follow the trail of thorny tendrils to their origin; perhaps there she would find the tree that grew the priceless talismans.

The path was narrow and unrelenting. Madlyn endured the nicks and cuts of the thorns that reached out to her from her sides, the scent of wild roses saturating her senses so that she barely felt the pain.

Before her it appeared, a tree larger than any she had ever seen, though perhaps not as tall as conifer, certainly its roots and branches reached further lateral distances than any rival. The branches were skeletal, save for sparse blossoms of black roses dotting along them. Madlyn saw nothing else, considered no danger and plunged headlong towards the base of the tree, where she pulled up panting for breath. A cavernous hollow in the trunk stared at her like an empty black eye socket and Madlyn could not help staring back into its void. It burrowed into the tree at her head's height and would certainly capacitate her entire skull were she to place it inside. Yet she dared not, as a shudder convulsed through her, a detesting of total darkness and claustrophobia.

Madlyn reached out with her hand and brushed her fingertips around the circumference of the hollow. The trunk was rough to touch; Madlyn was gazing absently into the void when on a sudden, a vine lashed out from within the hole and coiled violently around her wrist. Madlyn gasped and tried to pull her arm free but the artery-like tendril grasped her like a hungry leech.

She panicked, the tendril secreting an otherworldly screech, as around her the branches of the tree lowered. To her horror, the lowered branches brought into view the swinging of numerous corpses that hung from the branches as gallows.

Her heart beat furiously, the eyes of the ancient dead bored into her with abhorrence from the rotted flesh of their faces. Below the hideous screech of the tree and the crackling of the dead-adorned branches, there rose a throaty thrumming behind her. Madlyn flung her head around and saw she was surrounded by wood golems. Their grotesque humanoid forms left her aghast and Madlyn felt a long lost emotion return to her - a feeling she had repressed since childhood. The feeling of raw fear; of unequalled fright that held her in paralysis.

From the hollow of the tree, more tendrils oozed outwards towards her and as she tried to fight back, she felt the wood golems draw ever nearer. A scream burst from her throat, previously choked back by unbridled terror but it was not long until her cries were muted by a tendril that wound about her throat. The world faded darker than she had ever known and the last thing she saw was the glimmer of steel flash once before her, though it may have only been a fabrication of her failing senses.

Back inside Tenebrae Manor, the atmosphere crackled with an ominous chill. Bordeaux - the master of affairs, servant to the castle's concord, waited in the shadows behind a candelabrum on the highest stairwell. Regardless of his impatience, he had to bide his time and just as the silence grew to an unbearable pitch, a soft sound cut through the gloom and evolved into the sounds of footfalls coming ever closer.

The crimson demon froze, holding his breath for fear of disclosure, until Lady Libra shuffled past him and out of view down the stairs. He had not been seen.

Still he waited, lurking there in the shadow of billowy curtains that draped about the floor length window in the hall. The wait became agonizing; Bordeaux whispered a treble count before sliding swiftly from his hiding place and into Libra's room.

The door was closed quietly with painstaking precision, the demon wasting no time in advancing to the corner of the room where Libra had concealed a secret passageway.

"Here..." he whispered, standing before the great dusty wardrobe.

He braced himself against the side of the cupboard and pushed hard. It was certainly heavier than he expected and as it budged from its resting place, the groan of it scraping the floor resonated through the room. Bordeaux cursed the sound, pausing for a moment to make sure nothing stirred.

With the wardrobe moved; an eerie light shone from the exposed entry, throwing the shadows of Bordeaux's ankles along the floor. The demon winced at the sight of grime on his burgundy coat, rubbed off from the face of the wardrobe with his pushing. Pedant even in this hasty mission, Bordeaux did not fancy dust on his refined clothes. Intrigued though he was with the light issuing at his feet, he still sighed awkwardly at his next task.

He got down on his knees and peered through the opening, the room on the other side was quite small, perhaps the size of a storage closet. Libra had not been able to fit through but Bordeaux had no doubt he could. He considered removing his coat to prevent further begriming, though he realised that his time may be limited.

Stealing himself, Bordeaux threw himself down to the floor and shuffled urgently through the opening, his broad shoulders being of only minor difficulty.

When he had pulled his legs through, he stood up and brushed down his arms and shoulders, grimacing at his now filthy hands. Bordeaux believed he had reason for suspicion of Libra; her protective defense and prolonged secrecy of this hidden room surely had some significance. And it was now before his very eyes that his accusation found proper footing.

Atop a small shrine there sat, as an egg is cradled in a nest, a beautiful relic, which glowed vibrant colours of red, amber and green. It was this very object from which the strange light was produced. Its beauty infatuated Bordeaux as he cautiously grasped it in his palms. The thing was roughly heart shaped and its glowing was not unlike that of a log in the fireplace, warm to the touch.

He shook himself out of the trance; time was not on his side at present. Libra could return at any moment. He pushed the thing through the entrance and followed in tail, crawling desperately back the way he had come. The colours that pulsed from the relic threw dim light on the floor surrounding and Bordeaux still on his knees, froze suddenly in terror.

Behind the relic, a dusky foot; now red, now amber, now green, belayed the presence of a figure looming above him. The Lady Libra's eyes struck fear in Bordeaux's heart as they tore into him with a hideous fury. The corner of her lip twitched and through her gritted teeth she hissed, "You."

"Libra," stammered Bordeaux. "This is..."

"Enough!" her voice was menacing. "I knew I should have stamped my authority sooner. I show you a little respect and suddenly you think yourself as my equal. Given my echelon, I knew reprimanding you without a more just cause would rob me of some dignity but you just couldn't accept it could you? Instead of pledging fealty like a good little insect with the basic will of maintaining order, you keep coming after me! Well, you will not make a fool of me, Bordeaux. You want to know what you are dealing with? Let it be!"

Libra raised her arms slowly, her white limbs quivering with an unseen force. The room shook and Bordeaux cried out, his very being evaporating before his eyes. He felt himself plummet backwards, crashing headlong into a murky brine. A sharp gust of torrent cut his lungs as his vision vanished into a blackness deeper than the night of Tenebrae Manor.

END OF PART TWO.

Part Three

XXII: The Conclave

In a certain part of the forest where the trees stood somewhat wider apart than elsewhere, the makings of a crude trail lay buried beneath a littering of pine needles. Like the matted stubble of an unkempt peasant, the rotting needles stuck to the soil, weather-beaten and uninspiring, blemished only by a protuberance of debris that broke the otherwise flat surface of ground. This debris, which lay directly in the centre of the badly worn path, appeared not unlike any other tree branch presenting itself so disconcertedly mangled in attempt to impede a jaded traveller. Of its construction, twisted wooden roots molding into the thicker bole of stump, riddled with rotten holes and knots, one would not give it a second glance. Yet given the now severe threat of wooden monsters in the area, closer inspection revealed it to be a perished wood golem that lay strewn across the road. Yes, its squatted humanoid shape was discernible, that horrid mouth of crooked stitches

240

ghastly to behold. And in the hollow sockets of its
displeasing face, where the eyes of the beast should have
been, a rodent crawled quietly betwixt. Its whiskers
twitched in the night air as it ventured ever cautiously
across the gnarled body of monster.

A veil of ebony now swept upon it, as a savage raven
drove its hideous beak into the core of the rodent's life.
The dying rodent expired and as its life fled from its frame
further death descended, as a flurry of black birds
swooped down to try and claim the first raven's prize.
They pecked and cawed and argued amongst themselves,
kicking the wooden corpse apart.

Mindless to all but instinct, the birds took flight on a
sudden, dispatched into chaos by a galloping horse that
charged straight through their squabbling. The skewbald
mare dashed onwards with the vigor of a wild bronco,
though the urgency of her march was restrained by the
rider, Crow.

The wood hermit closed in on Tenebrae Manor, the
path ridden was one forged by him in years gone by,
though not one he had traversed in some time. He looked
to the sky and read the stars fluently; the manor was not
far away now. Crow's chestnut curls streamed behind him
in the slipstream, across his back the gilded beauty of his
completed sword and shield lay strapped. The magnificent
leaf shaped shield glittered in the dim starlight, as this light
played along the iron edges overlaying the matted green
wood.

His journey was hardly one of jubilance. Sprawled
with him on the back of his horse, balanced precariously in
his lap, a tragedy was wrapped in ragged blanket.

The mare slowed to a trot as it passed the old

mailbox and reached the imposing front threshold of Tenebrae Manor; Crow swung from his horse and tied her hastily to a tree. Had he the time to consider the branches that leant inward and clung to the manor, he would have been greatly perturbed but now was not the time to take in the scenery. With nurturing arms he took the bundle of blankets in his grasp and ran into the front foyer.

"Usher, where are the others? Bordeaux? Anyone?"

"A few have congregated in the dining hall, sir," said Usher without tone or colour. "First floor on the right."

Crow could sense a commotion as he climbed the stairs and, on entering the room, saw Edweena, Arpage and Sinders ensconced around a tea tray.

"Ah ha! The crow man himself," cried Sinders. "Are you scared, crow man?"

"Be silent," Crow quipped, instantly hushing the rascal scarecrow.

The composer Arpage sat with a teacup quivering in his shaking hands and he was only further startled when Crow placed the bundled heap on the table before him.

"Crow..." Edweena whispered. "That can't be..."

"The kitchen girl," finished Crow.

Huddled indeed within the blankets, the lifeless body of Madlyn stared with empty eyes. Her skin was of bluish tinge, her neck bruised from the stranglehold that had been her end.

"I found her deep in the trees," said Crow. "Those golems attacked her. There was nothing else I could do."

They stood silent around the table; bewildered and in disbelief. Madlyn was dead and, unlike the other apparitions that hovered in Tenebrae's darkness with varying levels of higher mortality, there was no bringing her back.

"Someone inform Bordeaux," said Crow.

"He seems to have vanished somewhere, perhaps out in the forest. Though I cannot imagine a pleasant stroll, given the way things are," replied Edweena. "I paid visit to Libra however, concerning other issues, whether she turns up here or not is another matter."

"Not that she'd be of much use," mused Crow.

The dim candlelight of the overhead chandelier offered little comfort to the mournful assembly. It could have been said that Madlyn's face looked no different, as she had so often drifted into vacant daydream, though she was not one to succeed in fooling anyone. This was no act of feigned death; she was most certainly perished.

The silence that settled was broken by the ingress of Lady Libra, who immediately noticed the jittery Arpage sitting on the opposite side of the table. The composer jumped; his teacup flung in such a matter that its scalding contents stung his hands and the cup shattered on the dark red carpet.

"The composer dares to show his face in my home," said Libra. "Here I was, thinking the cold would have killed you by now."

"Die?" replied Arpage. "Oh that I could. That is, I think I could. Who could say? The years go by and I still l-live, m-miss."

"Shut up," said Libra. "Why are you here?"

Sinders rose. "Shut up, she says. Then demands locution. Little wonder he is so bemused."

"Have it your way, pumpkin head," replied Libra. "If the little music man has lost his voice, then you tell me. Why are you in my house?"

Sinders clasped his head in sudden despair. "What pain it is to say, my home is gone! Ruined!"

"Sacked by golems," added Arpage.

"They poured in on us unawares," said Sinders. "I had to set fire to my beautiful home so we could escape."

"You lit a fire in the forest?" said Crow. "Fool! You could end us all!"

Crow drew his sword and Sinders instantly lost the air of storyteller and huddled behind the equally cowardly Arpage.

"Sheathe your steel, Crow," said Edweena. "They know they've done an ill deed."

"Just so, kindly vampiress," Arpage tittered. "We've learnt our lesson, honestly."

"Then perhaps you should inform Libra of the consequences of your irrational act."

Both turned their heads cautiously towards Lady Libra, who stood expectantly akimbo. The pair hesitated in the awkward silence, Sinders removing his tattered black hat as if to shield himself.

"Well?"

"The man escaped," shot Sinders.

It took Libra a moment to absorb this news, before she flew at both of them and grabbed at their collars.

"You let him escape?"

Arpage sobbed and Sinders kicked his legs, sending straw showering to the floor.

"Please miss!" cried Arpage. "In the chaos of the moment, he ran! There were flames everywhere and monsters and smoke! Oh my eyes, how it stung. I could not see him for my tears."

"You imbeciles have not only brought on the danger

of forest fire; you've unleashed into the world a man with knowledge of Tenebrae Manor, of our eternal night! What if he reaches a town? We'll be exposed!" Libra bristled with fury.

"You need not worry about the former," Edweena interjected. "I saw the smoke while I was out hunting. By the time I arrived there, the place was a charred shell - the fire is out."

"Libra, though this matter of this escapee is no doubt important, perhaps you should take a look over here," said Crow.

From her current position, Libra could only discern the bundle of rags on the tabletop, where candle wax was beginning to drip down from the chandelier above. She dropped Arpage and Sinders to the floor and walked over to the table.

The others stared at her face as she considered the body of Madlyn. For some time she said nothing, her features betrayed no form of reaction. Then, calmed, though not without the hint of sorrow on her heavy heart, she turned to the door and took a step towards it.

"We will bury her in the cemetery."

Edweena moved forward and placed a hand on Libra's back. "The wood golems, Libra. It isn't safe to leave the manor anymore."

"The girl deserves a respectable interment. See that this is arranged."

None of them would respond, perhaps they were bewildered by the strange compassion that the lady of the manor usually lacked. Libra left and although she had not turned back to face any of the others who remained in the dining room, all could not deny the glimmer of a tear that trickled down her face.

XXIII: A Sepulchral Valediction

With funerals so few in number in the chronology of Tenebrae, the very idea of preparing such an event threw the bemused characters into further disarray. In a place where the dead already wandered the halls and spirits seemingly incapable of perishing awaited a more promising afterlife, little knowledge of human entombment remained.

As such, most of the organisation was left to the zombie Rune, whose seemingly redundant wisdom was called upon to bear the brunt of such a distressing affair. Meanwhile, those that remained in mourning offered their assistance in varying ways, though the realisation of a duo of disappearances concerned them. Where was Bordeaux? And Deadsol? Lady Libra answered to their obvious omissions with a curious mixture of feigned ignorance and unprovoked aggression.

"The troublemaker Deadsol is serving a suitable punishment... For mocking the queen of Tenebrae

Manor."

And of Bordeaux? With her heavy foot placed down so defiantly in regards to Deadsol's incarceration, it was unusual that she would be so elusive about Bordeaux's whereabouts.

"Bordeaux is..."

Libra would trail off in any manner available. A change of subject where suited, though she preferred to stamp her authority with added venom in her responses, so that eventually none dared approach her.

All the while, the mummy shuffled onwards. Rune rumbled purposefully about the mansion readying Madlyn's ceremony. With such peerless ethic with regards to the task assigned, one would easily believe it to be a swift and concise ceremony - respectful to a fault. Yet it was Rune's crippling capacity, both physically and mentally, that led the dirge of preparation towards clutter and confoundedness. Heartfelt intentions aside, poor Rune was at a loss to manage the situation entirely by himself - with the manor so large and isolated, his steps so painfully slow, he was unable to wring the appropriate level of help from any other. As such, the moon rose and set several times as Rune embarked on his work. Though the world had spun several times, the endless hours of night blended into one, so that the others took little notice of his tardiness. A coffin had been found amongst an abundance of disused palls in the lower crypts beneath the house. Numerous as they had been, Rune had had to settle for a rather large box that blocked access to any others in the back of the crypt. Dust stricken and cramped with decades of cobwebs, Rune had to enlist the services of both Sinders and Arpage to remove the coffin and carry it upstairs. Though not the most capable of handymen, the pair made their feeble attempt - the coffin made its journey from the crypt to the first flight of stairs. And when Sinders' straw-stuffed arms gave way and sent the wooden box tumbling onto the feeble Arpage, Rune decided the job would be better suited to that of Edweena and Crow.

The latter pair obliged willingly and also took it upon themselves to repair one of the carriages that lay dormant along the western side of the manor. It was during this undertaking that Arpage was assigned a job more appropriate to his effeminate station, the writing of a short requiem on his violin and the arrangement of a wreath of flowers.

The sky swirled as though it was cloaked with smoke. A billowy screen of cloud poisoned the clear purity of night and spread like a used paintbrush spilling its dregs into clean water.

On an hour when it seemed that the gloom could not be more impenetrable, the horse drawn carriage set out from Tenebrae Manor into the ramose trees of the forest. Through the night there brayed the snorts of Crow's horses, three of which dragged the august freight not unlike a locomotive. From his perch atop the carriage, the Usher slouched with incredible bulk, clutching at the reins with his massive and scarred hands.

The carriage gave off no semblance of colour; its blackness glossy in the half-light, reflected by paint and velvet curtain. Tailing behind it was the coffin, gingerly confined on a trolley-like platform that rattled on its axles. The wheels of the freight cycled on with a rhythm disrupted by the unevenness of the terrain. Often times, the spinning silver spokes would halt abruptly; caught on a tree root or natural concave of ground. Though the horses muttered their protest; Usher needed not the use of his whip, for the equine engine carried on regardless. Perhaps the horses were conversing with their other sister through their whinnying; the skewbald mare rode in wide circles about the carriage, where the sword drawn Crow scouted for hazards. It had been agreed that the woods were undoubtedly dangerous and the comely hermit took it as his duty to keep guard over the others whilst on route to the graveyard.

The forest wept with the groans of a nearby terror unseen, though Crow was not alone in his scouting. At the pinnacle of the canopy there lurked a lithe shadow - the vampiress Edweena, scouring the floor from a lofty bough. A movement fluttered the dark curtains of the carriage and at that moment, a small shaft of night threw its light on the apparitions that sat within. They brooded in the listless umbra, ensconced on two leather-lined benches adjacent, so that the quintet were left facing each other in uncomfortable congestion. Sitting with their backs turned to the destination - Rune, Sinders, Comets; the frightening abhuman trio of Tenebrae. Aligned on the bench, they were a terrifying treble to Arpage sitting opposite. The three stared down at the composer, who tittered nervously from his cramped position next to Libra. The magnificent bulk of the gourmand easily took up the space of two and, as such, Arpage was left overwhelmed and crammed between the carriage door and Libra's right hip. After a moment's mourning the composer had conceded to the destruction of his violin bow - crushed under the weight of Libra as she sat herself down in the carriage and he was now trying to ward off the staring eyes of the opposing trio.

"He he, a rather imposing lot, one might say? Something out of a child's nightmare, no?"

Arpage was met with silence until Sinders spoke. "What of it?"

"Ah! What of what? Only that I find myself in the company of you fine monsters, you brilliant fabrications of distorted horror! My sanity is long gone, so I dare not vouch for my own deceiving eyes; yet how can it be that you three are... Shall we say, tangible before me? Truly you are fictional figments in my clouded sight."

"Laudable reality - I am very real, music man," said Sinders. "Animated straw indeed! And the head of decomposed vegetable matter, my life is a curse. You can blame Malistorm this for miserly existence."

The mention of the name caused Libra to stir in her seat.

"Ah yes, the old baron," mused Arpage. "A somewhat less chaotic reign."

The black veil across Libra's face concealed her eyes; though her plump red lips were visible, the bottom half of her pale face appeared to float in the sombre darkness as she treated her company with sedated apathy.

"And this specimen?" continued Arpage, grasping at a loose ribbon of Rune's wrappings. "I don't think we've ever spoken properly."

Rune's eyes had glassed over with a pasty yellow that polluted his irises. The slackness of his jaw grew presently, the listless thing slowly losing the battle against gravity. He had not noticed the conversation fall into his lap. Having been so generously ignored, Arpage grew nervous and again began to fidget with his broken bowstring. All attention fell towards Rune as he lurched forward on a sudden, broken free of his trance by a swat to the head from Comets. The runty jester had proven far more civil hitherto - no doubt due to the absence of Deadsol but the opportunity to rile his senior had established as far too tempting to resist.

"He's talking to you, silly," cried Comets.

"Talk?" replied Rune.

"Arpage!"

"... Page."

"Dreaming of books again," said Sinders. "You will never behold a senility so..."

"I was an accident," said Rune. "An embalming mishap. It wasn't Malistorm though, oh no. This was many centuries ago. I can't recall the name of Tenebrae's chieftain at the time but he used me for an experiment."

"He heard it all," muttered Sinders. "And still interrupted me..."

"Fascinating! Man plays god and you - the manifestation!" chortled Arpage. "What a laugh! And what of young Meteors?"

"Comets," came a husky voice.

"Eh, what?"

"His name is Comets, you halfwit." Libra's voice silenced them all.

Arpage felt his heart flutter with fright; he tried to steal a few inches of space on the bench. Yet he could only wish for more room, wish that the billowing that pressed against him was merely drapes of material from her dress but Libra could not and would not budge.

"He is truly enigmatic," Libra conceded. "We've no idea where he came from."

Infrequently sojourned, the cemetery stood at an isolated mile from Tenebrae Manor and, small though it was, the crippling decay of its ruins were no less imposing than the aforementioned mansion. Alone it brooded atop the crest of a light incline, yet despite its position, it remained difficult to distinguish at a distance from the trees encompassing.

The party crawled up the hill, the horses growing steadily more fatigued as they passed the rusted iron gates that swung lifelessly from their hinges. Once within the crumbling stone fence of the graveyard, a comforting sense overcame the characters; there had been no ambush along their journey and they found themselves feeling safely cradled in the cemetery's deathly embrace.

Headstones lay ruinous and disintegrated, jutting their mangled peaks from the dry brown grass that had overrun the entire place. The trees in the cemetery bore no foliage at all and their skeletal branches stretched in all directions. In an age long past, the graveyard had been tended to by various servants of Tenebrae but pertaining to its immortal nature, the few occurrences of death within the castle deemed the occupation as redundant. Indeed, the graves were few, for the mortals that stumbled upon the immemorial home were usually wont to suicide or disappearance. Their mark was left on no one and proper ceremony was unnecessary.

The grounds were rough and uneven; the stone pathways that crossed between headstones had burst in all directions by tree roots beneath. Having reason to be wary of their tread, for the ground was laden with the pits of open graves, they eventually uncovered a suitable burial place for Madlyn. The hole was less weather beaten by snow and rain than others, though it was the size that rendered it the most appropriate. Madlyn's coffin was of awkwardly large proportions to an extent most tragically comical; her tiny body shrunken so that such spacious confines seemed a touch disrespectful.

Clothed in a black tunic that dulled the green vibrancy of his youth, Crow lowered the box into the grave with help of Edweena, whose dusky attire was no different to what she usually wore. And as the characters gathered in a circle, the wood hermit hurled soil onto the wooden coffin, as Rune recited a eulogy from a leather book.

"As darkest shadows we gather, under a night without end. Where the umbrageous pitch conceals us from the light of day, so long forgotten to these ageless trees. We have naught to guide us but our lunar orb, whose very lustre is but only reflection. And thus we linger in the shadows of the world, where our fellow ghoul has met her end. We relegate Madlyn to the artless weeds of decay. We open the door to her subterranean gateway, where she must go alone and soil seals the gate in deepest darkness."

Having awaited his cue, Arpage then began his funeral requiem, though due to his lacking of a bow he could only resort to plucking at the strings of his violin. The effect of the elegy was somewhat jarring - though the tune carried a pretty melody, the unorthodox manner of leaping between notes by way of pizzicato did not display the same smooth emotion that would have come from the glide of a bow.

The others stood uncomfortably, seemingly awaiting the song's awkward end. And when the dirge ended, Comets began to clap, though he was swiftly silenced by the glare of Rune.

For a moment, the only sound was that of a series of dull thumps, of dirt striking wood as Crow filled the grave. Another thump - Rune closing the heavy book, a noise that struck a chord in the hearts of the others, who stood crestfallen. Rune twitched involuntarily and reached for a certain spot on his scalp; his hand came away soggy.

"Rain," came Libra's voice from the coach.

Unbeknownst to the others, the lady had already returned to the coach, despite her possession of the only umbrella and awaited departure.

"We should go," said Edweena, echoing their thoughts, though her deadpan expression was heart wrenching to hear out loud.

The coffin was gone and with it Madlyn; the last shovel of soil concealing her to her resting place. As they left, the rain began to fall soft and heavy, bruising the lonely grave with bloated droplets.

By the time the coach reached the midway of the journey home, the rain was turning torrential. Though no wind assisted its violent lashings, it fell in such a screen of haze that navigation became troublesome. The horses struggled to haul the carriage wheels through the muddy turf and Edweena found her steps increasingly heavy as she walked beside Crow and his mare. The downpour hissed in her ears, making conversation with the wood hermit seem ridiculous, yet a nagging cry in her mind forced her to speak.

"Where has she gone?"

Crow took a moment to register the question. "The girl? You're asking me?"

"I can't help but think it," replied Edweena. "You

mortals. Can it be that you really just disintegrate to dust?"

"It would seem that way to me as man... Surely your years as a vampire have unearthed some truth about this supposed afterlife."

Edweena's sapphire eyes swam with sorrow as the rain tore down her face. "This, I do not consider an afterlife. I am just like you, only with more years at my back. The idea that Madlyn has ascended to some eternal paradise is as much a flight of fancy to me as I'm sure it is to you."

"I'm afraid I cannot offer much in way of consolation," said Crow. "For I am certain that I will die. You, however..."

"I know."

The seconds poured onwards. Edweena spoke again. "Where will you go?"

Crow thought a moment, as though such an idea had never arisen in his mind. "I do not know. I am content to find that out when it comes."

Inside the coach, where the mood was just as heavy with sorrow, Arpage gazed out the window. Having been further crammed against the wall by Libra's impressive rump, he sat hypnotised by the downpour.

"That was well played, Arpage," said Sinders. "Given the circumstances."

Arpage twitched from his trance, "Circumstance? Oh my, by nature of the event and nature of my now stunted instrument, I say yes."

He looked at his broken bowstring, then at Libra as though imploring for an apology but she did not respond. Attempting to adjust the ruff about his neck, he discerned a sudden thud and the coach came to a shuddering halt.

"Are we there?" asked Comets.

The jester looked out the window, the great frontage of Tenebrae Manor looming before him confirmed his suspicions. "We are!"

Though the coach had stopped, the thud came again. It was as though something was beating on the roof above them, something heavier than rain and those inside became uneasy.

"Something isn't right," hissed Libra. "Usher you twit, what is going on out there?"

Her response came in the form of the carriage roof bursting open; the clawed arm of a wood golem came whistling through. Arpage squealed like a child and threw the door open and, stopping not to observe the fate of his companions, ran, arms flailing, into the house.

The golem stared down at them from the hole in the roof, wasting no time in taking another swipe at the helpless passengers below. The rain poured into the coach as the rest scrambled to exit.

Crow had dismounted his horse and was fighting off an entourage of beasts with his sword.

"Get inside!" he cried.

Pertaining to the state they were left in by the cowardly composer, the mighty doors of the manor stood wide open. The golems pursued with an unusual speed and the Lady Libra, being of hefty proportion and lagging fitness, struggled to reach the entrance. Accompanying this was the rain soaked swathes of her heavy dress and she was soon forced to feebly beat away her attackers with her umbrella. This she performed admirably, until a wayward golem escaped her notice and hooked its arm around her neck in a stranglehold. She tried to scream; breath cut frantically short, she attempted to free herself from the monster's grasp. The beast was wickedly strong and just as Libra began to fail, she felt the air rush back into her lungs. Edweena had leapt at the wood golem and clawed the thing to submission with fang and nail. Libra sat stunned at the gesture of selflessness displayed by her old friend.

"Go!" cried Edweena.

Lost for words, Libra rose to her feet and delved into the safety of the mansion's walls; Crow and Edweena following in tow. Usher locked the doors fast.

"So aggressive," gasped Sinders.

"And faster..." replied Edweena.

XXIV: Aubade

A rush of panic enveloped Bordeaux as he crashed into the drowning wake, an adrenalin that cloaked him in a salty embrace. Twirling about an ever-shifting axis, he fought for his bearings against the violent current. The initial shock had erred him into a stuttered inhale that filled his lungs with a stinging pain. Such sharp daggers of pulpy water filled him with the sensation of a long lost memory - the sea.

The waves tossed his exhausted body like a rag doll; he felt the incredible weight of fatigue hauling him into the depths. Once or twice when his head broke the surface, he tried to open his eyes but his flaming hair lay matted across his face and extinguished his vision. Hoping to jettison excess weight, Bordeaux tried desperately to remove his maroon coat. The ocean had soaked it to his skin and he was unable to tear it from his arms.

Consigning himself to fate, his energy failed him, though it seemed that the sea had grown tired of the taste of his struggles. Tumbling from the reflective crest; a white cap bloated with waxing gibbous, the gorged moon hurled him from the tide.

Like a weaning babe, he gaped at the air and gripped his fingers into the sands to ensure their existence. The murky film of the monumental sea slid up to caress him again, as the waves crashed onto the shoreline. Around his sunken head they crawled, the waves stretching for him, trying to haul him back into oblivion.

Bordeaux lay motionless, still of limb - his heavy breathing the only trace of life. Although he felt the nagging threat of high tide swell dragging him away, he was too exhausted to move.

His sufferance had been of a potent poison; never had he felt so drained. A small influx of energy mustered within brought Bordeaux to his hands and knees before he clambered to his feet to survey his environment.

The beach spread either side of him and coiled into toothy cliffs at his lateral horizons, opening wide to engulf the moonlit bay. The light of the moon teased with the shadows, an accentuating sharpness that distinguished even the smallest grain of sand, the smallest seashell.

The crimson demon stood bewildered. What had happened? Where was he? He trudged forward as a somnambulant, kicking the dunes beneath his weary steps and disturbing the bustle of tiny blue crabs that scuttled in their traffic on the sands.

Libra; yes, he remembered Libra, a face of bridled fury boring into him. And then...

The dune grew sharper in its incline and soon Bordeaux was once again on hand and knee, crawling to the summit of sand to get a better vantage point of his locale. The grass grew long like reeds about him, their celadon stalks rustling softly in the ocean breeze.

Bordeaux thought he could hear wind chimes - their resplendent carol drifting through the tide in glorious percussion. The music seemed the perfect partner to the gnarled trees that stood bare and stooped; beaten by sea, glass whistles in a sculptured Thule.

Bordeaux sank to his haunches, soothed immeasurably by the seaside lull; it was not long before he drifted to sleep.

Sleep came to him in drifts. The cold gusts of the dream toyed at him, pulling his mind this way and that, as though he were merely a puppet in a carnival show. All colour fled from his thoughts, all save that grey and green of the beach. The celadon washed over him like the notes of a piano and filled his dreams with recollection. Lady Libra and her magical prowess; Bordeaux had not realised the extent of it. She had banished him, somewhere far from Tenebrae Manor. He dreamt of her hands waving before him hypnotically and for a moment, recalled the pain he had felt tearing at him. It had been an unbearable affliction and, on remembering it, he kicked fitfully in his sleep. How could it have been that Libra had such ability - ability that could throw him from dimensions and maroon him at any impossible distance from home?

His mind went black again as he plunged in a deeper period of slumber. Bordeaux felt his ears fill with the distant cry of the savage. The tribe beat at war drums and the light of a fire pierced apart the darkness. Though wood or flint did not kindle this fire. Its core was aglow with that beautiful heart-shaped talisman Bordeaux had found in Libra's secret room. The flames burned with shades of red, amber and green. And around the great fire, he could discern the twisted shapes of terrifying monsters.

The wood golems danced an ancient ritual about the flaming heart, which lit up the ghastly deadpan of their faces. Those expressionless eyes bulged with blind malice and, from their heads, they tore at the branches that sprouted. The wooden bodies ripped the sticks and roots off their bodies and beat them together as they shuffled a slow dance around the wood heart. The sinuous shape of claws faded into existence about the heart, though they were, in fact, the branches of a mighty tree. As the golems danced, the tree grew until it towered over them, the wooden heart ablaze in its trunk. Roses blossomed along the branches and from various points, vines dropped to the ground below. These tendrils slithered about the roots - the dreaming Bordeaux watched as one constricted itself around a nearby tree stump and hauled it from the ground. A stump revealed itself to be the head of a new golem, the body of which was wrenched above ground by the noose about its neck.

The wind had increased when Bordeaux awoke at length. A certain freshness in the air revived him as such as he was able to stand up again. It was then that he saw that the portion of beach on which he stood was in fact a sandbar, a sort of natural barrier dividing the tumult of the sea from a still inland lagoon. Though their similarities were obvious to the naked eye, Bordeaux felt strangely unsettled from his vantage point. To his left, the sea roared restlessly and shifted evermore in its being. The lagoon on his right, filled with the very same salty water, lay in pristine tranquility reflecting the sky like a mirror. The mangroves cut inverted patterns on the surface of the pool, while the clouds whispered across a canvas of stars.

Overwhelmed as he was, a realisation had dawned on him; the threat to his home, the onslaught of beasts that had placed the livelihood of Tenebrae Manor in doubt - it was internal. The great gem that he had found in Libra's possession; he had read of it in Rune's book. It was the heart of that ancient magic, the black rose tree. The wood golems were merely trying to retrieve that which belonged to their creator and it was Lady Libra who withheld it from them.

Across his tired face Bordeaux fashioned a grin and cursed his ignorance. The strange happenings in the forest, the numeral increase of monsters, the ascension of Lady Libra to the apex of Tenebrae's hierarchy - they all coincided perfectly. Libra has not overtaken him on her own merit - that powerful talisman had endowed higher magic prowess onto her! Bordeaux clasped at his skull in anger; it had been Libra who had brought peril to Tenebrae Manor. She had thieved that treasure and hoarded its powers for herself alone.

The wind paid no mind to his revelation; the demon stood at a loss. The answers were his but how helpless he was in this exile! How futile the knowledge that revealed itself to him! Would that he could beat upon the dunes with his fists, although his attention was presently arrested. The sea breeze had ushered in a change felt not by Bordeaux for ages.

He looked to the lagoon that stood bruised in the purple twilight of the setting moon. The leaves of the mangroves shone with a fiery brilliance, the twisted ruggedness of their muddy branches accentuated by the reflection of a light long foreign to him. Bordeaux turned to the sea and was awestruck.

Teasing the waves with golden highlights, the dawn poured onto the beach and it was not unlike the coveted painting that hung in his chambers back at the manor. But this was reality observed; Bordeaux squinted his crimson eyes and saw the sun rise for the first time in centuries.

XXV: Edweena & Crow Quarrel With Libra

For Edweena, it was the opportunity wasted that frustrated her most. So much as it seemed to linger about her stormy person with the loveless impressions of rain unrelenting. An opportunity that, had she indulged upon it, would have seen her any amount of leagues away from the disintegration of the mansion that confined her. Dragging her down with it toward crumbling foundation, Edweena felt more than ever before, a predetermined binding to this place - this place called 'home' through gritted teeth. Were she to pursue the harvest of her dream, she must surely now wait for a timelier hour. It had been Bordeaux that she had called upon through the sufferance of such internal anguish but pertaining to his costly vanishing, she had only herself with which to wallow in her brooding; and it was the challenge of channeling her anger towards a more fruitful solution that Edweena found most difficult.

She had been thankful for Crow, the one who had provided her with some consolation in wake of such mounting melancholia. Yet it was obvious to her that he lacked the wisdom of years. In Bordeaux, she had another eternal refuge from death with which to transpire the similar struggles of a life forever locked in its twilight. Edweena considered Libra; her oldest friend with whom the early years of her damnation had been received with some joy. The vampiress observed the way Libra coped - through means of suppressed denial and lust for dominion over what was still obtainable to one of her stature. But Edweena could not be pushed into these realms of the oblivious; a heightened sense of being had her constantly questioning her existence, a trait that she cursed.

Yes, the bats had flown and she was not amongst their black leather flight; Edweena felt now that responsibility beckoned her. Although she wanted to turn her dusky head to see where the bats had flown, she was instead called to protect those few who were her friends and the many whom she considered weaker than her. She had resisted the calling, ignoring the outstretched arm that would pull her from the quicksand. But the consideration of her decision had been made more difficult by the ruining of her favourite drawing room on the third floor. It had become so overrun with vines that she was now unable to gain entry.

This occurrence had driven her to the armoury of the household, a rusted hovel wrapped in stone and buried deep in the maze like topography of the manor. It was here amongst the disorderly regime of rusted swords and time eaten shields that she mused upon her sufferance. It was a cold and indifferent cave, not unlike those other moth-riddled rooms that populated the manor. When Edweena had properly lit the room, she had been as a child gazing at presents. Each weapon personified the sharpness of her angst and it was the deliverance of the sword strokes she proceeded to swing that brought release to her anger. She had chosen a sword less brittle in its archaism and, observed only by the faces of shields hanging on the walls, she was applauded as her stealthy arm threw the blade into a deadly rhythm. The silver sliver of the rapier cut the air and flowed like ribbons and, being so deeply entranced by her imaginary fight, Edweena was startled to see Libra standing at the doorway.

"Oh, my lady. I did not think anyone else…"

"Let us just forget the formalities, Edweena," said Libra in a surprisingly soft tone.

"Indeed, Libra."

"What were you doing with that old sword?"

"I supposed it might be beneficial," Edweena replied. "To fight away any threats. Those monsters seem more aggressive…"

Libra nodded empathetically. "That is a good idea."

They stood silent a moment, their eyes darting about in avoidance of eye contact.

"I, uh, I wanted to ask – why did to rescue me from that beast before?" queried Libra.

The vampiress shrugged. "I would not abandon a friend."

Edweena resumed her air swings, the blade whistling an echoing song.

Libra felt a compassionate throb in her chest, one she was not used to acknowledging; the idea that someone would put themselves ahead of another. The fact that she had been spared by what was a strained friendship softened her heart further.

"Thank you, Edweena."

The vampiress did not turn to face Libra for fear of revealing a smile, yet she shrugged again in response and grunted with each sword swing. Presently she spun about, half expecting the Lady to have departed from her presence but still she stood there. The corner of Edweena's mouth upturned as she proceeded to the pile of rusted swords and threw another at Libra's feet.

"I don't suppose you would honour me? They are dull, I assure you," she said.

Libra slowly stooped to retrieve the sword in her hand and she appeared instantly ill at ease with the weapon. She observed Edweena's lithe body with a jealous pang of her former years. There had been a time when they were both of equal stature.

"I, I couldn't. Not anymore."

Edweena rushed towards her with a belligerent swing that Libra had no choice but to block. The swords rang with a piercing pitch that echoed for some time as Edweena smirked venomously at her stunned opponent. Libra felt her blood boil with a zeal for dominance. She could not be beaten now, not in any faculty. She returned with her own smirk and laborious swing of the sword. A stealthy block from the vampiress absorbed the blow and she leapt back swiftly and eyed down Libra.

"Do you remember when Malistorm taught us to fight?" said Edweena.

"He told us ladies should not be so helpless," laughed Libra.

They flew at one another again and the swords, in

spite of their dilapidation, rang through the armoury with the shrewdness of newly tempered blades. The friendly battle was grossly one sided, pertaining in part to the restriction belayed by Libra's charcoal dress standard and physical sluggishness. The ability of the gorgon was desperately subpar, having rusted away with inactivity in similar fashion to the weapons the pair held. Libra could do little but block Edweena's swift cuts, whilst her own attacks were predictable and laboured.

The vampiress progressively forced Libra backwards, until only a few feet stood between them and the stonewall.

"I had forgotten," said Edweena between swings, "That you are left handed!"

"What of it?" Libra grunted and absorbed another volley.

"They say a left handed swordsman is doomed to fall – for they cannot guard their heart!"

With intention of sealing victory, Edweena took a further swing, one more violent than before. Though no sooner had she let fall her blow did she feel some strange resistance.

Her sword remained upheld in mid-slice, Libra's hand held aloft with quivering fingers shielding her with an invisible magic.

"Well, may I beat you to the punch, that the heartless need not worry about a heart," said Libra. "I find that sorcery serves me now."

Libra could see her opponent sweated with frustration. Edweena exhaled her vexation as the sword she held turned suddenly to ice and shattered to pieces on the floor.

The women backed away from one another. Flushed
a perspiring crimson, Libra gasped for air as she adjusted
the disheveled curls of her dark hair. Edweena gritted her
teeth from her thwarted attempt of relegating Libra back
to her former echelon. Her blue eyes turned to a certain
wall adorned with axes and mail and she retrieved a
weighty axe for herself.

"Axes?" said Libra. "Surely one scuffle is enough… I
am exhausted."

"Not for you," replied Edweena. "As much as I'd
enjoy it… This is for another purpose. My favourite room
is choked with that obnoxious overgrowth. I'm sure you've
noticed it smothering our home, though I'm not too sure
what the view is like from way up in your fancy
chambers."

From another shelf she grasped a more estimable
rapier embedded with brilliant onyxes and, leaving Libra in
her wake, made for the door.

"Well, then I bid my luck to you, *break a leg*,"
muttered Libra.

The vampiress allowed Libra to have the last word,
for she knew that was a match she could not hope to win.

The Lady gorgon huffed to herself and stamped her
foot to hear its sound reverberate about the room. The
lower of her cherry lips thrust forward in a pout and,
removing herself from an akimbo stance, took for herself
her own axe. Though lighter than the one Edweena had
taken, she found the thing manageable for her own
strengths and left the armoury in the darkness left behind
by the snuffed candles.

Libra's tread became an aimless shuffling between
rooms. That she intended to return to her quarters was

known, yet it was the journey manifested before this destination that inhibited her progress. And, coupling the apathy towards walking this considerable distance was her crestfallen disposition; so that, when she may have previously crept like a cat or sauntered like a proud pelican, she instead trudged with a jaded gait.

The passage that stretched from the armoury to the stairs unfolded in the darkness and appeared more like a tunnel than a hall. It was lit only at its ends by two candles weakening in their sconces. Like black satin, she drifted through the requiem of the halls and it seemed her melancholic sighs were the very energy that propelled her dreary body forward. The axe swung lazily by her side, occasionally snatching a reflection of light on its sickly sharp face from whatever change came in the intensity of the shadows. Minutes continued to tick by and Libra felt that the grip of her dictatorship over the residents of the manor weaken with the passing time.

She had reached the end of the armoury tunnel and bemoaned the sight of the stairs she now had to climb. Previously, she had been able to call on Madlyn to undertake such mundane errands. It was true that the girl's death had had a sobering effect on Lady Libra, although many would say that it was her losing a tool of servitude rather than the loss of a personal friend that grieved her.

The summit of the stairs gave way to the more elegant ground floor of Tenebrae Manor; Libra stopped for a moment to absorb the magnificence of the foyer around her. She leant upon the handle of the axe, brushed dust from her thigh and drank in the wondrous decor of her ruinous home. The cobwebs that hung from the chandeliers muted the baroque colours with a dusty veil that soothed the restless Libra. This was what she had wanted, the ruling of this mansion, to be queen of her own castle. Regardless of the dismal isolation that came with it, she had wanted it. And she had grasped it for her own - could it be that she was to lose what she fought for?

The restless frustration of her musings was joined by the shadow of company that appeared suddenly in the room. The apparition had been gliding swiftly towards an opposite door until, on observing Libra, checked its path and strode towards her.

The arrival of Crow brought the paramount of her bitterness to the front of her mind, something in the green of his tunic made Libra sick with repugnance. A mutual disdain for one another had kept previous engagements between the pair at a low, for both considered the other pretentious, with such insults being shared verbatim.

"My Lady, I was on my way to see you," said Crow, tipping himself into a bow that had to be forced from his mannered being.

"Can I not buy a moment of respite, Crow?"

"Such pleasure cannot be afforded at present, I am afraid."

"Then carry on and be swift about it," Libra drawled.

Crow had appeared hasty hitherto but Libra's uncouth belittling of him brought a vengeful sluggishness to his actions. He sauntered towards a rather ugly chair, leant upon its side and folded his arms.

"I had wanted to collaborate a plan of action, miss. With regards to the dire circumstances befalling us," said Crow, scratching at his chestnut curls.

Libra chose to stare absently about him, her bloated apathy taking on the form of disinterest.

"And why do you care so much? You don't live here."

Crow looked bemused. "I live in the same forest. Under the same trees, the same night. Please Libra; let us work together to bring order to this place. Let us make a plan!"

"For?"

"You cannot be serious!"

Libra smirked; childish as she knew her actions to be, the chance to fluster the wood hermit amused her. She tilted her head in mock pity and gave a pout that sparked anger in Crow.

"This house is disintegrating, the forest is overrun with violent monsters - you have already lost young Madlyn to this plague. Not to mention that other human that escaped from Sinders' grasp."

"One more human to go, I suppose," replied Libra.

Crow sighed. "I am ready to ignore that remark; I implore you, Libra. Take a stand. You want to be the leader over us all? Then deliver us from this!"

"You're the echo of a cymbal, Crow. Do you not think I know of all this? What would you have me do?"

"I have tried to like you, Libra. Respecting your rank is hard enough. I do not know what Malistorm saw in you; surely it is obvious that Bordeaux would have handled leadership better. Why he has not, can not, challenge your post baffles me - but that is now a futile matter."

Libra felt her hand tighten around the axe handle.

"Hear my plan," continued Crow. "Edweena and I propose a watch. With the able bodies of the manor, we take shifts circumnavigating the house and fighting back any interrogation - be it golem or those trees strangling the place to the ground."

"Do what you will."

"I plan to but know that you are not exempt. With the spells you boast, you should help us - many of us have only physical strength."

Libra moaned irritably, though she feigned enough acceptance of Crow's proposal that he seemed pleased.

"Edweena and I shall head two regiments. Rune is the only incapable resident. I would ask that you release Deadsol from imprisonment so he can assist us. I know not what has become of Bordeaux, though I've little doubt you have something to do with it. Relinquish him as well! Will you help me, Libra?"

"Is that all?" sighed Libra.

Crow held his tongue behind gritted teeth. "I hope to hear from you."

With a flutter of his cape, Crow left Libra to the dust and cobwebs of her musing.

Her temperament successfully flustered, Libra continued on towards her room. Such was the expanse of Tenebrae Manor that the densely packed rooms could be compared to the suburbs of a greater city.

Sidling through a gallery of paintings, she bemoaned her crippled status with the fierce portraits of former royalty.

They are no longer threatened by me.

The peril that surrounded the mansion had relegated her to the lesser menace, the smaller of two evils.

She passed by a somewhat ironic sunroom, whose comforts had never been adored. Even her banishment of Bordeaux and Deadsol had failed to strike fear in them. When Libra had gone through the small study and its collection of idle bookshelves, she knew she was almost there. Libra did not want the responsibility. Hitherto she had hidden behind her prominent power, delegating to others; the idea of showing admirable sovereignty in this hour of need filled her with dissatisfaction - this was not the reign Libra had designed for herself.

The final stairs to her room loomed insurmountable before her. But with a flush of bitter frustration, paired by considering herself worthy of a momentary reprieve, she hurled herself upwards and closed her doors.

XXVI: Adventures Afar

Adrift along the reeds that wove
Their tendrils on the silver cove,
A stranger stood aghast and mused
Upon the paths pursued.

A fright of fear and fraught with worry
Or be it optimistic flurry
Hurries on impatient wing
Bound for home or foreign fling?

The effect of sunlight on Bordeaux's physical being was one of crippling lethargy, a sapping of energy that meant he sat quite motionless on the dunes for several hours. As the midday sun burned down on his back, he lay in the maze of wind swept grey grass and observed the tricks of the light. It threw the shadows of grass stalks across the gold sand and gave the impression of tiger stripes; so accentuated were these shadows, that Bordeaux was engrossed by memories long past and, in his daze, the hours flew by in minutes.

He could not say how long it had been since he had last swum through the daylight. It was only once the sun had drifted past its pinnacle and begun to glide back down to the horizon that he felt sufficient enough strength to rise up and consider his situation.

The sea was magnificent; its great and heaving body sprawled across the expanse of the planet. And just when it seemed that the blue beast were about to rise up and swallow everything, its energy would wane and the waves would crash back down onto the shore with bubbled hiss. The lax nature of the ocean in some ways settled the heart of Bordeaux but the utter freedom now at his disposal presented a bigger problem. He now stood in the aftermath of chaos and though he was separated entirely from the dire predicament of Tenebrae Manor, there still remained the question of what he was now to do.

Knowing that the peril upon his old home persisted and that he was in possession of the likely solution, filled him with an urgent desire to race back to the mansion and rescue its residents from oblivion. Responsibility told him that such a rescue mission should be placed at the zenith of priorities. But how in the world could he do as such? On this foreign coastline, bereft of civilization, the horizon stretched in all directions. And to just assume that any random choice of direction would lead him back to Tenebrae was foolish. He would most certainly need a plan, yet the difficulties involved in locating himself and the manor invoked another idea.

The creeping relief of freedom teased at Bordeaux, it whispered to him that this was his chance. The world stood at his feet. He could forget Tenebrae Manor; forget the night, his friends and his post. A new life of change and endless possibility lay before him, though when he smiled at the idea of wayfaring, he swiftly turned to frowning. What point was there in him floating from place to place; like driftwood in these vast seas? Had Bordeaux not settled at Tenebrae to get away from such a life, to cast down an anchor in the night tide?

And to what point did he do anything? In such a large expanse, Bordeaux had never felt so trapped. At that moment, his entire life seemed futile and meaningless, his years but a chasing of the winds. The world turned, the orbs rose and set as had always done, yet now this sunlight, so beautiful to him a few hours earlier, now shone down with a certain staleness that exposed all the coldness of his feelings of isolation. There it hung at the sky's zenith; the pinnacle light bleeding onto the earth and leaving shadow with little place to hide. It cared not for Bordeaux's presence and it had not missed him through the centuries spent in eternal night.

Perhaps he had outstayed his welcome on the earth. As a demon he could not die, though he could destroy himself. The curse of his immortality plagued at Bordeaux's mind; would he dare take his own life? Age would not annihilate him. Were he to embrace a different kind of darkness, it would have to be by his own or another's hand. With him as a spirit, though miles away in physicality, the manor would fall with him. Those others doomed to wander the earth immortal would be homeless and left open to exposure.

No! He would not abandon his friends! So long as his consciousness remained rooted to this tangible reality, he would endure. If only for those he had governed in the darkness, he would deliver - such must be his purpose. The words of Lady Libra echoed in his ears; Eternity is a frightfully long time to spend alone...

Bordeaux stood up with renewed vigour and turned his back on the ocean. As he climbed through rugged sea cliffs and away from the beach, he planted in his mind the seed of an idea that he could only hope would blossom. If he were any hope of finding Tenebrae Manor again, he would need to first uncover a civilization of any kind. A town, a village - even one person who could speak and understand him would help.

The sun set on his first day in exile and with the rising moon came a gush of acclimatized energy. Soon he found himself atop the sea cliffs on a sort of plateau and moving quickly along its grassy top with increasing speed.

The open plain that draped itself in gentle slope settled the fretful Bordeaux and seemingly instilled a greater mobility upon him. It was as though the weight of his angst had eased and he was running for some time without fatigue as a result. Eventually, the terrain began to resist him, the grass grew thicker, the soil boggier and soon enough he found himself trudging through an oozy marshland. The moon was beginning to set and as the bruised sky lit up its corners, Bordeaux knew the dawn would arrive again in time. He cursed the slowing of his trek, for his apprehension increased with it and winced at the sight of his leather shoes becoming impossibly caked with mud. Pedant to a fault, he could not stand the sight of an unkempt personal appearance.

He sighed as he trudged, the shoulders of his burgundy coat crisp with salt, having earlier wrung the ocean from its fibers. Pungent morass surrounded him on all sides like a vast stretch of cloth thrown to the floor. The hillocks rose and fell unchanged in their treeless covering of swampy grass, given definition only by the shadows that sighed between them. The wind whispered by with ease and when the plain seemed to contract with dizzying inhale, the wind would change and the hills would bloat again with sickening distention.

Thus the day passed again. Twilight had dissipated into the blackness of evening when Bordeaux began to consider stopping for rest. His heart fluttered with hopelessness, surely this would be his end; trapped in impenetrable isolation. Yet a thread of hope would presently appear before him. It fashioned itself as a ribbon of road and fence running parallel and breaking the monotony of the endless and empty miles of marsh.

Bordeaux stared blankly; this road, though simple in its windings, readily became the first sign of advanced development he had seen in centuries; Tenebrae aside. It lay convex, an elevated portion of gravel and ran alongside a stone fence that came up to Bordeaux's waist.

Running a nail of his emaciated hand over the rough brick of wall he shuddered and ruminated another direction. The road stretched its arm either side of him and as far as his vision permitted. It separated the marshy hills like a natural border, leading the crimson demon to believe himself to be a pinhead stuck down onto an enormous map.

In a moment, the flush of panic enveloped him again, for he knew not which way down the road he should take. But soon as he readily reassured himself of the major purpose of any road - namely to connect two places, he realised that it did not matter which way he chose. As such, he set out in the direction that altered his trajectory more obtusely than the other.

To feel the solid ground underfoot proved welcome relief to the tiring Bordeaux. Ever onward he trudged, his pace soon becoming a weary drag and he took on the guise of one somnambulating. The sun rose again, however he took little notice of it. Rolling itself to the highest point in the oceanic sky and shining down onto his pale forehead, Bordeaux was able to discern that he must be headed in a southerly direction. He recalled the subtle things he had forgotten; the daylight calls of birds, the verdant reflection of light shimmering off tufts of grass greener than he could remember. But most prominently he recalled how quickly the time flew when he had both night and day dividing it.

He refused to stop in his wanderings. Though hunger and fatigue gnawed at his body, he persisted until nightfall came around again and with it, another revelation. When the hills had taken on their violet cloak given them by the darkness and the stars had lit their lanterns and hung as silent observers, Bordeaux noticed a light glowing in the distance. A dull glow of orange that, given the vast range of vision around him, must have still been several miles off if it were indeed what he thought it to be - a campfire. He had at first dismissed the light as a trick of his fraying consciousness, though the further he walked, the larger the glowing grew until there was no denying it to be a small fire. A fire which, as he crept closer in the darkness, presented itself as the centerpiece of a camp site of two travelers.

Around the flames they sat, casting lengthy shadows that exaggerated the minimal bulk of the pair. Bordeaux crouched so that the lengthy grass concealed him, paying no heed to the repugnant smell given off by the proximity of mud.

Two men, one much older than the other, huddled quietly about their little fire, which gave shape to the cart and horses that stood reined by the roadside. Bordeaux lay still for some time, the men none the wiser to the stranger in their presence. Both were dowdy, forgettable in appearance and no doubt peasants or simple workmen. The older man, with shoulders weighted heavily with age, plucked at the knots in his unkempt beard with a blade; his friend, an equally disheveled youth, stoked the flames with a stick. The scent of soup permeated the air and overran the odours of the marsh, channeling from a kettle that hung over the fire. The smell taunted Bordeaux and he readily mused over a course of action.

Surely these two strangers would assist a fellow vagabond lost in the marshes. The play unfolded in his mind; he would approach them and pledge peace and they would permit him to travel with them. Perhaps they could then inform him of his whereabouts and with such a basis,

Bordeaux might be able to discover the way back to
Tenebrae Manor.

Just as he was about to rise from the reeds and
approach, he stole back in a flash on an impulse of
realisation. Having heard the sound, the youth turned his
head from the fire and scanned the vicinity but the
shadows concealed the demon efficiently.

Bordeaux reached for his temple and probed at the
arisen issue - his horns. He was not dissimilar to the men
in any other way, however the two curled protuberances,
small though they were, would instantly give himself away
as a character of suspicion. Bordeaux had dealt with
simple-minded villagers in ages past, many times evading
the accusations of his demoniac notions through varying
measures. He wondered whether times had changed since
he had been at Tenebrae. The year was unknown to him,
the culture of the outside world completely alien. Perhaps
it would not be an issue?

No, he could not risk it and with no means to cover
his small horns, he was at a loss to determine the right
action. He would not need to decide, for another problem
arose when the old man suddenly opened his mouth and
muttered to his companion - they did not speak in a
language Bordeaux understood.

They spoke in short bursts, with Bordeaux unable to
denote the pauses between certain words so that their
voices slurred into an unintelligible drone. The crimson
demon focused intently; it was not in French that they
spoke, nor any of the Latin based tongues. No, this was
something different.

Although he could not be sure, Bordeaux assumed
the language to be that of a Slavic decent. The assumption

proved to be of little help; not only did he remain unaware of his location, he could in no way inquire of the two gentlemen before him. Deadsol had been of Russian decent; Bordeaux had often heard him speak the harsh tongue and pen the Cyrillic letters but even though there were similarities in the strangers' accents, he was not sure.

Bordeaux realised that his best bet would be to hide himself amongst their cargo and travel in secrecy. He circumnavigated the campsite, keeping at a distance that left him in the darkness. Cursing the sound of his legs swaying through the grass, he scooped up a pile of mud and hurled it away from him, so that the thud caught the attention of the wayfarers. They turned towards the noise and spoke to each other. The horses brayed uncomfortably and in the minor commotion of it all, Bordeaux threw his body onto the cart and hid amongst the load of barrels and sacks that sat there.

He had fallen into a fitful slumber. Aptly covered by a tarpaulin, Bordeaux awoke to the rocking of the cart as it rumbled down the road. The sun pierced through the fabric of his covering and stung his lethargy into play yet again. His stomach nagged with hunger and he could see a sack in front of him with a small tear in it, where a handful of grain that Bordeaux assumed to be rice poured through. He lifted his head quietly; the wayfarers had their backs turned to the cargo and were chatting to each other as the horses carried on. The scenery had not changed; the swampy hills carried on for miles around with the wind whistling so loudly that he could scarcely hear anything else.

But when Bordeaux had eagerly shoved the rice into his mouth, he noticed something peculiar that made him gag. Perhaps it was that he had not eaten in so long, or that the grain he ate was hardly nourishing, or more likely; that the carriage was traveling back the way he had come the day before. He felt at a loss; for how long would he be trapped in these marshes? The miles he had covered on foot yesterday were for naught, now that the cart drove in the opposite direction. Defeated, he let his head fall back down and again fell into a restless sleep.

The days passed in minutes. The crimson demon had lost count of how many times he had seen the sun and moon. There were times when he would wake and wonder if it was a new daylight he felt on his pale face or merely the same day he had counted before plunging into delirium. His strength was failing him. The rice from the broken sack was revolting and it took every effort not to expel every mouthful.

"Is this my punishment?" he mused to himself. "Maybe Tenebrae Manor was my purgatory... And this swamp, this endless rotting wasteland must be..."

Yet just when the crimson demon had consigned himself to the idea of an entire torture in the marshes, the winds ushered in a change so refreshing that his resolve steeled ever slightly. A crisp scent cut his nostrils and invigorated his person; the cart had reached a coast. The travelers seemed revived too; their long journey coming to a close, they spoke gaily amongst themselves, still unaware of the stranger in their cargo.

Bordeaux watched seagulls float in lazy circles above him and, eventually, he could hear the sounds of the sea as it crashed against a small harbour town that would be their destination. Perhaps salvation had come for Bordeaux or at least a further reprieve.

The voices of people, despite their foreign tongue, sung like music to his ears. Society, the bustle of a small port. Bordeaux could hardly believe such things still existed for him. Presently the cart came to a halt, the horses brayed and Bordeaux heard the crunch of the two men's footsteps around the cargo. He swiftly clambered into the empty rice sack and lay perfectly still. Bordeaux could hear the men grunting as they lobbed the cargo down onto the docks. Soon it was his own limp body that was thrown and he stifled a cry as he hit the deck with a thump. Bordeaux had arrived.

XXVII: Freeing Those Imprisoned

It was true that Tenebrae Manor suffered the strains of considerable tension at this point and that each character had innately scrambled to their own methods of weathering the menace of disturbance. In many cases, it had been a resorting to unification and standing firm against peril but for the spindly Arpage, it had been his natural affiliation to cowardice that had him scattered of mind and body.

When the golems had attacked the carriage as it returned from the cemetery, he had cannoned into the house without a thread of care for his friends and had not been seen since. The expanse of the mansion meant that none could track him down, were he indeed still within its walls; although one began to suspect that Arpage was lost in a sense that he could not find his own way about rather than having someone unsuccessfully trace him.

Notwithstanding his disappearance, he was indeed still inside Tenebrae Manor and yet he could find no other creature or room that he recognised. While he had momentarily wanted to vanish and to be safe from danger, Arpage was now yearning to find someone or something that he knew in this place he thought was home. How it could be that he could be lost in his own abode puzzled him greatly. However, the vacuous silence that met his cries filled him with sickening dread. The musician conceived horrid images of the friends slain at the hands of those monsters. And he, the dribbling coward, had escaped to an empty shell of a house. Perhaps he had been thrown into utter isolation, the only lively being of the manor. Like a hermit crab, he longed for his loft in the auditorium. To stroke the keys of his monstrous piano again, to nap on his dilapidated couch with inked smeared score sheets covering the dusty floorboards around him. Were he to absorb the sombrous acoustics of the auditorium again, he would feel complete. It would not matter what became of his friends. Arpage could hide in his guilt indefinitely. For he knew that if someone were to find him, surely they would reprimand him to such extent that isolation would be his only desire.

But the indecipherable mansion lay its artery-like corridors all about him and being of a disheveled state of mind, Arpage could not discern the correct path that would take him to his hovel at the higher stretches of Tenebrae. Heightening his frustrations was the omnipresent taunt of the auditorium itself; he could see its carbuncled protuberance from various vantage points around the house. Here, he could see its outer walls from the floor length window of an abandoned sitting room. There, he could see it from the covered walkway bridging two turrets. And as he sidled up a spiral stairwell through the shadows, the auditorium was there again, further away this time, seen through one of multiple arrow slit windows.

Up and around the stairs he climbed, until he was running frantically down another corridor. To his left, the moon shone down onto the sheer cliff face where the manor was perched, so Arpage was finally able to realise that he had reached its rear side. The pines jutted like spearheads across the valley and immediately below him was nothing but black void. How far he would fall before reaching the knuckled bottom, he did not know, for the moon played tricks with the shadows playing through the valley. So onwards he ran, in his attempt to plunge deeper into the bowels of Tenebrae, where he assumed his safety would be augmented.

Down more stairs he ran until he burst out into a cloistered courtyard enclosed on all sides by the high rising of architecture. And there was the auditorium again, high above him, camouflaged amongst the cityscape of roofs and windows of the ancient home. The auditorium taunted him - ominous, panoptic. He fell to his knees in despair.

"Curse the mountebanks who built this place! Damn their tangled artistry! That a man can be lost in his own home, the very idea!"

Arpage curled forward so that his forehead brushed the cobblestones as convulsing sobs drenched his flaccid hair with tears. So engrossed was he in his bemoaning that he did not notice the dark flash of a velvet ghoul watching him from the wall face high above him. From deathly blue eyes it stared, waiting with a spidery patience from a cobweb of ivy that strangled the castle wall. The apparition scuttled across the bricks and leapt over the quadrangle with chilling speed.

Arpage, having seen the shadow flash over his head, quivered with wretched timidity. He looked up at the walls above the cloisters and shook uncontrollably upon seeing the ivy rustling in varying places. The spider needed concealment no longer, for the prey was trapped. Its shadow crawled about Arpage in a wide circle, as though spinning a quietus of silk around him.

Before he could scream, the being advanced to him and when he peered from his fetal huddle to observe his captor, he saw only the arachnid grace of the vampiress Edweena.

"Lost?" she said, her voice husky as bruised onyx.

"Madam Edweena, indeed!" he cried and crawled forward so he could wrap his arms around her ankles.

"Such torment I have not known," he gasped as he kissed her feet. "It is worse than the desert of writer's block! Such loneliness! But now! You are here, oh sweet Edweena!"

Edweena placed her hands on her hips and huffed, "Stupid little man, it has been one week."

"A week?" cried Arpage. "And here was I thinking that time was lost at Tenebrae. Certainly given the drawling torture that was this week, it feels a thousand years have passed since I laid eyes on another!"

"It is a very big house, I suppose. Those forgotten architects certainly had their work cut out for them. But it is in fact good that I have found you," said Edweena.

She broke free of Arpage's clinging hands and glided towards the cloisters. She wrapped herself around a pillar and disappeared into the shadows.

"Good, yes. Good doesn't quite cover it, I'm afraid," said Arpage. "Splendid, wondrous, what have you."

"Follow me."

Arpage scrambled to his feet and ran after her into the darkness of a long hall, where the red carpet ran bloodstained beneath the cruel portraits of ancient barons. A sort of strange light encompassed Edweena and from the vantage point of the composer, she appeared as a brilliant shadow, shaped from the light of the candle she carried. The shape of her slim shoulders seemed so accentuated in the darkness that one would assume them carved from the sinuous candlelight. Her steps moved in glissando fashion, gliding like a finger across the keys of a great piano, brushed in a swoop of baritone.

"You will take me to my loft in the auditorium won't you, my sweet Halloween?" asked Arpage.

"That dusty old hovel?"

The composer struggled to keep up with the lithe vampiress and she refused to slow down or acknowledge him with the turn of her head.

"Yes, my dear," continued Arpage. "Like the dawn that lost its way to Tenebrae's trees, I too am lost. And my hovel, as you say, eludes me as this house eludes the earth and sun."

They continued their way through tallow soaked corridors and up slick staircases.

"After your foolishness at the farm, I'd say you do not deserve such a reprieve," said Edweena.

"The farm! Madam, I assure you, it was all the work of those other two! That scarecrow, that man!"

"Perhaps. But now the man, what was his name? He has escaped. What will you say if he finds civilization? What if the world buys his story?"

"The man Jethro, oh my word! I know the err

undertaken, be it my fault or another's," Arpage
bemoaned.

"You'd best hope that he is dubbed insane," said
Edweena. "Or better yet, that the fool falls to the dangers
of the forest and perishes swiftly."

"You would wish such a fate on a man? A painful
death?"

"To run through a deathly fire, knowing that rest
awaited on the other side. To die would be a peace…"

They came to a certain room that Arpage immediately
recognised; the room where Crow had brought in the body
of Madlyn, after Sinders and Arpage had escaped the fire.
The disorderly tea tray remained where it had been left and
mice had congregated around the crumbs that remained
scattered about tepid teacups.

And now they were back out in the front hall before
the grand staircase. Arpage flew to the foot of the stairs,
knowing that the auditorium was at the summit on the
right. Usher stood soldier still and watched the pair in
silence.

"Oh you did it!" squealed Arpage. "The path is
revealed, my precious auditorium at the zenith of these
very stairs!"

"Hold it, Arpage," said Edweena coldly.

The composer had placed one foot on the first step
and convulsed at her demanding tone. He half turned and
peered over his shoulder at her.

"I was not leading you to your loft, mister,"
continued Edweena. "Come. You and Sinders are to assist
me in patrolling the house."

"What? No!" cried the composer and he attempted to
dash up the stairs.

In a flash, Edweena had grabbed him by the ruff around his neck.

"Yes, I am afraid. No one is exempt. The manor needs every hand to help."

Arpage had begun to cry. "But me? Stopping those things? Impossible! And Sinders! It is through false smiles that I treat him civilly. I've grown an impatient indifference towards that scarecrow…"

"Well, if you want a loft to come back to," said Edweena, "you will come with me now."

Off in another direction she dragged the composer and, showing little resistance in defeat, Arpage allowed her to do so.

Commotion cluttered the halls of Tenebrae; the house groaned from its state of hibernation and, like ancient machinery, stirred into life. Yet beneath the castle, deep in the dark reaches of forgotten tombs, all was still. Only through the spinning of the spiders or the scurry of rats did life unveil itself. The silence was deafening. So encompassing that it played tricks and feigned noise. Was there a thud heard in a far off room? Could a clinking of chains be heard shivering from the blackness? Were any present to hear it, they would indeed hear a low and tortured wail echoing through the gloom. The cry of one in severe torment, though it seemed so far away that its source could never be located.

In the dungeons, Deadsol moaned in the pain of

isolation. He hung from the wall of the dank cell, an epitome of rust. Like the corroded bars of iron that enclosed him, he too was disintegrating. His own chains would not yield under his strains, for they were new and glistened with the reflections of whatever rare light they could catch.

Long since his feet gave way beneath him had Deadsol hung limp from his chained arms. The skin of his wrists stung with tender red welts from where he had tried to pull free. His face, once primped with a well-trimmed moustache now sagged under the shock of beard that spewed from his face. All was as it had been since he had broken free of his trance; Deadsol did not remember how he had come to be here, if he were to search the recesses of his mind for that moment when he'd rambled away from Comets under the hypnotic spell, he would come up empty. The only memory that lingered was the heavy shape of Libra before him; his groggy memory recalled her blurred shape chaining him to this wall before all had gone black.

The dungeons were damp with terrible isolation. Deadsol cried until his throat was raw in the vain hope that someone would find him. Yet he was always met with the same chilling quiet. And so it was that he hung there, lifeless and defeated, until there came a moment where he thought he could hear a noise nearby. It was a tiny step, scuffling on the dirt - a tread too heavy to be the scattering of a rat. No, this certainly sounded like the gait of a biped, Deadsol felt his heart race with anticipation.

"Hello? Friend?" he called. "Oh please, should there be anyone nearby who can hear me! Know my plea, unchain me from this iron evil!"

Knowing there stood a chance that his senses were failing him; that he could be only imagining the scuffling of nearby feet or the glow of a candle, Deadsol struggled to resist the temptation of believing salvation was near. A copper coloured flame burned steadily brighter and soon the shadows of the iron bars were thrown across his face. He squinted his eyes and made out the shape of a squatted human with a rabbit-eared hat and his ears sang with the familiar sound of bells ringing.

"The great Deadsol. What are you doing here?"

"Comets! Am I glad to see you! Awed, even! You've certainly come to save me, have you not?"

The jester put the lantern down in the floor and ran his gloved hands over the corroded prison bars. A jangling of his motley cap sounded as he pushed his tumid head between the bars.

"Perhaps Libra won't be pleased," he said. "But the Crow man has need of our services."

"Gentle boy!" sighed Deadsol. "I am indebted to you. Yet I must ask how you plan to deal with these chains?"

Comets tried to pull his head back through the bars but found himself pinned behind the ears. He exhumed a grunt and twisted his bulbous head to an inhumane angle so that he was able to free himself. Taking a step back, he stood with grand stature and withdrew a key from his red and yellow sleeve.

"Shall I reveal my secrets like the foolish magician? I have been rummaging through Lady Libra's bedroom."

"Scoundrel!" chuckled Deadsol. "Magnificent scoundrel! Come then, boy. Don't delay, the manor demands it."

Catlike, Comets jumped up and hung from the chains

of the ceiling so that he could reach Deadsol's locks. The shackles groaned and snapped open with Deadsol, forgetting to place his feet flat upon the ground, falling to his face. A sprightly leap and he was again on his feet, bristling with the renewed energy that came with the sweet taste of freedom.

"Now then!" said Deadsol. "You say that Crow wants us? We shan't keep him waiting, left to defend our walls by himself. Tenebrae Manor is in need! All puns intended, this is our darkest hour. To the crow's nest!"

"You look terrible," replied Comets.

"Such awful words, beast. I should clock you. Though you are correct, one surely cannot pose for victory looking like this!"

It was as though he had never been imprisoned; Deadsol sprinted recklessly into the darkness with Comets struggling to keep up. The copper demon, reunited with his diligent lackey, ran until his lungs burned. His laughter filled the sobered void of the manor.

They reached their favourite drawing room and Deadsol pranced into an adjoining ensuite.

"What a disgrace this is," he muttered.

"How can you complain now?"

"Ah, true that the dungeon was dank. But it is nothing compared to the state of this bathroom. Look at this grime!"

"It hasn't been used since you left," replied Comets. Deadsol turned the handle of a gold tap where, after a considerable pause, followed but an expulsion of dirty fluid, clear water ran freely. His reflection in the mirror portrayed a haggard ruffian that was startling to gaze upon.

"This will not do at all, deary," he said. Turning to

Comets, he continued. "Really Comets, can I buy a moment of peace to attend to this unshaven monster in dire need of whittling?"

The jester did not need to be told twice, leaving Deadsol to attend to his ablutions. As the door slammed briskly behind him, Comets ensconced on the nearby floor and waited patiently. A cheery conglomerate of hums and whistles entangled with the rushing water and whispered under the doorframe in a wisp of steam.

Deadsol's voice was muffled by the wall that divided them. "It seems a grey fire has spread atop the forest of my scalp! Far more salt than pepper these days, my boy."

"Do hurry up, D," replied Comets.

Deadsol appeared to have ignored his friend and resumed his humming. The crisp glass clink of a razor on basin was heard, not before the snip of scissors and the duck-like snort of Deadsol as he rinsed his face in his hands.

"This dishevelment is a most unpardonable offense."

The minutes ticked by and Comets grew impatient.

"Why do you tarry so?"

"Art cannot be rushed, dear lad. I must prim myself for battle."

In the corner of the drawing room, a great clock bellowed out its hour call and Comets could not wait any longer. He slammed his fists against the door with such force that the wood might splinter.

"Move, move!"

The door opened just as Comets swung his fists again and he fell to the floor. Gazing up, he saw the copper demon standing akimbo with unmatched pomp. Deadsol had removed his beard so all that remained was his thick moustache, which was trimmed straight to impeccable perfection. His hair had been combed with a neat part on the side, enwrapping his stately head. A clean cravat blossomed from the chest of an ironed brown coat and complemented his accessories - fresh leather shoes and a magnificent rose gold ring on his right hand.

Comets stared in awe at his friend. He knew Deadsol to be proper in his own lunacy but never had he seen him dressed so well.

"Excuse my delay, Comets. Our lady Tenebrae needs us and a gentleman should always give importance to his appearance."

"You are excused," replied Comets, who suddenly felt more bedraggled than he had ever felt before.

Deadsol strode gaily to the mantelpiece, where his favourite walking cane awaited his grasp. Its reddish gold handle matched the beauty of his ring and, after bouncing the point of the cane on the ground he raised it above his head, "To the crow's nest!"

And Comets cawed with tenacity.

Even with the winds of chaos lashing at the house, below it the mute chef remained oblivious. Ignorant as he remained to the peril placed under his home - and by extension himself, he had pottered about his kitchens. Like a crab on the floor of the deep sea, he scuttled and who was he to be perturbed by the vicious currents that stirred the upper waters? None had informed him of any intercepting command that would conflict with his usual station and as such, he continued to carry on in his duties.

It was only once he had taken note of a certain silence that he pursed his bulldog-like brow and began feeling discomforted. A certain silence that had little to do with noise itself but rather a change in the bustle of the sweat stained kitchens. Even in his deafness the chef could discern this silence. It was as though the seemingly living organism that was the kitchen had been dissected of something. A benign something, to be sure, as one who loses a tooth can acknowledge its absence and continue with full functionality of mouth.

Disoriented by this void, the chef sorely felt a phantom strike at his nerve endings. Not even the realisation of what nagged him could satisfy this itch; when he finally noticed that the girl was missing, his thoughts shifted immediately to the where and why.

Madlyn had disappeared so discreetly from his life that he scarcely paid mind, to the point that he had reveled in the systematic order it procured. His work had been far more efficient without her clumsiness and the mere fact that Libra had not complained to him recently stood as proof.

Ever busy, he remained in the tireless effort involved in quenching Libra's appetite. This, coinciding with his job of providing food for the other house members meant that he was working endlessly. When Madlyn had come into his life little over a year previous, the chef had seen it as an opportunity to relinquish some responsibility onto another; giving him some well earned rest in the process. But Madlyn's frailty of mind and ability eventually meant that the chef was doing even more work to make up for the girl's shortcomings. All the same, he had noticed her absence and felt the fluttering of nostalgia in his heart. He wouldn't mind having her around again, she was hopeless to be sure but he certainly enjoyed the company. It was true that he could not talk or hear; yet the presence of another was most welcome to his aging and lonely heart, particularly given their similarly hindered intellect.

The mute chef did not know Madlyn had died. In the heat of the moment, none had thought to inform the man who spent the most time with her and, as such, he obliviously waddled to the small room where Madlyn had slept. The room had always been bare, though now it seemed emptier than ever. Where was Madlyn? Why hadn't anybody told the chef of her fate?

There was nothing on the old rotted desk, save a small sheet of paper that, in the absence of wind or other disturbance, had sat unprovoked with the dust settling on its surface. The mute chef picked the paper up in his meaty fingers. He was not much for a vocabulary, nor did his sight permit extensive reading. Yet he could read the elementary scribbles of Madlyn quite easily. The note was addressed to him -

Dear Chefy,

I am gone forever.

- M.

The mute chef, despite his ignorance towards Madlyn's death, took this note as a permanent parting word. And when he had finished reading, his body convulsed into huge and heavy sobs.

And at that moment, the years of loneliness overwhelmed him completely.

XXVIII: Old Town

Above him came the clatter of busy feet on the boardwalks. For his eyes, the fulgurant sunlight that threw its luminance in stripes betwixt the wooden planks, shifting and changing as the shadows of people slid along atop. Throughout the dreary narcosis, befriended by the muffled voices of other beings, the low droning of the sea washed onwards. Bordeaux drifted in and out of sleep like a newborn, comforted by the cradling bay waters that slapped carelessly against nearby boat hulls. He could not move yet. Having been thrown into some sort of loading dock, the demon chose to await the coming night before venturing further. The sweet cries of seagulls rang like Christmas bells; the warm air about him evoked a sensation of bustling festivity. Though exceedingly eager, yet Bordeaux remained in concealment lest he was prematurely discovered for the demon he was. And suffering of crippling fatigue, his body convinced his mind to stay still a little while longer.

As the sea carried on its restless rocking, the bustle of
the harbour began to subside as the evening interluded.
Bordeaux steadily stood on his feet and stretched his
limbs, sucking in the calm of the salty air. Physically he was
looking a tad worse for wear; his coat was dirty, his shoes
were scuffed and the first signs of five o'clock shadow
speckled his gaunt jaw. Yet he remained primarily
concerned with the covering of his small horns. He ruffled
the long red curls of his hair so that the horns were
disguised somewhat, before climbing a small rope ladder
to the wharf above. No living being met his entrance, lest
one were to count the now silent seagulls nesting high on
the masts of boats.

The crimson demon surveyed his surroundings; he
had been brought to some small port town. The bay was
tangled with the buoyant traffic of sailboats whose masts
crisscrossed the scene as they bounced on the water's
surface. Ropes were strewn everywhere across a cluttering
of barrels and crates.

The night was sick with the stench of low tide and an
enormous ship that sat anchored in the bay caught
Bordeaux's attention. Its sails were flaccid in the still calm,
yet it exuded dominance over the entire town. Buildings
spread from the shore and up a mountain that nestled in
the backdrop.

Bordeaux gazed with awe at the first town he had
seen in centuries. The steps he took towards the streets
were slow and cautious, though it seemed that the
townsfolk had retired indoors for the night. As such, he
was soon walking freely in the dim glow of moth clustered
street lanterns, until the sound of a door opening made
him leap for the shadows of an alleyway. Bordeaux saw the

door in question, the frontage of a double storey wooden building that he took for a shop or hotel. A man had stepped through the threshold and stood farewelling an unseen figure within. They spoke in that same distant language that Bordeaux could not understand; yet it was the hat and coat held by the man that the demon desired. Pleasantries finished, the door closed and the man stood in darkness readying himself to put on his coat. Bordeaux saw his chance and dashed towards him, snatching both hat and coat from the startled man, who had little time to react to such thievery. Though the man shouted at Bordeaux and wrung his fists, the demon had already disappeared into the dank alley mists and was gone.

When he was convinced that no one had followed him, Bordeaux squatted in a lane and analysed his bounty. The fedora hat was beige, as was the rather shabby coat. He concluded that the man must have been of a middle class status, likely to be able to buy himself a new coat and hat. These thoughts abated Bordeaux's guilt, though it was soon renewed when he found a certain coat pocket full of currency. His palm opened and he prodded at its contents like one cradling an injured bird. Two bank notes unfurled, housing a fistful of copper and silver coins. Bordeaux praised his luck, albeit he did not know just how valuable the money he had was. Stuffing the money back into the coat, he stood and dressed himself with the hat using a puddle to observe his reflection. The hat fit him well, perhaps both it and the coat were a little too large for him but they at least left him looking like nothing more than an ordinary man.

It was with great anxiety that Bordeaux braved the social pool of an old tavern; nonetheless the night was wearing on at this point, which meant that only a few straggling drunkards remained at the bar. Despite his fears, none turned to take notice of his entrance, so he moved toward the bar and took a seat. A rather roughshod bartender acknowledged him and Bordeaux clasped at his throat to feign an inability to talk. He motioned for a drink and held his money in his open palm at the bartender. A seemingly perfunctory response came from the bartender, much to Bordeaux's relief and, taking a few of the coins from the demon's hand, he returned in time with a stein of beer and a small loaf of bread. It was a simple act of servitude, yet it had such an effect on Bordeaux that he felt his eyes become wet with gratitude.

He tore ravenously at the bread and although he had no seasoning or spread, after days of malnourishment, it was, to him, the sweetest thing he had ever eaten. This overwhelming of his senses was ever increasing, inasmuch as he feared he would be unable to restrain himself and cry out - cry with glee, torment, sorrow; he could not tell which. The remaining coins lay on the table next to his beer mug. By looking at them it became apparent that they were dull with years of use. Depicting some figure of royalty unknown to him, the circling letters on the coin faces were also foreign. He was however, able to read the years that the coins were minted and was shocked at the results.

"1793... 1801... 1779..." he muttered in awe.

Had he really been gone from the world so long? In a night so unending, he had never taken note of time at Tenebrae Manor. The demon had long considered the mansion a permanent home and the very concept of time had grown so alien to him. These coins told the story of the outside world; several centuries had passed since Bordeaux had last bothered to remember the year. It made him shudder to think of the world around him that may as well have been another planet.

"I have to get home," he whispered.

For days he had mused on the best plan of action. He wondered whether a map would help him. But who could say how many miles separated him from the manor? There was every chance that any map he discovered would be of slim help. Stargazing was another option; perhaps he could look to the heavens and see a constellation he recognised, one that could lead him in the correct direction. Again this idea seemed too small a thought. This was a massive world, Bordeaux knew as such from his travellings in the days before Tenebrae. Days when he was newly demonic and his life as a human had recently ended. His best and only hope remained in simply choosing a direction that felt right; it may be that instinct would reign over all.

The thought of lodging in a comfortable bed tempted Bordeaux, until he realised the sheer foolishness of spending his remaining money. Bearing that, he returned to the loading dock by the wharves and curled up behind a few sacks and barrels.

However, he did not sleep for long. Soon he awoke in the full light of mid-morning and decided that he should explore this town and plan his next move. His hat and coat meant he was disguised splendidly, for he looked like nothing more than a pale stranger. The harbour was alive with commotion. Children ran through a forest of legs, laughing as they tried to hide from their friends in the crowd. Women yelled from awning-covered stalls and advertised their wares of food and fabric. Burly mariners loaded their rowboats, ready to stride out to the massive sail ship that awaited them. At his feet, chickens sauntered aimlessly with seagulls, pecking at the ground for vagabond grains with the same pluckiness of pick pockets that lurked amongst the townsfolk.

It took Bordeaux an entire morning to circle the bay-hugged crescent of the village. From his wanderings he discovered two roads that led out of town, one at either end to the north and south. The south road, which coincidentally revealed itself to him first, appeared to be that very road in which he had entered as a stowaway. This, he knew, would throw him back into the swampy hills from whence he had come. A sense of foreboding shuddered down his back as the stale sun shone down on the road. It was no doubt the fear of being lost in those ghastly marshes again that made him turn back into the town and try again to find an exit route.

The northern road was different. Granted, he could not see very far along it until it curved around a grassy mound. A dusty trail that lay flat until it curved away from the coast and into parts unseen behind a row of tall juniper trees. In all, there was nothing unusual about this road. Yet Bordeaux was impossibly transfixed on it and that point where it turned behind the hill and out of sight beckoned him to pursue. Could he trust his instincts?

There was no time to lose. The longer he tarried, the less likely he was to find Tenebrae Manor and greater the chance of his friends perishing at the hands of that rebelling forest. Bordeaux needed a means of transportation if he were to cover enough ground. Starting down the road in a brisk walk he pondered to himself.

"I could stow away on that ship... No! I am certain

that I am still within reach of Tenebrae by land. Surely Libra's power was not so great as to throw me across oceans. But I cannot wait for another cargo cart as before! What I need is a horse..."

If it were indeed a Slavonic dialect he was hearing from the townsfolk, then that would surely place him within his known world; that he was somewhere on that great Eurasian landmass.

Bordeaux strained to recall those final few years before he had concealed himself in Tenebrae Forest. How was it that he could not remember the location of the manor? Trees - conifers everywhere, Tenebrae Manor may as well have been a desert island in an endless ocean. The crimson demon remembered little about how he came to be in the grasp of the eternal night; all that remained behind in the residue of his mind was a ghostly image of Malistorm, the former baron. The one who had introduced him to that infernal world of shadows and dark flames.

Memories clouded the vision of Bordeaux, so that he soon had to check himself and pull to a halt on the road. He was not thinking straight; it would be unwise to just hurl himself down this road and hope for the best. What would he eat? How would he shelter himself? How did he assume to cover so much ground on foot?

He looked back towards the town, then again at the road beyond, when something caught his eye. Perhaps merely the fleeting hallucination of weariness, or a phantom's trickery, Bordeaux could have sworn that he discerned the figure of a familiar girl on the road ahead. But when he looked properly, there was of course nothing to see but the muddy trail across the winding hills.

With a nagging tug at his heartstrings, he turned his

feet back towards the harbour and headed back into the village.

XXIX: Libra's Lament

In Libra's room, stillness dominated over all. The chaise lounge lay in the static. At the vanity, bottles of perfumes stood silent as soldiers, crystalline as the sky after the storm passes. Libra's enormous bed was, not surprisingly, unmade and its disheveled sheets flowed in billowy swathes to the floor. Yet they did not flow as per definition of the word - they were still. Like a river frozen over winter, they were silenced and only insinuated the thought of ever flowing like water.

Another dark sheet floated in the middle of the room. It hovered like a ghost and any betrayal of a footing on which it stood was lost to the shadows at its base. It was a pedestal of course, covered by a sheet, yet even the boldest heart would for a moment doubt their sight when first laying eyes on it. They would feel their heart lurch but for a second and all the childish terrors of their infancy would flood back to them, only to be abated by matured reality.

The silence breathed in sharply, as though of shock, stifling as one who steps into icy waters. What followed was a bloated exhale and as the walls seemed to breathe, a creaking scuttle echoed in the dim. A cockroach crawled aimlessly over the floor. In the candlelight, it looked as if the flagstones themselves were moving or that an ever-shifting stain marked the carpet. Its antennae twitched; the roach had detected something. Was it another sigh or another flint of movement striking the scene? The insect resumed its shuffle and never saw the great silk-slippered foot descend upon it and crush it to death most instantly.

Lady Libra, who had been sitting statuesque at the window the entire time, grimaced at the repulsive sight of the crushed creature and scraped her shoe clean with the butt end of the axe. Propping the axe back up against the wall, she returned to her vacant gazing of the forest below her window. The vines suffocating the manor had almost reached her window at the very top. While the others had rushed to defending the walls she had remained stationary, her apathy spoke greatly of her personal defeat, of the turmoil she continued to suffer.

Libra had glanced at the sheet-draped pedestal when her thoughts were interrupted by a knock at her door.

Her voice had lain long in disuse, so she twice had to croak, "Come in."

The door opened to the svelte shadow of Edweena. The vampiress stormed in like a draught of cold air in the warm room, completely disrupting the cautious stagnation of Libra's musing. She sheathed her rapier and threw the severed head of a wood golem at Libra's feet.

"They've surrounded us entirely. Impossibly sluggish at the best of times, though some are more adroit than others. A few would advance at us unawares and try to catch us off guard."

Lady Libra regarded the head with minimal interest. She nudged the root-mangled thing with her foot and watched as clots of soil fell from its face.

"Hmm. And the trees latching to my home; did you prune them?"

Edweena almost laughed, "Prune is one way of placing it. Swords slice through them with ease but they're painfully persistent. Some vines had already begun to grow again by the time Crow's regiment relieved us."

Libra's voice was dismissive and slow. "Well, good. You got what you want from this silly watch. Anything else?"

"Anything else?" said Edweena with rising anger. "Libra please see sense! This cannot be ongoing. We are buying time only. It is your responsibility to guide us from this mess. A mess that you must have insight of in some way."

"So you opt to accuse me?"

"Much as I hate to delate you, Libra; but you surely must have noticed that these rebelling forest monsters coincided perfectly with your ascension. Tenebrae Manor was locked in darkled calm for centuries, you know this!"

"Not my fault!" huffed Libra.

"I have never known such childishness! You impossible thing! Whether you had something to do with it, I do not know. Frankly, that is irrelevant. But 'sorcery serves', as you said. You have the spells, the aptitude and the rank to put an end to this. We can only hold out a little longer - lest Tenebrae become doomed."

Libra lagged for a moment. "Why do you care

anyway? You were always in such a hurry to stray from the stagnant. Why would it matter to you what happened to this dusty old place?"

"Because it is our home!" Edweena's voice dropped to a more compassionate tone. "My friends live here. What can I say to make you help us?"

Libra paused. "I am considering a few ideas..."

Edweena threw her hands to her hips and huffed with vexation. She looked visibly fatigued by her efforts. "The scarecrow and Arpage are of little help," she said. "They are far more likely to fall sooner rather than later. Would you really lose more after what happened to Madlyn?"

"I said," replied Libra slowly, "I am considering a few ideas."

"You will only move when a fire is lit under you."

Edweena then left Libra, having added bruising words to her brooding.

Libra sat perfectly still for but a few seconds, waiting until the steps of Edweena dwindled into nothingness. When she was certain her rival was gone, Libra raced to the door and slammed the lock shut. Her eyes locked greedily onto the pedestal as her hands tugged at the cloth to unveil her frightening amulet, which glowed with an eerie beauty. The thing was illuminated with an indifferent kaleidoscope of colours, flashing calmly between hues. This relic, the wood heart, was the sole reason for the chaos that gripped the manor; the impetus to Libra's dominance over the other residents of the house, the reason she had been able to rule uncontested as their supreme despot. To run her hands over it was to feel extraordinary energy channel into her veins and this power left her in a lulling calm. With such force at her disposal

Libra felt invincible and she certainly was peerless in her quest to reign over Tenebrae.

But now she found herself in a prominent predicament; the wood golems wanted the heart back. She had known it from the very beginning, having stolen it unrightfully for herself several years previous when Malistorm still ruled the mansion. It appeared that the wood heart, in spite of its awesome power, would not resist being lured back to the hands of the golems, who would return it to the Black Rose Tree where it belonged.

Lady Libra was at a loss and in the purest of denial of her influence in the situation. To hand back the thing would rob her of all magical force and leave her monarchy ripe for the plucking by any of the other residents of the manor. Yet she knew that things could not continue as at present – the golems were slowly destroying the house. Their pace was ever increasing; it would not be long until the trees had asphyxiated it to its very foundations and the house become any more than a ruinous blemish in the endless trees.

Much as she had tried to wash the blood from her hands, to sweep the entire issue under the rug, Libra was under intense pressure from all sides to relinquish her denial and fix what she had broken. She knew that the fate of the house and all those who resided with was entirely up to her.

Libra found her thoughts turning to Bordeaux. The crimson demon had been an enviable presence to her; his humility and leadership something she coveted greatly. But it was just not in her to rule with such sovereign concord. She wanted to be worshiped as greatness! Where could Bordeaux have ended up? In her fury, she had merely channeled the power of the wood heart into what had been her most powerful magic spell yet. Bordeaux had been flung across dimensions, teleported for lack of a better word and of where he had ended up, Libra was completely ignorant.

She now regretted the actions of her anger; if Bordeaux were here, he would be able to bring order to the forest. Although it may have seemed that Libra had rid herself of her most threatening competitor, she had in actuality banished their best source of salvation. And now, when she would have normally cast off all responsibility onto others, she was now expected to bear the burden herself.

She turned back to the wood heart, the glow of which painted the walls with fantastic flames that inflicted Libra with an unshakeable nostalgia. Memories blazed in her dusky head as her amber eyes dove deep into the flames; she fell into a sort of trance at the sight of such unreckoned beauty.

The flames flickered, the flames flashed and from her tangled memory, she thought she heard a familiar voice echo through the void.

"Your tenacity is admirable, Libra; you would make a defiant leader."

A svelte, younger Libra simpered at such flattery.

"Better than Bordeaux?" she replied.

Malistorm stood at the window and stared out into the darkled trees. Though heavily sunken with fatigue, his eyes pierced with terrifying ascendancy.

"There are two kinds of sovereignty, Libra. Those who rule with intimidation and those who rule with humility. The difference between the two is that humility will please all, intimidation will please only one."

He had never said which one was better. Always a figure of mystique, even during his life at Tenebrae Manor, Malistorm never revealed more than his intention. It remained unknown to her how Tenebrae came to be built, perhaps Malistorm himself did not know. He alone stood as the oldest resident of the archaic walls, its peerless leader. From the highest spire of the house, he looked down on his moonlit province like a purple eidolon, in a state where he could disappear with the shake of his cloak in the event that anyone should disturb his brooding. His ruling was like that of a strict parent, never did he express any personal emotion lest he surrender his coerce authority.

The flames receded, the flames reformed and from her cobwebbed mind, another memory was born.

"The world is a place much darker than here..." he had said. "Let this forest be your recluse. This is our domain, this place closer to the other dimensions than anywhere else. Wondrous terror is attainable only here, while the rest of the world is abandoning the supernatural to the scientific..."

Whether he was once man or some eternal sentinel, how Malistorm came to be remained unknown, even to those who knew him best - Bordeaux, Edweena, Rune. Yet he reserved a special fondness for Libra. And to her, he was a sort of dark angel, her guardian.

"You are brash, young lady. A valuable trait in a world painfully suspicious of sin and witchcraft. We are banished, Libra. This dark corner of the world is our only solitude."

"But why here?" replied Libra. "Why this isolation?

Who chose this site for our abode? Who built this house and when?"

"Unimportant."

"I must know!"

The magician heaved a sigh that divulged the true decaying of his aging face. Yet it was not with age that Malistorm's wrinkles grew deeper, it seemed more related to the heaviness he carried in his heart at all times. Libra's excessive yearning for self-illumination wore him down in one sense and reminded him of years earlier when he too had swam in the same waters of youthful persistence.

"I will show you something very important, Libra," he said. "You must divulge it to nobody…"

The gorgon's eyes blossomed with greed; it did not matter what Malistorm had to say, the fact that she was the only one to hear it was important.

Malistorm had led her to the library, where they had retrieved a book so old that it had begun to unravel at the spine. The pages were clotted with cavities, the leather brushing away like dust along its cover. The pair had then returned to Malistorm's study at the top of the manor, the very room Libra now clamed as her own fantastic bedroom. And Libra, bristling with anticipation, felt the greed that burned in her core singe the back of her throat.

"In this book, Libra… You will find the very spell that keeps the shroud of darkness over our Tenebrae Manor."

"That very spell?" gasped Libra; "I had thought you only knew it by heart!"

"It may have seemed like me to do as such, alas no." He trailed off and again stared out into the forest. "I do not know what the years ahead hold for me. It was best that I write the spell down somewhere, lest my pretty little minions be exposed to the hideous daylight."

"And you are going to teach me?"

"It is a difficult spell but not something you haven't trained for. Should I be, shall we say, indisposed, I believe you will be capable of carrying on the spell in my stead." Libra leaned towards him. "And be queen over Tenebrae Manor?"

Malistorm held his skeletal palm aloft to hush her and standing a good foot taller than her, needed no words to reinforce his governance.

"I did not say you would be a queen," he said. "I would merely have you in charge of our most vital spell. This is no small task!"

Libra pouted playfully but Malistorm had not finished and she took instant umbrage to the words that followed.

"I envisage Bordeaux succeeding me."

Her eyes bulged, the white around those amber irises burning irate.

"Do not look at me so, Libra," continued Malistorm. "Some are natural governors and I see this as the best use of Bordeaux's abilities."

Under the tempering flames of her anger, the beauty of her face took on a new life of exquisiteness and she wanted nothing more than to slay Malistorm in that instant and take reign for herself. But no, she could not do that. Surely she would not be capable of such a black deed, even in her rage. She thought of bursting from the room in a huff, though that too would not be beneficial. A piece of the most priceless knowledge of Tenebrae Manor was being presented to her; she would be a fool to ignore it. The flames receded, the flames reformed and from her cobwebbed mind, another memory was born.

Time flew past in rushes and lulls, though neither could be properly discerned in the constant night. Libra had gloated to Bordeaux and Edweena, taunting them with Malistorm's trust. The magician had carried about his stern yet gentle governance, the brush of his violet cloak shielding them from the harmfulness of the outside world.

Libra continued to practice her magic and sword skills, remaining a diligent pupil in hopes of one day proving her master wrong. She could rule Tenebrae. And she would.

Soon, Malistorm began speaking to Libra of another mystery.

"A black rose tree…" he pointed at a sketch in a mighty tome.

"It is beautiful."

"There is no tree quite like it. Its blossoms are said to be the most extravagant one could hope to lay eyes on."

"Where can we find one?"

"I do not know," replied Malistorm. "I do know that they grow sparsely in this forest. Perhaps there is only one. Perhaps it is merely an abnormality formed from centuries spent in darkness. But look closer…"

Libra leaned towards the page and observed the glowing hollow in the trunk of the tree.

"A wooden heart," said Malistorm. "It glows with a flame that will never be extinguished. It is as though this kindling can never be exhausted and it is said to be unbelievably powerful."

"How powerful?"

Malistorm strode to the window. "None could oppose you."

The flames receded, the flames reformed and from her cobwebbed mind, another memory was born.

The two of them had conspired to retrieve it, after which, several scouting missions proved fruitless. Libra was sucked into the same seclusion of temperament portrayed in Malistorm, so that even Edweena, her best friend, could not decipher her.

"Where have you been hiding yourself, Libra?" said Edweena. "The forest is ripe with mischief, yet I cannot find you recently."

"I'm... Busy," came the distracted reply.

"I loathe such inactivity! When such energy flows through me, I simply must give into it... Though I am missing your company."

Libra was barely listening.

"I am going out for a while, Libra," came Malistorm's ghostly murmur.

"Where?"

He did not answer. Simply pulling up the collar of his cloak, he vanished from the house like a king of vampire bats. Though his words had been vague as usual, Libra had taken notice of a certain oddity in his tone which she didn't understand, even in the present time. Malistorm did not return to Tenebrae Manor.

The flames receded, the flames reformed and from her cobwebbed mind, another memory was born.

Stricken by his vanishing, leaderless in the shadows,

those apparitions left behind waited in uncertainty. What had become of their baron, they would never know.

All was not lost, so long as Libra knew the spell of eternal night. But it was Libra who wore a sneaking suspicion as to Malistorm's fate.

She foraged through the notes in his study, searching for any lead to his whereabouts. Upon uncovering his final scribbled notes, including a crudely drafted map of a certain area of forest, Libra set off on her own hunt. She remembered the ease in which her fit body had torn through the woods. Lithe as a black panther, she raced to an unexplored part of the trees without so little as a sweat. The tree carried grotesque grandeur, so much that Libra wondered how it had not been discovered earlier. Although she soon realised that to find one particular tree in a forest was indeed similar to finding a needle in a haystack.

It was undeniably the very treasure she had been searching for. Gnarled branches twisted from its thick bole so that the furthest twigs spanned in an impressive circumference. Along its branches there sprouted an unusual blossom; roses glistened with midnight dew, shining sharp as swords. The ground beneath the tree was littered with the footholds and potholes created by those great roots that burst from the dusty ground in all directions, dotted with fallen blooms of the aforementioned roses.

Libra readily stooped down and picked one up, admiring its beauty, before gazing at the tree it fell from. One feature stood dominant over all - that of blackness as dark as all night, all coal, onyx and ebony. The black rose tree; it was distinguishably dark even under the night sky, where vision was difficult.

Libra trembled at the ominous sight, for she could discern her prize from where she stood, some fifty feet from the tree. Separating itself from the monochromatic scheme of its surroundings, the wood heart glowed from within a hollow of the trunk, beckoning her with its beauty. This was it and her eyes did not deceive her; the very relic she and Malistorm had yearned for sat before her. With it, she would be unmatched. Even Bordeaux would not be able to match her in power. She would rule the manor by force if she had to. The wood heart! She had to take it.

As Libra stepped towards the tree, she felt as though it acknowledged her presence, for the branches shuddered on a sudden, unaided by the windless atmosphere. Libra crept warily but still had to stop several times to unhitch her black pants that kept snagging on tendrils of thorns that littered the forest floor. Momentarily she halted all together and pinned her hair up behind her, rolling her sleeves up as she did so. This endeavour would undoubtedly take a lot of concentration.

Closer she crept; the heart was only a few feet away. The light emanating from it lit up her pale face, a jarring force of white beauty in the otherwise dark region where she stood. And as the wood heart switched palettes between a spectrum of colours, so too did Libra's beauty reflect the same luminance. Would its touch scald her? Was it heavy? Was it sealed in the tree and irremovable? The properties of this treasure thrilled her and with bated anticipation did she hope to claim it for herself.

Libra stood at the base of the tree and started suddenly, fearing she had heard a noise or detected some disturbance. But no, it must have been her over stimulated imagination. She reached both hands out to the heart and grabbed it. As though it were meant to be hers, it was removed easily from its hollow. She spent a moment absorbing the exquisite detail of her prize, feeling an unbridled energy enter her person. Her senses sparked with sharper life and she no longer felt the fatigue of her journey.

Yet as she turned to escape back to the manor, a stinging lash that wrapped around her ankle restrained Libra. She stumbled, almost dropping the wood heart. A barbed tendril had latched around her leg and now bound her to the tree trunk. Her eyes followed the vine and saw it had spewed forth from the empty cavity where the heart had sat moments earlier.

A panic bubbled in her chest and to her horror, more tentacles shot from the hollow and from the roots below her and began to constrict her in a deathly grip. The tree knew she had stolen the wood heart.

Libra tore at the vines with one arm, trying to shield the heart under the other, yet they grasped with wicked strength. There was a rustle and a groan from around her and Libra saw grotesque, squatted humanoids approach her sluggishly. They seemed to be made of wood and mud, horrific with their bulged and vacant eyes.

By the time Libra could shake away the fear, she was entwined by innumerable tendrils, one of which had wrapped about her throat and squeezed like an anaconda. She felt the life drain from her eyes as she slowly suffocated. Her vision began to fail her and when it seemed she would surely perish, an adrenalin of determination surged through her.

With a pulsing and furious malice, a refusal of defeat, the wood heart glowed in her hands and from its core, a ring of fire shot forth.

In an instant, the vines that bound her were incinerated and those wood golems that had surrounded her crumpled to ash. Charred remnants of vinery lay twitching at her feet and the tree itself seemed to groan involuntarily.

Libra inhaled deeply and quenched her lungs with air, her nerves steadily calming. Hesitating no further, she ran from the sight of the tree and back to the manor.

What awesome power dwells within this relic!

Tenebrae Manor greeted her with merciful silence. She returned to Malistorm's room and placed the wood heart on his abandoned desk, before an indomitable smirk crossed her face.

The flames receded, the flames reformed and one last memory surfaced from the ashes.

She had ruminated on a hiding place for the wood heart for some time. It seemed to her such a shame that an object of such beauty should be hidden away but Libra could not risk it being thieved. Without it, she would be brought back to even footing with those competing for leadership.

But how would she avoid suspicion? An instant claim would be too hasty, so she chose to seal herself in Malistorm's study. Claiming it as her own quarters, Libra ignored the door knocks of all visitors, attributing an increase of magical study to her isolation. True in a sense, for with the wood heart she was capable of unspeakable sorcery and, within several months, she had actively announced to the other residents that she would be their queen and that all would answer to her. Protests towards her claim were met with malicious punishment that readily put the others in place below her.

As for the wood heart, she had stumbled across the secret room completely by accident. Disposing of much of Malistorm's belongings, she had uncovered the small passageway in her room when a loose brick had fallen away unexpectedly. A crude hiding place to be sure but discreet enough to keep the heart hidden and keep the source of her power away from prying eyes.

Years had passed since then, though in the grand scheme of Tenebrae, it could have been yesterday. To Libra, it certainly seemed as such. Having made her decision to pursue power over friendship, she gradually isolated herself from the residents until they were no more than associates. As her demands grew fiercer, so too did she expand in weight, her slothfulness increasing in tow. And once Madlyn entered the scene, a frightened and stupid girl that was so easily manipulated, Libra had a lackey who would complete all the errands befitting of her status. The fruit of her hedonism had ripened and was ready for harvest. Though where she had expected to shine like a quasar, she was instead thrown in the deepest umbra of the begrudged. Her rejected friends watched from the shadows of the rooms below, hurt and nonplussed as to whether or not this was the same Libra they had known. Their resenting of her crippled the household and soon, she was barely recognisable as the strong willed woman who had been their friend. In place, was the self-absorbed tyrant she had become.

XXX: Juniper

Bordeaux had turned back towards the town and readily felt his mind unravel; after the hours had gone by in thought, he sought a useful way to travel.

To return somehow to his immemorial home and save his friends in time,

He would need to cover ample ground swiftly and what better way than equine?

Atop a horse's hasty flight of hooves, he would be able to spread his wings

And hope against helplessness that his soaring would fling

Him in the correct direction, the accurate degree of the compass where his home

Waited in mid-peril for him, their saviour, to return from his unexpected roam.

So within the harbour town, he made his way through the bustling parade

Of markets and stalls and found a merchant with
whom he attempted to strike a trade.

Though they spoke no common tongue, Bordeaux's
remaining coins and a silver ring,

One of many he wore, were an absolute bounty to the
peasant, who stood grinning.

He was more than ecstatic to acquire such treasure
for a common horse

And Bordeaux was pleased that his exchange had not
required force.

Thus the crimson demon rode away from the coast
and left

The harbour town betwixt the sea and mountains in
that salty cleft

Where land and sea locked in embrace. The road he
had chosen became

Little more than dust and grass until he found the
path had dissipated into no more than a plain.

The sunlight shone down onto his back, igniting the
steppe of reeds and flowers

With a vibrant fluorescence of colours - green, blue,
yellow and they showered

Onto him, with the foreign intrusive red of his hair
and his horse with a pelt of auburn

Disrupting the harmony of those glowing colours
poured from the sunny urn.

The breeze whispered sea-bound and flew over his
shoulders,

Fleeing the steppe that lay littered with blossomed
bud and boulder.

And this wind was accompanied by the glassy
currents of the rivers

That ran like veins towards the heart, the sea, in glossy cool slivers.

Breaking the field of verdant green, those trees that stood few and far between

Were of a variety of juniper and Bordeaux had forgotten how open space could spark the serene.

Yet even with such velvet verdancy stretching towards his every horizon,

Each day that passed punctured his confidence and mounted his wizened

Appearance into something increasing haggard and poor;

A weather beating proven by the stubble that sprouted on his gaunt jaw.

Gradually the scene shifted, before eventually growing stale in his heart.

The open space of the fields that once thrilled him did start

To evoke loneliness akin to the forest that he yearned for in vain.

Gone was the freedom of riding across this lush and uninhibited terrain.

All that remained in its place was a crippling and desperate despair

That was magnified verbatim by the roaring rush of the lilies and above, the daylight glare.

Night had revived Bordeaux time and again, so that he pressed

On further until the steppe grew in shoots of tree and became woods. He addressed

The reality of his stark situation. Another change of scene and no hint for him to grope.

He found he was blindly reaching at the fraying strands of his hope.

"I am at a loss. My efforts are futile. I cannot continue on this way," he said.

"I've no idea where my home is and surely my friends may have already assumed me to be dead.

Is there any point to travelling further degrees of longitude on this planet?

Though where else can I go and live in tranquility unmet?"

Just as Bordeaux had begun giving up and thought he might cast

His anchor overboard, so to speak (for he felt like a rudderless boat) and avast

His travelling for favour of aimlessly drifting alone over the lands,

A certain movement of a creature, namely a tamely colt, captured his glance.

The beast, clearly domesticated, peered from his timid eyes

Beneath the drape of a brush, whose blue-black cones and grey-green fronds disguised

It in a considerable camouflage to the unobservant eye. Although hardly an unusual sight,

The horse made Bordeaux realise a possible end to his plight.

For the wayward appearance of this particular saddled thing could only mean

That a settlement, be it farm or town nearby, would break the monotonous bush land green.

Bordeaux forced his horse into a trot and rounded a corner of hill,

And there, just out of sight down the foot of the
slope was a windmill.

It stood as a beacon, towering over the small
farmhouse next to it.

The fields of trimmed grass surrounding were
inviting, he had to admit.

Straddled by a verandah, the house appeared ancient
and in need of repair

And Bordeaux wondered whether its inhabitants still
lived there.

As he drew nearer, he dismounted his horse and crept

Towards the flimsy fence near the house. On a
sudden his heart leapt,

For the movement of a human being startled
Bordeaux,

As she glided from the door of the cottage into the
afternoon glow.

The lass he observed was in the prime of youth,
simply adorned in a sky coloured dress.

Her entangled hair glowed a palette of auburn,
shifting shades with the sunlight's caress.

As she hung out linen to dry in the sun, Bordeaux
attempted to call out and speak.

The travelling had him worn with fatigue and a
nagging hunger made him weak,

But could there be harm in confiding with her? There
was no town for miles,

This Bordeaux knew, so perhaps she could offer safe
lodgings for a while.

So a demon posed as a man called out at the girl, who
showed little shock

At the sudden arrival of a stranger. A turn of her head

and a sway of her frock

Preceded a confident smile that startled him; for the ease of her beauty was akin to a nymph

Or any of those other mysterious dryads that hover through nature as sprightly glyphs.

As though he were little more than another tree in the forest, another post in the fence, she turned

And left him alone in the grass. The screen door closed and the wind was all that could be heard. She returned,

With a tan-furred dog at her feet that raced at Bordeaux, whose fearing eyes suddenly bulged wide.

But the dog's advance was friendly and when he looked up again at the girl, she beckoned him inside.

Bordeaux was never quite certain whether the girl spoke a foreign language or simply didn't talk at all

But never once did the girl say a word and her spritely mystery kept the demon in thrall.

Despite the lack of verbalism in their commune, Bordeaux spoke to her often and felt she still understood

The desperation of his situation. He named her Juniper, for the abundance of such plants in the surrounding woods.

Together, they tended to the health of the horse that had transported Bordeaux safely until now

And as the days drifted by in sweetly, Juniper carried about her errands feeding chickens and milking cows.

He had thought that Juniper must live alone; though found soon enough that she had her own demons.

In a certain sunny room of her humble house sat an invalid old man, who painfully cried for deathly haven.

The man must have been Juniper's father; he could

not stand on his own accord.

He was completely dependant and the man's tears were his only way of expressing thanks to his ward.

The sight of the sickly man struck a chord in Bordeaux's heart

And he tried to ask Juniper how she became tied to this part.

It seemed to upset the girl to reminisce, she showed Bordeaux a grave

That stood lonely at the bottom of the garden, at the back of the enclave.

With the headstone unmarked, Bordeaux could not discern whom the grave was for

But gathered it must have been her husband or mother, someone else who may have poured

Their heart into the tending of this farm and the caring of the sick old man.

Bordeaux realised that Juniper too, was trapped in a world of limited span.

As the sunlight filtered through the quiet days, he felt his heart become enveloped

With fires of love and tenderness, albeit somewhat impetuous and less developed.

Perhaps it was merely the farmland's secluded reality presenting idea of freedom

Or that Juniper represented the folklore of more relatable kingdom.

Their similarities were unassailable; she too was stuck in a world reliant on her servitude,

So maybe between them, they could share their inequitable load and belay the attitude

Owing to a life where their whims, fancies and

dreams would always be second

To the needs of others that lay languid in their introspective pond.

Yet these very thoughts ended up pivotal and soon Bordeaux's calling took its toll.

He realised that he was chasing an ideal life that he could never hope to control.

Although in his heart, he felt that staying with Juniper was no act of whim,

Nothing would change the fact that his own home and friends needed him.

The emotion welled in his chest and when he one day caught Juniper's gaze,

He exclaimed, "Juniper, this cannot work! I cannot stay. Though your beauty amaze,

You don't understand the words that I say and nor could I hope to properly know you.

Even though the agony we feel is certainly burdened well together, you know it to be true!

Between us there is mutual devotion, derived of my love of your heart, so altruistic!

No chimera could destroy my knightly ambition to nurture you, my fantastic!

But while my home calls for me, the idea of us united is indeed a chimera,

Aspired dream must give way to my responsibility, such cruel terror!

Oh chimera – a dream from whence I stumble on my words, darling Juniper.

Let me say - no other muse compares to you, you star of brighter luminance than Jupiter."

Juniper's eyes swelled with a torrent of tears as she

clutched at her heart.

The deluge of Bordeaux's avowal, even with their foreign linguistics, did impart

The expression intended. And her acceptance of his pleas shone through their mutual affection,

The realisation that both must go alone and attend to their own afflictions.

He longingly stared at her with sorrowful eyes and repeated, "I have to go."

Juniper kissed him softly on the cheek and whispered a word for him, "Bordeaux."

His horse was prepared in the symphonic nocturne of the evening, where the crickets

Rung their ornamental anthem sempre forte in the gnarled brambly thickets.

Bordeaux painfully uttered farewell and hoped to guide himself through the treacherous shoals

With the spritely image of Juniper forever etched into his soul.

XXXI: The Further Rascalities of Deadsol & Comets

A rather strange turning of events occurred at Tenebrae Manor and readily threw its residents into further anxiety. Indeed, it seemed to toy with inevitability to a certain extent; the wood golems persistent attacks at the Manor's facade led to a wall collapsing at one particular point, leaving a long abandoned bedroom on the ground floor victim to the outside elements. And further compounding its need for a savior, the branches that strangled the house had caused a section of roof to collapse in on itself, crunched under the bruising blow of tendrils. Vines had readily cracked many of the windows and the halls begun to echo with the ghostly winds that found ingress into them.

The watch employed by Crow and Edweena had bought but minimal time and as the hours wore on, it appeared that they were losing ground at an increasingly rapid rate.

It was from a stretch of parapet lined with a few meager torches that the triptych of Crow, Deadsol and Comets observed the dire happenings on the ground several stories below them. The wind carried with it a bite that cut through the fleecy pelt of Crow's coat, so that he sat huddled with a pipe in his mouth, eyes invariably scanning the forest. It was an almost canine obedience with which he had pursued his station of sentry, which had taken its toll on his weary body; the mortal sat nodding and fighting off the sleep that beckoned him. Beside him, the glistening steel of his sword reflected brilliantly the green of his ivy leaf shield.

Deadsol stood absently nearby, his endless polishing of a rather sharp saber providing a release of energy for the wildly rambunctious demon. And of rambunctiousness - Comets, the very definition of the word, balanced precariously on his toes and tottered along the castle wall, teasing the gaping maw of darkness that lurked below. In his hands, two pikes on which the heads of slain wood golems stared from deadpan eyes served as a means of balance for the sickening trapeze act undertaken by the jester.

The wind blew again in a silvery gust, startling Crow from his doze and very nearly dropping his pipe from his mouth.

He sat up groggily, grabbing both his sword and the attention of his two henchmen.

"Best be patrolling. I suppose I can trust you two to keep watch up here?"

Deadsol stopped polishing his saber and fashioned a rather devious grin. "Trust? Why, how could you doubt us now? We have proven worth, surely."

"Thinks we'll mess up, he does," mumbled Comets.

"You two, really... It was a passing comment," said Crow. "Trifle use it is to have all three of us up here; I'll go circumvent the place. No doubt I can pick off a few golems while I'm at it."

"But you are so fatigued, dear sir!" replied Deadsol. "Consider Comets and I going in your stead."

Crow rubbed his eyes, darkened about the rims with exhaustion. The moral dilemma nagged at him; he wondered whether he could trust the harlequins to perform astutely.

"I... I could not allow it. You boys have been splendid thus far but I believe I am more suited to slaying these beasts."

"Told you," said Comets. "Didn't I? Thinks we'll singlehandedly doom the place."

Deadsol produced a magnificent pout that seemed curiously out of place on his masculine jaw line, while Crow scratched thoughtfully at his chestnut curls.

"Three hours," said Crow. "That's all I require. Let me doze a while."

Deadsol thrust his sword skyward. "There's a fellow! Fear not, Crow! Comets and I care for this manor as much as you do."

"Besides, we'll be here a bit longer than you..." sneered Comets.

Crow grimaced at such a comment and remained in a state of cautiousness. Yet when he directed his glance towards the jester and saw the merciless lack of emotion emitted by Comets as he clapped the two golem heads together, he felt somewhat at ease.

"Keep close watch on that front door," said Crow.

"And where that wall collapsed. Fail me at your own peril."

Comets held the two pikes either side of his head, so that he looked like a ghastly cousin of Cerberus. From betwixt the frowning deadpan of the perished golems he peeled a chilling grin across his face. "Wouldn't dream of failing you, dear."

Deadsol had already left their side. As Comets chased after him, Crow stood silent in the wind with his cape blustering in the gale and wondered whether he had just made a clinical error.

It took Deadsol several minutes to make his way from the top of the manor to the ground floor and when he eventually burst out the front door, he stood with arms akimbo and breathed in the dark forest air. He bounced on his feet gaily and tapped his hand upon the hilt of his sword as though it were a trusty guard dog. A clattering was heard in the foyer behind him and presently Comets slammed the front door behind him and pulled up alongside. The jester carried a small mace in one hand and held a stuffed cloth sack over his shoulder. Crowning – or rather encompassing his bulbous head was a knight helmet with a red feathery plume jutting from the apex. The rabbit ears of his motley cap had been pressed down so as to accommodate his head within the mask, yet the bells still rang loudly as they dangled like earrings under his chin.

"Well my boy," said Deadsol. "When man must face up to his enemy, aggression is paramount and carnage – the key. I say, Comets! Where did you get all this?"

"What do you care?" replied Comets, flicking the visor of the helmet up.

"I see the benefits in such a helmet, young man. But can you see?"

"Of course! Watch this."

Comets closed the visor and swung the mace over his head, Deadsol having to step aside to avoid being clobbered. The jester ran in a straight line and lashed out at the first tree in his path. He threw lumbering shots at the trunk with his mace, which seemed a little on the heavy side for such a small wielder.

Deadsol laughed triumphantly, clutching his belly with mirth.

"Well done, son! We shall win back the mansion yet!"

"Then what?" asked Comets. "Libra hates us, Bordeaux is dead. Will we remain here with that gourmand above us?"

"Then we will wander as vagabonds in the perennial gloom! Until then, these beasties are threatening our home. Will you allow it?"

Comets shook his fist in the air with inhumane determination.

They began to patrol in a wide circle around the house.

We are the vagabond,
We wander place to place
With derelict aplomb
And apogee of grace.

We are the vagabond,
We are what we are.
But soon again we drift along
And chase our endless star.

We are the vagabond,
And who are you to judge

Our hate of higher echelon -
The venom of our grudge!

Inattentive to the dangers that surrounded them, Deadsol and Comets sang their song and ruthlessly destroyed anything that crossed their path. Though they made such a racket and drew the attention of the wood golems with ease, the monsters were strangely impotent in their retaliation.

Comets was particularly aggressive, as though he stood possessed by some unknown force, endowed with a brute strength that brutally punished his opponents. His mace splintered the heads of unwary golems with bruising obliteration, while Deadsol's razor sharp saber easily severed the vines that clung to Tenebrae Manor.

Their confidence increased with every kill; soon the boys had circled the manor several times. Deadsol grew fatigued and hoped that their three hours was soon coming to an end. Meanwhile, Comets, with boundless energy, continued to wreck a path of destruction through the forest.

"Hold fast, Comets!" called Deadsol, pulling up beside a small sapling whose branches had already begun to reach for Tenebrae Manor like a baby reaching for its mother.

"Slaying these creatures is a cake-walk, wouldn't you say?" said Comets.

"Exactly, my lad. It comes down to simple logic," replied Deadsol.

Comets tilted his head, perplexed.

"Consider this," said Deadsol, pointing his saber at the sapling. "What is this?"

"A tree," replied Comets.

"Precisely. But really, what is a tree?"

"A big stick with leaves on it."

"Brilliant," said Deadsol. "Absolutely brilliant."

For a moment, Deadsol stood admiring his own analogy to the extent that Comets flung his hands in the air and pleaded for his friend to get to the point.

"Ah, yes. As I was saying – a big stick is merely wood, yes? Now consider this saber."

"Steel," said Comets.

"Exactly. And what do they say of wood and steel – which would yield?"

"Enough perorating, Deadsol! The wood bows to the steel!"

"Ha!" cried Deadsol, swinging his saber at the sapling and slicing it in twain.

Comets clapped his hands in delight and laughed like a maniac at the moon.

Deadsol sheathed his saber, "So long as we have the intelligence and the menace, Tenebrae Manor will not be lost!"

Comets rummaged through his cloth sack and hurled several golem heads into the shrubbery before pulling out something of a similar size and cradling it in his arms.

"So long as I have this…" he murmured.

"Comets, what is that?" gaped Deadsol.

Comets stared cautiously at his friend, a certain emptiness in his eyes suddenly frightened Deadsol. The jester held forth the object – a glowing heart-shaped amulet.

"Stole it from Libra's room," he uttered quietly. "It's mine now."

"Allow me to see that, boy! What beauty!"

Deadsol reached out his hand but retracted it instantly as Comets savagely bit down on his fingers. The demon was startled, clutching his fingers in pain and when he looked again at Comets, the jester's eyes glowed blood red.

"Comets? Come now, let's give the pretty thing back to Libra."

"Never!" the jester barked. "Libra thinks she can hoard this for herself? It's mine, mine!"

Deadsol was now genuinely concerned for his friend, who was undeniably possessed by the power of the wood heart.

From the forest, the grueling moans of the wood golems seemed to increase. Comets perked up at the sound and stared from reddened eyes into the trees.

Before Deadsol was able to restrain him, the jester had run off, leaving his friend apprehensive for the first time in a long while.

XXXII: L'Unica Strada

The road could not be called as such anymore. Hitherto it had transitioned through stages of varying widths - at times broad as a great highway and at others, little more than a narrow lane way. Yet now it seemed to have funnelled in on itself, its sides had crept inward until they almost met and the dusty trail was barely distinguishable through the overhanging ferns. Perhaps it was merely the scratching of branches that proved irritating but in any account, Bordeaux's horse protested the journey along the tightrope of path. The beast had endured greater challenges thus far; whisked away from a seaside existence, she had carried Bordeaux through forests and rocky mountains, across grassy steppes and sleet-struck plateaux. But this wood had been the tipping point, the moment when the horse could tolerate no more.

Bordeaux attempted to calm her and allowed her to slow to a crawling pace. The demon's own back was

burdened by a heavy satchel, filled with various objects -
the hat and coat he had stolen, a few scraps of food.

As he turned his head to the canopy, where sunlight
filtered in swathes through the green, he reminisced the
days that had gone by and tried to remember how long he
had been in this forest. It had been several days since the
trees had closed around him and although the road had led
him well so far, Bordeaux now doubted its integrity. The
wind rushing between the trunks carried no other sound
but the rustling of leaves and Bordeaux shivered in the
silent isolation.

There was a thread of logic in Bordeaux's persistence
of avoiding towns and settlements; he undoubtedly knew
Tenebrae Manor stood in a far corner of the forgotten
trails of the world and to remain close to major roads or
populated countryside was to render his searching nearly
ineffectual. In practice it was far bleaker. A certain sense, a
feeling of whim kept him on his course, though it was
appearing less than likely that he would ever find his way
home. The cold indifference of the wind racing through
the conifers galvanized his doubt.

Bordeaux dismounted his horse and walked beside
her. The path he had followed had all but completely
vanished; he now found himself knee deep in ferns and
wading devoid of direction. The sun was beginning to set,
its fading twilight igniting the forest to a brilliant hue of
autumnal fire - of orange and gold.

With thoughts eyed towards retiring for the night at
any appropriate spot, Bordeaux was inattentive to the
foreign object in his path; that is until his foot struck it and
sent a clattering noise through the trees. His horse started,
whinnying nervously as the crimson demon scanned the

ground for that which he had kicked. The sharp clash of some metal object seemed most likely and he very soon found a cheap tin pail laying discarded amongst the ferns.

Bordeaux picked the thing up by the handle; it was rusted and dented and he wondered how it had gotten there and for how long it had been lost. Naught but trees surrounded him entirely, yet further steps through the forest eventually widened the trail again, until it unveiled an impossibly small village at its end.

Its revealing proved more bemusing than elating; to Bordeaux, it was the least likely settlement he could have imagined. Yet it was certainly populated, for several signs of civilized life gave way. It consisted of a single street, dividing perhaps a dozen buildings, the largest of which boasted a second storey. Each establishment - wooden and dark with grime. Somewhere nearby, Bordeaux could discern the lowing of cows and several hens strutted down the dirty street in erratic directions. Laundry hung from windows and flapped like wet flags in the wind. And all around the town, the trees loomed and threatened to swallow it whole.

A shudder lurched down Bordeaux's spine. There was something off putting about this whole place; this apparently nameless place, for he could not discern the town name carved into the decrepit signpost hanging above him. He had assumed the dull creaking sound that filled the air to be that of the sign swinging on its post but no - it was something far more sinister. Hung in various places about the town entrance, the disfigured corpses of hanged beings swayed in the evening breeze, the ropes that bound their necks groaning under decayed dead weight.

Bordeaux stood aghast; the dead were all women,

their thanatoid faces forever locked in an expression of despondent hatred. These sentinels, forever silenced by horrid gallows, seemed to issue a stern threat to outsiders - leave this place and forget you had ever seen a thing.

Yet for Bordeaux, they evoked a repressed memory in him most lamentable.

"Witches..." he muttered. "They must be a suspicious lot."

Bordeaux himself had dealt with such accusations in his past, having found no other choice but to flee from many places before he could call them home.

Such a horrid thought, to think that most of these women were probably innocent.

Although he could not feel sorrow for long, for he knew that they had obtained peace through death, while Bordeaux continued to wander the world without a grave to rest. Again he felt the twang of homesickness and realised then that Tenebrae Manor was his only home on this earth, the only place where he could live as he was - happy or no, he could still be himself. He had often confused these thoughts as a longing for his mortal past but only now was it confirmed properly in his mind.

Bordeaux cautiously advanced into the village until he saw a trough of rainwater by the roadside. Tying the reins of his horse to a nearby post, he allowed her to drink, an action undertaken most graciously by the animal. She portrayed the same unease in her composition, braying nervously as Bordeaux stroked her mane soothingly. By now the sun had well and truly set, giving way to a cold purple that would soon fade to black.

From the window of a hut, a small pair of eyes bored into him. When he turned and peered into that gaping

blackness in the wooden façade, he saw the eyes belonged
to a child. Her gaze gave way to very little expression; no
smile curled her lips, nor did her tiny brow contort into a
frown. Yet there was an obvious detachment; her eyes
were cold as death, looking at Bordeaux as one might look
upon an insect - an intrusive insect that must be
exterminated swiftly. Bordeaux felt, all at once, completely
exposed, standing interrogated in the middle of the street
until he moved swiftly onwards. But the girl's eyes never
left him and followed him until he was out of sight.

The double storey building would have been taken as
a rather simple structure on its own, had it not been
surrounded by a multitude of inferior huts. The clock, high
up on the front façade of the place was dilapidated at best.
Yet its hands still turned and the bell in the high tower
remained silent for now.

Rummaging through his satchel, Bordeaux pressed
the fedora hat over his horns and stood in the darkness
before the building. The night had swallowed all else; the
only lights shining in the village squirmed sinuously from
its windows. Bordeaux assumed it to be both a town hall
that doubled as a tavern of sorts, for he heard the voices of
a ruckus within and the clinking of glasses on bar top. The
voices were merry and, when he focused, Bordeaux felt his
heart skip a beat - he understood what they spoke. He
could not believe it! Here, of all places, after months of
silence, of miscommunication, he was within earshot of
people he could speak to.

In a moment, his wariness left him, yet it was not
long before it crept back. Needless to say, he was still a
stranger in this isolated town. Would they accept him or
eye him with suspicion? Shuddering at the recollection of

the hanged women, Bordeaux decided it would be the latter.

He peered through the door and eyed the crowd; it must have been everyone in the town. A plan formulated in his mind - he would slip into the crowd and remain scarce, perhaps he could overhear any important information and finally figure out where he was.

There was a certain haze permeating about the interior, the scent of beer and tobacco smoke adding to the soupy atmosphere. Outside, the bell sung with the coming hour and with it, a commotion scuttled through the room. People moved to find a seat wherever they could.

Bordeaux took a moment to grasp whatever activity this strange troupe of villagers were about to undertake. He watched as they gathered in a crowd around a sort of stage area, where two rather haggard men sat tuning crude musical instruments. From the darkest corner of the tavern there stood a man of such short stature that, were it not for the hint of recognition, Bordeaux may not have noticed him at all. And it seemed that this impish creature recognised him too, for he stared blankly from goggled eyes, his pockmarked mouth curling perplexedly. Then all at once the imp man looked away and instead chose to focus his attention to the stage.

The two musicians that had ensconced on stools upon the stage did not exactly carry the same sort of eloquence associated with men of such culture. Where someone like Arpage may have dusted the seat, plucked at the ruff of his neck and ceremoniously bowed deeply to the audience, these two men sat in a vile dishevelment that left them indistinguishable from the other villagers. One of them, a bulky and well-bearded man tested a few notes on a greasy flute - stained with years of use. The other man, sombre shouldered and despondent, turned the tuning pegs of a splintered guitar with an ear inclined towards the instrument, giving the appearance of a fatigued mother cradling a baby.

The rambunctious crowd was reaching an animalistic pitch when the flautist, with a voice that doused the fever of the audience, bellowed forth.

"My pretty people!"

The intoxicated crowd roared a rousing reply, "Fiddler!"

The Fiddler smiled humbly and capped the excitement with a motion of his palm. "Listen me pretties, lend your ears to your darling Fiddler and his most passionate accomplice, Razorback."

"Razorback!" roared the crowd and the guitarist raised his hand in response.

Then, as a teacher scolds a mischievous class, the Fiddler's face contorted in malice and he shouted, "Enough!"

The crowd fell quiet and the smile curled its way back onto the Fiddler's face. Those in the audience stared with adoration, with anticipation and Bordeaux was utterly nonplussed at the control these two bards had over the strange villagers.

Fiddler adjusted the sleeve of his more than haggard brown coat and proceeded to play a series of ornaments on his flute.

"The world has forgotten us, darlings," he continued.

The crowd booed.

"They say!" cried Fiddler. "They say our ways are

archaic to point of irrelevance! That we of this little shire are narrow-minded!"

"And worthy of neglect," added Razorback.

Again the crowd was irate and Razorback brushed his knuckled fingers over the strings of his guitar. Although the instrument was worn, it produced a beautiful tone and the minor chord he strummed again and again filled the room ominously.

"But we are not without our reasons," said Fiddler, "For we know, we know, this world is indeed darker than the heartless void of the devil's very chest!"

Here the crowd began to act peculiar; many of the women crossed themselves or muttered unintelligible oaths. The men, though they all appeared rugged, quivered at the knees and shook their heads.

"The forest is full of horrors," Razorback proclaimed.

"It's true!" bellowed an old man from the audience, "They took my Madeline!"

"Yes sir," said Fiddler. "The ghosts that lurk in those nightmarish trees are merciless - many have been lost."

For a moment the room was silent.

"Yet tonight we celebrate," said Fiddler. "Rejoice! For one of our own returns to us! One of us who we had given up as lost! But this is no phantom you see before you, nor some miraculous Lazarus. No! This is a man who was swallowed by the trees and lived to return; Jethro!"

As the audience cheered at a feverish level, a frail youth climbed onto the stage and smiled nervously. Even with his white and shocked hair, his hollow eyes fraught with terrors he could never forget; even with the emaciated features of his outcast face, Bordeaux instantly recognised the man. It was the very same Jethro, the man who had stumbled upon Tenebrae Manor and its ghoulish residents!

While the crowd shouted in jubilee, he could only attempt to ward away the paralysis of disbelief that constricted him. A mixture of varying emotions rushed through him; foremost being a knee-jerk thought, how had this man come to be here? And when that immediate reaction had subsided, Bordeaux realised he must indeed be very close to Tenebrae Manor, the thought filling him with glee. Yet if this were the very same Jethro, then Bordeaux was in far greater peril than he had anticipated; this man knew of the house where night covers eternal. What if he led the villagers to Tenebrae? What if they came with pitchfork and flame and drove him and his friends from their home? Furthermore; say the villagers approached common society with the matter. Tenebrae Manor would be exposed, no longer could its residents reside in exile. Such thoughts were most dreadful to Bordeaux.

Jethro stood on the stage and waved at the crowd, oblivious to the presence of Bordeaux. The effect of his sojourn under the endless night sky had aged him severely, yet now that he had escaped back to his hometown, he managed a weary smile. The once blonde hairs on his head had faded to a fear-induced white and he was visibly thin and frail. He was being bombarded with a barrage of questions.

"Where have you been?"

"What have you seen?"

The Fiddler placed a hand on Jethro's shoulder, the farmhand flinching involuntarily at the touch.

"Our prodigal son is but too exhausted to regale us with his adventure."

The crowd groaned.

"Fear not!" Fiddler snapped. "For he told this bard the entire story!"

He spat out a few notes on his flute in tune with Razorback's ever calling strums.

"He spoke of a night that never ends," said the Fiddler. "Though the world turns, this place knows no days - it is forever shrouded in a blanket of darkness!"

The crowd shuddered but clung to every word.

"And worse, those that lurk in this night... Shadows more monster than man!"

"What do these shadows look like?" gaped a woman from the audience.

"Where do they live?" cried another.

"Hush, my pets!" said Fiddler, "Patience is virtuous. These shadows live in a house of nightmares! Of horrible corridors that drag forever, of rooms long left to the mercy of spiders!"

"Then we must destroy this place! Expunge it from our world!" called a man.

"You won't get me galloping into darkness like a fool," replied another spectator. "Surely God will eradicate this evil for us! He will protect us!"

"There's witchcraft afoot, I knew it!"

"We cannot risk the vanquishing of our village..."

Here, the crowd fell into a bitter quarreling. Bordeaux dragged his hat down further onto his head; he too, felt the fear of the villagers, albeit for different reasons. He struggled to clear his mind but the ruckus was so loud that he clasped his skull.

"Everyone," cried a voice. "Everyone please be quiet!"

The voice was timorous above the commotion, yet when the villagers saw Jethro attempting to speak, they fell back to a low muttering.

"You don't understand," said Jethro. "I can't remember where I've been. I can hardly be sure it was real! I've been sick and delirious for days. We are so isolated and the forest is so big! I could never find this place again."

Those in the audience surrounding Bordeaux sighed with disappointment.

Grateful to have had no attention drawn to himself, the crimson demon slipped out the door of the tavern and slumped against the wall. The night was blacker than he had seen since his exile from Tenebrae Manor, paying to the utter isolation of the village. The stars in the sky were overwhelmingly infinite and with each one separated from the next by insurmountable distance, Bordeaux was soothed by their relatable loneliness.

The Fiddler and Razorback had commenced a long and mournful tune that drifted to Bordeaux's ears in a muffled drone. The music, on a sudden, became clearer as the door of the tavern opened and shut again quickly.

Bordeaux realised he was not alone in the darkness; he discerned the wispy shape of another being strolling slowly down the main street. He knew immediately that it was Jethro, the man must have had need to escape the groping of the villagers and clear his head. In any account he was walking with uncertainty, dream-like in his gait. The shock of his adventure would have carried a toll on him.

Yet Bordeaux felt nothing of the man's emotions. This was his chance to discover how to get back to the manor; he could not pass up such fortune. He took no patience with him in his stride, merely gliding up to Jethro and grasping at his shoulders.

"Jethro. I knew it was you."

Jethro shuddered. A raw fear overcame him, as it was apparent that he recognised the voice of the stranger approaching. And when he turned to confirm that it was, in fact, Bordeaux standing before him, he turned so pale he might have been transparent.

"Y-you, no…"

"Jethro listen, I won't hurt you," pleaded Bordeaux, "But you must tell me, which way to Tenebrae Manor? Surely you remember something!"

Jethro stammered, his face contorting to one of child-like terror. Although he tried to speak, Bordeaux could not be patient and shook him by the shoulders eagerly.

"Come on, man. You have to help me! I will leave you alone forever after this. Just tell me, how do I get home? Where am I?"

"N-no! No! Help!" blurted Jethro, paralysed with horror.

The commotion had collected the attention of several villagers who rushed to see what was going on.

"Demon!" cried Jethro.

Bordeaux tried to silence him but it was no use. Jethro thrashed like a drowning man, the villagers advancing to his aid and, in the commotion, Bordeaux's hat fell off.

Those surrounding him dropped back immediately and gasped. The crimson demon's horns were on display for all to see.

"Beast of Beelzebub!"

Several of the men raced towards him and struck him

fiercely with their fists, Bordeaux struggling to escape the gang and run away. What followed was a blur in Bordeaux's memory. He heard the shouts of angry townsfolk; saw the flash of torch fire as he plunged out of the town into the forest. Dogs snapped at his heals, those faster men caught up with him and struck him in the back with shovels and pitchforks. Yet still he ran, each abusive cry and blow breaking down his composure until he felt utterly hated. He cursed them with bitter cries, begged them to stop and leave him be. Onwards he ran, until the cries of the villagers grew fainter, his senses became hazy, until he eventually collapsed, exhausted into a muddy creek. The snarling of dogs roared in his ears and though the beasts were far away, their barking was all he could comprehend as his vision faded to nothing.

The villagers had long since returned to the village empty-handed, leaving Bordeaux face down and defeated in muddy creek. Despondent he lay, engulfed by a sense of maudlin rejection. He tried to lift himself up but fell quickly back into the dirty water. He felt as though his heart had caved in on itself, crushed by the blows of loneliness and depression. His face twitched involuntarily until tears began to secrete from his long dry eyes; soon he was sobbing wretchedly in the creek, kicked down one last time and left behind. It was not only the days he had spent banished from Tenebrae that crushed him; no, this was much more. The weight of his ever-suffering afterlife had become all at once, too heavy for his shoulders and he could not longer pretend that he was content in any way with how his years had played out, how long he had felt unloved and hated.

As he lay still in the grime, his mind was thrown back

in time as far as he could remember. Only snippets of his former life remained – the flash of a sunny vineyard, the afternoon light shining on his long hair, the smiles on the faces of his long dead family as they gazed at their simple house.

Bordeaux was overcome with sobs again; so many centuries had passed since he had passed from his first life, the life where he had lived happily in the most blissful ignorance. What deity had forsaken him to this unending eternity? No matter where he had been over the years, he had never been truly content. Tenebrae Manor had been a tolerable way to pass the hours but the demon could not deny that his happiest days had abandoned him long ago. Rolling onto his back, he stared at the patches of night sky that penetrated betwixt the looming conifers. From his perspective, the trees seemed to lean over him, peering down on him like he was some foreign creature washed up on a distant shoreline. Bordeaux remembered the god he had heard of in his previous life, the greater being that he had never really understood and was reminded suddenly of an old verse he had read, his lips mouthing the words deliriously from the creek bed;

Why is light given to those in misery,
And life to the bitter of soul,
To those who long for death that does not come,
Who search for it more than for hidden treasure,
Who are filled with gladness
And rejoice when they reach the grave?
Why is life given to a man whose way is hidden,
Whom God has hedged in?

His sobbing had stopped but still the tears fell quietly from his vacant eyes. He lay so perfectly still and expressionless, he may as well have been dead.

With the shadows of the trees and flickering of the stars holding Bordeaux hypnotised, he did not remember falling to sleep.

The sickening and revolting daylight woke him from his fitful sleep. Feeling completely sorry for himself and giving up his will to carry on, Bordeaux decided he would just lay right there forever.

But soon, as it always is with the impulsive nature of intelligent life, he grew bored and irritable. The sun cut his face with its rays, the dryness in his throat becoming too much. Then, as if only to pass the unending time he had, he stood up groggily and began to trudge through the difficult forest.

Bordeaux had lost his grip on higher consciousness, remiss in his counting of the days that passed overhead, merely walking in no particular direction until fatigue made him sleep again. The words of his prophet continued to play repeatedly in his head and Bordeaux soon knew that he was setting himself up to become the closest thing he could know of death. He was doomed, he would wander without food and drink and shelter until he was a husk of a man, a bitter and anti-supernal demon. Bitter acceptance shrouded him; he would wander forever in exile.

When it seemed his fate had been sealed and when all his hope had flown away from him, a change in the forest crept upon him. It was a change he, at first, wrote off as the ramblings of his decreasing sanity but soon began to believe again. An ember of hope had reignited from the ashes, in his mind he truly began to believe he was onto something.

It was but a simple observation - *he could not remember the last time he had seen the sun.*

Had delirium stretched the length of the night, so he assumed himself to be back within his homeland? Or was this, in fact, reality?

Bordeaux sat down on a rotted log on the forest floor, his head pounding with confusion. Yes, the night had been unusually long. He was close! He had to be! Bordeaux gritted his teeth in anguish; he was still so lost. The forest was deeper than the inkiest oceans; how he would ever find Tenebrae Manor he did not know.

Again his vision blurred, yet he believed himself to be in the presence of a silent shade shrouded in a dim blue light. The ghost hovered before him in the distance, although he could feel it staring at him with owl-like eyes – wide and impressionable. Like a pulse, the shroud of light ebbed and flowed and when it receded, Bordeaux knew that he recognised the face of the apparition.

His delirium weakened his memory but the gaunt face of the girl with eyes that bulged from sunken hovels was one that he indeed knew. And when she turned and floated away over a small incline, Bordeaux was instantly compelled to follow her.

The ghost floated betwixt the trees with her white hair flowing as though underwater, her eyes never leaving the demon that chased in tow.

Bordeaux's thoughts mounted with glee

That girl. Libra's servant. The kitchen girl. What was she doing here? I knew her once! I knew that face!

The girl drifted silently and never wavered in speed, despite Bordeaux's desperate racing to keep up. He tripped over roots, struggled down slopes and ran with all his might through thick grasses. He felt as though he was running through a dream, eyes fixed on the ghost until she, all at once, dissipated into the night.

Bordeaux soon gasped and fell to his knees. The girl was gone – though he scrambled across the ground and clawed vainly at the air, the apparition was no longer there. Again Bordeaux's vision begun to fade and the final thought preceding his drift into slumber was a pondering of the ground beneath him. Why, it almost feels like a road.

It was still dark when he awoke. Yet when he rolled onto his back it was not the starry sky that met his gaze, rather a roof of dank and dripping stones. He winced in his delirium and choked on the rank scent of mud. Beneath him was a strange indentation on the ground – wheel tracks.

Bordeaux sat up and as he did so, he met the gaze of a small pock-mouthed man staring at him from his perch on a horse-drawn carriage.

The imp from the tavern.

The goggle-eyed imp continued to stare intently at Bordeaux, until a flick of his head gestured the demon to turn about. When he did so, Bordeaux's heart swam with affection, for the elated Mute Chef stood there with a smile of disbelief and an offered hand.

Taking his hand, Bordeaux rose in tears and, after embracing the chef, turned to thank his engineer of his deliverance. But the pock-mouthed imp was already on his way, with the empty crates and barrels rattling upon the back of his cart.

Bordeaux knew words were wasted on the chef and

prayed the sagged gentleman in the greasy kitchen smock could read the appreciation in his face. Before him loomed a large door which led to the underbelly of that monumental and awe-inspiring spectacle. That nocturnal castle that teetered on the edge of time itself; surrounded by knuckled rock and jagged pine. Tenebrae Manor – Bordeaux was home!

XXXIII: Libra Tries To Kill Deadsol

The irrepressible Deadsol, once so cocksure of disposition, was now faced with a confrontation that left him shaking at the knees. Inasmuch as he stood sweating profusely with a damp palm wrapped about the handle of Libra's door. A fearful sense of dread consumed him, brought to a pinnacle by the cluttering commotion of noise on the other side of the door. In the end, it was a rare display of genuine concern for his little friend, Comets that urged him forward. For the imp had become possessed by some mysterious object of Libra's and so, swallowing the painful anxiety in his throat, Deadsol opened the door.

Libra's room was in shambles, trashed as though some unforeseen hurricane had swept its vapours through. It was this dishevelment that caused the complexion of Deadsol to become white as a sheet, yet he felt some solace to discover that it was not Comets but Libra herself who had made the mess. The Lady Libra could be seen upturning the entire contents of her room with considerable perturbation; the dark curls in disarray about her flustered face. She huffed as would a child who had lost a favourite toy, short and irritable bursts of profanity were expelled from her mouth.

Deadsol stood still as a statue; he and Libra had not encountered one another since his imprisonment. As far as he knew, Libra still considered him incarcerated. Yet when she looked up and saw him, Libra stood with arms akimbo and fumed as though she had just gotten rid of him but minutes earlier.

"You."

"Me," uttered Deadsol in reply.

"I thought I told you to knock."

"Indeed, I believe you did say that at one stage. My apologies, Miss Libra."

Libra's brow upturned., "What manner of decorum are you feigning, Deadsol? I thought I imprisoned you."

Deadsol sprung forward with his hands submissively clasped. "That you did, madam. Yet Tenebrae Manor called for me and I rose from the ashes in response!"

"I see that incarceration did nothing to stem that infuriating eloquence. Whatever. Leave me, I am not fit for visitors."

Here, Libra returned to rummaging. She was undoubtedly searching for the wood heart and Deadsol remained idle in the room with bated breath. All at once, Libra's vain search became too much and she struck at the wall with her fist.

"Where is it?" she fumed. "Where? Where!"

She plucked a perfume bottle from her vanity and threw it menacingly. It shattered but a foot from where

Deadsol stood.

"Miss Libra..."

"What?"

"That which you search for; it is not all that valuable, no?"

"Deadsol, you blighter, you fantastic idiot... I am looking for something very valuable of mine. And you standing there makes my gorge rise! Go away!"

Libra threw another bottle of perfume at him, the sweet scents filling the air slowly with sickening fumes.

"If I were to say," probed Deadsol, "That you were looking for a lovely, *heart-shaped amulet*... Would I be correct?"

Starting suddenly, Libra's mouth twisted with rage and through her teeth she snarled, "Where is it?"

Deadsol whimpered, "A thousand pardons, Miss. Comets has it. He ran away into the forest..."

The face of Lady Libra turned paler than before, the stony porcelain beauty of her face seemingly crystallizing into a frozen state, as though she had been immortalised in a painting utterly devoid of expression.

From her position near the vanity, she and Deadsol remained locked in a standoff, motionless as though posing for a portrait. For a moment it looked like they would remain forever thusly, until Deadsol noticed a minor change in the Lady's face that caused him to frown. It was a subtle change, although this smallest of tweaks had given Libra the appearance of a psychopath and her eyes drilling into Deadsol with punishing indifference to his wellbeing caused the copper demon to shudder involuntarily.

When Libra finally spoke, it was slow and deep. "You

allowed that insect to make off with my treasure?"

Deadsol shook from head to toe and cowered from his stance. When he nodded timidly in response, Libra turned her gaze away and squeezed her eyes shut. There was another subtle movement - this time her arm, which reached for the axe that leant against the stone wall. Again, she looked at Deadsol, her amber oculi burning hotter than the forgotten sun, scorching him to the core.

"Fool!" she roared. "Confound you to have blundered upon my very ruin!"

Here she rushed to him, launching the axe with a sickening force that would have split Deadsol in two had he not leapt out of the way.

The axe stung the ground and echoed resonantly with the shrill scrape of steel on stone. Libra gasped for breath through her grinding teeth. Again she threw the axe into motion, slicing the air horizontally and missing Deadsol by the hair of his moustache. The most minute of cuts split open on his cheek and the sight of blood hurled them both into a primal state of instinct. Libra; the ferocious predator, merciless as a great white shark. Deadsol; a defenseless rabbit bounding desperately from mortal peril. The demon danced in a panic around the room, dodging the onslaught of blows from Libra's axe. Her dispossession of the wood heart had blunted the potency of her magic, so she could only resort to a physical violence. She struggled to move her heavy body around, yet the blood-thirst that possessed her drove her on.

"You may be incapable of dying but that doesn't mean I can't chop you into pieces!" she bellowed.

Deadsol jumped on the bed and ran across it to put an object between himself and Libra. "Lady, please! I implore you to stop!"

"You've ruined me!" cried Libra. "Oh agony of abhorrence! My hate for you is unending, my blood boils at the sight of you!"

"Not my fault!" blurted Deadsol, so fearful, he was almost in tears.

He was backed into a corner, yet as Libra approached, she needed a moment to catch her breath. Both sweated profusely with exertion and the sight of Libra so powerless made Deadsol laugh hysterically on a sudden. His laughter only amplified Libra's rage; she readily composed herself and raised the axe again.

"Incorrigible fiend! You will not see the moon rise again! I will pry your heart from its dark cage! I will wrench that vile thing from the very pit of your ashen soul!"

She made to land the deathblow, before a voice stopped her hand.

"Enough of this."

In the doorway stood a familiar emaciated man with clothes most haggard and face covered with dark red stubble.

"Bordeaux!" cried Deadsol.

Libra dropped the axe in shock as Deadsol ran to hide behind his wayward friend.

"Odysseus returns!" he laughed.

As the pair embraced, Libra stood shaking in the corner, the axe lying idle at her feet. Her murderous dominance had escaped her at the sight of Bordeaux; she felt now that it was her that was vulnerable. Indeed, she had reason to believe herself to be under fire, for Bordeaux, looking much like death animated, turned to her with anger in his eyes.

"You had hoped to be rid of me?" he said.

"Bordeaux, I..."

"How you could lead Tenebrae into ruin so shamefully..."

"I didn't want it like this!" Libra interrupted. "I wanted to be worshipped! I should be worshipped! If I am to remain on this earth for eternity, then I damn well want to live my own way!"

Bordeaux paced towards her. "You should pay the highest price for what you've done. You've placed us all at risk and if Tenebrae Manor falls, you will topple down with us!"

Libra's resilience failed her and she slumped onto the chaise lounge and buried her face in her hands. Deadsol remained silent near the door, absorbing every word spoken.

"There is so much I want to know from you," said Bordeaux. "But I'll start with a simple question. One that I believe I already know the answer to. Why did you banish me? Are you so infatuated with yourself that you would erase a friend without so much as a thought?"

Libra pretended she didn't hear and only sat there shaking her head.

"What happened to Madlyn?" asked Bordeaux.

The Lady looked up at him, her face smeared with mascara and frustrated tears. "She's dead. Died in the forest. Crow found her. Nothing can be done of that."

"The monsters got her," added Deadsol.

"Shut up, Deadsol!" Libra snapped.

Bordeaux paced back and forth in an arc around Libra like a moon about a planet, seemingly readying another barrage of questioning, when Crow and Edweena burst into the room.

"They're in the house!" cried Edweena.

The three originally in the room were brought instantly to attention. Libra stood and felt her anger rise again.

"What did you do?" hissed Libra. "How did they get in?"

Crow was irate; "I told you we could not hold them back much longer!"

Both he and the vampiress noticed the disheveled figure in the presence of Libra and Deadsol and, when Edweena realised who it was, she flew to embrace him.

"Edweena," said Bordeaux. He could not help but smile for a moment.

Edweena hugged him fiercely. "What happened to you? We thought you'd left us for good!"

She slapped Bordeaux's shoulder with her palm as he and Crow shook hands warmly. But the wood hermit's face soon returned to its grave pallor.

"But it seems you've returned just in time to see us fall," said Crow.

From the floors below, deep down into the core of Tenenbrae Manor, a multitude of groans echoed up the stairs.

Deadsol fell to his knees, screaming like a little girl. He clung to Libra's dress and hid his frightened face behind a swath of charcoal skirt, much to the irritation of the Lady Libra.

"There's no more hope," he sobbed quietly.

"Steel yourself, Deadsol," said Bordeaux, "We have one last chance." The crimson demon grabbed his friend by the scruff of his coat and pulled him to attention.

"Libra! Hide nothing from us any further, our very existence depends upon it!" said Bordeaux. "That shining amulet, that wooden heart! You must give it back to the golems! That is what they want."

Libra sighed vexingly. "I don't have it anymore!"

"There is no time for this, Libra," said Edweena. "Throw aside your pride and relinquish the thing!"

"I said I do not have it anymore! If you don't believe me, ask Deadsol."

As all eyes fell onto him, Deadsol's own eyes widened. His moustache quivered like a sparrow's wing as the lips behind it trembled.

"I can't bear to think of it!" he wailed, "Dear Comets, my little friend! He has the heart! And he ran into the forest before I could stop him. I'd never seen him so obsessed, so vile!"

"Have you any idea where he could have gone?" asked Edweena.

Bordeaux's mind raced, a kaleidoscope of thoughts swirling erratically in the form of ink scratched across parchment. The pages of the great book he had read fluttered like bat-wings until one particular page tore itself from the spine and unfurled into the petals of a black-coloured rose. From its centre, a single eye opened and stared with deranged indifference. He recognised the eye, bulging owl-like from a sunken face. His heart shuddered and he exclaimed, "Wait!"

They turned to him as their saviour, the eyes of Bordeaux's friends imploring him to redeem them from their peril.

"I have an idea where Comets is." He turned to Crow. "Libra tells me you found Madlyn in the forest.

Where was it that you found her?"

Crow scratched his head. "At the foot of a massive tree. But my mind is a little hazy; I had to escape so swiftly. I don't know that I recall how to get there."

"The Black Rose Tree," came the voice of Lady Libra.

"Libra?"

"That is the tree he speaks of," she continued. "I know where it is."

"What makes you think Comets went there?" said Edweena.

Libra sighed, "The wood heart was a strange thing. The monsters seemed drawn towards it, I believe it is probably their lot to try and retrieve it. And, in turn, the heart itself must be drawn to its proper pedestal. Comets is a weak-willed little creature, he has likely been put under its spell with the hopes he will return it to the tree."

"I had hidden two of my horses outside," said Crow. "Pray the golems have not yet found them. They will take us to the tree. But we have to go now!"

"I will stay behind," said Libra. "But I will tell you how to find the tree."

"But you know where it is!" exclaimed Edweena. "You should come with us!"

Libra rolled her eyes. "Look, I'll give you this one jab at me. Do I look like one to sit on a horse? I'll only slow you. It is better that I don't accompany you."

Crow and Edweena drew their weapons and raced to the door, with Bordeaux following, slowed by his dragging of the reluctant Deadsol.

XXXIV: The Black Rose Tree

Stricken with a feverish energy, an unbridled chaos, the forest quivered with discomfort. As though it were trying to shake off a coat that does not fit properly, it shuddered with the increase of commotion under its canopy. Fog shrouded all. Through the haze, the boles of ageless conifers rose ominously like the undead, thrusting jet black from the opaque grey of fog.

As the horses charged on, the trees gave off the impression of marching. A poorly formed assemblage, for the trees sprouted wherever they pleased, yet they carried the same cold indifference pertaining to a ruthless army. Above the sound of hooves that stamped out a war-drum percussion, the cries of the forest monsters resonated. Their throaty bellows rocked the branches and caused the pine needles to shiver with a whispering rustle.

Even with the tumultuous uncertainty seeded in his heart, Bordeaux still breathed deep the air of his darkled home. The sickly sweet permeations of pine invigorated him and he found himself feeling more alive than he had in some time. Not deterring from the urgency of his mission, this euphoria he felt was not shared by his companions.

As he held the reins tightly, Bordeaux felt a similar gripping on his shaggy clothes, as Deadsol, who was sitting behind him, clung in fear to his friend's shoulders. Ahead of them, Crow rode at a furious pace with Edweena as his passenger.

The wood hermit cut through the trees one-way and then another in a desperate attempt to find the black rose tree. Part of him prayed he was heading in the correct direction.

The terrain rose and fell in no particular pattern and eventually the ground beneath them began to slope steadily downhill. The pounding of drums took on a clearer sound, so that soon the clacking of sticks could be discerned above the din. The horses tore on down the slope, until a clearing spread out before them.

The tree grew immense from the pit, overshadowing the ground that lay littered with roots and thorny tendrils.

"There is no mistaking," called Crow. "This must be the place."

It needn't be said, for each of them regaled some instance of recognition at the sight of the tree. Bordeaux instantly remembered the drawings he had seen in Rune's book. Edweena and Deadsol were certain they had seen similar tree-like shapes about Tenebrae Manor - on sigils and tapestry, jewelry and ornament.

There was an evident commotion at the foot of the tree. For while most of the wood golems circled the tree in some tribalistic ritual, several hovered around a certain part of the trunk, swinging their clubbed arms.

"There he is!" cried Deadsol.

The four of them dismounted and looked towards the chaos where Comets was thrashing about like a feral dog. His eyes were glassed over with a frighteningly absent shade of red; he gnashed and scratched at the golems like a creature threatened. The wood heart remained firmly in his grasp and in plain sight of the monsters, so that he was clutching the thing under one arm and throwing a flurry of punches with the other.

"We can't get to him. He is utterly surrounded!" cried Edweena.

"All they want is the wood heart," said Bordeaux.

"We just need him to give it up and get out of there."

"They seem uninterested in all else. We don't have much time," added Crow.

"There must be a simple way of going about this," Bordeaux began but before he could continue, he felt a push in his back.

From behind him, Deadsol had raced forward into the mess of monsters.

"Deadsol!"

"No time for this! I must help him!" blurted Deadsol.

The copper demon threw himself into the arena and began wading through the crowd of golems. They rose in waves all around him and he found himself wrestling away a few who tried to take him down.

"The idiot!" said Edweena. "Crow and I will get Deadsol. Bordeaux; get to Comets!"

Crow leapt into the fight with sword blows, while Edweena flew at the beasts with her claw-like hands, though it was immediately apparent that the golems grossly outnumbered them. So great were their numbers that not a segment of ground could be discerned amongst the tide of stitched face and knuckled wooden limbs. The glisten of steel from Crow's sword cut through the dull darkness and the sound of blows bellowed with each beast that was struck down.

Bordeaux, weaponless bar his fists (which in turn were rarely called upon for such hostilities), threw aside his usual pedantry for the sake of his friends and furiously charged towards Comets. The strength of his adrenalin startled him, as he scooped up and threw several of the golems surrounding Comets. He was closing in on the imp jester, who was still flailing like a cornered canine, utterly devoid of his own higher consciousness.

Bordeaux reached for him and wrested him up, where he thrashed like a disobedient child in his arms. The wood heart glowed ominously in his grasp, as wood golems began to attack Bordeaux more fiercely.

"Comets! Give up the shiny thing," he pleaded.

Comets growled deeply and kicked in primal fury, he clearly had no recognition of the man holding him. He scratched at Bordeaux's chest, before issuing a sharp bite on his arm.

Bordeaux cried in pain and dropped Comets, who, in turn, dropped the wood heart to the ground, where it tumbled in amongst the thorny tendrils.

Quickly recovering, Bordeaux scrambled for the heart, though he was beaten to the goal by Comets and several wood golems.

"Bordeaux!" cried Edweena from afar.

The crimson demon turned to see animated corpses now being lowered from the branches of the black rose tree. These horrifying spectres, hung by their necks, joined the squabble from above, like spiders descended from a thread. The twisted animations of their awkward punches and grasps chilled Bordeaux's blood. These fallen souls were trespassers who had tried to steal the wood heart in times past. Edweena writhed about in the clutches of a corpse, while Deadsol hopelessly beat at the thing with his fists.

Bordeaux was torn; he turned back to see that Comets had been upended by another of these corpses and thrashed hopelessly in its grasp several feet above the ground. Beneath him, the wood golems leapt angrily for the wood heart. Bordeaux turned back to Edweena and was about to run to her when Crow entered the scene and cut the strangling corpse from its noose. They fell to the ground in a heap, with Edweena having enough time to escape.

"Forget us, Bordeaux!" said Crow. "Get to Comets!"

Bordeaux wasted no time in rushing to the aid of the jester, leaping at the feet of the corpse and clabbering up its legs. The cadaver had Comets in a crushing stranglehold; the jester's face turning a despairing shade of purple as his life was choked from him. He seemed to be trying to drop the wood heart to the ground but from his position he could not shift the thing from under his arm.

Bordeaux struggled in vain to dislodge the iron grip of the corpse arm from around Comets' neck but the fiend held with such deathly tightness. The trio grappled at one another in midair, held by the tendril about the neck of the corpse.

Bordeaux felt his arms weaken and feared he could not hang on for much longer. He pulled desperately at the strangling arm, bringing himself up level with the face of the villain. And when their eyes locked, Bordeaux felt his heart lurch with disbelief. There was something in those sunken oculi - a terrifying ascendancy that Bordeaux recognised instantly. *He was staring into the very face of Malistorm, Tenebrae Manor's lost leader.*

Yes, that shock of white hair; now thinned and decaying; that purple cloak, torn and frayed from exposure to the elements. It was the very same Malistorm he had once submitted to.

Upon this revelation, Bordeaux became limp of limb and plummeted to the ground, where he could only gape in despair at the unfettered hatred displayed by the former baron.

The wood golems had begun clambering up the trunk of the tree in an attempt to reach the struggling pair, while Edweena rushed to Bordeaux's side. Behind them, Crow dragged a hysterical Deadsol away from the madness.

"Bordeaux, we have to leave," said Edweena. "They'll get their relic back."

Bordeaux gritted his teeth. "Is there nothing we can do for Comets?"

Edweena tugged at his arm gently, before starting on a sudden. Above all the noise and ruckus, she had not noticed a change in the sky. It was a subtle alteration, the edges of the sky above the trees glowed with a foreign brightness that she struggled to comprehend.

"Bordeaux - look."

The palette of the forest was transforming – the monochromatic darkness slowly being overcome with a wash of colours. The fog lifted, the trees became greener, the deepest violet of the skies diluting into an array of pink and orange; and at the furthest corners - the sky blue of the early dawn.

"Day!" gasped Bordeaux.

Were Edweena's pale pallor capable of further whiteness, it no doubt would have turned as such. The night grew weaker by the second, like a veil pulled, a lid lifted, a coffin unearthed. The trees yawned with the morning light, squinting with a quiver of branches, as the sun appeared from the horizon in a blinding dazzle.

Edweena ran for the coverage of a nearby tree, kicking fitfully at the creeping shadows that shortened all around her. As the day broke over Tenebrae forest, Bordeaux threw himself over Edweena as a shield as, above her screams of agony, another phenomenon occurred.

As the sun pierced its rays onto the black rose tree, it began to crystallize. The branches retracted, as do the legs of a drowned insect, the thorny roots groaning as they gripped the soil and hardened further. All the wood golems around the tree petrified at the first glimpse of light, the corpses hissing dreadfully as they disintegrated to nothingness.

Comets, true to his name, fell lifelessly earthbound with a thud, the shooting star glow of the wood heart growing faint in his limp grasp until it rolled away from him, indiscernible from any other colourless rock.

Then, all at once, the sky reversed on itself. From the apex of the heavens, the night returned. Its creeping black billows spread towards the horizons like a dust cloud until there was no trace that change had ever disrupted the eternal night. The pines stood silent again, the moans of the last dying golems drifted off into the leaves and

Bordeaux, Deadsol and Crow hurried to avail Comets and Edweena.

By the time the silence settled and the stars appeared, thousands of black rose blossoms shed their petals from the perished tree, where they fell in a shroud of dark snowflakes.

XXXV: Raison D'être

In her heavily sedated state, Edweena suffered fits of pain foreign to anything she had felt before. In spite of her vampiric nature, she thrashed like a mortal on death road. She knew herself to be dreaming, yet it seemed she could recall no other reality and she began to fear that perhaps she wasn't asleep at all and that this pain really was her lot.

The same vision haunted her time and again - she stood perilously close to a cliff face, where she felt herself forced closer to the brink by a wall of tendrils behind her. The formless void of the abyss, where it may otherwise be black as pitch, was instead, filled with a blinding light that stung Edweena's eyes to look upon. The bloodstained tears that fell from her despairing eyes singed her cheeks; she felt she was being punished for acknowledging the pain. When the lashing of vines became all too much, she fell into the white pit where flames would engulf her instantly and her subconscious faded to black to protect her from further torment.

All would then divulge into a myriad of patterns. Squares of uneven grey stone would dance in their chequer pattern amongst shifting shadows until they warped and contorted, only to become entwined in a windowpane that threw shafts of light across her. Edweena would feel as though tangled in cloth or perhaps the sticky web of a monstrous arachnid and despite her fitful kicks, she could not detangle herself. Soon, her weakness would overwhelm her and she would again fall to sleep. And all too soon, those tendrils would reappear in her mind's eye; the urge to cry out would envelop her, only this time she heard a voice call her name.

The tendrils before her now writhed and withered, before settling into the shape of a tree branch framed by a windowsill. The jagged square stones retracted until she realised she was gazing vacantly at the ceiling above.

"Edweena," the voice called again.

She knew the voice, the recognition of it swelling her heart with hope. All at once, she remembered what had happened and where she was.

Edweena's vision cleared until the stately form of her old friend Bordeaux took shape beside her. But could this really be him? This man cut a figure so dapper, so true to the Bordeaux she knew - but hadn't he become more disheveled? Hadn't he returned from an exile full faced with beard, clothes shabby and hair ragged? Yet there he stood in all his streamlined charm, his maroon suit devoid of blemish down to the most minutely misplaced stitch, his gaunt jaw line clean-shaven and framed by a tidy length of groomed red curls.

He was looking down at her and Edweena now

realised she was laying on a lounge in her old drawing room. Confusion settled over her, for she remembered this place to be completely overrun with vines and branches. It felt almost as if she had been hurled backwards through time.

"You've awoken."

Propping herself up on her elbows, Edweena shook the cobwebs from her mind. "How is it that I am here? Was this room not ruined?"

Bordeaux paced about the room and ran his hand along the peeling wallpaper. "Tarnished? Yes. Ruined? No. The vines died along with the monsters. It was simply a matter of clearing the trimmings in preparation for your awakening. I had hoped you could awake in a familiar place."

"That is sweet of you," Edweena smirked, sitting up.

"I could have placed you in a coffin like some common vampire," laughed Bordeaux. "But I am reasonably *au fait* that you despise such clichés."

"I am not one to be locked in a box."

"Not while blood flows hot through the hearts of your victims, eh what?"

Edweena gasped on a sudden. "*The wood heart!* What happened?"

Bordeaux turned to face her. "Destroyed, deary. Along with the golems and the black rose tree. Nobody will have possession of such a relic again and I fear that nobody ever should."

"Of course, the light," said Edweena, clasping her head at the recollection. "Daylight…"

"Indeed. You were rather badly burnt. We had all of us feared for your recovery."

Here, Edweena examined her arms, from which the flaking of her fragile skin peeled menacingly. To see such injuries reminded her of the intense pain she had felt, so that she shuddered involuntarily.

"All that evil, gone…"

"Perished with the sunlight," replied Bordeaux.

"Sunlight… How?"

With a brisk gesture of his hand, Bordeaux directed her attention to the door, where the Lady Libra had recently entered and stood timidly. She seemed to be attempting to maintain a dignified composure but to see that Edweena was awake filled her with a childish joy that left her trembling with excitement.

"Ah! You're back with us!" she beamed, before gathering her regality. "Good."

"Miss Libra, Edweena was just inquiring of the sunlight that saved our Tenebrae Manor."

Libra strode deeper into the room to Edweena's side and sat herself down on a nearby chair.

"Surely you will forgive me. The day was my doing. Those monsters only thrive in darkness; I hoped that to reverse the spell of our eternal night would dispatch them but…"

"But you knew it would place me in mortal peril," finished Edweena.

"You must have known it to be a difficult decision!" Libra pleaded earnestly. "But I had to try it. I had to take a stand. I was reminded of a certain comment, something along the lines of 'only moving when a fire is lit beneath me'."

Edweena stared intensely at Lady Libra for several seconds before her face softened into a smile. Libra, who had awaited her response with apprehension, sighed with relief.

"You are right, Libra. Risking one life for the sake of many others. And to save our home… It was the move of a good leader. I forgive you."

Lady Libra only smiled and shuffled awkwardly in her chair before she was snatched up in a hug from Edweena.

"Incidentally," said Libra, "You need not worry about my 'leadership' any further."

"Oh?"

"I have been speaking with Bordeaux," continued Libra. "And we both decided that he would be more fitting at managing the manor."

"At your service," smirked Bordeaux.

"And he will do a fine job," said Libra. "Malistorm would be pleased. Now would you excuse me? Worrying about your wellbeing has positively exhausted me."

Lady Libra, with the elegance native to her grandiose attitude, left the room with a dignified ambling, until the swishing of her dress faded away down the corridor.

Bordeaux had moved to the window, where he admired the beauty of the taiga beyond.

"That hideous creature that you fought with," said Edweena. "I know who it was. What became of our little Comets?"

Bordeaux's head dropped for a moment and left Edweena to fear the worst, before he spoke again, "Comets is fine." He turned his head towards the vampiress as she placed her hand on his shoulder.

"As exuberant as ever, I am pleased to report," he continued. "By the by, I have assigned him and Deadsol to begin repairing our rather damaged home."

"We will all help," said Edweena.

The rebuilding of Tenebrae Manor was a process both slow and difficult, yet with the abundance of time bestowed upon the lives of those who dwelt within, it was not an insurmountable task.

Comets, having recovered from the tumultuous events of recent past, was set to work on assisting the construction of broken rooms and windows, the clearing of debris and other tasks which fulfilled his lustful energy. Having zero recollection of his possession by the wood heart, he scampered about the place with his chum, Deadsol, who was pleased beyond belief that his friend had pulled through such turmoil. And in spite of the pair's boundless yearning for destruction and mischief, they wasted no time in seizing the opportunity to help restore Tenebrae Manor to its former archaic glory. Under the fair command of Bordeaux, they found little reason to object and were only too willing to oblige.

Compelled too was the scarecrow, Sinders. Having no desire to relocate back to his dingy and burned-out shack, he too took up the task assigned to Deadsol and Comets.

Yet Tenebrae Manor was an impossibly large place and, despite their best efforts, only those more important restorations were completed. For the mansion was undeniably gothic and the rule for any gothic setting is that of a ruinous mood, a lament of a bygone era.

As such, the trio soon grew bored and returned to

their rascally ways, leaving Bordeaux to reluctantly accept their resignation.

Rune, Tenebrae's archaic antiquarian, continued to go quietly about his ways in the windowless vault of the library. Always a being of inimitable wisdom wrapped in forgetfulness, he could hardly recall that his home was ever under any threat. The trials that he knew of were those faced by nameless folk in old books and in most books, there is always a hero who ties up the loose ends of any story. As such, old Rune never let himself be troubled by the happenings beyond the walls of his library, ultimately representing a recluse within a recluse. Having lived through so many years, the events of recent times – the wood golems, the slow destruction of the house around him, these were little more than a blip in his interminable existence.

The entry foyer had adorned the cloak of monochrome native to the current hour, known in some cultures as a witching hour of sorts. The Usher stood at his post. He had remained a statue for so long, the still subject of an artwork that nobody was painting. Certainly the scene was brilliant in its simplicity. But with the brush of a master artist, it could easily be transformed into a layered complexity.

The moon hung low in the sky where it threw long shadows across the tiled floor, like nets cast into the sea. The painter would need little more than black and white on his palette, between which a kaleidoscope of greys mixed into a nauseating haze. The clock ticked and for a moment, the big dusty shoulders of The Usher rose slowly and fell in a heavy sigh. The corner of his scarred mouth twitched, his eyes blinked slowly. Then suddenly he stepped forward and in doing so, stepped completely out of his comfort zone.

Usher opened the mighty front door of Tenebrae Manor, not because he had heard a knock, rather that he felt the impulse to do anything else but stand still. The cold night air gushed in, sending a fluttering of disturbance through the carpet and curtains; owls complained at the disruption of their warm dozing.

Usher stared out beyond the threshold of the manor. Nothing moved; no being was there to accept his invitation inside. Where another heavy sigh would have been appropriate, Usher instead gazed vacantly at the forest beyond, before closing the door and returning to his post.

Although the Mute Chef never quite recovered from the heavy sorrow of Madlyn's passing, he would eventually return to his bustling ways and soon the kitchen was as alive as it ever had been. And even though few stopped to admire his culinary talent, he felt evermore comforted by the strange presence that possessed his sweating home. Peculiar occurrences dotted his progress – plates were smashed, the suds of soapy dishwater were splashed onto the floor and certain objects went missing from his larder. But these events did not upset the chef at all, across his face there even peeled a smile. For there were also hours when the pots would boil on their own accord and within the mist of steam above he could discern a ghostly shape of girl he had once known and truly cared for in his own way.

And whenever he saw this apparition, he could not help but utter a series of mirthful chuckles disguised as uncontrollable wheezes; had he a working voice box, his happiness would no doubt echo throughout the manor.

The auditorium had been silent for so long that it was hard to believe anyone had ever inhabited its walls at all. Mice scurried across the carpet, as the empty red seats waited on a movement, any movement at all from the darkened stage. And when the ghostly audience fell crestfallen (for an absence of art is truly the greatest tragedy) and when all hope had been given up for the coming of a hero who might inject new ideas into cultural enlightenment, the great doors of the place swung open.

The composer, the great Arpage Espirando Notturno

puffed out his shallow chest, threw a slimy reed of his hair back into its place on his greasy scalp and walked forward into his domain. Sighing in purest ecstasy, he took great delight in the click of his shoes on the floor and the hush of his green cardigan tails trailing behind him. The mice fled from sight, fearing the cat had returned and that now was not the time for play. Were they capable of speech, of instilling fear into their disobedient offspring, they would have murmured, "There is the greatest musician of them all, the magnificent Arpage!"

But Arpage paid no attention to the rodents as he glided across the stage, his stage, where he blew kisses and thrust his arms skyward to his imaginary audience. For all his supposed pomp and grandeur, upon climbing the ladder and completing the long awaited reunion with his loft, he could not help skipping gaily on the spot.

Brushing his emaciated fingers along the keys of his organ, he struck at a single note, A for Arpage and shuddered at its crisp beauty. And when he passed the tattered couch and sat down at his note-cluttered drawing board, he whimpered blissfully, placing his face down onto its surface.

He fell asleep instantly, while crotchets and quavers danced inside of his head.

What of the Lady Libra, the once untouchable apex of Tenebrae's hierarchy? Having relinquished her position to what she reluctantly decided were 'more capable hands', she too decided to diminish the lavish excess of her life - in some aspects.

Choosing to ignore the valuable treasures she had collected, she kept a small livelihood with only her most favourite things. Yet she was unshakeably hedonistic, so that while she was able to give up the grand bedroom for the sake of a smaller quarters; the position of her new room just so happened to be directly above the kitchen halls. Thus meaning that she had direct access to a shaft where a winch and pulley delivered food directly to her room with minimal effort.

As such, her gluttony only escalated, her plumpness proliferated, until she grew so fat that she rarely left her room at all.

There came a time not long after when Edweena again began to feel the yearning for a new challenge, the stillness of the manor frustrated her greatly and she fought against the quicksands of stagnation with increased vigour. She moved irritably about the house, seeing little but abandoned rooms and silent corridors. It was not that she despised the place but merely felt that her time at Tenebrae Manor must end and perhaps end sooner than anticipated.

The fact that she had obtained closure from her old friend Libra and that the manor was now entirely free of immediate danger prompted her decision to venture into the world beyond the darkness of the trees. She wished she could steal away quietly, leaving little commotion in her absence, however she knew there would be one person who would truly lament an unexplained disappearance.

She leapt stealthily across the rooftops of Tenebrae Manor like a panther in a mountain range, landing on the window ledge of a certain turret, from where the flames of a candle flickered weakly.

The silence of her arrival did not startle Bordeaux, who turned from his reading desk as though he had expected her all along. He gazed knowingly at her, Edweena stepping down into the room and pacing about as if it was her own. She stopped before Bordeaux's favourite painting, the painting of the sunrise and observed the masterwork of the brushstrokes.

"I'm leaving."

Bordeaux sipped at his long ignored coffee cup and grimaced; its contents cold.

"I know."

Edweena looked at him expectantly. "So?"

Bordeaux heaved a heavy sigh. "I cannot stop you, Edweena."

"Come with me." She leant over the writing desk and stared earnestly at him.

"I... I cannot," he replied.

Rolling her eyes, Edweena stepped away. "I understand your station. But why stay? Did your exile not fill you with the expectation of a more exciting life?"

The crimson demon stood and led Edweena back to the painting, where neither of them spoke for some time.

Bordeaux finally broke the silence. "In times past, I was servant on a vineyard in Southern France. Our country lay in fields of verdant green, lined with miles upon miles of grape plantations. The leaves were like stars; I still remember how beautiful the land looked in the afternoon sun. I remember the breeze of the Mediterranean coast on my skin. Life was fleeting but life was wonderful. At five and twenty, I had an accident on the vineyard. The pain was so incredible; I knew myself to be dying. I know not how long it remained dark, only that I awoke again and my family was gone. My home had seemingly been abandoned long ago. I was still of this world. I could breathe. I could walk, talk. Yet something had changed. The earth seemed clearer, I could see and feel things I had never known and I thought that I must be alive. But I wasn't. I had died, I know I had died. And there was no God, no deity to meet me after death. Perhaps more frightening still, no Beelzebub or devil appeared to banish me into eternal hellfire either. There was nothing but I still was. Surely you have an idea what that feels like? To die and realise that there is nothing. No eternal afterlife of paradise, no confining to swelter in an underworld. Nothing. Why am I still here? Is this my curse? Is this hell? I have seen it all, Edweena. I have travelled through the Orient, the steppe of Asia Minor. I have stowed away on ships, an imposter sailing for the edges of the world, only to discover that there is just more land. I have seen the swamp eaten jungles of the new world, the polar extremes of the furthest Thule. My recent exile was nothing new. I have settled at Tenebrae Manor purposefully. Like many others under this roof, I cannot die with time, lest I am killed. At times I have thought of ending it but… I must stay here. I have duties here, at least for now. You must understand, Edweena."

Edweena could not respond for several moments,

tears forming in her eyes. Bordeaux looked down at the ground and felt his chest swell with despondence.

"I had no idea of your mortal life," she said. "Nor your previous travels."

"It is fine. Not all of us can so easily cast aside the memories held dear to them. Deadsol was a miserable Russian baron before death, before his sanity dwindled over the ages. Now look at him, he has never been so jovial. Arpage, he cannot even remember his life before Tenebrae. If only I was so fortunate."

"I too, curse my immortality, Bordeaux. I had no choice either. At times, I wish I could be like Madlyn. She, like all humans, has no idea what a privilege it is to die eventually. I feel such anger that my mortal death was taken from me. To sleep in blissful darkness forever… I would give all else to get that."

"Which is why you would leave now?"

"Yes," said Edweena. "I know that the night ends at a certain point. From then on, I am in great risk of perishing. It is the thrill of mortality, the idea of a life of arbitrary length. It compels me, Bordeaux."

"You would treat your life so recklessly?" asked Bordeaux.

"I have had my share of years, Bordeaux. Lord knows how many years excess. This life I have now may as well be death of sorts. Should I die, you will know that I died having truly lived."

Bordeaux sighed. "I understand."

Tenderly, with the fondness of a true friend, Edweena kissed Bordeaux upon his gaunt cheek, heartache consuming her. Without the need for further words, she stepped away from him, pausing briefly at the window ledge before vanishing into the trees outside.

Bordeaux was seized by a paralysis of mind; his knees shook and only once he had fought for any sort of composure did he move to the window to see if he could still see Edweena somewhere in the distant trees.

But she was gone and the night carried on as it always had.

END OF PART THREE.

Epilogue

The winter had arrived late that year but when its winds arrived, they bit hard with punishing indifference. Their polar currents cut through the still forest like wights exhuming a ghastly wail, perhaps lamenting their lack of orientation betwixt the trees, for the gales blew this way and that at their own will. The trees, silenced by a blanket of crystalline white, slouched in pneumonic sleep, immersed so deeply into the night around that they recalled nothing but darkness. It was as if colour had never existed; grey dominated the stony sky and evanescent wisps of cloud flitted high in the domed atmosphere.

Nestled in its small clearing, a wooden hut stood strong against the wintry blasts, yet it was slowly losing its stance to the piling of snows about its walls and the smoke that drifted from the chimney was instantly snuffed by the winds. For this hut, its feeling of isolation was exaggerated in the gloom, it cowered to the gusts and allowed it to dominate the forest.

The moon was a waning gibbous and it could be said that its waning was a result of the cold currents extinguishing its lunar flames, for it shone dimly through the windows of the shack and across the wooden floors draped with a fur rug.

The old man sat in his chair, nestled feebly from the elements by a thick layer of woolen blankets. And certainly his snowy beard aided his warmth despite its resemblance to the powder outside. The fire crackled in the hearth, providing more than adequate heat to the room. Yet even with the main log burning nicely, the old man could not help but notice his diminishing pile of kindling to the side of the fireplace and he sighed begrudgingly. His bones ached, though whether this was due to his age, the cold or even both, he could not tell.

Supposing that it did not really matter, he shivered in his blankets and stretched in his chair. He would have to gather firewood eventually; nobody else would in this hermit's abode.

"Mayhaps it will be good to go outside," he said to himself. "If only to feel the elements in these old bones again." He would only be a moment; the larder of firewood was only a few metres from his hut.

With a struggle, he rose and donned his green cloak. His slouched profile looked not unlike the snow-capped conifers outside the door, weighted down with the season's drifts.

The difference in temperature between the inside of the hut and out was tremendous, as the old man felt instantly the blows of gale lashing at his weathered face. Still, he shuffled out into the dusk and when he had reached his woodpile, he stopped and admired the majestic silence of the pines that encompassed his home. Certainly it was cold but would that really matter, say, if he were to venture but a little further to admire the forest?

"A little further. What harm, other than freezing to death?" he chuckled, before breaking into a series of autumnal coughs.

He waded through the drifts, passed his old forge, passed the stables where his last horse had died decades earlier. The trees towered around him, as though they were parental figures watching over his comparably tiny frame. To feel the cold and such cold it was, invigorated the old man. Memories of his youth flew on the gusts, times when he could ride just as fast through the tree trunks, when he knew the ins and outs of this nighttime forest like the back of his hand.

There presently came a moment when he decided that he would turn back but upon commencing his return journey, he realised his trail had been covered with new snow. A younger man may have panicked in such a situation but not this nonagenarian. He had lived out his years; the idea of death no longer frightened him. No, he rather cursed his own dull wit. What a fool he had been, venturing out into this weather at his age.

"I will deservedly perish. Stupid old fool," he muttered.

The trees gave no assistance in gauging his whereabouts; they all looked the same to him.

Onwards he wandered until he came upon a place where the trees stopped all of a sudden and a sharp cliff face echoed in the void beyond. He clambered up a great boulder until he was able to sit on the ledge of the precipice, where the trees below carried on uninhibited until they met mountains on the far horizon.

He sat in silence, shivering in his cloak with wisps of

his white hair blowing across his wrinkled face.

"Surely you should be some place warm."

The old man flinched at the voice and when he turned his ancient head, he saw the demon standing beside him.

"Bordeaux," said the old man.

"Crow."

The old man stared at the crimson demon, who appeared more than content to admire the view of the forest below. It was the very same Bordeaux he known from years earlier, his immaculate dark red suit, his charcoal scarf blowing in the frigid breeze; how long had it been since he had last seen him?

"I suppose I just wanted to feel… alive again," said Crow.

Bordeaux chuckled. "Don't we all."

"You look the same," was all Crow could muster to say.

"And why would I have changed, sir?"

"I had thought you might not be around anymore," replied Crow. "The manor still stands?"

"A foolish idea to think otherwise."

Crow chuckled in response. He and Bordeaux remained quiet for some time, listening to the sounds of the whistling wind in the pine branches.

"You are indeed fortunate, Crow," said Bordeaux. "You will receive rest shortly and what wouldn't I give to take it from you."

Crow felt a slight fear in his chest but Bordeaux continued to gaze out over the abyss with no sign of movement.

"I stood on the threshold of Tenebrae Manor some

time ago," continued Bordeaux, "And, for a fleeting second, I nearly ran, wishing nothing more than to see a new place. To perhaps, find Edweena. To see whether the world has changed further from the last time I saw it."

"And you didn't?"

Bordeaux laughed menacingly. "Ha, no sir. I did not. Again, the question begged, why? I have nowhere to be. Any home elsewhere would merely become stagnant again, in time."

"I suppose I cannot relate," said Crow. "I have no grasp of such a lengthy life and never will."

"Ah Crow, old friend. I could throw myself from this very cliff but then what? I had thought myself dead when my mortal existence was taken from me and now I cannot tell how many centuries I have passed in this purgatory."

No more words were uttered for some time, until Crow began to shiver more so. Bordeaux stirred from his perch like an eagle rustling from hours of watching in patience.

"Follow the flames home," said Bordeaux.

Crow stirred. "What? Bordeaux?"

He turned to where the demon had stood seconds earlier but Bordeaux was gone.

When Crow looked back into the trees, a trail of ghostly orange flames seemed to hover in a line until they disappeared from view further ahead.

Thankful for the kindliness of his strange friend, Crow gathered himself up and wandered back into the forest, following the flames that would, no doubt, bring him back to his hut. The winds and the snows continued with no difference to their nonchalance, the trees remained covered in their blanket of eternal night.

And it is there that those pines would continue to stand, in a forest that some may call the darkest corner of earth. But no – that is the wrong choice of words, for a corner is a place where two ends meet. This is rather a nothingness, born of mystery and existing in a greater emptiness. A place on the planet that may never be discovered and, to any who would listen, may never need to be discovered.

Somewhere in that forest stands Tenebrae Manor, immortal as an artwork. And, like the arts, where anything can come from nothing, the mansion is still there, quintessential of the gloom that protects it and paramount to the ongoing reprieve of sufferance it represents.

END

Appendix

Character Profiles

Bordeaux

Of all the residents that dwell within Tenebrae Manor, Bordeaux is the closest one might hazard to label as protagonist. Looked upon as a master of affairs and servant to the castle's concord, he casts a world-weary figure of despondent melancholia. Pedant to a fault, he is oft one to place the needs of others before his own. His steadfast loyalty and obedience to his station begs the notion of how a stagnant and unchanging life can lead to despair.

Lady Libra

If Bordeaux represents the embodiment of sovereign leadership, then the Lady Libra would certainly be the antithesis. While it would seem that the self-proclaimed queen of Tenebrae Manor borders the brink of evil, it is merely her extreme selfishness that portrays her as a sort of anti-hero. A powerful magician, Libra holds the residents of the manor under her thumb and abuses her echelon with strict and self-centred orders of servitude. Yet it all comes at a high price – for the Lady Libra is utterly despised by many who had once called her a friend.

Deadsol

The mischievous Deadsol is a figure of colourful whimsy within the otherwise gloomy abode that is Tenebrae Manor. His mannerisms are that of a harlequin, to such a point that he is rarely taken seriously. This matters little to the copper demon, who, with Comets as his diligent lackey, cause all kinds of trouble to the jaded residents that share the walls of the manor. Inspired by the geniuses of Russian literature, Deadsol's character is one that impresses upon the reader that life, even in moments of perpetual darkness, can be made jovial.

Edweena

Encompassed in a fierce passion, the vampire Edweena is the personification of stubborn. Though she is one of the older residents of Tenebrae Manor, her mind and body are that of youthful athleticism. In spite of her facade of strong will, she battles an ongoing inner torment; she despises the monster that she is and though Tenebrae Manor offers salvation to those doomed to immortality, Edweena often wonders whether it is worth it at all. She toys with the idea of the ultimate challenge – leaving the refuge of eternal night and pursuing a risk-filled life of adventure. But is that what she truly desires?

Comets

Easily the most mysterious character of Tenebrae Manor, Comets is also endowed with an unrivaled lunacy. He is eloquent to a fault, yet often the words that spew forth from his mouth make little to no sense. He acts as a sort of lackey to Deadsol; the two of them infamous for much mischief within the mansion walls....

Madlyn

Despite being an adolescent human girl, Madlyn is even more bizarre than the monsters that dwell with her. She stumbled into Tenebrae Manor lost and devoid of her senses; Bordeaux taking pity on the girl and putting her to work in the kitchens in hope of re-establishing her mind. Servant to the demanding Lady Libra, who has taken advantage of the poor girl's innocence and forces Madlyn to answer her every whim. A born dreamer, Madlyn lives the fairytales in head as if they were reality; seemingly not realising that she is in fact already living in a tangible fantasy.

Crow

Preferring his own company, Crow has lived as a hermit in Tenebrae Forest for many years. His life and background are a mystery; why he should choose to conceal himself in the forest of eternal night bewilders even the most macabre of Tenebrae Manor's residents. A jack of all trades, Crow is an apt swordsman, skilled in equestrian matters and a fine blacksmith. Keeping to himself has meant he is highly independent, living in a small hut deep in the trees away from the manor. Bordeaux's concerns are shared by Crow, who wishes to maintain the peaceful life he has created for himself.

Arpage

Though not much of a 'major player' in Tenebrae Manor,
the composer Arpage certainly encapsulates the whimsical
nature of the mansion's residents. Living in a shambled
loft above a long isolated auditorium, Arpage spends his
hours in the throes of frustration native to any artist or
musician. A violently passionate man, though somewhat
insipid and cowardly, the composer is a character who
struggles to keep his emotions in check, often flying into
frazzled   fits   of   immature   tantrums.

The Usher

A simple-minded servant, The Usher spends most of his time as doorman to the great oak doors at Tenebrae Manor's threshold. He is a man who takes his job very seriously, in spite of the fact that Tenebrae quite obviously receives few visitors. It is at this point that Usher becomes perplexed. For what would be the outcome is he were to slack off and miss the opportunity to perform his duties? The Usher dares not chance his hand, and instead chooses to do what he knows – that of serving others. He is a gentle giant and one of the more pitiable residents of the manor.

Sinders

An enigmatic apparition, the origins of the scarecrow Sinders are lost to the night. The man himself chooses to torment others with an apparent abundance of wit and knowledge, but even that might be the work of a charlatan. Luckily for everyone else Sinders does not reside within Tenebrae Manor, instead living an isolated life in an ivy-choked shack deep in the forest.

Rune – The Antiquarian

The most inclusive being of Tenebrae Manor is also seldom seen. Rune appears as an archaic geriatric who spends almost all of his time alone in Tenebrae's library. His mind is so full of knowledge that it overflows to the point where it would seem that he can't learn anything new – becoming seemingly senile. But no, there is far more going on inside that bandaged head; Rune's knowledge of Tenebrae Manor is without peer.

The Mute Chef

Although being one of the more obscure characters of Tenebrae Manor, the Mute Chef has proven to be somewhat of a fan favourite among readers. Perhaps it is his plight that touches the hearts of fans; the poor elderly man is both deaf and mute, and is a slave to his job like so many of us. But he is a man of perfection who takes immense pride in his vocation, to such extent that it would seem that he enjoys his quiet life in the dank kitchens of the manor.

Malistorm

A mysterious paternal apparition, Malistorm has resided in Tenebrae Manor longer than anyone can remember. Perhaps he was the very being who cast the eternal night across the sky like a shroud, the very architect who conjured the manor from among the pines – none know for certain. His disappearance from Tenebrae Manor was cloaked in the very same mystery – and the house has struggled for it. Now that new dangers threaten the manor they are in need of Malistorm's leadership all the more, but have come to accept that he is not returning anytime soon...

The Wood Golems

Mindless and sinister, the Wood Golems are a major antagonist to the residents of Tenebrae Manor. Despite their cumbersome movement and awkward appearance, they are deadly when given a chance and parasitic to boot – the Wood Golems have been vastly increasing in number, threatening to overrun Tenebrae Manor. If left uninhibited, it won't be long until the manor is destroyed beyond repair and left no more discernable than the ocean of trees that surround it.

Compendium of Poetry

Illustrations & Sketches

Bordeaux's Abode

The Composer

Spiders on the Lawn

Bordeaux (concept)

Deadsol and the Usher (concept)

425

Comets and the Wood Golem

Arpage and Madlyn (concept)

Edweena (concept)

Interview with the Author

The following interview was undertaken 29 June 2014 between Feathered Quill Book Reviews and P.S.Clinen.

FQ: Does the word Tenebrae have a specific meaning?

CLINEN: Tenebrae is a Latin word - literally meaning 'darkness.' The word appealed to me for a number of reasons, most obviously the setting of the novel - a house where night is eternal. But Tenebrae also carries religious motives as a Christian service usually celebrated before Good Friday. As Tenebrae Manor deals with the ideals of eternity and salvation versus suffering, I felt it was an appropriate name.

FQ: Was there an actual mansion or structure that provided the inspiration for Tenebrae Manor?

CLINEN: The mansion itself is an assemblance of numerous inspirations. I have always been fascinated with Gothic; as a child I loved anything with ghosts or haunted houses, and today I am fascinated by old architecture. Tenebrae Manor itself drew inspiration from many of my favourite darker stories such as

429

Poe's *The Fall Of The House Of Usher*, Lovecraft's sunken city of R'yleh in the *Cthulhu Mythos*, as well as Stoker's *Dracula* and Mervyn Peake's *Gormenghast*.

FQ: Tenebrae Manor is full of frightful characters but each seems to have their own similarities to human emotions. Was this something you intended for them to have?

CLINEN: It was my intent for the novel to be a little bit weird. The characters appear monstrous, but their individual personalities bring up the old saying 'don't judge someone until you know them.' All of them are underdogs in their own way, each have their troubles that a reader can relate well with. They were born out of imagination - again I can cite my childhood as the source of inspiration, with Tim Burton's films and Roald Dahl's books leaving wonderful impressions in my mind, reminding me that it is okay to be strange as long as you are true to yourself!

FQ: The character of Usher displayed a profound innocence in the dark world he was surrounded by, so what was your purpose for including him in this story?

CLINEN: At a first glance The Usher may seem little more than a minor character, but his actions exemplify some of Tenebrae Manor's major themes. He is the doorman and main servant of the manor, so simple of mind that he knows nothing more than to do his job and do it without complaint. In a world where other characters are questioning their purpose,

Usher knows exactly what he has been called to do. However, like the others, he does go through stages where he believes there may be something else out there for him. His character illustrates a reluctance towards change, even when one's world has become stagnant.

FQ: Why did you decide to place Libra, a woman, as head of Tenebrae Manor as many times male characters dominate dictating roles?

CLINEN: I don't know that it has anything to do with gender as such; Libra is just a strong and self-centred character who chased her ambitions - something characters like Bordeaux and Edweena struggle to do. Libra is the illustration of how too much of a good thing can have negative effects. And her name - Libra - embodying balance (or anything but!) shows how putting one's self before others can lead to ruin, which is a major part of Gothic literature. While Libra may appear villainous, she really is more of an anti-hero, and though many may love to hate her the reader can't help but relate to her in one way or another.

FQ: There are many small mysteries throughout this story pertaining to Tenebrae and its residents. Was this something you intended for this book, perhaps to add to the mysterious allure of this story?

CLINEN: When diving into the world of Tenebrae Manor I want my readers to feel as though they are in a dream. Dreams are a place where anything is possible and sometimes things make very little sense, yet it remains a place where things are at their most honest and truthful, which can lead to a greater enlightenment. The world-building of mysteries is mostly just adding flavour to my attempt at producing a literary fable; there are some things in Tenebrae Manor that don't need to be revealed, doing so could very easily disrupt the intrigue. I think it is important not to show all your cards; real life doesn't give us all the answers, so a book that does the same thing becomes much more relatable.

FQ: The two main human characters of Madlyn and Jethro were very different in their outlook of Tenebrae Manor. Were these two characters in a way representing two sides of human emotion?

CLINEN: Definitely. Although Madlyn was much more of a major character than Jethro. Jethro was your average person, as such he was very much incapable of accepting such a bizarre and frightening world as Tenebrae Manor. Madlyn on the other hand was fragile in temperament. She lived in a world of impossible fantasy, yet still chose to fly off into her romantic daydreams. It is Madlyn's beautiful innocence that shields her from the horrors that Jethro is unable to handle, creating a strange counterweight where the weaker-minded person has a distinct advantage over a sound mind.

FQ: Not much was said about Jethro at the end of this story, could he possibly come back in a

second book about Tenebrae Manor?

CLINEN: Perhaps, though if there is a sequel I doubt he could breakthrough as a major character. Jethro was more of a segway into the main storyline of Tenebrae Manor. He is intentionally an uninteresting character, as such he slips into the background towards the end of the story while the whimsical Bordeaux, Libra, Deadsol, etc. really get their chance to shine. A number of readers have inquired about a sequel to Tenebrae Manor. At present I have no plans to continue it; I feel the story ends in a good spot and anything further added may take away from the impression left by the book on a whole. I am currently working on my next novel, although I have no release date in sight yet. Having said that though, I very much adored the characters of Tenebrae Manorand loved writing about them. So who knows? Maybe one day down the track we'll hear more about Bordeaux, Libra and Tenebrae Manor! Thank you very much for your time.

ABOUT THE AUTHOR

Patrick Stephen Clinen is a writer and artist from New South Wales, Australia. *Tenebrae Manor* was his first novel, originally published in 2014. Since then he has published an illustrated children's book, *A Boy Named Art* and released his second novel, *The Will of the Wisp*. This revised edition of *Tenebrae Manor* was released in 2017. All of his published works are available on Amazon. For more information about P.S.Clinen, including poems, stories and artwork, visit www.psclinen.com